Anna B. Kingsford

Clothed With the Sun

Anna B. Kingsford

Clothed With the Sun

ISBN/EAN: 9783348024242

Printed in Europe, USA, Canada, Australia, Japan

Cover: Foto ©Andreas Hilbeck / pixelio.de

More available books at **www.hansebooks.com**

"CLOTHED WITH THE SUN"

BEING THE BOOK OF THE ILLUMINATIONS

OF

ANNA (BONUS) KINGSFORD

EDITED BY

EDWARD MAITLAND

"Illumination is the Light of Wi...
secrets.

"Which Light is the Spirit of G...
things of God."

L O...
GEORG...
15 YORK STR...

Dedication.

To the numerous and world-wide circle of genuine students of Divine things, who recognised in Anna Kingsford a Seer, an Interpreter, and a Prophet of the rarest lucidity and inspiration, and a foremost herald of the dawning better age ; and especially to the Friend whose instant and enthusiastic appreciation proved an invaluable support in a position of peculiar difficulty, and beneath whose roof some of the illuminations herein contained were received, but who desires to remain unnamed ; and also to the " friend, disciple, and literary heir of the renowned magian, the late Abbé Constant (" Eliphas Levi ")"—namely, to the Baron Guiseppe Spedalieri, for manifold tokens of high approbation and devoted friendship,—this book is affectionately inscribed.

" And I saw another angel flying in mid-heaven, having an eternal gospel to proclaim unto them that dwell on the earth, and unto every nation, and tribe, and tongue, and people ; and he saith with a great voice, Fear God, and give him glory ; for the hour of his judgment is come : and worship him that made the heaven and the earth, and sea and fountains of waters."

APOC. xiv. 6, 7 (R.V.).

TABLE OF CONTENTS.

	PAGES
Dedication .	v
Preface .	xi.-xxix

PART THE FIRST.

ILLUMINATION
No.

I. Concerning the three Veils between Man and God	1-5
II. Part 1. Concerning Inspiration and Prophesying .	5-7
Part 2. A prophecy of the Kingdom of the Soul, mystically called the Day of the Woman . .	8-9
III. Concerning the prophecy of the Immaculate Conception	10-13
IV. Concerning Revelation	13-15
V. Concerning the Interpretation of the Mystical Scriptures . . . . —Part 1	16-19
Do. Do. —Part 2	19-21
VI. Concerning the Mosaic Cosmogony . . .	22-25
VII. Concerning the Fall	25-28
VIII. Concerning the prophecy of the Deluge . .	29-30
IX. Concerning the prophecy of the Book of Esther .	30-32
X. Concerning the prophecy of the vision of Nebuchadnezzar	33-35
XI. Concerning the prophecy of the time of the End .	35-41
XII. Concerning the Soul: its origin, nature, and potentialities	41-52
XIII. Concerning Persephone, or the Soul's descent into matter	52-55

viii *Contents.*

ILLUMINATION
No.

PAGES

XIV. Concerning the Genius or Daimon—Part 1 . 55-61
Do. Do. —Part 2 . 61-66
XV. Concerning the "Powers of the Air"—Part 1 . 66-70
Do. Do. —Part 2 . 70-71
XVI. Concerning the Devil and devils . 72-73
XVII. Concerning the Gods 73-74
XVIII. Concerning the Greek Mysteries . . 74-81
XIX. Concerning the origin of Evil, and the Tree as
the type of Creation . —Part 1 82-83
Do. Do. . —Part 2 83-85
XX. Concerning the Great Pyramid, and the Initia-
tions therein 85-89
XXI. Concerning the "Man of Power" . . 90-94
XXII. Concerning the "Work of Power" . 94-98
XXIII. Concerning Regeneration . . 99-102
XXIV. Concerning the Man Regenerate . 102-107
XXV. Concerning the Christ and the Logos . . 107-109
XXVI. Concerning the perfectionment of the Christ . 109-111
XXVII. Concerning Christian Pantheism . 111-112
XXVIII. Concerning the "Blood of Christ" . . 112-115
XXIX. Concerning "Vicarious Atonement" . . 116-122
XXX. Concerning Paul and the Disciples of Jesus . 122-125
XXXI. Concerning the Manichæanism of Paul . . 126
XXXII. Concerning the Gospels : their origin and com-
position 127-131
XXXIII. Concerning the actual Jesus . . . 131-136
XXXIV. Concerning the previous lives of Jesus . . 136-138
XXXV. Concerning the Holy Family . . . 139-140
XXXVI. Concerning the Metempsychosis or Avatâr . 141-144
XXXVII. Concerning the Æon of the Christ . . 144-146
XXXVIII. Concerning the doctrine of Grace . . 146-147
XXXIX. Concerning the "Four Atmospheres" . . 147-149
XL. Concerning the Hereafter . . . 150-155

ILLUMINATION
No.   PAGES
XLI. Concerning the true Ego . . . 156-158
XLII. Concerning God 159-163
XLIII. Concerning Psyche, or the Superior Human Soul 164-170
XLIV. Concerning the Poet, as type of the heavenly
    personality 170-174
XLV. Concerning Psyche (continued from No. XLIII.) 174-177
XLVI. Concerning Consciousness and Memory in relation
    to Personality 178-183
XLVII. Concerning the Substantial Ego as the true Sub-
    ject . . . . . —Part 1 183-187
    Do. Do. —Part 2 187-189
XLVIII. Concerning the Christian Mysteries—Part 1 . 189-191
    Do. Do. —Part 2 . 191-193
XLIX. Concerning Dying 194-197
L. Concerning the One Life, being a recapitulation . 197-205

PART THE SECOND.

THE BOOK OF THE MYSTERIES OF GOD.

I. The Credo; being a summary of the spiritual his-
    tory of the Sons of God, and the mysteries of
    the kingdoms of the Seven Spheres . . 210
II. The "Lord's Prayer;" being a prayer of the
    Elect for interior perfectionment . . 211
III. Concerning Holy Writ 212-213
IV. Concerning Sin and Death . . . 213-215
V. Concerning the "Great Work," the Redemption,
    and the share of Christ Jesus therein . . 215-221
VI. Concerning Original Being, or "Before the
    Beginning" 221-223
VII. Alpha, or "In the Beginning" . . . 223-224
VIII. Beta, or Adonai the Manifestor . . . 224-225
IX. Gamma, or the Mystery of Redemption . . 225-227

ILLUMINATION
  No.   PAGES

    X. Delta, or the Mystery of Generation .   .   . 227-230

   XI. Epsilon, or the First of the Gods—Proem   .   .   231

       Hymn to Phoibos   232-233

  XII. Zeta, or the Second of the Gods—Part 1. Proem,   . 234-235

       Hymn to Hermes   236-237

       Part 2. An exhortation of Hermes to his Neophytes   238-240

 XIII. Eta, or (mystically) the Third of the Gods—Part 1.
       Proem   240

       Hymn to the Planet God   240-249

       Part 2.—Hymns to the Elemental Divinities—
          (α) To Hephaistos   250-252
          (β) To Demeter   252
          (γ) To Poseidon   253
          (δ) To Pallas Athena   254
          Epode 254-255

  XIV. Theta, or (mystically) the Fourth of the Gods—
       Part 1. The Hymn of Aphrodite   .   . 255-258

       Part 2. A Discourse of the Communion of Soules,
          and of the Uses of Love between Creature and
          Creature; being part of the Goldene Booke of
          Venus   258-262

   XV. Lambda, or the Last of the Gods; being the Secret
       of Satan   263-269

  XVI. The Seven Spirits of God and their Correspondences,   269

 XVII. The Mysteries of the Kingdoms of the Seven
   .   Spheres   270-271

PART THE THIRD.

Concerning the Divine Image; or the Vision of Adonai   . 275-284

APPENDIX.

Notes   287-304
Definitions and Explanations   .   .   . 304-314

PREFACE.

IN the preface to "Dreams and Dream-Stories" Mrs Kingsford speaks of the "priceless insights and illuminations, acquired by means of dreams, which had elucidated for her many difficulties and enigmas of life, and even of religion, by throwing on them a light which penetrated to their very springs and causes." By far the greater number of the insights and illuminations thus referred to were received during the period of some fourteen years, in which it was my high privilege to collaborate with her in the work principally represented by our joint book, " The Perfect Way ; or, the Finding of Christ," having been expressly vouchsafed, first, to bring about our association in that work, and, next, to aid us in its accomplishment. Many of them were accordingly used, either in whole or in part, in our book,—those that were not so used being reserved either as not coming within its assigned scope, or because their publication at that time would, we were instructed, be premature. The present volume comprises both those which were so used, —such of them as were there given in part being here given in full,—and those also which were withheld,—the motive for their reservation being no longer operative ; together with others, some of which have appeared elsewhere, and some were received subsequently. And the publication is made in fulfilment of the twofold purpose of separating Mrs Kingsford's illuminations alike from her ordinary writings and from mine as her collaborator ; and in accordance with her express injunctions, emphatically renewed on finding her departure imminent. The present volume, however, does not exhaust the store of similar treasures left by her, but only such portion as comports with the form of publication here adopted. There still remain sundry lectures and occasional papers, and the majority of her conversations with her Genius ;—for, as is shown in this book, she was privileged in this respect far in excess of any instance known to history ;—conversations which, while also constituting illuminations, were of too personal a character for inclusion in these pages, comprising as they did not only instructions for guidance in circumstances of difficulty, but also intimations — fully borne out by evidence — respecting her own previous existences. For in this respect also Anna Kingsford was a demonstration of the great doctrine, the rehabilitation of which was an important part of her mission,— the doctrine of the pre-existence of the soul or Ego ; of its persistence through all changes of form and conditions, and of its power while still in the body, to recover and communicate to its exterior selfhood, its recollections of its past existences. Belonging, however, to the category of the biographical rather than of the exegetical, all precise references in this relation are withheld from these pages, such allusions only being retained as are necessitated by the context.

Although the questions of the derivation and significance of the matter herein contained, have been treated with considerable fulness in "The Perfect Way,"—particularly in the preface to the revised and enlarged edition,—some account is not the less called for here ; and this, not only for the sake of those readers who may not have prior acquaintance with that book ; but also because the removal of the personality concerned has made it possible to speak with greater explicitness than was fitting in her lifetime.

A comparatively brief statement, however, will suffice, since the questions to be satisfied are but two in number, and the answers to them will be addressed to such persons only as are already sufficiently developed in respect of the consciousness of things spiritual, as at the least to be capable of entertaining propositions involving the reality of the region and experiences concerned. For this is a restriction which obviates the necessity of arguments and explanations, which could not be other than protracted, conceived in deference to those who, being totally devoid of the spiritual consciousness, are wont to make their own defect of sensibility an argument against such reality, and to regard denials based upon non-experience as effectually disposing of affirmations based upon experience.

The two questions to be elucidated are—(1) The source and method of these illuminations; and (2) the nature and import of the revelation contained in them, supposing it to be, as confidently regarded by ourselves, a new and divine revelation. And this, whether judged by the method of its communication, or by its intrinsic nature. For the test, no less than the testimony, is twofold.

As respects the first head. These illuminations are in no way due to artificial stimulation of faculty, whether by means of drugs, or by "animal magnetism," "mesmerism," or "hypnotism," or to the induction of any abnormal state through the act of the recipient herself or of some other person; all that was or could be done on this behalf being the promotion of the interior conditions favourable to the reception of them. And these conditions consisted, not in the search for phenomenal experiences—though these would sometimes occur—but in the intense direction of the will and desire towards the highest, and an unchanging resolve to be satisfied with nothing less than the highest,

namely, the inmost and central *idea* of the fact or doctrine
to be interpreted ; the motive also being the highest,
namely, the emancipation, satisfaction, and benediction
of souls, our own and those of others. As will be seen
from this book, the majority of her illuminations were
received during natural sleep, some in satisfaction of their
recipient's own difficulties, and some in immediate response
to needs and mental requests of mine, of which she had
no cognisance and surpassing her ability to have satisfied.
And not unfrequently the responses surpassed the ability
of either of us to comprehend them at the time,—though
invariably coming through the consciousness,—and only
on our subsequent advance in perceptivity did they fully
disclose their significance, thereby proving their independence
of our own limitations. They never failed, however, sooner
or later, to demonstrate themselves to us as necessary and
self-evident truths, founded indefeasibly in the very nature
of existence ; and never did we finally accept and use them
until thus demonstrated to and recognised by us both.
And such, precisely, is the authority to which appeal is
made on their behalf, and in no way to book, person or
institution—however sacred or venerable—or even to the
manner of their communication, veritably miraculous though
this was, as the term miracle is wont to be understood. For,
to cite the preface to " The Perfect Way," we held it to be
"contrary to the nature of truth to prevail by force of authority, or of aught other than the understanding ; since truth,
how transcendent soever it be, has its witness in the mind,
and no other testimony can avail it. . . . What is indispensable is, that appeal be made to the *whole* mind, and not
to one department of it only." Now, that mind only we
had learnt to account a whole mind which comprises the
two modes of the mind, the intellect and the intuition, and
these duly trained and developed.

Having such derivation and character, these illuminations are the product, simply and purely, of the process which has ever, by those versed in Divine things, been recognised as that whereby Divine communication occurs,—namely, the spontaneous operation of the Spirit in a soul duly luminous and responsive. Through such operation the perceptive point of the mind is indrawn and uplifted to a sphere transcending both the physical and the astral or magnetic, and one altogether superior—because interior—to those accessible to the mere lucid, sensitive, or clairvoyant; in that it is the inmost and highest sphere of man's manifold nature, the celestial, or "kingdom within." Attaining to this degree of inwardness, the soul is "clothed with the sun"[1] of full intelligence, recovering all memories and discerning all principles and significations, in measure according to its capacity as developed by the experiences gained in its many earth-lives and in the intervals between, and is enabled also to communicate of them to its superficial personality. The condition is, moreover, one to enter which is to hold direct communion with the "spirits of the Just made perfect," and to be qualified to become the mouthpiece of the Church invisible and triumphant. So many and of such kind were the experiences received by Mrs Kingsford that when, after conjecture had been exhausted in the endeavour to frame a satisfactory hypothesis concerning them, assurance at length came from her own angel-genius, declaring the method of this revelation to be entirely interior, in that his "client" was a "soul of vast experience, knowing all things of herself and needing not to

---

[1] The "woman" of the Apocalypse and all other mystical Scriptures is never a person, but always the soul. Hence the significance of the present title. Any such exaltation of a person would be an act of idolatry.

b

be told ; who was being divinely enabled to recover in this
incarnation the memory of all that was in the past, expressly
in order to give the world the benefit of the holy and inner
truth of which she was the depositary ; "—so far from the
statement—extraordinary and remote from anticipation as it
was—being found difficult of credence, it was at once recognised as affording the only solution which reconciled all the
difficulties and accounted for all the facts.

And so far, it may be well to add, from these experiences
occurring in the first instance to persons predisposed to
accept them, we were—both of us—at their commencement
utterly sceptical as to their possibility, or as to there being
any basis of reality for any spiritual phenomena whatsoever.
Not that we were materialists.   In neither of us had perception ever been at that low ebb.   Rather were we idealists,
but idealists who had yet to learn that the ideal *is* the real,
and that the ideal world is a spiritual and personal world.
They came, too—as already said—in course of a quest,
not for phenomena, but for truth ; and were possible only
because the veil of matter interposed between the worlds
of sense and of reality had already, by dint of persistent
earnest seeking inwards, and by the adoption of the mode
of life which has always, by proficients in spiritual science,
been insisted on as essential to the higher perceptions,
become for us so rare and tenuous as to be readily penetrable.   The period, moreover, was anterior to that of the
recent impulse given to such studies by the importation of
kindred knowledges from the East.   And from first to last
our work was carried on in complete independence of
extraneous sources and influences, such recourse as was
had to books or to persons being on behalf of parallels,
correspondences, and confirmations in regard to our own
experiences and results.

The search for such parallels and confirmations in the records of the remote past, proved satisfactory in a measure far surpassing aught that we had ventured to anticipate. For, over and above the full recognition of our methods, facts, and doctrines in quarters worthy the highest respect, we discovered clear and positive announcements, both Biblical and extra-Biblical, of precisely such an illumination to take place at the exact time of its occurrence to us, and possessing exactly the features by which it was characterised for us,—the event itself being variously described as constituting a new illumination, the return of the Gods, the reign of Michael, the breaking of the seals and opening of the Book, the Second Advent, the " number "—or period —of the " Beast "; and the end of the World,—each alike implying the downfall of the world's materialistic system, both in philosophy and in religion, through the demonstration of the falsity of the materialistic hypothesis. The period assigned was that from 1878 to 1882, and it was precisely the period of our reception of the chief part of our doctrine and of its first promulgation, " The Perfect Way —which consists of lectures delivered in 1881—having been published in the winter of 1881-2. So that whether judged by the dates, or by the world's condition, nothing was wanting to the accomplishment of the predictions. And of these we knew only after the event.

To come to our second head—the nature and import of that which was thus received. It was from the very outset made clear to us—and every fresh accession of experience, perception, and knowledge served but to confirm the intimation—that the event constituted nothing less than the re-delivery, from the source and by the method to which it was originally due, of the ancient revelation which, under the name of the Hermetic or Kabalistic *Gnosis*, constituted the Sacred Mysteries, and underlay and controlled the expression of all the sacred religions and Scriptures, of antiquity, and formed at once a perfect system of thought and rule of life, in that it was founded in the very nature of existence as uniformly discerned under Divine illumination by the advanced souls of all times and places. From which it will be seen that the claim to be a new revelation does not imply a claim to be a new gospel, but a gospel only of interpretation, and therein of restoration and reconciliation. For the position maintained is that Christianity has failed, not because it was false, but because it has been falsified ; its official guardians having, after the wont of their order, " taken away the key of knowledge (*Gnosis*), and not only not entered in themselves, but hindered those who would have entered in."

The following remarks on the chief points in this indictment of the Church visible on behalf of the Church invisible, will serve to facilitate the comprehension of this book.

Christianity—which is rightly definable as a symbolic synthesis of the fundamental truths contained in all religions—early fell into bad hands. Like its Founder, it was crucified between two thieves, who were no other than the types of its crucifiers. These were, on the one hand, Superstition, which is the distortion of spiritual perception ; and on the other hand, Materialism, which is the privation of spiritual perception. These are the " two beasts " of mystical Scripture, which come up, respectively, from the " sea " and the " earth," to ravage the hopes of humanity. And the two are one under the name of Sacerdotalism, being but varied modes of its manifestation. It was Sacerdotalism that crucified both Christ and the doctrine of Christ with its two hands Superstition and Materialism.

For, operating as Superstition, Sacerdotalism perverted

into mystery, and rendered not merely unintelligible but irrational, a gospel which in itself was absolutely simple, obvious, and reasonable. This is the doctrine that the true life and substance of Humanity are not material and created, but spiritual and divine; and that it is possible for man, by co-operating with the spirit within him, and subordinating his lower nature to his higher, to rise wholly into and be reconstituted—which is "regenerated"—of his higher, and become thereby divine, having in himself the power of life eternal. And that whereby this is effected—namely, inward purification—is the sole secret of the Christs. Wherefore he in whom this process finds full accomplishment, *has* and *is* Christ, and attains the summit of human evolution, the point of junction between Humanity and Divinity. Thus demonstrating to men in his own person their divine potentialities, and the manner of the realisation thereof, and by his loving self-devotion on their behalf softening their hearts and winning them to follow in his steps, he becomes their "Saviour." And that he is said to save them by his blood, is because "the blood is the life," and the true life-blood of the Christ is a spirit absolutely pure,—the inward God in the man,—and by the attainment of this pure spirit man is redeemed. And that the Christ is said to suffer and die for others, is because through his abounding sympathy he suffers even to death in and with them;—not instead of them—"for" does not here mean "instead of"—for that would be to deprive them of their means of redemption, since only through his own suffering can anyone repent and become perfected.

This doctrine, so reasonable and obvious, and satisfying alike to head and heart, Sacerdotalism, operating as Superstition, superseded by shifting the whole edifice of Christianity from its proper—because its only intelligible and consistent basis in Pantheism, or the doctrine that God is all and in all—to that of an impossible Manichæanism—or the doctrine of two eternal, self-subsistent opposing principles of good and evil,—a doctrine which by making evil a positive thing, and thus exalting it to an equal rank with God, at once dethrones God and eternises evil. It deprives God also of His supreme quality of Justice, by representing Him as accepting physical suffering as an equivalent for moral guilt, and the punishment of the innocent in lieu of that of the guilty. While by removing Christ from the category of the highest human to that of the superhuman, it robs all of their potential divinity in favour of the exclusive divinity of one; and thereby effectually neutralises the significance and value of his mission, the express purpose of which was to show his fellow-men, not what could be achieved by some great supernatural personage, with whom they could have nothing in common, but what they themselves have it in them in due time to become, simply by giving fair play to their own best, namely, the ideal of perfection disclosed to them by their own intuition. For the fulfilment of the intuition is the realisation of the ideal; and the realisation of the ideal is the " Finding af Christ."

Operating as Materialism, and preferring the letter to the spirit, the symbol to the verity, the form to the substance, Sacerdotalism ignored and suppressed the real, because the mystical and spiritual, import of Christianity, by means of the idolatrous exaltation, as the agents of salvation, of its persons, events, forms, and other things physical, in place of its spiritual realities, the principles, processes, and states implied by these and of which they were the symbolic representatives. The obvious truth that religion, as a thing relating not to the senses but to the soul, and appealing, therefore, only to the soul, must consist in things cognate

to the soul, in that they are of like nature with the soul,
and not in things material and physical,—was altogether
set aside, all logical proprieties being violated, as just shown,
by positing physical bloodshed and suffering as the compen-
sation for moral guilt, and these, too, of another than the
guilty—instead of the repentance and amendment to which
they are ordained to minister. While every expression in
Scriptures avowedly mystical and parabolical, was enforced
in its literal sense, in defiance of repeated injunctions in
Scripture to the contrary. And that which was really "an
eternal gospel" by virtue of its being founded in the unchanging nature of things, and everlastingly demonstrable
to the mind and verifiable by inward experience, was made
dependent on the perishable records of physical events in
themselves exceptional, and liable—whatever the testimony
—sooner or later to be called into question.

Christianity was further mutilated, dwarfed, and distorted
by the exclusion from recognition and worship due, of
those Divine Principles or modes of Deity, variously desig-
nated the Gods and the Spirits of God, by whose immediate
operation in the soul the man regenerate and made perfect
is built up, the spiritual chaos is transformed into a kosmos,
and Christ becomes Christ. The very process of Regeneration, moreover, although emphatically declared by
Jesus to be the sole condition of Salvation,—a process
wholly spiritual and interior to the individual,—came to be
either altogether ignored or thrust into the background, in
favour of that of atonement by vicarious physical bloodshed,
through the loss of the knowledge of the meaning alike of
regeneration and of atonement, and the consequent failure
to recognise those terms as denoting one and the same process, and this a process, as just said, wholly spiritual and
interior to the individual.

While, as presented by Sacerdotalism, or—to adopt the modern equivalent of this term as more appropriate for the rest of these remarks—Ecclesiasticism, Christianity is thus but a congeries of arbitrary and unintelligible propositions, bearing no discernible relation to the needs, aspirations, or perceptions, whether of the mind or of the soul; as presented in the recovered Gnosis, it is at once intelligible and irrefragable, constituting a perfect system of thought and rule of life, and satisfying alike the demands of the keenest mind, the longings of the tenderest heart, and the aspirations of the most ardent soul.   These are characteristics which not the most hardy champions of Ecclesiasticism venture to claim for the orthodox presentation; but on the contrary they freely acknowledge it to be a problem insoluble by reason, and one to be accepted on authority of Church or Book, even at the cost of intellectual suicide.   Said one of them recently—a dignitary of the Anglican Church—speaking, apparently, not alone for his order, but for mankind at large, " We weary ourselves vainly in endeavouring to shape these truths into a system.   We have no faculties for such speculation.   It is enough for us to rest in the language of the Apostles."[1]   Such is the frank admission of the official guardians of the faith according to Ecclesiasticism, and the admission is one in respect of which it is hard to determine whether its candour or its courage is the most conspicuous. Its candour, because of its complete indifference to the consequences to their order which can hardly fail to follow the confession that it does not understand its own teaching; and its courage, because of its palpable disregard of the emphatic injunctions wherein Scripture expressly reprobates such " resting in its language," affirming that the " letter kills,"— as indeed it has killed the very faculty of the perception of

[1] Canon Westcott on the Atonement.—*Historic Faith* (p. 133).

things spiritual in all who have "rested in" it,—and strenuously repudiating meanwhile the notion of the incomprehensibility of its doctrines, as when it calls on men to "prove all things" and to render a "reasonable service," and insists on the necessity of "hearing ears and seeing eyes," that is, of a "spirit of understanding" in respect of divine things, as the indispensable basis of the faith that saves. But to this it has come, that after having rendered the doctrine of Scripture unintelligible by insisting, against the express injunctions of Scripture, on the literal meaning of the words of Scripture, Ecclesiasticism now complains that owing to the limitations of human faculty, there is no alternative but to rest in the letter of Scripture! Obviously it is not Ecclesiasticism that is entitled to resent the advent of an interpretation which, by restoring the Spirit to the letter of Scripture, shall restore the doctrine and rehabilitate the credit of Scripture.

But whatever may be the attitude of Ecclesiasticism towards the new—or rather the recovered—interpretation, that of the world at large is scarcely doubtful. The world, it is true, has followed the Church in its fall into materiality in respect of things spiritual—a fall which, but for the Church's initiative, the world had not undergone. But there are tokens manifold and indisputable to prove that the heart of the world is, nevertheless, in the main right; and, consequently, that—like the Prodigal of the parable—having once eaten of the husks of mere materiality—whether religious or scientific—it has learned to loathe them, and is already coming to its proper, because better, self, and turning wistful thoughts homewards. And hence it is that for those who in virtue of their "ploughing with the heifer" of the spiritual consciousness, are able to "expound the riddle"[1] of

---

[1] Judges xiv. 12-18.

the age, the epoch is no other than " Othniel "—God's good time; the world is "Caleb"—one whose heart is right; " Kirjath-sepher "—the city of the letter—has already sur- rendered; and " Achsah ".—the rending of the veil (that hid the Spirit), is about to become the bride of the victor, bringing to him as her dowry the "upper and nether springs" of those blessed results in soul and mind and heart and life which ever flow from the full understanding of Divine things.[1]   From which it may be surely inferred that unless Ecclesiasticism also accept the new interpreta- tion, which also is the old, and like a living garment participate in the growth of its wearer, it will find itself discarded as obsolete; while the new humanity—to which it will thus have served but for matrix—will constitute itself a new, and more than ever a true, Church, and one that can never fail and fall, inasmuch as it will have for foundation, not the incohesive sands of authority and the letter, but the indefeasible Rock of the Spirit and the Understanding.

    .   .   .   .

The chief means proposed in this book in furtherance of its ends, may be summarised as follows :—

1. The re-establishment of the Understanding as the basis of Faith.

2. The restoration to its true place as the object of veneration, of the thing signified—that is, of the spirit, substance, verity, or reality—instead of the symbol or appearance of it; and therein the abolition of idolatry both in religion and science, whether the object be a person, a book, or an institution, the form, the letter, or the rite, or matter itself,—to the end that God only may be worshipped.

[1] Joshua xv. 16-19.

3. The restoration of the doctrine of the Duality of the Divine Unity, or Original Being; and therein the recognition of the essential divinity of both constituents of existence, its life, or force, and its substance; with the result of removing matter from its wrongful position as an independent, self-subsistent entity, to its proper rank as a mode of the Divine Being, wherein it represents Spirit, by the power of the Divine Will projected into conditions and limitations, and made exteriorly cognisable.

The restoration of this doctrine involves the deposition alike of Materialism, and the no less atheistic Manichæanism also widely in vogue, in favour of that true Pantheism which, while it regards God as the all in all of Being, does not regard all Being as in the *condition* of God.

4. The restoration of the true doctrine of Creation and Redemption by means of Evolution, (1) by re-establishing the doctrine of the permanence of the true Ego of the individual, and its persistence through all changes of exterior form and condition, thus positing as the subject of Evolution, an entity competent to retain the impressions, and to progress by means, of its experiences; and (2) by exhibiting one and the same method as that both of Creation and of Redemption, the difference being only of medium—or "vehicle"—and of direction; inasmuch as the former occurs by a centrifugal operation in matter; and the latter by a centripetal operation in substance (or spirit),—a process which constitutes *in*volutional evolution, both processes occurring in the same individual. Herein consists the reconciliation of science and religion, inasmuch as Redemption is thus the logical complement of Creation and outcome of Evolution, in that the process whereby it occurs—which is mystically called Regeneration—consists in the reconstitution of the individual by and of the higher

elements of his own system, the Soul and Spirit, and—instead of dispensing with experience—is accomplished by means of the experiences acquired in a multiplicity of earth-lives, the number of which is determined by the exigencies of the individual case, their purpose being to afford the requisite opportunities for the " suffering "—which is *felt* experience—through which alone perfection, and thereby salvation, are attainable.

The restoration of the doctrine of a multiplicity of earth-lives involves as its corollary that of the doctrine of acquired destiny, called by the Hindûs " Karma." [1]

5. The interpretation of Christianity and of religion generally, in such manner as to exhibit the identity of the needs and perceptions of the soul in all ages ; as well also as the identity of the theological doctrine of salvation by " vicarious atonement " with the mystical, but none the less scientific, doctrine of redemption by regeneration as defined in the foregoing paragraph.

6. The solution of the problems of inspiration, prophecy, and miracles, and the practical demonstration of the so-called supernatural as natural to man, in that it appertains, not to the superhuman, but to the higher human.

7. The disclosure of the Christian *origines* as regards both the person of Jesus and the composition of the Gospels.

8. The enlargement of Christian faith and practice by means of the restoration of the Gods to their due place in man's recognition and veneration ; and the combination of the Greek and Buddhist with the Christian ideals, thereby restoring to man the sense of beauty, joy, and hopefulness which comes of the recognition of the universal indwelling Divinity—(which is Greek) ; and providing a perfect system and rule in respect of things physical, intellectual, and moral

[1] See Appendix, " Definitions and Explanations."

—(which is Buddhist), as the foundation for the higher, because more interior, spirituality (which is Christian).

Going so far as do the illuminations in this book to realise the most sanguine anticipations of that "new birth of Esoteric Christianity, or new and higher religion in which philosophy, religion, and poetry shall be fused into a unity,"[1] to the full satisfaction of man's highest needs and aspirations, their lamented recipient, Anna Kingsford, must, sooner or later, be recognised by all competent judges, as having made at once to science, philosophy, morality, religion, and literature at large, and especially to that of our own country and language, a contribution of an order unique, unsurpassed, and in certain respects of supreme moment, unequalled and even unapproached.

In the arrangement of the contents of this volume, the method followed is that of subordinating the chronological to the logical, and regulating the sequence in accordance with the mutual dependence of the subjects treated. It is on this principle that precedence is given to those illuminations which may best serve as the writer's personal credentials in respect of her mission. The second place is assigned to those which, in virtue of their being derived from Scripture, and prophetic of precisely such an event in the world's spiritual history as to occur at this time, serve—at least for the faithful—to relieve the idea of a new revelation of any *a priori* improbability. The others—with the exception of Part II., which is arranged according to express instructions —follow in an order the *rationale* of which will be obvious to the intelligent reader. And all of them are given as originally written down either by their recipient herself, or by myself acting as amanuensis,—a function which—

[1] Schelling.

as her sole associate in the spiritual task with which we were jointly charged—I alone exercised.   It need hardly be added that, regarding as we did that task as a sacred one, and the highest that could devolve upon mortals, no pains were spared either to observe the conditions necessary for it, or to secure absolute accuracy in our relation of the "things seen and heard" in the prosecution of it.   For the annotations and explanations—which are in accordance with the teaching received—I alone am responsible, that is, restricting the term "alone" to its ordinary acceptation.

Concerning the hiatus in the "Hymns of the Gods" in Part II., Mrs Kingsford wrote in her diary under date August 23, 1887, being the eleventh month of her last illness, and the seventh before its termination :—

"I wish I knew whether I am to recover or not.   It seems, judging from physical signs, as if I could not live long; but then strange things hap where prophetesses are concerned!   I am so sure that the prophecy is not finished, and that a vast amount of work remains to do which must be done by me or not at all, that I cannot but think the Gods will restore me in time. . . .

"Why do not the Gods give me the three hymns which are yet wanting to their series?   I have the hymns of Phoibos, of Hermes, of Aphrodite, of Dionysos, of Saturn. I yet want the hymns of Ares, Zeus, and Artemis.   If these hymns be not given to me, they will never be given to any other. . . .

"I had hoped to have been one of the pioneers of the new awakening of the world.   I had thought to have helped in the overthrow of the idolatrous altars and the purging of the temple ; and now I must die just as the day of battle dawns and the sound of the chariot wheels is heard.   Is it, perhaps, all premature?   Have we thought the time nearer than it really is? Must I go, and sleep, and come again before the hour sounds?" [1]

It remains only to add in regard to Part III. and the Appendix, that the references to my own experiences are admitted with great reluctance, and in spite of every effort to deprive the book, not merely of a biographical character, but far more so of an autobiographical character. It was only on finding that the omission of such references would operate disadvantageously by mutilating or weakening the record—(as by leaving it to appear as if I were unable of my own knowledge to testify to the possibility of such experiences)—that I consented to renounce my design and strong preference in the matter.

Edward Maitland.

London, *Whitsuntide*, 1889.

[1] I cite this last paragraph as showing how small in her own view appeared the work which she accomplished as compared to that which remained, and which she felt she had it in her to accomplish were only time and strength allowed ; and also as showing the intensity of her realisation of its importance, as well as her conviction of the truth of the doctrine of a multiplicity of earth-lives.

ILLUMINATIONS.

PART THE FIRST.

No. I.

CONCERNING THE THREE VEILS BETWEEN MAN AND GOD.[1]

A GOLDEN chalice, like those used in Catholic rites, but having three linings, was given to me in my sleep by an Angel. These linings, he told me signified the three degrees of the heavens,—purity of life, purity of heart, and purity of doctrine. Immediately afterwards there appeared to me a great dome-covered temple, Moslem in style, and on the threshold of it a tall angel clad in white linen, who with an air of command was directing a party of men engaged in destroying and throwing into the street numerous crucifixes, bibles, prayer-books, altar-utensils, and other sacred emblems. As I stood watching, somewhat scandalised at the apparent sacrilege, a voice at a great height in the air, cried

[1] London, March 1881.

A

with startling distinctness, "All the idols He shall
utterly destroy!" Then the same voice, seeming
to ascend still higher, cried to me, "Come hither and
see!" Immediately it appeared to me that I was
lifted up by my hair and carried above the earth.
And suddenly there arose in mid-air the apparition
of a man of majestic aspect, in an antique garb, and
surrounded by a throng of prostrate worshippers.
At first the appearance of this figure was strange
to me ; but while I looked intently at it, a change
came over the face and dress, and I thought I
recognised Buddha,—the Messiah of India. But
scarcely had I convinced myself of this, when a great
voice, like a thousand voices shouting in unison,
cried to the worshippers : " Stand upright on your
feet :—Worship God only !" And again the figure
changed, as though a cloud had passed before it, and
now it seemed to assume the shape of Jesus. Again
I saw the kneeling adorers, and again the mighty
voice cried, "Arise ! Worship God only !" The
sound of this voice was like thunder, and I noted
that it had seven echoes. Seven times the cry re-
verberated, ascending with each utterance as though
mounting from sphere to sphere. Then suddenly I
fell through the air, as though a hand had been withdrawn from sustaining me : and again touching the
earth, I stood within the temple I had seen in the
first part of my vision. At its east end was a great
altar, from above and behind which came faintly a
white and beautiful light, the radiance of which was
arrested and obscured by a dark curtain suspended

from the dome before the altar. And the body of the temple, which, but for the curtain, would have been fully illumined, was plunged in gloom, broken only by the fitful gleams of a few half-expiring oil-lamps, hanging here and there from the vast cupola. At the right of the altar stood the same tall angel I had before seen on the temple threshold, holding in his hand a smoking censer. Then, observing that he was looking earnestly at me, I said to him : "Tell me, what curtain is this before the light, and why is the temple in darkness?" And he answered, " This veil is not One, but Three ; and the Three are Blood, Idolatry, and the Curse of Eve. And to you it is given to withdraw them ; be faithful and courageous ; the time has come." Now the first curtain was red, and very heavy ; and with a great effort I drew it aside, and said, " I have put away the veil of blood from before Thy Face. Shine, O Lord God ! " But a voice from behind the folds of the two remaining coverings answered me, " I cannot shine, because of the idols." And lo, before me a curtain of many colours, woven about with all manner of images, crucifixes, madonnas, Old and New Testaments, prayer-books, and other religious symbols, some strange and hideous like the idols of China and Japan, some beautiful like those of the Greeks and Christians. And the weight of the curtain was like lead, for it was thick with gold and silver embroideries. But with both hands I tore it away, and cried, "I have put away the idols from before Thy Face. Shine, O Lord God ! " And now the light was clearer and

brighter. But yet before me hung a third veil, all of
black ; and upon it was traced in outline the figure of
four lilies on a single stem inverted, their cups
opening downwards. And from behind this veil the
voice answered me again, " I cannot shine, because of
the curse of Eve." Then I put forth all my strength,
and with a great will rent away the curtain, crying,
" I have put away her curse from before Thee. Shine,
O Lord God ! "

And there was no more a veil, but a landscape,
more glorious and perfect than words can paint, a
garden of absolute beauty, filled with trees of palm,
and olive, and fig, rivers of clear water and lawns of
tender green ; and distant groves and forests framed
about by mountains crowned with snow ; and on the
brow of their shining peaks a rising sun, whose light
it was I had seen behind the veils. And about the
sun, in mid-air hung white misty shapes of great
angels, as clouds at morning float above the place of
dawn. And beneath, under a mighty tree of cedar,
stood a white elephant, bearing in his golden houdah
a beautiful woman robed as a queen, and wearing a
crown. But while I looked, entranced, and longing
to look for ever, the garden, the altar, and the temple
were carried up from me into Heaven. Then as I
stood gazing upwards, came again the voice, at first
high in the air, but falling earthwards as I listened.
And behold, before me appeared the white pinnacle
of a minaret, and around and beneath it the sky was
all gold and red with the glory of the rising sun.
And I perceived that now the voice was that of a

solitary Muezzin standing on the minaret with uplifted hands and crying :—

> " Put away Blood from among you !
> Destroy your Idols !
> Restore your Queen ! "

And straightway a voice, like that of an infinite multitude, coming as though from above and around and
beneath my feet,—a voice like a wind rising upwards
from caverns under the hills to their loftiest far-off
heights among the stars,—responded—

> " Worship God alone ! "

No. II.

PART I.

CONCERNING INSPIRATION AND PROPHESYING.[1]

I HEARD last night in my sleep a voice speaking
to me, and saying—

1. You ask the method and nature of Inspiration,
and the means whereby God revealeth the Truth.

2. Know that there is no enlightenment from without : the secret of things is revealed from within.

3. From without cometh no Divine Revelation :
but the Spirit within beareth witness.

4. Think not I tell you that which you know not :
for except you know it, it cannot be given to you.

5. To him that hath it is given, and he hath the
more abundantly.

[1] Paris, February 7, 1880.

6. None is a prophet save he who knoweth : the instructor of the people is a man of many lives.

7. Inborn knowledge and the perception of things, these are the sources of revelation : the soul of the man instructeth him, having already learned by experience.

8. Intuition is inborn experience ; that which the soul knoweth of old and of former years.

9. And Illumination is the Light of Wisdom, whereby a man perceiveth heavenly secrets.

10. Which Light is the Spirit of God within the man, showing unto him the things of God.

11. Do not think that I tell you anything you know not ; all cometh from within : the Spirit that informeth is the Spirit of God in the prophet.

12. What, then, you ask, is the *Medium ;* and how are to be regarded the utterances of one speaking in trance ?

13. God speaketh through no man in the way you suppose ; for the Spirit of the Prophet beholdeth God with open eyes. If he fall into a trance, his eyes are open, and his interior man knoweth what is spoken by him.

14. But when a man speaketh that which he knoweth not, he is obsessed : an impure spirit, or one that is bound, hath entered into him.

15. There are many such, but their words are as the words of men who know not : these are not prophets nor inspired.

16. God obsesseth no man ; God is revealed : and he to whom God is revealed speaketh that which he knoweth.

17. Christ Jesus [1] understandeth God : he knoweth that of which he beareth witness.

18. But they who, being mediums, utter in trance things of which they have no knowledge, and of which their own spirit is uninformed : these are obsessed with a spirit of divination, a strange spirit, not their own.

19. Of such beware, for they speak many lies, and are deceivers, working often for gain or for pleasure sake : and they are a grief and a snare to the faithful.

20. Inspiration may indeed be mediumship, but it is conscious ; and the knowledge of the prophet instructeth him.

21. Even though he speak in an ecstasy, he uttereth nothing that he knoweth not.

22. Thou who art a prophet hast had many lives : yea, thou hast taught many nations, and hast stood before kings.

23. And God hath instructed thee in the years that are past ; and in the former times of the earth.

24. By prayer, by fasting, by meditation, by painful seeking, hast thou attained that thou knowest.

25. There is no knowledge but by labour ; there is no intuition but by experience.

26. I have seen thee on the hills of the East : I have followed thy steps in the wilderness : I have seen thee adore at sunrise : I have marked thy night watches in the caves of the mountains.

27. Thou hast attained with patience, O prophet ! God hath revealed the truth to thee from within.

[1] Here implying the Christ Jesus within, or the regenerated human nature, in whomsoever occurring.

PART 2.

*A Prophecy of the Kingdom of the Soul, mystically
called the Day of the Woman.*

1. And now I show you a mystery and a new
thing, which is part of the mystery of the fourth
day of creation.

2. The word which shall come to save the world,
shall be uttered by a woman.

3. A woman shall conceive, and shall bring forth
the tidings of salvation.

4. For the reign of Adam is at its last hour; and
God shall crown all things by the creation of Eve.

5. Hitherto the man hath been alone, and hath
had dominion over the earth.

6. But when the woman shall be created, God shall
give unto her the kingdom; and she shall be first in
rule and highest in dignity.

7. Yea, the last shall be first; and the elder shall
serve the younger.

8. So that women shall no more lament for their
womanhood: but men shall rather say, "O that we
had been born women!"

9. For the strong shall be put down from their
seat; and the meek shall be exalted to their place.

10. The days of the covenant of manifestation
are passing away: the gospel of interpretation
cometh.

11. There shall nothing new be told; but that
which is ancient shall be interpreted.

12. So that man the manifestor shall resign his office ; and woman the interpreter shall give light to the world.

13. Hers is the fourth office : she revealeth that which the Lord hath manifested.

14. Hers is the light of the heavens, and the brightest of the planets of the holy seven.

15. She is the fourth dimension ; the eyes which enlighten ; the power which draweth inward to God.

16. And her kingdom cometh ; the day of the exaltation of woman.

17. And her reign shall be greater than the reign of the man : for Adam shall be put down from his place ; and she shall have dominion for ever.

18. And she who is alone shall bring forth more children to God, than she who hath an husband.

19. There shall no more be a reproach against women : but against men shall be the reproach.

20. For the woman is the crown of man, and the final manifestation of humanity.

21. She is the nearest to the throne of God, when she shall be revealed.

22. But the creation of woman is not yet complete : but it shall be complete in the time which is at hand.

23. All things are thine, O Mother of God : all things are thine, O Thou who risest from the sea ; and Thou shalt have dominion over all the worlds.

No. III.

CONCERNING THE PROPHECY OF THE IMMACU-
LATE CONCEPTION.[1]

I STAND upon the sea-shore. The moon overhead is at the full. A soft and warm breath, like that of the summer wind, blows in my face. The aroma of it is salt with the breath of the sea. O Sea! O Moon! from you I shall gather what I seek! You shall recount to me the story of the Immaculate Conception of Maria, whose symbols ye are!

Allegory of stupendous significance! with which the Church of God has so long been familiar, but which yet never penetrated its understanding, like the holy fire which enveloped the sacred Bush, but which nevertheless, the Bush withstood and resisted.

Yet has there been one who comprehended, and who interpreted aright the parable of the Immaculate Conception ; and he found it through US, by the light of his own intense love, for he was the disciple of love, and his name is still—the Beloved ;—John, the Seer of the Apocalypse. For he, in the vision of the woman clothed with the sun, set forth the true significance of the Immaculate Conception. For the Im-

---

[1] Paris, July 26, 1877. Received in the night and written down under trance, the seeress being transported in spirit to the sea-side, but maintaining with the body a connection sufficient to enable her to write. The changes of person from singular to plural are due to the overshadowing influence speaking at one time as a unity, and at another as a plurality.

maculate Conception is none other than the prophecy
of the means whereby the universe shall at last be
redeemed. Maria—the sea of limitless space—Maria
the Virgin, born herself immaculate and without spot,
of the womb of the ages, shall in the fulness of time
bring forth the perfect man, who shall redeem the race.
He is not one man, but ten thousand times ten thousand, the Son of Man, who shall overcome the limitations of matter, and the evil which is the result of
the materialisation of spirit. His Mother is spirit,
his Father is spirit, yet he is himself incarnate; and
how then shall he overcome evil, and restore matter
to the condition of spirit? By force of love. It is
love which is the centripetal power of the universe;
it is by love that all creation returns to the bosom of
God. The force which projected all things is will,
and will is the centrifugal power of the universe.
Will alone could not overcome the evil which results
from the limitations of matter; but it shall be overcome in the end by sympathy, which is the knowledge
of God in others,—the recognition of the omnipresent
self. This is love. And it is with the children of
the spirit, the servants of love, that the dragon of
matter makes war.

Now, whether or not the world be strong enough
to bear this yet, we know not. This is not the first
time we have revealed these things to men. An
ancient heresy, cursed by the Church, arose out of a
true inspiration; for the disciples are ever weaker
than the master, and they have not his spiritual
discernment. I speak of the Gnostics. To the

Master of the Gnostics we revealed the truth of the
Immaculate Conception.   We told him that Im-
manuel should be the God-Man who, transcending
the limitations of matter, should efface the evil of
materialisation by the force of love, and should see
and hear and speak and feel as though he were pure
spirit, and had annihilated the boundaries of matter.
This, then, he taught; but they who heard his
teaching, applying his words only to the individual
Jesus, affirmed that Jesus had had no material body,
but that he was an emanation of a spiritual nature;
an Æon who, without substance or true being in the
flesh, had borne a phantom part in the world of men.
Beware lest in like manner ye also are misread.   It
is so hard for men to be spiritual.   It is as hard for
us to declare ourselves without mystery.   The Church
knows not the source of its dogmas.   We marvel also
at the blindness of the hearers, who indeed hear, but
who have not eyes to see.   We speak in vain,—ye
discern not spiritual things.   Ye are so materialised
that ye perceive only the material.   The Spirit comes
and goes; ye hear the sound of its voice: but ye
cannot tell whither it goeth nor whence it cometh.
All that is true is spiritual.   No dogma of the Church
is true that seems to bear a physical meaning.   For
matter shall cease, and all that is of it, but the Word
of the Lord shall remain for ever.   And how shall it
remain except it be purely spiritual; since, when
matter ceases, it would then be no longer comprehensible?   I tell you again, and of a truth,—no
dogma is real that is not spiritual.   If it be true, and

yet seem to you to have a material signification, know that you have not solved it. It is a mystery: seek its interpretation. That which is true, is for spirit alone.

No. IV.

CONCERNING REVELATION.[1]

ALL true and worthy illuminations are *reveila-tions*, or re-veilings. Mark the meaning of this word. There can be no true or worthy illumination which destroys distances and exposes the details of things.

Look at this landscape. Behold how its mountains and forests are suffused with soft and delicate mist, which half conceals and half discloses their shapes and tints. See how this mist like a tender veil enwraps the distances, and merges the reaches of the land with the clouds of heaven!

How beautiful it is, how orderly and wholesome its fitness, and the delicacy of its appeal to the eye and heart! And how false would be that sense which should desire to tear away this clinging veil, to bring far objects near, and to reduce everything to foreground in which details only should be apparent, and all outlines sharply defined!

Distance and mist make the beauty of Nature:

---

[1] Home, November 27, 1883. Received in sleep.

and no poet would desire to behold her otherwise than through this lovely and modest veil.

And as with exoteric, so with esoteric nature. The secrets of every human soul are sacred and known only to herself. The ego is inviolable, and its personality is its own right for ever.

Therefore mathematical rules and algebraic formulæ cannot be forced into the study of human lives; nor can human personalities be dealt with as though they were mere ciphers or arithmetical quantities.

The soul is too subtle, too instinct with life and will for treatment such as this.

One may dissect a corpse; one may analyse and classify chemical constituents; but it is impossible to dissect or analyse any living thing.

The moment it is so treated it escapes. Life is not subject to dissection.

The opening of the shrine will always find it empty: the God is gone.

A soul may know her own past, and may see in her own light: but none can see it for her if she see it not.

Herein is the beauty and sanctity of personality.

The ego is self-centered and not diffused; for the tendency of all evolution is towards centralisation and individualism.

And life is so various, and so beautifully diverse in its unity, that no hard and fast mathematical law-making can imprison its manifoldness.

All is order: but the elements of this order harmonise by means of their infinite diversities and gradations.

The true mysteries remained always content with nature's harmony : they sought not to drag distances into foregrounds ; or to dissipate the mountain nebula, in whose bosom the sun is reflected.

For these sacred mists are the *media* of light, and the glorifiers of nature.

Therefore the doctrine of the mysteries is truly *reveilation,*—a veiling and a re-veiling of that which it is not possible for eye to behold without violating all the order and sanctities of nature.

For distance and visual rays, causing the diversities of far and near, of perspective and mergent tints, of horizon and foreground, are part of natural order and sequence : and the law expressed in their properties cannot be violated.

For no law is ever broken.

The hues and aspects of distance and mist indeed may vary and dissolve according to the quality and quantity of the light which falls upon them : but they are there always, and no human eye can annul or annihilate them.

Even words, even pictures are symbols and veils. Truth itself is unutterable, save by God to God.

No. V.

CONCERNING THE INTERPRETATION OF THE MYSTICAL SCRIPTURES.

PART I.[1]

" **I**F, therefore, they be Mystic Books, they ought also to have a Mystic Consideration. But the Fault of most Writers lieth in this,—that they distinguish not between the Books of Moses the Prophet, and those Books which are of an historical Nature. And this is the more surprising because not a few of such Critics have rightly discerned the esoteric Character, if not indeed the true Interpretation, of the Story of Eden; yet have they not applied to the Remainder of the Allegory the same Method which they found to fit the Beginning; but so soon as they

---

[1] Paris, June 6, 1878. Read in sleep, in a library purporting to be that of Emmanuel Swedenborg, in the spiritual world, Swedenborg himself being present. As we subsequently ascertained, it represents the doctrine of that famous seer, but without his limitations. Like most of the writings thus beheld by the seeress, it was in German text and archaic spelling, and also, like several others, was given in immediate response to a mental request for light on the subjects treated, made by me without her knowledge either of my request or of my need, or being able of herself to have supplied the want. On seeking—also from transcendental sources—to know more respecting this experience, we received for answer that "a portion of Swedenborg is still in this sphere, through which he can communicate with those with whom he is in affinity;" and that under his magnetism, the seeress had been enabled—as stated in the preface—to recover these recollections. The capitals of the original are retained, but the spelling is modernised.

are over the earlier Stanzas of the Poem, they would have the Rest of it to be of another Nature.

" It is, then, pretty well established and accepted of most Authors, that the Legend of Adam and Eve, and of the Miraculous Tree and the Fruit which was the Occasion of Death, is, like the story of Eros and Psyche, and so many others of all Religions, a Parable with a hidden, that is, with a Mystic Meaning. But so also is the Legend which follows concerning the Sons of these Mystical Parents, the Story of Cain and Abel his Brother, the Story of the Flood, of the Ark, of the saving of the clean and unclean Beasts, of the Rainbow, of the twelve Sons of Jacob, and, not stopping there, of the whole Relation concerning the Flight out of Egypt. For it is not to be supposed that the two Sacrifices offered to God by the Sons of Adam, were real Sacrifices, any more than it is to be supposed that the Apple which caused the Doom of Mankind, was a real Apple. It ought to be known, indeed, for the right Understanding of the Mystical Books, that in their esoteric Sense they deal, not with material Things, but with spiritual Realities ; and that as Adam is not a Man, nor Eve a Woman, nor the Tree a Plant in its true Significa-tion, so also are not the Beasts named in the same Books real Beasts, but that the Mystic Intention of them is implied. When, therefore, it is written that Abel took of the Firstlings of his Flock to offer unto the Lord, it is signified that he offered that which a Lamb implies, and which is the holiest and highest of spiritual Gifts. Nor is Abel himself a real Person,

B

but the Type and spiritual Presentation of the Race of the Prophets; of whom, also, Moses was a Member, together with the Patriarchs. Were the Prophets, then, Shedders of Blood? God forbid; they dealt not with Things material, but with spiritual Significations. Their Lambs without Spot, their white Doves, their Goats, their Rams, and other sacred Creatures, are so many Signs and Symbols of the various Graces and Gifts which a Mystic People should offer to Heaven. Without such Sacrifices is no Remission of Sin. But when the Mystic Sense was lost, then Carnage followed, the Prophets ceased out of the Land, and the Priests bore rule over the People. Then, when again the Voice of the Prophets arose, they were constrained to speak plainly, and declared in a Tongue foreign to their Method, that the Sacrifices of God are not the Flesh of Bulls or the Blood of Goats, but holy Vows and sacred Thanksgivings, their Mystical Counterparts. As God is a Spirit, so also are His Sacrifices Spiritual. What Folly, what Ignorance, to offer material Flesh and Drink to pure Power and essential Being! Surely in vain have the Prophets spoken, and in vain have the Christs been manifested!

"Why will you have Adam to be Spirit and Eve Matter, since the Mystic Books deal only with spiritual Entities? The Tempter himself even is not Matter, but that which gives Matter the Precedence. Adam is, rather, intellectual Force: he is of Earth. Eve is the moral Conscience: she is the Mother of the Living. Intellect, then, is the male, and Intuition the female Principle. And the Sons of Intuition, herself fallen, shall at last recover Truth and redeem all Things. By her Fault, indeed, is the moral Conscience of Humanity made subject to the intellectual Force, and thereby all Manner of Evil and Confusion abounds, since her Desire is unto him, and he rules over her until now. But the End foretold by the Seer is not far off. Then shall the Woman be exalted, clothed with the Sun, and carried to the Throne of God. And her Sons shall make War with the Dragon, and have Victory over him. Intuition, therefore, pure and a Virgin, shall be the Mother and Redemptress of her fallen Sons, whom she bore under Bondage to her Husband the intellectual Force."

PART 2.

" Moses, therefore, knowing the Mysteries of the Religion of the Egyptians, and having learned of their Occultists the Value and Signification of all sacred Birds and Beasts, delivered like Mysteries to his own People. But certain of the sacred Animals of Egypt he retained not in Honour, for Motives which were equally of Mystic Origin. And he taught his Initiated the Spirit of the heavenly Hieroglyphs, and bade them, when they made Festival before God, to carry with them in Procession, with Music and with Danc-

---

[1] This portion, which was received, also in sleep, two nights after the foregoing, is a part remembered of a lecture—evidently out of the same book—delivered by a man in priestly garb, in an amphitheatre of white stone, to a class of students, of whom the seeress was one.

ing, such of the sacred Animals as were, by their
interior Significance, related to the Occasion.   Now,
of these Beasts, he chiefly selected Males of the first
Year, without Spot or Blemish, to signify that it is
beyond all Things needful that Man should dedicate
to the Lord his Intellect and his Reason, and this
from the Beginning, and without the least Reserve.
And that he was very wise in teaching this, is evident from the History of the World in all Ages,
and particularly in these last days.   For what is it
that has led Men to renounce the Realities of the
Spirit, and to propagate false Theories and corrupt
Sciences, denying all Things save the Appearance
which can be apprehended by the outer Senses, and
making themselves one with the Dust of the Ground?
It is their Intellect which, being unsanctified, has led
them astray; it is the Force of the Mind in them,
which, being corrupt, is the Cause of their own Ruin,
and of that of their Disciples.   As, then, the Intellect
is apt to be the great Traitor against Heaven, so also
is it the Force by which Men, following their pure
Intuition, may also grasp and apprehend the Truth.
For which Reason it is written that the Christs are
subject to their Mothers.   Not that by any means
the Intellect is to be dishonoured; for it is the Heir
of all Things, if only it be truly begotten and be
no Bastard.

"And besides all these Symbols, Moses taught the
People to have beyond all Things an Abhorrence of
Idolatry.   What, then, is Idolatry, and what are False
Gods?

" To make an Idol is to materialise spiritual Mysteries. The Priests, then, were Idolaters, who coming after Moses, and committing to Writing those Things which he by Word of Mouth had delivered unto Israel, replaced the true Things signified, by their material Symbols, and shed innocent Blood on the pure Altars of the Lord.

" They also are Idolaters who understand the Things of Sense where the Things of the Spirit are alone implied, and who conceal the true Features of the Gods with material and spurious Presentations. Idolatry is Materialism, the common and original Sin of Men, which replaces Spirit by Appearance, Substance by Illusion, and leads both the moral and intellectual Being into Error, so that they substitute the Nether for the Upper, and the Depth for the Height. It is that false Fruit which attracts the outer Senses, the Bait of the Serpent in the Beginning of the World. Until the Mystic Man and Woman had eaten of this Fruit, they knew only the Things of the Spirit, and found them suffice. But after their Fall, they began to apprehend Matter also, and gave it the Preference, making themselves Idolaters. And their Sin, and the Taint begotten of that false Fruit, have corrupted the Blood of the whole Race of Men, from which Corruption the Sons of God would have redeemed them."

No. VI.

CONCERNING THE MOSAIC COSMOGONY.[1]

THE opening chapters of Genesis have, in some of their applications, a reference to the Mysteries. The following are some of their manifold meanings.

In the first chapter (and beginning of the second) is related the creation of human nature in its two divisions, intellect and intuition, body and soul, man and woman, each creation occurring by development or evolution out of lower forms, through the successive incarnations of the individual.

In the second chapter (beginning at verse 4) is described humanity (or Adam), male and female, in a state of mere intellectualism or external reason, and before the advent of revelation or religious perception. Here the allegory refers to the race and to the individual alike, and treats of man as sense and soul, priest and prophet, world and church.

The Tree of Life is the Central Will or Divine Life, the God, that is, whether of the universe or of the individual. And the Tree of Knowledge is experience which comes of trespass, or a descent from the region of spirit to that of matter. It is thus Maya, or illusion ; and the serpent, or tempter, is the impulse by yielding to which the inward reality of

[1] Boulogne, August 1880. Received in sleep.

Being is abandoned for the outward appearance, and idolatry is committed through the preference of the symbol to the verity, of the form to the substance, The phrase "coats of skin" implies a deeper descent into materiality, and the consequent need of multiplied penances and transmigrations.

The Tree of Life signifies also the secret of regeneration, or final transmutation into pure spirit, and the consequent attainment of eternal life, which can come only when all the necessary processes have been performed, and the soul—Eve—is once more pure and free, when she becomes "Mary."

In the Mysteries the Adam of the second chapter signifies also the ordinary earth-man, devoid of spiritual perception or consciousness, and unable, therefore, at all to comprehend the mysteries. And Eve signifies the seer and prophet, who, being illuminated in soul and taught of the Spirit, has in his keeping the knowledge of things sacred, but is on no account to divulge that knowledge to the outer world of mankind at large. Springing from the heart of humanity, when its outer sense and reason and passions are laid in sleep, or mystic trance, Eve is the Sibyl, or "Mother," who has the sacred tree in charge, but may not communicate of it. But being tempted by the prospect of sensuous reward, she yields to the serpent of matter—or astral impulses—and communicates the Mysteries to the vulgar, and thereby loses her supremacy over men, and from being their mistress and ruler, becomes their slave, while the prophets, her offspring, are persecuted and slain, so

that all her revelations and proper ministrations are
made in pain and sorrow and labour.   For it is
characteristic of the vulgar, that they reverence only
what is unfamiliar and mysterious to them.

The Four Rivers springing from one source are the
four elements which enter into the composition
alike of the whole and the part, the universe, the
planet, the individual, and the single (physiological)
cell.   Together they constitute the fourfold being.
Pison, which surrounds and encloses the earth or
mineral zone, and contains the materials of wealth
and fame, is the body, or material region.   Gihon,
the river which runs through the land of burning,
denotes the Vale of Gehenna or purgatorial region,
and is the " fiery body," the magnetic belt between
the body and the soul.   Hiddekel, the river with the
double symbol of Two Languages, is that which leads
back to the ancient time and place of the soul's
" innocence."   For, being representative of the soul,
it occupies the soul's place between the material and
the spiritual part.   The last is called the Euphrates,
and implies the innermost and highest, the Spirit, or
Will.   These four " rivers " go forth into and constitute the whole universe, and all therein that is of a
fourfold nature.   A portion of each is necessary to
constitute a molecule, or monad, of the substance of
creation, whether a planet, a man, or a cell.   For the
cell is the type of the kosmos.

Now the signification of the Rivers of Eden is fourfold, denoting, First, the four generations of the soul's
evolution, individually and collectively.

Secondly, The four stages of the soul's initiation and perfectionment.

Thirdly, The four interpretations of Scripture.

Fourthly, The four elemental spheres of nature in which the soul has its generation and education.

No. VII.

CONCERNING THE FALL.[1]

THE friend with whom I was staying having asked me to obtain for her, if possible, while in her house a precise and practical instruction on this subject, I found myself surrounded in my sleep by a group of spirits, who conversed together upon it evidently for my benefit. They began by saying that all the mistakes made about the Bible arise out of the mystic books being referred to times, places, and persons material, instead of being regarded as containing only eternal verities about things spiritual. The opening chapters of the sacred books, they said, exhibit the meaning and object of religion, and the method of salvation. They are an epitome of the whole Bible, a kind of argument prefixed to the divine drama of the spiritual history of man.

The key to their interpretation is to be found in the word *Now*. There is no past in the Divine Mind, no future in the Divine Economy. To each

[1] Paris, July 29, 1880.

is one thing forbidden under penalty of death. This
one thing is disobedience to the Divine Will.
Death is the natural and inevitable result of rebellion
against the Central Will, which is the Tree of Life.
Death ensues in the body when the central will of
the system no longer binds in harmony the component elements of the body. And death ensues
in the soul when it is no longer desirous of union with
the Divine Will. Wherefore disobedience and rebellion are death. But to desire ardently that which God
wills, and to give oneself even to the death to fulfil
God's Will, is life. For "he who will find his life
shall lose it;" which means that he who seeks his own
in opposition to the Divine Will, shall perish. "And
he who loses his life, shall find it;" which means that
he who giveth himself to the death to fulfil the
Divine Will, shall have—nay, already hath—eternal
life.

Now, the injunction laid on every human soul is,
not to disobey the Divine Will. For, in the day that
the soul wilfully opposes itself to God, she shall
surely die. This means that the natural death or
dissolution of the body shall, in such case, entail the
dissolution and dispersion of the soul. For the
Divine Breath, or Spirit, is the central life of the
human soul, or true man ; and if the elements of this
personality be no longer bound in obedience to the
Divine Fire, they will become dissolved and dispersed in the void, and so the individual perish.
"Dying, thou shalt die." The rebellious Adam hath
not eternal life. Death in the body is for him death

in the soul. The soul is a purer and finer essence than the mere matter of the body. But when she is rebellious, and her elements are no longer bound to their central fire; they continue, after the death of the body, to disunite and disintegrate, until, at length, the Holy Spirit being withdrawn, the soul dissolves into the void and is no more. This is eternal death. On the other hand, the soul redeemed by obedience to the Divine Will, withdraws itself, and aspires ever more and more to its centre, until—absorbed therein —it becomes like unto God, wholly spiritual. This is eternal life.

Now, "the Gift of God is eternal life through Christ Jesus our Lord." " For, as in the earthly and rebellious Adam we die; so in the Christ we are made alive for evermore." That is, that inasmuch as by disobedience to the Divine Will the soul brings on itself dissolution and eternal death ; so, when it is regenerate and strives continually to attain the Christ nature, it obtains thereby eternal life. For it arises necessarily out of the law of the universe that nothing can continue to exist which is out of harmony with the Divine Central Will. Now, the nature which is in most perfect harmony with the Divine Will is the Christ-nature. Wherefore, of the redeemed universe the perfect chord is, Thy Will be done.

But had it been permitted to the rebellious and fallen Adam, after his act of disobedience in plucking and eating of the forbidden fruit, to "put forth his hand and take also of the Tree of Life, and to live for ever," the result would have been an eternal

hell. For then the soul would have continued to
exist for ever while in a state of separation by disobedience from God, and while insulting and defying
God. Such division of the universe against itself
would have involved its destruction,—a catastrophe
which can by no possibility occur. And the condition
would have involved the soul in a perpetual hell of
misery ; wherefore, in merciful arrest of such a doom,
God drove out the fallen soul from the reach of
eternal life. But even while doing so, God pronounced the words of hope and redemption. For
with the curse comes the promise, " Adam falling,
Christ redeems."

For the soul having accomplished the act of disobedience, has its " eyes opened." And it now
perceives that alone and divorced from the Divine
Will it is " wretched, and miserable, and poor, and
blind, and naked," as said of the Church of Laodicea
in the Apocalypse ; and Adam, knowing he is fallen,
" hides " himself. For apart from God, Who is its
life, the soul is nothing. And this knowledge of her
shameful condition is all the soul gains by rebellion.
And so the lesson to the soul· is this :—If thou
disunite thyself from God and make thy desire
earthwards, thou art as the dust of the ground, and
must die the death of the body. But if thou desire
only God, and make God's law thy will, and its
accomplishment thy delight, thou becomest as God,
and hast eternal life.

No. VIII.

CONCERNING THE PROPHECY OF THE DELUGE.[1]

WHEN reading this morning the work of Eliphas Levi on "Magic," I came upon the following sentence :—" In the Zohar, one of the chief books of the holy Kabbala, it is written, ' The Magic Serpent, son of the Sun, was about to devour the World, when the Sea, daughter of the Moon, put her foot on his head and crushed him.' "

At this instant a writing was presented to my spiritual eyes, in which I read the following explanation of the Deluge of Noah :—

" The Flood came," says the Scripture, "and swept away the wicked." The Flood, therefore, is not the wickedness itself, as some have supposed, but that which destroyed wickedness, and bore the righteous unharmed on its bosom. The Flood is Aphrodite the Sea-queen and Maria the Star of the Sea ; or, as the name signifies, Sea-salt, or Bitterness of the Deep. " The Woman shall crush the head of the Serpent." Maria, the God-woman, or feminine presentation of the supreme power and goodness, delivers mankind and destroys evildoers. She is the Water of Regeneration ; the Sea through which, as Paul the Mystic says, we must all pass. She was in the beginning, because she is God, and the Spirit of God, or Divine Cloud, dwelt upon her. " We all passed through the

[1] Paris, September 28, 1878.

Sea and through the Cloud." Jesus the Saviour went
down into her, and received in her His chrism, while
at the same time the Divine Hermes overshadowed
Him.

Maria the Sea is the water mystically appointed for
the washing away of Sin. Therefore as the Flood
she purifies the world, and bears on her immaculate
breast the Ark of the Divine Covenant which contains the Elect." [1]

And when I had read this, it was impressed on my
mind as a prophecy having special significance for
the present age.

No. IX.

CONCERNING THE PROPHECY OF THE BOOK OF ESTHER. [2]

THE most important book in the Bible for you
to study now, and that most nearly about to be
fulfilled, is one of the most mystic books in the Old
Testament, the book of Esther.

This book is a mystic prophecy, written in the form
of an actual history. If I give you the key, the clue

---

[1] Like Eve, Maria and the Sea are mystical synonyms for the Soul,
which is called " Bitterness of the Deep " because—consisting of the
universal substance—she attains her perfection through painful experience. Concerning Hermes, see Part II., Nos. XII. and XIII., (6).

[2] Paris, Easter Sunday, 1880. Repeated from dictation heard
interiorly while in trance.

of the thread of it, it will be the easiest thing in the world to unravel the whole.

The great King Assuerus, who had all the world under his dominion, and possessed the wealth of all the nations, is the genius of the age.

Queen Vasthi, who for her disobedience to the king was deposed from her royal seat, is the orthodox Catholic Church.

The Jews, scattered among the nations under the dominion of the king, are the true Israel of God.

Mardochi the Jew represents the spirit of intuitive reason and understanding.

His enemy Aman, is the spirit of materialism, taken into the favour and protection of the genius of the age, and exalted to the highest place in the world's councils after the deposition of the orthodox religion.

Now Aman has a wife and ten sons.

Esther—who, under the care and tuition of Mardochi, is brought up pure and virgin—is that spirit of love and sympathetic interpretation which shall redeem the world.

I have told you that it shall be redeemed by a "woman."

Now the several philosophical systems by which the councillors of the age propose to replace the dethroned Church, are one by one submitted to the judgment of the age; and Esther, coming last, shall find favour.

Six years shall she be anointed with oil of myrrh, that is, with study and training severe and bitter, that she may be proficient in intellectual knowledge, as must all systems which seek the favour of the age.

And six years with sweet perfumes, that is with the gracious loveliness of the imagery and poetry of the faiths of the past, that religion may not be lacking in sweetness and beauty.

But she shall not seek to put on any of those adornments of dogma, or of mere sense, which, by trick of priestcraft, former systems have used to gain power or favour with the world and the age, and for which they have been found wanting.

Now there come out of the darkness and the storm which shall arise upon the earth, two dragons.

And they fight and tear each other, until there arises a star, a fountain of light, a queen, who is Esther.

I have given you the key. Unlock the meaning of all that is written.

I do not tell you if in the history of the past these voices had part in the world of men.

If they had, guess now who were Mardochi and Esther.

But I tell you that which shall be in the days about to come.[1]

---

[1] The name Esther—which is one with Easter—denotes a star, or fountain of light, a dawn or rising. The feast of Purim, instituted in token of the deliverance wrought through Esther, coincides in date with Easter. In the Protestant Bible the later portion of the Book of Esther is placed in the Apocrypha. The spelling followed is that of the Douay version. The penultimate sentence obviously refers to the work in which we were engaged, but not necessarily to the workers themselves. The two dragons are materialism and superstition (see Preface).

No. X.

CONCERNING THE PROPHECY OF THE VISION OF NEBUCHADNEZZAR.[1]

THE King Nebuchadnezzar is mystically identical with king Assuerus, in that each alike denotes the spirit of the latter age, that, namely, of mere Intellectualism, as distinguished from and opposed to Intuitionalism. And both narratives, as well also as that of the Deluge and of the book of Esther, are prophecies which now are beginning to have their accomplishment on a scale greater than ever before. For, the image shown to the king in his dream represents the various systems of thought and belief which find favour with the world. Of these the intellectual philosophy which rests upon the basis of a science merely physical, is the head, and is symbolised by the gold. And this rightly, so far as concerns the intellect; for it is indeed king of kings, and all the children of men, the beasts of the field, and the birds of the air, are given into its hands. This is to say, all the activities of society, its learning, its industry, and its art, are made subordinate to the intellect. The breast and arms of the image are of silver. This is the domain of morality and sentiment, which under the reign of the mere intellect hold a subordinate place. Belonging to the region of the heart, it is feminine;

---

[1] London, February 22, 1881. Received in sleep.

C

and implying the intuition, which is of the woman, and her assigned inferiority, it is of silver. The thighs and the belly are of brass, and this kingdom is said to rule over the whole world. By this is meant the universality under a regime wholly animal and non-moral, of falsehood, cruelty, impurity, blasphemy, and all those deprivations of the true humanity, which characterise an age of materialism. The iron of which the legs are made, represents force, and denotes the negation of love, and the consequent prevalence of might over right, and the universal rule of selfishness. By the mingling of iron and clay in the feet is implied the weakness and instability of the whole structure, the clay representing matter, which is made the foundation of the system instead of spirit, which alone is stable and enduring.

The Stone cut out without hands, which destroys this image, and becomes a great mountain filling the whole earth, is that "Stone of the Philosophers," a perfected spirit, and the true gospel of the inner knowledge which appertains thereto. This it is which smites the age upon its feet, or fundamental basis, its materialistic hypothesis. And with the demonstration of the falseness of its doctrine, now being made to the world, shall fall the whole fabric of society, with its empire of force, its exaltation of the masculine mode of the mind, its subjection of women, its torture of animals, and its oppression of the poor. With its clay, its iron, its brass, its silver, and its gold, all swept away as chaff by

the wind, the true knowledge and spirit of understanding which are of the intuition, shall usher
in the kingdom of God, and the "stone," become
a mountain, shall fill the whole earth.

No. XI.

CONCERNING THE PROPHECY OF THE TIME OF THE END.[1]

AS there was a return of the spirit, or angel, of
Elias in the person of John the Baptist before
the advent of Jesus, so there will be a return of the
angel of Daniel, before the next manifestation of the
Christ. Daniel's angel is he who specially foretold
the culmination and the hour of overthrow of the
world's materialistic system. And when he had completed his prediction he told Daniel that he—Daniel
—should rest for the present, but when the time was
accomplished and the end was at hand, he should
return and stand again in his place, and prophesy
before the world. And the token whereby the approach of the end should be known would be the
spectacle of the "abomination of desolation standing
in the holy place." A like assurance was given also
to John. Now, the holy place is always—whether in
the universal or the individual, in the macrocosm or
the microcosm—the place of God and the Soul; and

[1] See note on next page but one.

the abomination of desolation, or which maketh desolate, is that system of thought which, putting matter in the chief place, and making it the source, substance, and object of existence, abolishes God out of the universe, and the soul out of man, and thus, depriving existence of its light and life, makes it empty, desolate and barren, a very abomination of desolation.

Jesus, recalling this prophecy, and citing the words of Daniel's angel, also foretold the same event as marking the end of that "adulterous" generation [a term identical with idolatrous as denoting the worship of and illicit association with matter], and the coming of the kingdom of God; and warned the elect in mystic phrase, thus to be interpreted :—

"When, therefore, ye shall see matter exalted to the holy place of God and the soul, and made the all and in all of existence;

"Then let the spiritual Israel betake themselves to the hills where alone salvation is to be found, even the heights and fastnesses of the divine life.

"And let him who has overcome the body, beware lest he return to the love of the flesh, or seek the things of the world.

"Neither let him who is freed from the body, become again re-incarnate.

"And woe to the soul whose travail is yet unaccomplished, and which has not yet become weaned from the body.

"And beseech God that these things find you not

at a season either of spiritual depression and feebleness, or of spiritual repose and unwatchfulness.

"For the tribulation shall be without parallel;

"And such that except those days shall be few in
number, escape from the body would be impossible.

"But for the elect's sake they shall be few.

"And if any shall then declare that here, or there,
the Christ has appeared as a person, believe it not.
For there shall arise delusive apparitions and manifestations, together with great signs and marvels, such
as might well deceive even the elect.   Remember, I
have told you beforehand.   Wherefore, if they shall
say unto you, Behold he is in the desert, whether of
the East or of the West,—join him not.   Or, Behold
he is in darkened rooms and secret assemblies,—pay
no regard.

"For, like lightning coming out of the East and
illuminating the West, so shall be the world's spiritual
awakening to the recognition of the Divine in
Humanity.

"But wheresoever the dead carcase of error remains,
around it, like vultures, will gather both deceivers and
deceived.[1]

"And upon them, the profane, there shall be dark-

[1] The foregoing part of this utterance was received at Paris, December 6, 1879, in sleep, the inspiring influence impressing itself upon the
seeress as being the angel Gabriel,—a circumstance which caused
some perplexity—her usual instructor being Hermes (= Raphael)—until
it was remembered that Gabriel was the inspiring angel of Daniel,
whose return had been foretold.   The remainder was received under
waking illumination in July 1886, while preparing the second edition
of "The Perfect Way," in which it appeared.

ness ; the Spirit shall be quenched and the soul
extinct ; and there shall be no more any light in
heaven, or in heavenly science any truth and meaning.   And the power of heaven upon men shall be
shaken.

"Then shall appear the new sign, the Man in
Heaven, upon the rain-clouds of the last chrism and
mystery, with great power and glory.

"And his missioners shall gather the elect with a
great voice, from the four winds and from the farthest
bounds of heaven.

"Behold the FIG-TREE, and learn her parable.
When the branch thereof shall become tender, and
her buds appear, know that the day of God is upon
you."

Wherefore, then, saith the Lord that the budding
of the fig-tree shall foretell the end ?

Because the fig-tree is the symbol of the divine
woman, as the vine of the divine man.

The fig is the similitude of the matrix, containing
inward buds, bearing blossoms on its placenta, and
bringing forth fruit in darkness.   It is the cup of
life, and its flesh is the seed-ground of new births.

The stems of the fig-tree run with milk : her
leaves are as human hands, like the leaves of her
brother the vine.

And when the fig-tree shall bear figs, then shall
be the second advent, the new sign of the man
bearing water, and the manifestation of the virgin-
mother crowned.

For when the Lord would enter the holy city, to celebrate his Last Supper with his disciples, he sent before him the fisherman Peter to meet the man of the coming sign.

"There shall meet you a man bearing a pitcher of water."

Because, as the Lord was first manifest at a wine-feast in the morning, so must he consummate his work at a wine-feast in the evening.

It is his Pass-Over; for thereafter the sun must pass into a new sign.

After the Fish, the Water-Carrier; but the Lamb of God remains always in the place of victory, being slain from the foundation of the world.

For his place is the place of the sun's triumph.

After the vine the fig; for Adam is first formed, then Eve.

And because our Lady is not yet manifest, our Lord is crucified.

Therefore came he vainly seeking fruit upon the fig-tree, "for the time of figs was not yet."

And from that day forth, because of the curse of Eve, no man has eaten fruit of the fig-tree.

For the inward understanding has withered away, there is no discernment any more in men. They have crucified the Lord because of their ignorance, not knowing what they did.

Wherefore, indeed, said our Lord to our Lady:—
"Woman, what is between me and thee? For even *my* hour is not yet come."

Because until the hour of the man is accomplished

and fulfilled, the hour of the woman must be deferred.

Jesus is the vine; Mary is the fig-tree. And the vintage must be completed and the wine trodden out, or ever the harvest of the figs be gathered.

But when the hour of our Lord is achieved, hanging on his Cross, he gives our Lady to the faithful.

The chalice is drained, the lees are wrung out: then says he to his elect :—" Behold thy Mother ! "

But so long as the grapes remain unplucked, the vine has nought to do with the fig-tree, nor Jesus with Mary.

He is first revealed, for he is the Word ; afterwards shall come the hour of its interpretation.

And in that day every man shall sit under the vine and the fig-tree ; the dayspring shall arise in the orient, and the fig-tree shall bear her fruit.[1]

For, from the beginning, the fig-leaf covered the shame of incarnation, because the riddle of existence can be expounded only by him who has the woman's secret. It is the riddle of the Sphinx.

Look for that tree which alone of all trees bears a fruit blossoming interiorly, in concealment, and thou shalt discover the fig.

Look for the sufficient meaning of the manifest universe and of the written Word, and thou shalt find only their mystical sense.

Cover the nakedness of matter and of nature with the fig-leaf; and thou hast hidden all their shame. For the fig is the interpreter.

---

[1] Zech. iii. 10 ; Mic. iv. 4 ; Cant. ii. 13.

So when the hour of interpretation comes, and the fig-tree puts forth her buds, know that the time of the end and the dawning of the new day are at hand,—"even at the doors."

No. XII.

CONCERNING THE SOUL:

its Origin, Nature, and Potentialities.[1]

THE Soul, in its first beginning, is not something added to the body, but is generated in the body by the polarisation of the astral elements. Once generated, it enters and passes through many bodies, until finally perfected.

As there are two of the outer, so also of the inner. The two of the inner are spirit and soul. In the translation of the Scriptures the word spirit is often used where soul is meant. For only the man created in God's own image is a living soul, that is, a soul which has the Spirit superadded to it.[2]

The clearest understanding may be obtained of the soul by defining it as the divine idea. Before anything can exist outwardly and materially, the idea -of it must subsist in the Divine Mind. The

---

[1] London. Spoken in trance at different times in the spring of 1881.

[2] Spirit, being the substance of all things, is in all things, but does not become *the* Spirit until, from being diffuse and abstract, it becomes, by polarisation, concentrate and formulate,—from heat becoming flame.

soul, therefore, may be understood to be divine and
everlasting in its nature.   But the soul does not act
directly upon matter.   It is put forth by the Divine
Mind ; but the body is put forth by the sideral
or fiery body.   As the spirit on the celestial plane
is the parent of the soul, so the fire on the material
plane begets the body.

The soul, being in its nature eternal, passes from
one form to another until, in its highest stage, it
polarises sufficiently to receive the spirit.   It is in
all organised things.   Nothing of an organic nature
exists without a soul.   It is the individual, and
it perishes if abandoned of the spirit.

As already said, at the moment when the soul
appears in any hitherto inorganic entity, it is by
means of the convergence of the magnetic poles of the
constituent molecules of that entity.   The focusing
of these poles gives rise to a circular magnetic
current, and an electric combustion is the result.
This vital spark is organic life, or the soul.   This
spontaneous combustion, or generation, is not a new
creation ; for nothing can be either added to or
withdrawn from the universe.   It is but a new
condition of the one substance.   The soul is to
the material organ what the tune is to the musical
instrument.   The tune subsists in the mind of the
composer (God), before the keys or strings of the
instrument can give it expression.   But unless for
this expression it could not become manifest to
sense.   This tune can be played on many instruments,
and transferred from one to another.   We are thus

brought to the great facts, the immortality of the soul, its transmigrations, and the metempsychosis.

The process of incarnation, and the method by which the soul takes new forms, are in this wise. When two persons ally themselves in the flesh and beget a child, the moment of impregnation is usually —though not invariably—the moment which attaches a soul to the newly conceived body. Hence, much depends upon the influences, astral and magnetic, under which impregnation and conception take place. The pregnant woman is the centre of a whirl of magnetic forces, and she attracts within her sphere a soul whose previous conduct and odic condition correspond either to her own or to the magnetic influences under which she conceives. This soul, if the pregnancy continues and progresses, remains attached to her sphere, but does not enter the embryo until the time of quickening, when it usually takes possession of the body, and continues to inhabit it until the time of delivery. A pregnant woman is swayed not by her own will alone, but as often by the will of the soul newly attached to her sphere; and the opposition and cross-magnetisms of these two wills often occasion many strange and seemingly unaccountable whims, alternations of character, and longings, on the part of the woman. Sometimes, however, the moment of impregnation or conception passes without attracting any soul, and the woman may even carry a false conception for some time, in which cases abortion occurs. There are innumerable accidents which may happen in this regard. Or, the soul, which has been attracted to her, may, under new influences, be with-drawn from her sphere, and from the embryo which, having quickened, may consume away; or, the soul originally drawn to her orbit may be replaced later by another, and so forth. Some clairvoyant women have been conscious of the soul attached to them, and have seen it, at times as a beautiful infant, at times in other shapes. Children begotten by ardent and mutual love are usually the best and healthiest, spiritually and physically, because the radical moment is seized by love, when the astral and magnetic in-fluences are strongest and most ardent, and they attract the strongest and noblest souls. ·

For you to understand yet more clearly and fully the origin and nature of the soul, whence it comes, and how it passes from one body to another, you must know that the plane on which the celestials and the creatures touch each other, is the astral plane. The substance of all created things is the begetter alike of body and soul. The soul, as I have said, is formed by polarisation of the elements of the astral body, and it is a gradual process; but when once formed it is an entity capable of passing from one body to another. Imagine the magnetic forces of innumerable elements directed and focused to one centre, and streams of electric power passing along all their convergent poles to that centre. Imagine these streams so focused as to create a fire in that central part,—a kind of crystallisation of magnetic force. This is the soul. This is the sacred fire of Hestia or Vesta, which burns continually. The body and person may fall away and disappear : but the soul, once begotten, is immortal until its perverse will extinguish it. For the fire of the soul, or central hearth, must be kept alive by the higher air or Divine Breath, if it is to endure for ever. It must converge, not diverge. If it diverge it will be dissipated. The end of progress is unity ; the end of degradation is division. The soul, therefore, which ascends, tends more and more to union with the Divine.

And this is the manner thereof. Conceive of God as of a vast spiritual body constituted of many individual elements, but all these elements as having one will, and therefore being one. This condition of oneness with the Divine Will and Being constitutes the celestial Nirvâna. Again, conceive of the degraded soul as dividing more and more until at length it is scattered into many, and ceases to be as an individual, being, as it were, split and broken up, and dispersed into many pieces. This is the Nirvâna of the Amen, or annihilation of the individual.[1]

"And whence," you inquire, "is the supply of new souls for the continual increase of the world's population ?" Souls, as you know, work up from animals and plants ; for it is in the lowest forms of organic life that the soul is first engendered. Formerly the way of escape for human souls was more open and the path clearer, because, although ignorance of intellectual things abounded among the poorer sort, yet the knowledge of divine things and the light of faith

---

[1] See Appendix, note A.

were stronger and purer.   Wherefore the souls of
those ages of the world, not being enchained to earth
as they now are, were enabled to pass more quickly
through their avatârs, and but few incarnations sufficed
where now many are necessary.

For in these days the ignorance of the mind is
weighted by materialism instead of being lightened
by faith.   It is sunk to earth by love of the body
and by atheism, and excessive care for the things of
sense.   And being crushed thereby, it lingers long
in the atmosphere of earth, seeking many fresh lodg-
ments, and so multiplies bodies.

And, furthermore, you must not conceive of Creation, or the putting-forth of things, as an act once
accomplished and then ended.   For the celestial
Olympus is continually creating and continually becoming.   God never ceases giving of God for God's
creatures.   This also is the mystery of the divine
incarnation and oblation.   The celestial substance is
continually individualising itself that it may build
itself up into one perfect individual.   Thus is the
circle of life accomplished, and thus its ends meet
the one with the other.

You have asked me—" How, if the planet consist of
body, perisoul, soul, and spirit, can there be born
of it entities which are not like it fourfold, but
threefold or even twofold, as are minerals and severed
parts of bodies, things made by art, and the like."   I
answer you that your error lies in looking on the
planet as a thing apart from its offspring.   Certainly,
the planet is fourfold, and certainly also its offspring

is fourfold. But of its offspring some lie in the astral region only, and are but twofold ; and some in the watery region, and are but threefold ; and some lie in the human region, and are fourfold. The body and perisoul are the metallic and gaseous envelope of the planet. The organic region composes its soul, and the human region its spirit, or divine part. For when it was but metallic, it had no soul. When it was but organic, it had no spirit. But when man was made in the image of God, then was its spirit breathed into its soul. Now, the metals have no soul ; therefore they are not individuals. And not being individuals, they cannot transmigrate. But the plants and animals have souls. They are individuals, and do transmigrate and progress. And man has also a spirit ; and so long as he is man—that is, truly human—he cannot re-descend into the body of an animal, or of any creature in the sphere beneath him, since that would be an indignity to the spirit. But if he lose his spirit, and become again animal, he may descend, yea, he may become altogether gross and horrible, and a creeping and detestable thing, begotten of filth and corruption. This is the end of persistently evil men. For God is not the God of creeping things, but Baal Zebub[1] is their God. And there were none of these in the Age of Gold : neither shall there be any when the earth is fully purged. O Men ! your exceeding wickedness is the creator of your evil beasts ; yea, your filthy torments are your own sons and abominable progenitors !

[1] Impurity, or the active principle in putrefaction and corruption.

Remember that there is but one substance. Body, sideral body, soul, and spirit, all these are one in their essence. And the first three are differentialities of polarisation. The fourth is God's Self. When the Gods put forth the world, they put forth substance with its three potentialities, but all three in the condition of odic light. I have called the substantial light sometimes the sideral body, sometimes the perisoul ; and this because it is both. For it is that which makes, that which becomes. It is fire, or the human spirit (not the divine), out of which and by which earth and water are generated. It is the fiery manifestation of soul, the magnetic factor of the body. It is space ; it is substance ; it is foundation. So that from it proceed the gases and the minerals, which are soulless, and also the organic world, which hath a soul. But man it could not make. For man is fourfold and of the divine ether or upper air, which is the province of Zeus, Father of Gods and men.

The outer envelope of the macrocosm and microcosm alike, which is represented by Demeter, is in reality not elemental at all, but is a compound of the other three elements. Her fertility is due to the "water," and her transmuting or chemical power to the fire. This water is the soul or protoplasma, which is put forth by Deity and constitutes the individual. Nor are you to look on fire as a true element. For fire is to the body what spirit is to the soul. As the soul is without the divine life until vivified by the spirit, so the body, or matter, is

without physical life in the absence of fire. No
matter is really "dead matter," for the fire-element
is in all matter. But matter would be "dead" (that
is, would cease to exist as matter) if motion were
suspended,—which is, if there were no fire. For, as
wherever there is motion there is heat, and consequently fire, and motion is the *condition* of matter,
so without fire would be no matter.

The soul is not astral fluid, but is manifest by
means of the astral fluid ; for the soul itself is, like
the idea, invisible and intangible. You will see the
meaning best by following out the genesis of any
particular action. The stroke of the pen on paper is
the phenomenon ; that is the outer body. The action
which produces the stroke is the astral body, and,
though physical, is not a thing, but a transition or
medium between the result (the stroke) and its cause
(the idea). The idea manifested in the act is not
physical, but mental, and is the soul of the act. But
even this is not the first cause. For the idea is put
forth by the will, and this is the spirit. Thus, you
will an idea as God wills the macrocosm. The real
body (or immediate result) is the astral body ; while
the phenomenal body (or ultimate form) is the effect
of motion and heat. If you could arrest motion, you
would have as the result fire, and thereby would
convert Demeter into Hephaistos. But fire itself
also is material, since it is visible to the outer sense,
as is the earth-body. But it has many degrees of
subtlety. The astral or odic substance, therefore, is
not the soul itself, but is the medium or manifestor

D

of the soul, as the act is of the idea. If, however, the phrase misleads you, it is better to modify it, as thus :—

The act is the *condition* of the idea, in the same way as fire or incandescence is the condition of any given object. Light is of spirit, heat is of matter. Water is the result of the operation of Wisdom the Mother, or oxygen, and Justice the Father, or hydrogen. Air is the result of the mixture, not combination, of wisdom and force. These two are properly elements. They are soul and spirit. But Earth is not, properly speaking, an element at all. She is the result of the water and the fire, and her rocks and strata are either watery or igneous. She is water and air fused and crystallised. Fire also, the real maker of the body, is a mode and condition, and not a true element. See, then, that the only real and true and permanent elements are air and water, spirit and soul, will and idea, divine and substantial, father and mother; and out of these all the elements of earth are made by the aid of the condition of matter, which is, interchangeably, heat and motion.

Wisdom, Justice, and Force, or oxygen, hydrogen, and azoth, are the three out of which the two true elements are produced. But water is a combination, air is a mixture. Wherefore the only two real entities, water and air, are unreal to the phenomenal; while the untrue elements, earth and fire, or body and electric fluid, are real in the phenomenal.

Souls are re-incarnated hundreds and thousands of

times ; but not the *person* (which implies the body), for the body perishes. These things were known to the Gnostics, Therapeutæ, Essenes, and to Jesus ; and the doctrine is embodied in the parable of the Talents, as thus explained :—Into the soul of the individual is breathed the Spirit of God, divine, pure, and without blemish. It is God. And the individual has, in his earth-life, to nourish that Spirit, and feed it as a flame with oil. When you put oil into a lamp, the essence passes into and becomes flame. So is it with the soul of him who nourishes the Spirit. It grows gradually pure, and *becomes* the Spirit. By this means the Spirit becomes the richer. And, as in the parable of the Talents, where God has given five talents, man pays back ten ; or he returns nothing, and perishes.

When a soul has once become regenerate, it returns to the body only by its own free will, and as a Redeemer or Messenger. Such a one regains in the flesh the memory of his past. Regeneration or transmutation may take place in an instant ; but it is rarely a sudden thing, and it is best that it come gradually, so that the " Marriage " of the Spirit be only after a prolonged engagement.

The doctrine of " Counterparts," so familiar to certain classes of " Spiritualists," is a travesty, due to delusive spirits, of the " Marriage of Regeneration."

Regeneration does not affect the interior man only. A regenerate person may have his body such that no wounds will cause death.

When a person dies, a portion of the soul

remains unconsumed,—untransmuted, that is, into
spirit.   The soul is fluid, and between it and vapour
is this analogy.   When there is a large quantity of
vapour in a small space it becomes condensed, and is
thick and gross.   But when a portion is removed, the
rest becomes refined, and is rarer and purer.   So it is
with the soul.   By the transmutation of a portion
of its material the rest becomes finer, rarer, and
purer, and continues to do so more and more until
—after many incarnations, made good use of—the
whole of the soul is absorbed into the Divine Spirit,
and becomes one with God, making God so much the
richer for the usury.   This is the celestial Nirvâna.
But, though becoming pure Spirit, or God, the individual retains his individuality; so that instead of all
being merged in the One, the One becomes Many.
Thus has God become millions.   We, too, are legion,
and therein resemble God.   God is multitudes and
nations, and kingdoms, and tongues.   And the sound
of God is as the sound of many waters.

No. XIII.

CONCERNING PERSEPHONE, OR THE SOUL'S DESCENT
INTO MATTER.[1]

I SEE God under two modes, one static or passive,
the other dynamic or active.   As the former,
God is original Life, Will, Power.   As the latter, God

[1] London, March 23, 1881.   Spoken in trance.

is the Holy Spirit. And the Spirit and the Substance of God are one. At first there is perfect rest.
Then comes a movement of rotation round itself, and
Substance becomes first ether, and at length matter.
Every ultimate particle of matter moves in ether, as
do the planets, and has two poles, that is in the
intercellular ether. Their rotation is intensely rapid ;
it makes me giddy to look ; and by this movement
comes creation. This is accomplished in six periods,
and then there is Rest, and the whole is re-absorbed.
Wherefore there is an incessant Putting-Forth for six
"days," and a recurring Sabbath of Rest.

The more rapid the movement of the particles of
his body, the more material is the man. Hence the
object of the saint is to attain perfect quiescence, and
thereby union with the Divine One. The "Philosopher's Stone" signifies in one aspect perfect quiescence,
or the re-absorption of matter into spirit through the
absence of motion.

Thus the rigidity we know as matter is caused by
the incessant, intense movement of spirit. This
truth, for the Greeks, is represented by Demeter,
who is all that is in motion and solid. And whereas
motion is begotten of the Holy Spirit in time, her
parents are Rhea and Saturn. Rhea is "the mother"
of the Gods, and is the same as Nox, the original
Darkness or Invisible Light of Divinity prior to manifestation in creation. And Persephone, or Proserpine,
is the daughter of Demeter or Motion—or that which
makes visible—by Ether. Persephone is the liquid or
psychic part of man, which consists both of his true

soul and his "fiery" or magnetic perisoul. And the
story of the stealing of Persephone, or rape of Proserpine, relates to the "fixing of the volatile," whereby
the astral part becomes coagulated into the material.
Belonging thus, half to the body, or lower world, and
half to the heavens and upper world, and thus linking
the two together, she is said to spend six months of the
year in Hades and six on Olympus. And she would
be updrawn altogether to the latter, but that as the
consequence of her eating a pomegranate, which—
like the apple of Eve—is the symbol of illusion or
matter, she is fixed in the lower world or body,
whence her mother, Demeter, seeks to withdraw her.

You are to understand, further, that this descent of
Persephone into Hades comes about not only through
the continued motion of the particles of the soul, but
also through their depolarisation from the central and
Divine Will. The body ought to be in such a state
that the man can indraw and re-absorb it. But Persephone, through following her own will, reversed the
poles of her constituent substance, and caused this to
become fixed. Whenever, as was the case with Jesus,
the man is in union with the central will of his system, he has power to indraw and re-absorb his body.
And one of the purposes of the Gospel story of the
water being changed into wine, was to typify this
transmutation. Animals never have this power, as
they have no divine spirit, and, therefore, no central
will, to polarise. Man has it only by the Spirit's
descent into him. The eating of the pomegranate
implies the reversal of the poles, and the illusion

whereby the outer becomes the inner, and the individual polarises outwardly instead of centrally, and, so, becomes fixed and material.

No. XIV.

CONCERNING THE GENIUS OR DAIMON.[1]

PART I.

EVERY human spirit-soul has attached to him a genius or daimon, as with Socrates; a ministering spirit, as with the apostles; or an angel, as with Jesus. All these are but different names for the same thing. My genius says that he does not care for the term angel because it is misinterpreted. He prefers the Christian nomenclature, and to be called minister, as their office is to guide, admonish, and illumine.

My genius looks like Dante, and like him is always in red. And he has a cactus in his hand, which he says is my emblem. (Speaking of Dante, I see that Beatrice represents the soul. She is to him what the woman should be to the man.) He tells me to say that the best weapon against the astrals is prayer. Prayer means the intense direction of the will and desire towards the Highest; an unchanging intent to know nothing but the Highest. So long as

[1] London, November 1880. Spoken in trance.

Moses held up his hands towards heaven, the Israelites prevailed.   When he dropped them, then the
Amalekites.   The genii are not fighting spirits, and
cannot prevent evils.   They were allowed to minister
to Jesus only after his exhaustion in combat with the
lower spirits.   Only they are attacked by these, who
are worth attacking.

I am to inform you that the genius never "controls"
his client, never suffers the soul to step aside from the
body to allow the entrance of another spirit.   The
person controlled by an astral or elemental, on the
contrary, speaks not in his own person, but in that of
the spirit controlling; and the gestures, expression,
intonation, and pitch of voice, change with the obses-
sing spirit.   A person prophesying speaks always in
the first person, and says, either, "Thus saith the
Lord," or "So says some one else," never losing his
own personality.   This is one sign of difference whereby to distinguish between the various orders of spirits.

Another sign, he says, whereby to distinguish
extraneous spirits from one's genius, is this,—the
genius is never absent.   Provided the mind is in
a condition to see, he is always present.   Other spirits
need times to be appointed and engagements to be
made for certain hours, because they may be elsewhere at any moment.   These spirits, moreover,
know nothing of the Gods.   Their very names are
secrets from them, and if they have heard them they
are but names to them.[1]   They are unable to grasp or

---

[1] One of their commonest modes of deception is by the assumption of
divine names; but their utterances are always pretentious and inane.

conceive of anything beyond the atmosphere of their own circle. It is true that they speak of God, but it is without understanding the meaning of the word. The more negative the mind of the individual, the more ready and apt he is to receive these spirits. And, on the contrary, the more positive and pronounced the will of the individual, the more open he is to divine communication. The command always is—"To labour is to pray"; "To ask is to receive"; "To knock is to have the door open." "I have often said," says my genius, "Think for yourself. When you think inwardly, pray intensely, and imagine centrally, then you converse with God."

He knows, he says, concerning our immediate future, but will not tell. All he will say is this,— "Be sure there is trouble. No man ever got to the Land of Promise without going through the desert." Again he holds up to me the cactus, and he says: "Do not fret yourself about trying to get into the lucid state. In a short time it will be unnecessary to become somnolent at all." He tells me that to-night I shall recollect a great part of what has been said, and the next time more, and so on until my mind is quite clear on the subject. It is a weakness and an imperfection when the mind does not retain what has been said. At night, when my brain is free from disturbing influences, I recollect more perfectly all I have seen and heard. And this, he says, should always be the case, because my place is not taken by any other entity. No other spirit steps in to dispossess me. But it is I myself who see and hear and speak,—my spiritual self, that is.

The genius is linked to his client by a bond of soul-substance. Persistent ill-living weakens this bond, and after several incarnations—even to "seventy times seven"—thus ill-spent, the genius is freed and the soul definitively lost. It is not isolated crime, as murder, adultery, or incest, or even a repetition of these, which breaks this bond ; but a continued condition of the heart in which the will of the individual is in persistent opposition to the Divine Will. For this is a state in which repentance is impossible. The condition most favourable to salvation and speedy emancipation from successive incarnations, is the attitude of willing obedience,—freedom and submission. The great object to be attained is emancipation from the body,—from the power and need of the body, that is.

In order the better to comprehend the procession of Spirit, it must be understood that Life may be represented by a triangle, at the apex of which is God. Of this triangle the two sides are formed by two streams, the one flowing outwards, the other upwards. The base may be taken to represent the material plane. Thus, from God proceed the Gods. From the Gods proceed all the hierarchy of heaven, with the various orders from the highest to the lowest. And the lowest is the order of the genii, or guardian angels. These rest on the material plane, but do not enter it. The other side of the triangle is a continuation of the base. The initiatory forms of the base of the triangle are the lowest expressions of life. These are the first expressions of incarnation, and of the stream which, unlike the first, flows inwards and upwards. The side of the triangle represented by this stream, culminates in the Christ, and empties itself into pure spirit, which is God. There are, consequently, spirits who, by their nature, never have been and never can be incarnate. And there are others who reach their perfection through incarnation. You will see, then, that the genii and the astrals have nothing in common. For the space contained in the triangle, and separating on the one hand the apex from the base, and on the other hand the two opposing sides, is a space occupied by the planetary fluid.

There are but two eternal generations,—that of the celestials who begin from the Spirit and are "begotten;" and that of the created entities who accrete a body exteriorly. The astrals are between these two. They are as planes which cannot focus the Divine Spirit, since their rays are reflected in all directions, and do not converge to a central point. They cannot know God. They are not microcosms. Man alone of the created entities is a microcosm, and he is this because the Divine Spirit, the nucleolus, contains necessarily the potentiality of the whole celestial cell. In God are all the Gods included; and the nucleolus in the perfected created cell is, therefore, multiple. Every man is a planet, having sun, moon, and stars.

The genius of a man is his satellite. Man is a planet. God—the God of the man—is his sun, and the moon of this planet is Isis, its initiator, or genius.

The genius is made to minister to the man, and to give him light. But the light he gives is from God, and not of himself. He is not a planet but a moon, and his function is to light up the dark places of his planet.

The day and night of the microcosm, man, are its positive and passive, or projective and reflective states. In the projective state we seek actively outwards ; we aspire and will forcibly ; we hold active communion with the God without. In the reflective state we look inwards, we commune with our own heart ; we indraw and concentrate ourselves secretly and interiorly. During this condition the "Moon" enlightens our hidden chamber with her torch, and shows us ourselves in our interior recess.

Who or what, then, is this moon? It is part of ourselves, and revolves with us. It is our celestial affinity,—of whose order is it said, "Their angels do always behold the face of My Father."

Every human soul has a celestial affinity, which is part of his system and a type of his spiritual nature. This angelic counterpart is the bond of union between the man and God ; and it is in virtue of his spiritual nature that this angel is attached to him. Rudimentary creatures have no celestial affinity ; but from the moment that the soul quickens, the cord of union is established.

It is in virtue of man's being a planet that he has a moon. If he were not fourfold, as is the planet, he could not have one. Rudimentary men are not fourfold. They have not the Spirit.

The genius is the moon to the planet man, reflecting to him the sun, or God, within him. For the divine Spirit which animates and eternises the man, is the God of the man, the sun that enlightens him. And this sun it is, and not the outer and planetary man, that his genius, as satellite, reflects to him. Thus attached to the planet, the genius is the complement of the man ; and his " sex " is always the converse of the planet's. And because he reflects, not the planet, but the sun, not the man (as do the astrals), but the God, his light is always to be trusted.

The genius knows well only the things relating to the person to whom he ministers. About other things he has opinions only. The relation of the ministering spirit to his client, is very well represented by that of the Catholic confessor to his penitent. He is bound to keep towards every penitent profound secrecy as regards the affairs of other souls. If this were not the case, there would be no order, and no secret would be safe. The genius of each one knows about another person only so much as that other's genius chooses to reveal.

PART 2.[1]

Now, there are two kinds of memory, the memory of the organism and the memory of the soul. The first is possessed by all creatures. The second, which is obtained by Recovery, belongs to the fully regenerate man. For the Divine Spirit of a man is not

[1] London, May 28, 1881. Received in sleep.

one with his soul until regeneration, which is the
intimate union constituting what, mystically, is called
the "marriage of the hierophant."

When this union takes place, there is no longer
need of an initiator ; for then the office of the genius
is ended. For, as the moon, Isis, or " Mother," of
the planet man, the genius reflects to the soul the
Divine Spirit, with which she is not yet fully united.
In all things is order. Wherefore, as with the planets,
so with the microcosm. They who are nearest
Divinity, need no moon. But so long as they have
night,—so long, that is, as any part of the soul
remains unilluminated, and her memory or perception
obscure,—so long the mirror of the angel continues
to reflect the sun to the soul.

For the memory of the soul is recovered by a
three-fold operation,—that of the soul herself, of the
moon, and of the sun. The genius is not an informing
spirit. He can tell nothing to the soul. All that
she receives is already within herself. But in the
darkness of the night, it would remain there undiscovered, but for the torch of the angel who enlightens.
"Yea," says the angel genius to his client, " I
illuminate thee, but I instruct thee not. I warn
thee, but I fight not. I attend, but I lead not. Thy
treasure is within thyself. My light showeth where it
lieth."

When regeneration is fully attained, the divine
Spirit alone instructs the hierophant. " For the
gates of his city shall never be shut ; there shall
be no night there ; the night shall be no more. And

they shall not need the light of the lamp, because the Lord God shall enlighten them." The prophet is a man illumined by his angel. The Christ is a man married to the Spirit. And he returns out of pure love to redeem, needing no more to return to the flesh for his own sake. Wherefore he is said to come down from heaven. For he hath attained, and is a medium for the Highest. He baptiseth with the holy Ghost, and with the Divine Fire itself. He is always "in heaven." And in that he ascendeth, it is because the Spirit uplifteth him, even the Spirit who descendeth upon him. "And in that he descendeth, it is because he has first ascended beyond all spheres into the highest Presence. For he that ascendeth, ascendeth because he also descended first into the lower parts of the earth. He that descended is the same also who ascendeth above all the heavens, to fill all things." Such an one returns, therefore, from a higher world; he belongs no more to the domain of Dionysos. But he comes from the "sun" itself, or from some nearer sphere to the sun than ours; having passed from the lowest upwards.

And what of the genius himself? I asked. Is he sorry when his client attains perfection, and needs him no more?

And he said, "He that hath the bride is the bridegroom. And he that standeth by rejoiceth greatly because of the bridegroom's voice." I return, therefore, to my source, for my mission is ended, and my Sabbath is come. And I am one with the twain.

Here he led me into a large chamber where I saw four bullocks lying slaughtered upon altars, and a number of persons standing round in the act of adoration. And above, in the fumes arising from the spirits of the blood, were misty colossal shapes, half-formed, from the waist upwards, and resembling the Gods. And he said "These are Astrals. And thus will they do until the end of the world."

After this instruction concerning the degradation of religion through the materialisation of the spiritual doctrine of sacrifice, he resumed :—

The genius, then, remains with his client so long as the man is fourfold. A beast has no genius. A Christ has none. For first, all is latent light. That is one. And this one becomes two ; that is, body and astral body. And these two become three ; that is, a rational soul is born in the midst of the astral body. This rational soul is the true Person. From that moment, therefore, this personality is an individual existence, as a plant or as an animal. These three become four ; that is, human. And the fourth is the *Nous*, not yet one with the soul, but overshadowing it, and transmitting light as it were through a glass, that is, through the initiator. But when the four become three,—that is, when the "marriage" takes place, and the soul and spirit are indissolubly united,—there is no longer need either of migration or of genius. For the Nous has become one with the soul, and the cord of union is dissolved. And yet again, the three become twain at the dissolution of the body ; and again, the twain become one, that is, the Christ-spirit-soul. The Divine Spirit and the genius, therefore, are not to be regarded as diverse, nor yet as identical. The genius is flame, and is celestial ; that is, he is spirit, and one in nature with the Divine ; for his light is the divine light. He is as a glass, as a cord, as a bond between the soul and her divine part. He is the clear atmosphere through which the divine ray passes, making a path for it in the astral medium.

In the celestial plane, all things are personal. And therefore the bond between the soul and spirit is a person. But when a man is "born again," he no longer needs the bond which unites him to his divine source. The genius, or flame, therefore, returns to that source ; and this being itself united to the soul, the genius also becomes one with the twain. For the genius is the divine light in the sense that he is but a divided tongue of it, having no isolating vehicle. But the tincture of this flame differs according to the celestial atmosphere of the particular soul. The divine light, indeed, is white, being seven in one. But the genius is a flame of a single colour only. And this colour he takes from the soul, and by that ray transmits to her the light of the Nous, her divine spouse. The angel-genii are of all the tinctures of all the colours.

I have said that in the celestial plane all things are personal, but in the astral plane they are reflects. The genius is a person because he is a celestial, and of soul-spirit, or substantial nature. But the astrals

are of fluidic nature, having no personal part.   In the
celestial plane, spirit and substance are one, dual in
unity ; and thus are all celestials constituted.   But in
the astral plane they have no individual, and no
divine part.   They are protoplasmic only, without
either nucleus or nucleolus.

The voice of the genius is the voice of God ; for
God speaks through him as a man through the horn
of a trumpet.   Thou mayest not adore him, for he is
the instrument of God, and thy minister.   But thou
must obey him, for he hath no voice of his own, but
sheweth thee the will of the Spirit.

No. XV.

CONCERNING THE "POWERS OF THE AIR." [1]

PART I.

I SAW last night in my sleep my genius clothed
with a red flame and standing in a dark place.
He held in his hand a cup, into which he bade me
look.   I did so, and as I looked a mist gathered in
the cup like a cloud ; and I saw in the cloud spirits
wrestling with each other.   Then the cup seemed to
widen, until it became a great table upon which
scenes and words were written.   And I saw the
vapour filled with astral spirits, ephemeral, flame-like,
chimerical ; and upon the mist which enveloped and

[1] London, November 17, 1880.

swept around them was written, " The Powers of the Air."

And I said to my genius, " Are these the spirits which control mediums ? " And he said, " Do not use that word *Medium ;* for it is misleading. These are the powers which affect and influence *Sensitives.*[1] They do not control, for they have no force. They are light as vapour. See ! " Then he breathed on the table, and they were dispersed on all sides like smoke. And I said, " Whence do these spirits come, and what is their origin and nature ? " And he answered,—" They are Reflects. They have no real entity in themselves. They resemble mists which rise from the damp earth of low-lying lands, and which the heat of the sun disperses. Again, they are like vapours in high altitudes, upon which if a man's shadow falls he beholds himself as a giant. For these spirits invariably flatter and magnify a man to himself. And this is a sign whereby you may know them. They tell one that he is a king ; another, that he is a Christ ; another, that he is the wisest of mortals, and the like. For, being born of the fluids of the body, they are unspiritual and live *of* the body."

" Do they, then," I asked, " come from within the man ? "

" All things," he replied, " come from within. A man's foes are they of his own household."

" And how," I asked, " may we discern the astrals from the higher spirits ? "

---

[1] That this is not intended to be an exhaustive account of the experiences of Sensitives will be seen from Nos. XXXIX., XL., and XLVI.

" I have told you of one sign ;—they are flattering spirits. Now I will tell you of another. They always depreciate woman. And they do this because their deadliest foe is the Intuition. And these, too, are their signs. Is there anything strong ? they will make it weak. Is there anything wise ? they will make it foolish. Is there anything sublime ? they will distort and travesty it. And this they do because they are exhalations of matter, and have no spiritual nature. Hence they pursue and persecute the Woman continually, sending after her a flood of eloquence like a torrent to sweep her away. But it shall be in vain. For God shall carry her to His throne, and she shall tread on the necks of them.

" Therefore the high Gods will give through a woman the interpretation which alone can save the world. A woman shall open the gates of the kingdom to mankind, because intuition only can redeem. Between the woman and the astrals there is always enmity ; for they seek to destroy her and her office, and to put themselves in her place. They are the delusive shapes who tempted the saints of old with exceeding beauty and wiles of love, and great show of affection and flattery. Oh, beware of them when they flatter, for they spread a net for thy soul."

" Am I, then," I asked, " in danger from them ? Am I, too, a Sensitive ? " And he said,—

" No, you are a Poet. And in that is your strength and your salvation. Poets are the children of the Sun, and the Sun illumines them. No poet can be vain or self-exalted; for he knows that he speaks only

the words of God. 'I sing,' he says, 'because I must.'
Learn a truth which is known only to the Sons of
God. The Spirit within you is divine. It is God.
When you prophesy and when you sing, it is the
Spirit within you which gives you utterance. It is the
'New Wine of Dionysos.' By this Spirit your body is
enlightened, as a lamp by the flame within it. Now,
the flame is not the oil, for the oil may be there
without the light. Yet the flame cannot be there
without the oil. Your body, then, is the lamp-case
into which the oil is poured. And this—the oil—is
your soul, a fine and combustible fluid. And the
flame is the divine Spirit, which is not born of the oil,
but is conveyed to it by the hand of God. You may
quench this Spirit utterly, and thenceforward you will
have no immortality; but when the lamp-case breaks,
the oil will be spilt on the earth, and a few fumes will
for a time arise from it, and then it will expend itself
and leave at last no trace. Some oils are finer and
more spontaneous than others. The finest is that of
the soul of the poet. And in such a medium the
flame of God's Spirit burns more clearly, and power-
fully, and brightly, so that sometimes mortal eyes
can hardly endure its brightness. Of such a one the
soul is filled with holy raptures. He sees as no other
man sees, and the atmosphere about him is enkindled.
His soul becomes transmuted into flame; and when
the lamp of his body is shattered, his flame mounts
and soars, and is united to the Divine Fire. Can
such a one, think you, be vain-glorious, or self-
exalted, and lifted up? Oh, no, he is one with God,

and knows that without God he is nothing. I tell no
man that he is a reincarnation of Moses, of Elias, or
of Christ. But I tell him that he may have the
Spirit of these if, like them, he be humble and self-
abased, and obedient to the Divine Word.

"Do not, then, seek after 'controls.' Keep your
temple for the Lord God of Hosts; and turn out
of it the money-changers, the dove-sellers, and the
dealers in curious arts, yea, with a scourge of cords if
need be."

PART 2.

"The astral existences, although they are not intelligent personalities, are frequently the media of
intelligent ideas, and operate as means of communication between intelligent personalities. Ideas, words,
sentences, whole systems of philosophy, may be borne
in on the consciousness by means of the currents of
magnetic force, as solid bodies are conveyed on a
stream, though water is no intelligent agent. The
minutest cell is an entity, for it has the power of self-
propagation, which the astral has not. It is an
imprint only, a shadow, a reflect, an echo.

"The atmosphere with which a man surrounds
himself—his soul's respiration—affects the astral fluid.
Reverberations of his own ideas come back to him.
His soul's breath colours and savours what a sensitive
conveys to him. But he may also meet with contra-
dictions, with a systematic presentation of doctrine or

of counsels at variance with his own personal views,
through his mind not being sufficiently positive to
control all the manifestations of the electric agent.
The influence of the medium, moreover, through
which the words come, interposes. Or, as is often
the case, a magnetic battery of thought has over-
charged the element and imparted to it a certain
current. Thus, new doctrines are "in the air," and
spread like wildfire. One or two strongly positive
minds give the initiative ; and the impulse flies
through the whole mass of latent light, correspond-
ingly influencing all who are in relation with it.

" In man the astral fluid becomes transformed into
human life at the moment of conception. It is the
envelope of the soul, and constitutes the sideral body,
which, in its turn, is the generator of the external
body. The internal man—he who ultimately is
immortal—consists of soul and spirit. The sideral
phantom and the outer body are perishable, save
when they undergo transmutation during the tenancy
of the soul and spirit. Hence the sideral body, being
the generator of sense, is the "Tempter," which—
inclining to matter—gives matter the precedence
over spirit. Of time and of sense, it beguiles the
intuitive part of man. In this way spirit and matter
represent, respectively, good and evil. For, in the
day that thou givest thyself over to matter, thou
becomest liable to extinction."

No. XVI.

CONCERNING THE DEVIL AND DEVILS.[1]

BEING unable to reconcile the statement that there is no personal Devil, but that what is called the Devil is simply the negation of God, with the evidences of the possession of individuals by devils or evil spirits, I received in my sleep this explanation.

"There is no supreme personal positive evil existence such as the Devil is ordinarily supposed to be. There is only the negation of God, which is to God what darkness is to light, the outermost void to the solar system. But there are evil spirits, the souls of bad men on their downward road to final extinction. And these are wont to associate themselves with persons in the flesh for whom they have affinity, partly in order to gratify their evil propensities by inciting them to wickedness and mischief, and partly to obtain from them the vitality necessary to prolong their own existence. Sometimes they are so low in vitality that a sentence of expulsion from the person in whom they have taken refuge, involves their immediate extinction, unless they can find other location, though it be only in an animal. And this was the case with the devils whom Jesus, on expelling them, suffered to enter into the herd of swine. For it is the fact that the disorders of men

---

[1] Paris, October 26, 1877.

do in some cases result from their possession by distinct personal entities as foreign and evil spirits, and are not merely disorders of their own physical constitution. Evil spirits have no chief, no organisation, or solidarity, nothing that corresponds to God. The worse they are the lower they are, and the nearer to extinction. The conditions which attract them are due to men themselves."

No. XVII.

CONCERNING THE GODS.[1]

A TRUE Idea is the reflect of a true Substance. It is because religious ideas are true ideas that they are common to all ages and peoples; the differences being of expression merely, and due to the variation of density and character of the magnetic atmosphere through which the image passes. The fact that every nation in every age has conceived, in some shape, of the Gods, constitutes of itself a proof that the Gods really *are*. For Nothing projects no image upon the magnetic light; and where an image is universally perceived, there is certainly an object which projects it. An Idea, inborn, ineradicable, constant, which sophism, ridicule, or false science has power to break only, but not to dispel :—an image which, however disturbed, invariably returns on itself and reforms, as does the image of the sky or the

[1] London, December 20, 1880. Spoken in trance.

stars in a lake, however the reflecting water may be momentarily shaken by a stone or a passing vessel : —such an image as this is necessa**[**y the reflection of a real and true thing, and no illusion begotten of the water itself.

In the same manner the constant idea of the Gods, persistent in all minds in all ages, is a true image ; for it is verily, and in no metaphoric sense, the projection upon the human perception of the *Eidola* of the Divine persons. The *Eidolon* is the reflection of a true object in the magnetic atmosphere ; and the magnetic atmosphere is a transparent medium, through which the soul receives sensations. For sensation is the only means of knowledge, whether for the body or for the reason. The body perceives by means of the five avenues of touch. The soul perceives in like manner by the same sense, but of a finer sort, and put into action by subtler agents. The soul can know nothing not perceptible ; and nothing not perceptible is real. For that which is not can give no image. Only that which *is* can be reflected.

No. XVIII.

CONCERNING THE GREEK MYSTERIES.[1]

IN the celebration of the mysteries of Phoibos Apollo, it was forbidden to eat anything upon which terrestrial fire had passéd. Wherefore all the

[1] London, March 27, 1881. Received in sleep.

food of his votaries was sun-baked, and his chief sacrifice consisted in fruits from high trees ripened by the sun's rays.

With these mysteries of Apollo were associated those of Zeus and Hera, the King and Queen, because both man and woman are admitted to the highest; and also because Eve and Adam, being thus initiated, were eaters only of fruits uncooked; and, in one of the historical senses of the allegory, Eve and Adam were the first Messengers. It was, therefore, an offence against Phoibos and Zeus for their votaries to eat anything on which fire had passed, or any fermented wine. Their wine was the pure juice of the grape drunken new, and their bread was unleavened and sun-baked.

The last Messengers must be initiated, as were Eve and Adam, into these inmost and highest mysteries of the perfect humanity, which constitute the highest of all castes, and entitle those who attain to them to sit on the golden seats.[1]

These mysteries have also an inward significance which is not hard to find.

In the mysteries of Phoibos and Zeus, the initiated attained to the condition of a grand Hierophant. ("See! I tell you all things.") He was enlightened by the "sun," and was in the fourth interior circle of spirits, which is that of the Christs of God.[2] To this interior circle Jesus of Nazareth aimed to pass after his resuscitation; as was implied when he said, " I

[1] See No. XXIV. ; also "Dreams and Dream-Stories," No. IX.
[2] Comp. Hymn to Phoibos, Part II., No. XI.

will drink no more of the grape until I drink its blood
new in the kingdom of God."

In the mysteries of Hermes, the second circle,—
the God who guards the Soul,—it was forbidden to eat
any creature which had life, or, rather, which had
seeing eyes.[1] For Hermes is the Seer. His votaries
partook only of vegetable food, which might be
cooked with terrestrial fire, and of wine, which might
be fermented.

Next in order were the orgies of Her who rose from
the sea; and in these the initiates might eat fish which
are truly fish, having fins and scales, but baked with
fire, not raw.   Wherefore as that Goddess is the Angel
of Harmony, or of the Sweet Song, the eating of fish
became a symbol of brotherly love and union ; and
two small fishes together was the mystical type of
little children dwelling together in unity or charity.[2]
For fishes swim in pairs ; and He who fished for men
drew them unto him by love. And all fishers were
under the protection of the Sea-Queen.   There are
two mystical truths belonging to the mysteries of
Maria the Sea-Star; and they are, in their interior
sense, the two fishes which Jesus imparted to the
multitude.   Of this I shall tell you more afterwards
when I speak to you of the twelve baskets of bread.
For these are the baskets which the twelve virgins
carried in the divine orgies.

In the mysteries of Bacchos it was permitted to the
outer circle to eat, if indeed they would, of all flesh

[1] Comp. Hermes to his Neophytes, Part II., No. XII. pt. 2.
[2] Comp. Hymn of Aphrodite, Part II., No. XIV. (2.)

save of the unclean. This is, they might eat of all
clean beasts of the field and birds of the air. This
was the fourth and lowest caste. But the votaries of
Iacchos (the mystic Bacchos), having known all the
higher rites, abstained from these things, though they
allowed them to the multitude who are in the body
only. For none of those who worshipped Dionysos
(or Iacchos) were uninitiated in the rites of Demeter
and Aphrodite. And for this reason there were substituted for the mysteries of Dionysos those of Ceres,
the Earth-Mother, in which the use of flesh was
entirely prohibited. For this reason also one hears
not of the mysteries of Bacchos save in connection
with wine, whether fermented or not ; for the interior
significance of his rites had reference to the truth and
meaning of things. The orgies of Ceres and Bacchos
were therefore united, the Goddess being honoured in
her bread, and the God in his chalice of truth. For
in that these are body and spirit, solid and fluid,
outer and inner, they comprise all things in earth and
in heaven.

And beyond the circle of Dionysos lay yet another
—that of a God who also had indeed his orgies, but
these were forbidden save in certain fierce nations and
barbarous times. For in the mysteries of Ares, the
Man of War, they sacrificed and ate human flesh and
the flesh of horses, which also war together with man.
For this circle is outside the kingdom of the fourfold
circles, and belongeth to the beasts of prey. And his
star is red, as with the blood of the slain. But the
orgies of Ares the Ram-headed no man celebrated

save in war; and he who knew the God spared not
his life, but freely sacrificed himself. For it was an
abomination to eat at the altar of Ares in time of
peace.

Yet hath Ares also his interior meaning:— O
Knowledge, thou art hard of access! The Horse
(which is the symbol of the intellect) dieth for thee,
and the Warrior is pierced. Thou art the Man of
War, and of iron are the wheels of thy chariot!

The Hebrew Scriptures describe the Lord Jehovah,
or Logos, as operating as the Spirit of the fifth circle,
when they speak of God as a Man of War. And the
book of Wisdom (xviii. 15) thus represents Him.
For the Divine Word takes many forms, appearing
sometimes as one, sometimes as another, of His
Seven Angels, or Elohim. These are only Seven,
because this number comprises all the Spirits of God.
So that when the seventh is passed, the octave
begins again, and the same series of processes is
repeated without, as reflects—becoming by distance
weaker and weaker—of the same Seven Lights.

See that above all things you teach the doctrine of
Caste. The Christians made a serious mistake in
requiring the same rule of all persons. Castes are
as ladders whereby to ascend from the lower to the
higher. They are, properly, spiritual grades, and
bear no relation to the outward condition of life.
Like all other doctrines, that of caste has been
materialised. The castes are four in number, and
correspond to the fourfold nature of man.

The Daimons, Guardian Angels, or Genii belong to

the order of Seraphs, or Serpents of Light, which surround and spring from the supreme orb. Hence the idea of the serpent as a fallen angel, the astrals being serpents of fire, springing from Hades, or the lower—the material and astral—world, which is the obverse of the upper.

Venus, or Aphrodite, is celestial Harmony,—that binding power of sympathy which purifies, enlightens, and beautifies. The Apple in her hand is the Kosmos (denoting the world sustained and redeemed by Love).

The Owl, sacred to Pallas, and the Cat to Hermes, are types of the Seer. For Wisdom and Understanding can behold things in dark places.

The Spoiling of the Egyptians has a secondary reference to the appropriation of their sacred mysteries by the Hebrews. The primary reference is to the enrichment and edification of the soul by means of the lessons obtained through the experiences of the body, symbolised as Egypt.

Air, Pallas, is the offspring of Ether, Jupiter, or original Substance in its masculine aspect. Ether is universally diffused, penetrating everywhere, or, rather, impossible to be excluded from anywhere. The whirling atoms of the densest solids revolve in ether, as do the planets in space. In a sense Ether *is* space.

The Soul, Persephone, is the daughter of Earth, Demeter or Motion, and of Ether, Zeus or Rest, respectively the visible and invisible. To him who knows the mysteries of Demeter or Ceres, the eating of flesh is an abomination.

These mysteries contained, among other things, the relation of the soul to the elements by which on either side it is beset,—namely, to motion and matter on the outer side, and to rest and spirit on the inner. Hence Demeter and her mysteries are of profound import, and relate to secrets the most interior. As the force which causes spirit to become manifest as matter or earth, she is the Earth-Mother and the power whereby germination occurs. Constituting all that is fixed and solid, she is creation, or manifestation through action or motion, the invisible made visible. And to her is due the phenomenal or illusive by which her daughter Persephone—or the soul—is drawn outwards and downwards. Illusion, the "fiery" or electric body generated of motion, and operating as a veil to hide the inner reality, is Maya and Glamour ; and the soul following this is carried off to Hades by its ruler Pluto (the God especially of riches, themselves, illusive as products of the earth). Eating of the Mystic Pomegranate (the "Apple" of Eve), the volatile becomes alchemically fixed, the soul is incorporated with the body, and in part, at least, materialised, and is no longer "virgin" or pure, because wedded to flesh and sense. At the entreaty of her mother, who fears her total immersion in matter, and consequent final loss, Zeus grants that she may divide her existence between the two worlds or conditions, the earthly and the heavenly, being —while in the lower—Queen of the Shades or those who sleep, being unconscious of things spiritual.

Thus the volatile or astral body, which is the immediate manifestation of the soul, is the daughter—or product—of Motion ; and Motion is the daughter of Time (Kronos or Saturn), and of Substance, which is Rhea, or the Holy Spirit in its feminine aspect. This last is the Great Mother, the original Panthea. The production of the material body by the fixing of the particles of the volatile body comes of the reversal of the poles of those particles through the outward tendency of the will of the individual, and its separation or divergence from the divine or central will.

The force whereby Zeus, the central spirit, produces the soul or ethereal body, and which also the soul uses to project itself still further, is the same force whereby the system is transmuted and indrawn again to its divine centre and made volatile. The force is one, it is the will and direction that are various.

In one application Persephone is the grain of wheat, Ceres the soil, and Hades the darkness which hides the seed, until under solar influence it emerges and returns to the light. It was through a misunderstanding of the mysteries of Ceres, and of the true meaning of the resurrection of the body, that the custom of burning the dead was given up for that of burying them.

The Gods of the elements, Athena (air), Poseidon (water), Hephaistos (fire), and Demeter (earth), are among the greatest, and are close to the throne, having universal sway, inasmuch as their empire is universal.[1]

[1] See Part II., No. XIII. pt. 2, and Appendix, note R.

F

No. XIX.

CONCERNING THE ORIGIN OF EVIL, AND THE TREE AS THE TYPE OF CREATION.

PART I.[1]

" I SPEAK of the Tree and of its meaning. Of this the Hindûs understand more than you, for they represent their gods with many arms. This is because they recognise the fact that the type of all existence is a Tree, and that God's universal symbol is that of the vegetable kingdom. It is for this reason that the Tree was planted in the midst of the garden, forasmuch as it was and is the type of all existence, the centre from which radiates the whole of creation. Let the insight of the Hindûs instruct you on this matter.

"You have demanded also the origin of Evil. This is a great subject, and we would have withheld it from you longer, but that it seems to us now that you are in need of it. Understand, then, that evil is the result of creation. For creation is the projection of spirit into matter; and with this projection came the first germ of evil. We would have you know that there is no such thing as purely spiritual evil, but that evil is the result of the materialisation of spirit. If you examine carefully all we have said to you con-

---

[1] Paris, July 21, 1877. This part was written down by the seeress herself while in trance. Part 2. was spoken in the same condition immediately afterwards.

cerning the various forms of evil, you will see that every one is the result of the limitations of matter. Falsehood is the limitation of the faculty of perception ; selfishness is the result of the limitation of the power to perceive that the whole universe is but the larger Self ; and so of all the rest. It is, then, true that God created evil ; but yet it is true that God is Spirit, and being Spirit, is incapable of evil. Evil is then, purely and solely, the result of the materialisation of God. This is a great mystery. We can but indicate it to-night."

PART 2.

I see a lake, vast and deep and bright. I am not certain whether it is lake or sea. It has no borders that I can perceive. Its waters are so clear that I could see the pebbles shining at the bottom, if it had one. It is overspread by a flood of nebulous light, evenly diffused in all parts ; and now, as I look, the light has become concentrated into flowers, and between them are spaces of darkness caused by the withdrawal of the light into the flowers. It is a vast floating garden of flowers, and in the midst of the garden is a Tree. The tree spreads out its arms everywhere. The garden is creation, the tree is God. And the tree seems in some way to be the flowers, and the flowers belong to the tree. I cannot discern the material of the tree ; it evades me as I look. It is not matter ; it is the substance of matter, the divinity underlying it. God is not light, but that of which light itself is the

manifestation. God willed it to be. Light is the result
of God's will. God said, " Let light be " ; and it was.
Matter is the intensification of Idea. All things are
made of God's thought. God is Spirit, and the substance of things. I see two forces ever in operation.
They are the centrifugal and the centripetal. And they
are one ; yes, one and the same, for I see the force re-
bound back to God. Creation is ever being projected
from God as from a luminous centre ; it is always
being drawn back again also. Some parts refuse to
return ; they go into outer space ; they are lost. Let
me see,—can it be that they pass beyond the sphere
of the Divine attraction ? Yes ; I see that it is so,
and oh ! they are lost. The Spirit is withdrawn ; it
is as if it were sucked out of them, and they wander
away into darkness, and expend themselves. The
rest, who approach God, develop the Spirit in them,
becoming more and more like God. God is the richer
for them. They continue to exist. They return, but
do not become lost in God.

I thought I was describing orbs in space, projected
from a central sun around which they circled ; but,
looking closer, I see them as individuals. They have
become persons. It must be that the method of
creation is the same for all.

God subsisted prior to creation ; there was a time
when God did not create ; it was God's Sabbath of rest.
Such Sabbaths recur,—when there is no material universe. This is when the Divine mind ceases from
thinking. For God to think is to create. Matter itself is a result of the Divine thought ; it was first pro-

duced by the intensification of Idea. It appears to me that its first form was like water—fluidic. Spirit is Divinity itself. God is dual. I see, on looking closer, that through this duality God produces creation. Evil is caused by creation, or the projection of spirit into matter ; that is, it is spirit which, by being projected far enough from the Divine centre,[1] becomes matter. Perception is one ; the senses are specialised modes of perception. God is perception itself. God is universal percipience. God is both that which sees and that which is seen. If we all could see all, hear all, touch all, and so forth, there would be no evil, for evil comes of the limitation of perception. Such limitation was necessary, if God was to produce aught other than God. Aught other than God must be less than God. Without evil, therefore, God would have remained alone. All things are God, according to the measure of the spirit in them. And now I see that the nearest of all to God is a woman.[2]

No. XX.

CONCERNING THE GREAT PYRAMID, AND THE INITIATIONS THEREIN.[3]

I SEE the Great Pyramid, and can tell you all about it. My genius informs me that the number of the pyramids in Egypt corresponds to the number of

---

[1] The centre, that is, of the Divine operation, not of the Divine Being.

[2] As type of the feminine or love aspect of the Divine Nature.

[3] London, March 22, 1881. Spoken in trance.

the mysteries of the Gods. No one has yet rightly found out the purpose of the great one. It was built simply in order to serve in initiations. I see a candidate and seven or eight hierophants going in procession with torches through the passages. Each passage represents a mystery, the chief one leading to the " king's chamber." This represents the greater mysteries. The " queen's chamber " represents the lesser mysteries. The coffer in the king's chamber is a measure representing the standard of the perfect Humanity. And in this the candidate was laid on his final initiation.

It appears to me that I was once there myself. My sensations about it are like a memory. It was not built to be a prophecy, but it may serve as a prophecy. In it is symbolised all the Wanderings in the Desert,—the history, that is, of the soul in the wilderness of the body. In representing the soul of the individual, it represents the soul also of the race, and thus is really a prophecy.

The new birth takes place in the king's chamber. It is the last stage. A person may be initiated several times in various incarnations ; but he is re-generated once for all. The " baptism " took place in the queen's chamber. It belonged to the lesser mysteries. It is neither initiation nor regeneration, but purification. There are four stages to be passed before final initiation. They correspond to the four elements, earth, fire, water, and air ; and they relate respectively to the four corresponding divisions of man's nature,—the body, the phantom or perisoul, the soul, and the spirit, which are the four rivers of Eden. And the candidate has to be tested and proved in each of them by the "tempter."

The initiate was accompanied by his sponsor or "mother," a priestess or Sibyl. The central secret of the Mysteries was the tree of life in the midst of the garden; Immortality, the secret of Transmutation, or of changing "water" (substance) into "wine" (spirit). This, "Issa"—the son of Isis—or Jesus, is alone able to do. O incomprehensible secret, who shall understand thee! A soul, as has already been said, may be initiated more than once, in several lives, but only once regenerated. For she—the soul —can only once be born of the spirit, or "wisdom." To be regenerate is to be born into spiritual life, and to have united the individual will with the Divine Will.

This union of the two wills constitutes the spiritual marriage, the accomplishment of which is in the Gospels represented under the parable of the marriage at Cana of Galilee. This divine marriage, or union of the human and Divine Wills, is indissoluble; whence the idea of the indissolubility of human marriage. And inasmuch as it is a marriage of the spirit of man to that of God, and of the Spirit of God to that of man, it is a double marriage.

I see the ceremony actually taking place. The hierophant represents the Divine Spirit; and he and the candidate face each other, and crossing their arms grasp each with each hand a hand of the other. A soul may be partially and transiently illuminated by the Spirit ; the Spirit may even descend upon an individual and make him a prophet, and pass away leaving him unregenerate, and out of the kingdom of God,—as occurred to John the Baptist. But it is the divine marriage only which constitutes regeneration, the sacrament of eternal marriage. Of this intimate union the soul itself is reborn, and its inmost recesses divinely illuminated. Of such marriage as this the Patriarchs were ignorant. Their connection with the Spirit was fitful and transient, and they were therefore represented as living in concubinage.

We have herein the reason why the Cup is denied to the laity. "Of every tree," it is said to the uninitiate Adam, "thou mayest freely communicate. But of the tree of knowledge thou mayest not communicate." The wine is the spirit of interior truth, the understanding of which gives eternal life ; and to this the people cannot yet attain. They may receive only the bread, which represents only the element of substance. This, however, contains also the spirit, although unmanifested and unrecognised.

I now see the pyramid distinctly. It was built entirely for initiations, so far as its builders were concerned. In these ceremonials the Reed played an important part, and in sacred mythos generally. Thus, Moses was placed in a basket of reeds. The Hindû divinity Kartikya was sheltered in infancy by reeds. The mysteries of Ceres, or Demeter, were carried in baskets of reeds, called *canephoræ ;* and the final stage in the initiation of Jesus is placed at *Cana.* A reed also was placed in his hand at his condemnation. And the virgin in the sacred marriage initiation also bore a reed with a cup on it. This is because, growing in and out of the water, which denotes the soul, and being a straight rod, the reed denotes the spirit. In India the Lotus has the same significance. I perceive that Jesus had been initiated in the mysteries of India and Egypt long before he was incarnated as Jesus, and he appears to me as having been a Brahmin.

The Egyptians and Hindûs appear to be of the same race, having their mysteries in common. For I am shown one of each people riding together on an elephant. Both countries were *colonised* at the same time from Thibet, and from thence all the mysteries proceeded.[1] In Egypt the initiations were generally in pyramids and temples. In India and Palestine they were underground, in caves. In Cana of Galilee there is a large cave, which was used for the purpose, with a "banqueting" room.

I am counting the pyramids. I see thirty-six, but I think there are more.[2]

---

[1] Herein is suggested yet another application of the parable of the Deluge. Thibet, like Thebes, signifies Ark ; and if, as long supposed, it was once the sole home of spiritual knowledge in the world and centre whence it was diffused, it may be said of the ancient Thibetan mysteries as of the dwellers in the Ark, "Of them was the whole earth overspread." The facts are noteworthy that Thibet is the highest table-land on the globe, and that the word *Ararat* is identical with the word *Arhat*, the Hindû term for the summit of spiritual attainment.

[2] Concerning the method of recovery of these recollections, see note at end of No. XXXII.

No. XXI.

CONCERNING THE " MAN OF POWER." [1]

I HAVE said that everything is fourfold, and as is the planet, so also is the man. The perfect man has a fourfold outer body,—gaseous, mineral, vegetable, and animal : a fourfold sideral body,—magnetic, odic, sympathetic, elemental : a fourfold soul,—partaking of the soulic elements of all the grades through which he has passed, being elemental, instinctive, vital, rational : and a triune Spirit,—because there is no external to Spirit,—desirous, willing, obedient. There is nothing in the universe save Man ; and the Perfect Man is " Christ Jesus."

" Mercury " fecundated by " sulphur " becomes the master and regenerator of " salt." It is azoth, or the universal magnesia (of the Alchemists), the great magical agent, the light of light fecundated by animating force, or intellectual energy, which is the sulphur. As to salt, it is simple matter. Everything which is matter contains salt ; and all salt may be converted into pure gold by the combined action of sulphur and mercury. These sometimes act so rapidly that the transmutation may be made in an hour, an instant, almost without labour and

---

[1] London, December 1880. Spoken in trance, but not, as in the foregoing, in the speaker's own person, but under dictation heard interiorly; and so also with the three utterances which follow.

without cost. At other times, owing to the contrary dispositions of the atmospheric medium, the operation may necessitate days, months, or years. Salt is fixed; mercury is volatile. The fixation of the volatile is the synthesis; the volatilisation of the fixed is the analysis. On applying to the fixed the sulphuretted mercury, or the astral fluid rendered powerful by the secret operation of the soul, the mastery over nature is obtained. The two terms of the process are materialisation and transmutation. These two terms are those of the "Great Work,"— the redemption of spirit from matter.

Miracles are natural effects of exceptional causes. The man who has arrived at wishing for nothing and fearing nothing, is master of all.

The Initiate of the highest grade—one who has power to command the elemental spirits, and thereby to hush the storm and still the waves—can, through the same agency, heal the disorders and regenerate the functions of the body. And this he does by an exercise of his will which sets in motion the magnetic fluid.

Such a person, an Adept or Hierarch of magnetic science, is, necessarily, a person of many incarnations. And it is principally in the East that these are to be found. For it is there that the oldest souls are wont to congregate. It is in the East that human science first arose; and the soil and astral fluid there are charged with power as a vast battery of many piles. So that the Hierarch of the Orient both is himself an older soul and has the magnetic support of a chain

of older souls, and the earth beneath his feet and
the medium around him are charged with electric
force in a degree not to be found elsewhere.

Now, the odic or sideral body is the real body of
the man. The phenomenal body is secondary. The
odic body is not necessarily of the same shape or
appearance as the outward body, but it is of the
nature of the soul. The creation of man in the
image of God " before the transgression," is the picture
of the man having power ; that is, having an odic
body in which the elements were not fixed,—a body
such as that of the " risen Christ." What I have
said concerning the volatilisation of salt, will help to
the understanding of this. But when the " sin of
idolatry " had been committed, then man ceased to
have power over his own body, and thus became a
" pillar of salt," fixed and material. He was " naked."

The man thus referred to attained power over his
body by evolution from rudimentary being ; and at
last, becoming polarised, received the Divine Flame
of Deity, and thereby the power over " salt." But
by reason of perverse will to the outer, he depolarised,
and thereby fixed the volatile. Then he knew that
he was " naked," and so lost " Paradise."

Can Paradise be regained ? Yes, through the
Cross and Resurrection of " Christ." For, as in
" Adam " all die, so in " Christ " shall all be made
alive.   And forasmuch as the earthly dies, the
celestial lives. The body can be transmuted into
its prototype, the magnetic body. This is the work
of the adept. The magnetic body can be abandoned

to the odic fluid, and the soul set free. This is the work of *post mortem* evolution. But to transmute phenomenal body, magnetic body, and soul alike into spirit,—this is the work of "Christ." "I have power," said Jesus, "over my body, to lay it down and to take it up again."

You have said to me, "If the odic or sideral body be the maker of the physical body, how can this differ in form from it ? How can a man be outwardly human, and really a wolf, a hare, or a dog ? "

When you become an adept you will know that such fact involves no contradiction. The transitions of the sideral body are not sudden. It *becomes* gradually, and does not undergo changes by cataclysm. It is already partly human before it has ceased to wear the form of a rudimentary man,—that is, of an animal. You have seen this in visions when you beheld the human shape in creatures under torture in the laboratory.[1] And it is still partly rudimentary when it puts on the human. Indulgence in its lower propensities may strengthen it in its old likeness, and accentuate its former propensities. On the other hand, aspiration towards the divine will accelerate the change, and cause it to lose altogether its lower attributes. That which is born of flesh is in the image of the flesh ; but that which cometh from the beyond is of the beyond. The womb can bring forth only its own kind, in the semblance

[1] See "Dreams and Dream-Stories," No. XIV., "The Laboratory Underground."

of the generators; and as soon as the human is
attained, even in the least degree, the soul has power
to put on the body of humanity.   Hence the odic
body always possesses some attribute of humanity.
But it may lose this by sin; and in such case it
returns, by a fresh incarnation, to the form of the
beast.   Of such returns to the lower form, some are
purely penitential; but most are retributory.   The
adept can see the human in the beast, and can
tell whether the soul therein is an ascending or
a descending soul.   He can also see the soul in
a man; and all men are not to him of the same
shape or appearance.   If your eyes were opened,
you would be astonished at the number of animals
you meet in the streets, and the scarcity of men.
The parable of the Enchanted City, in the eastern
fables, is descriptive of this mystery.

No. XXII.

CONCERNING THE "WORK OF POWER."[1]

YOU have asked me if the Work of Power is a
difficult one, and if it is open to all.

It is open to all potentially and eventually, but not
actually and in the present.   In order to regain power
and the resurrection, a man must be a Hierarch;
that is to say, he must have attained the *magical* age

[1] London, December 1880.   Received in sleep.

of thirty-three. This age is attained by having accomplished the Twelve Labours, passed the Twelve
Gates, overcome the Five Senses, and obtained
dominion over the Four Spirits of the elements. He
must have been born Immaculate, baptised with
Water and with Fire, tempted in the Wilderness,
crucified and buried. He must have borne Five
Wounds on the Cross, and he must have answered
the riddle of the Sphinx. When this is accomplished
he is free of matter, and will never again have a
phenomenal body.

Who shall attain to this perfection? The Man
who is without fear and without concupiscence; who
has courage to be absolutely poor and absolutely
chaste. When it is all one to you whether you have
gold or whether you have none, whether you have a
house and lands or whether you have them not,
whether you have worldly reputation or whether you
are an outcast,—then you are voluntarily poor. It is
not necessary to have nothing, but it is necessary to
care for nothing. When it is all one to you whether
you have a wife or husband, or whether you are
celibate, then you are free from concupiscence. It is
not necessary to be a virgin; it is necessary to set no
value on the flesh. There is nothing so difficult to
attain as this equilibrium. Who is he who can part
with his goods without regret? Who is he who is
never consumed by the desires of the flesh? But
when you have ceased both to wish to retain and to
burn, then you have the remedy in your own hands,
and the remedy is a hard and a sharp one, and a

terrible ordeal. Nevertheless, be not afraid. Deny
the five senses, and above all the taste and the
touch. The power is within you if you will to
attain it. The Two Seats are vacant at the Celestial
Table,[1] if you will put on Christ. Eat no dead thing.
Drink no fermented drink. Make living elements of
all the elements of your body. Mortify the members
of earth. Take your food full of life, and let not the
touch of death pass upon it. You understand me,
but you shrink. Remember that without self-im-
molation, there is no power over death. Deny the
touch. Seek no bodily pleasure in sexual communion; let desire be magnetic and soulic. If you
indulge the body, you perpetuate the body, and the
end of the body is corruption. You understand me
again, but you shrink. Remember that without self-
denial and restraint there is no power over death.
Deny the taste first, and it will become easier to
deny the touch. For to be a virgin is the crown
of discipline. I have shown you the excellent way,
and it is the *Via Dolorosa.* Judge whether the
resurrection be worth the passion; whether the
kingdom be worth the obedience; whether the
power be worth the suffering. When the time of
your calling comes, you will no longer hesitate.

When a man has attained power over his body, the
process of ordeal is no longer necessary. The Initiate
is under a vow; the Hierarch is free. Jesus, therefore,
came eating and drinking; for all things were lawful

[1] See No. XVIII., "Concerning the Greek Mysteries." Also,
"Dreams and Dream-Stories," No. IX., "The Banquet of the Gods."

to him. He had undergone, and had freed his will.
For the object of the trial and the vow is polarisation. When the fixed is volatilised, the Magian is
free. But before Christ was Christ he was subject;
and his initiation lasted thirty years. All things are
lawful to the Hierarch ; for he knows the nature and
value of all.

When the elements of the body are endowed with
power, they are masters of the elemental spirits, and
can overcome them. But while they are yet under
bondage, they are the slaves of the elementals, and the
elementals have power over them. Now, Hephaistos is
a destroyer, and the breath of fire is a touch of death.
The fire that passes on the elements of your food, deprives them of their vital spirit, and gives you a corpse
instead of living substance. And not only so, but the
spirit of the fire enters into the elements of your body,
and sets up in all its molecules a consuming and a
burning, impelling to concupiscence, and to the desire
of the flesh. The spirit of the fire is a subtle spirit,
a penetrative and diffusive spirit, and it enters into
the substance of all matter upon which it acts. When,
therefore, you take such substance into your organism,
you take with it the spirit of the fire, and you assimi-
late it together with the matter of which it has become
a part.

I speak to you of excellent things. If you would
become a man of power, you must be master of the
fire. The man who seeks to be a hierophant, must
not dwell in cities. He may begin his initiation in a
city, but he cannot complete it there. For he must

not breathe dead and burnt air. In a city you respire
air upon which the flame has passed ; you breathe
fire, and it consumes your blood. The man who seeks
all power must be a wanderer, a dweller in the plain
and the garden and the mountains. He must seek
the sun, and the breath of night. He must commune
with the moon and stars, and maintain direct contact
with the great electric currents of the unburnt air, and
with the grass and unpaved soil of the planet. It is
in unfrequented places, or in lands such as those of
the East, in parts where the abominations of Babylon
are unknown, and where the magnetic chain between
earth and heaven is strong,—that the man who
seeks power, and who would achieve the Great Work,
must accomplish his initiation.

The number of the human microcosm is thirteen ;
four for the outward body, four for the sideral body,
four for the soul, and one for the Divine Spirit. For,
although the Spirit is Triune it is One, and can be
but One ; because it is God, and God is One. At the
Last Supper, therefore, in which the Magians sym-
bolise the Banquet of the Microcosm, there are twelve
apostolic elements and one Christ. But if one of
the elements be disobedient and a traitor, the Spirit
is quenched and death ensues.

No. XXIII.

CONCERNING REGENERATION.[1]

THE difference between the "Son of God" and the mere prophet is that the former is born regenerate, and is therefore said to be "born of a virgin."[2] But regeneration is a union of the soul and spirit, and is not a process in which the body bears a part. In the "Baptism" Jesus received the Æon, or "Dove," and was filled with the Holy Ghost, becoming a Medium for the Highest. The Christ is informed from within, and "needeth not that any man should tell him ; for he knows what is in man." But the adept receives from without, and is instructed by others.

The adept, or "occultist," is at best a religious scientist ; he is not a "saint." If occultism were all, and held the key of heaven, there would be no need of "Christ." But occultism, although it holds the "power," holds neither the "kingdom" nor the "glory." For these are of Christ. The adept knows not the kingdom of heaven, and "the least in this kingdom are greater than he." "Desire *first* the

---

[1] London, June 1881. Received in sleep, in answer to an inquiry respecting the advisability of studying occult science.

[2] *I.e.*, his own soul purified from taint of materiality,—the soul being always the "mother" of the mystic or interior man. See "Definitions."

kingdom of God and God's righteousness ; and all these things shall be added unto you." As Jesus said of Prometheus,[1] "Take no thought for to-morrow. Behold the lilies of the field and the birds of the air, and trust God as these." For the saint has faith ; the adept has knowledge. If the adepts in oc-cultism or in physical science could suffice to man, I would have committed no message to you. But the two are not in opposition. All things are yours, even the kingdom and the power, but the glory is to God. Do not be ignorant of their teaching, for I would have you know all. Take, therefore, every means to know. This knowledge is of man, and cometh from the mind. Go, therefore, to man to learn it. " If you will be perfect, learn also of these." "Yet the wisdom which is from above, is above all." For one man may begin from within, that is, with wisdom, and wisdom is one with love. Blessed is the man who chooseth wisdom, for she leaveneth all things. And another man may begin from without, and that which is without is power. To such there shall be a thorn in the flesh.[2] For it is hard in such case to attain to the within. But if a man be first wise inwardly, he shall the more easily have this also added unto him. For he is born again and is free. Whereas at a great price must the adept buy freedom. Nevertheless, I bid you seek ;—and in this

---

[1] A term which signifies forethought. The remonstrance is against undue anxiety and alarm on the soul's behalf while in the path of duty, as implying distrust of the divine sufficiency. See Appendix, note J.

[2] *I.e.*, the flesh itself is their thorn.

also you shall find. But I have shown you a more excellent way than theirs. Yet both Ishmael and Isaac are sons of one father, and of all her children is Wisdom justified. So neither are they wrong, nor are you led astray. The goal is the same ; but their way is harder than yours. They take the kingdom by violence, if they take it, and by much toil and agony of the flesh. But from the time of Christ within you, the kingdom is open to the sons of God. Receive what you can receive ; I would have you know all things. And if you have served seven years for wisdom, count it not loss to serve seven years for power also. For if Rachel bear the best beloved, Leah hath many sons, and is exceeding fruitful. But her eye is not single ; she looketh two ways, and seeketh not that which is above only. But to you Rachel is given first, and perchance her beauty may suffice. I say not, let it suffice ; it is better to know all things, for if you know not all, how can you judge all ? For as a man heareth, so must he judge. Will you therefore be regenerate in the without, as well as in the within ? For they are renewed in the body, but you in the soul. It is well to be baptised into John's baptism, if a man receive also the Holy Ghost. But some know not so much as that there is any Holy Ghost. Yet Jesus also, being himself regenerate in the spirit, sought unto the baptism of John, for thus it became him to fulfil himself in all things. And having fulfilled, behold, the "Dove" descended on him. If then you will be perfect, seek both that which is within and that which

is without ; and the circle of being, which is the
" wheel of life," shall be complete in you.[1]

No. XXIV.

CONCERNING THE MAN REGENERATE.[2]

YOU have been told that Jesus and those like
him came back voluntarily and were born
under conditions different from the ordinary, in that
they had accomplished some degrees of their regeneration.   These degrees are twelve in all, and
constitute twelve labours, twelve gates, or twelve
pearls, all of which are of equal value.   Jesus was
born regenerate in certain degrees, and the whole
were completed only after his "resurrection," during
the retirement which ended in his "ascension."   The
last degrees are the most difficult.   There are four
for the soul, four for the perisoul (or astral), and four
for the body, this being the last.   And it was this
that Paul was so anxious to accomplish, but failed to
do.   With some the body is never redeemed ; but
this does not hinder the "divine marriage" of the
soul and spirit.   This marriage facilitates the redemption of the body, but may take place without
it.

[1] The above interpretation concerning Rachel and Leah, as we subsequently ascertained, is on the lines of the Kabala.

[2] London, July 9, 1881. Received in sleep. See also No. XXXIII.

There are four zones or divisions in the astral light, and the reflect of Jesus is in the highest only, and cannot be seen by those who have access only to the lower ; and not being strengthened by the shadow of the body of Jesus, it has become fainter, until now it is hardly perceptible. This is because his body was indrawn.[1]

Jesus had a great advantage in his birth, owing partly to his own regenerate condition, and partly to that of his parents. Owing to the purity of his mother's blood, she is said to have come of a priestly family. For the same reason his father is said to have come of a royal descent, for the terms "Tribe of Levi" and "House of David" have a mystic meaning.[2]

The sanctity of any particular Christ is dependent upon the advance made by him previously to his birth. Jesus had in this respect an advantage over Buddha. He was regenerate in more degrees, and he had no sexual relations as had Buddha. The Twelve Labours refer each to some concupiscence, which is depicted under the figure of a ravenous bird, horse, or some other animal which requires to be subdued. And Jesus had previously accomplished the Labour denoting that particular kind of con-cupiscence.

Now, of men some must needs be satisfied first

[1] Some occultists have made their own failure to discern the reflect of Jesus—a failure here accounted for—a ground for denying his existence.

[2] For another and more profound meaning of the derivation from David, see note to No. XXXVIII.

intellectually.   These are regenerate first in the mind ;
and afterwards they attain to the kingdom.

But some begin from within ; and these are the
most blessed.   For they seek the kingdom first, and
the rest is added to them afterwards.

These last begin the Great Work in the heart,
by means of the affection.   And the grace of love
attracts the Holy Spirit, and transmutes them from
glory to glory, so that the reason, or mind, is
suddenly enlightened by the inner reason ; and with
such the work of regeneration is instantaneous,—" in
the twinkling of an eye."   These are of the type of
the woman.

But others—and these are of the masculine type—
must perform their work more laboriously ; for in
them the mind is first illuminated.   They pass from
without inwards ; from the circumference to the
centre.   And this is but a difference of method, not
of ultimates ; for the Reason is the heir of all things.

With these the Great Work is a slow process ; but
their gold is one in kind with that of the first.   For
when at last the divine marriage consummates their
labours, the mind and the body are already redeemed,
and beyond the power of death, because they have
already the power.

But with those who are regenerate first within,
there is suffering of the body, and often death.   For
two opposing currents meet with violence, and the
result may be the rending apart of body and spirit.
But yet their death is not as the death of the unregenerate.   Because in the very shock of it trans-

mutation takes place: matter, that is, is sublimated, and the man needs no further incarnation. He is free, for he has conquered matter. Wherefore the bond is severed between him and the earthly, and he will return to the earthly no more.

He who is regenerate first in the body and mind, usually lives long, even beyond the limit of mortal life, and absorbs in that period his entire astral being, and often even his body. Thus did Enoch, thus Elias, and some others. I do not name them. And Jesus remained to do this also. For he would leave nothing undone, being in the end Lord of the kingdom, the power, and the glory.

But when he arose from the dead, not having seen corruption, nor fallen under the dominion of death, there remained to him one degree of regeneration to be accomplished,—he was not yet "ascended."

For there were then but the eleven; because the twelfth—"Judas"—was imperfect. And because of this Judas, Jesus fell under the power of the cross.

[For Judas was the type of his own weakness; since the flesh, not being wholly regenerate, was, in that unfulfilled degree, weak.

And the regeneration of his body not being complete before his crucifixion, his flesh-will still warred against his spirit-will, and he could still find room to say, "Not my will, but Thine be done."

The Martyrs who followed his teaching were braver in the face of death than Jesus, though their pains were, for the most part of them, far sharper.

Tender women, maidens, and youths went fearless

and smiling to the stake or the rack, without tear or sigh ; but Jesus shrank and wept piteously at the foot of his cross.

Yet a man may be victor in the spirit though his body remain unredeemed. For this redemption of the body—when fully accomplished—is transmutation, and its beginning is the At-one-ment of the will of the flesh with the will of the spirit].

But when Jesus completed his regeneration, then there were again twelve.

But until Jesus, no man ever attained these twelve degrees and the divine marriage from within. Hitherto the taking of the kingdom had been from without, by violence and labour, after the manner of the Patriarchs.

Now, these twelve degrees are fourfold for almost every part of man ; being four for the body, four for the astral, four for the soul, but one for the spirit.

And until Jesus there had been no regeneration of the twelve in this order,—from within. Buddha at his death had attained to the ten only.

For of some the regeneration is fourfold ; being one degree for each kingdom, and the last for the marriage of the spirit.

And with some it is sevenfold ; being two for each kingdom, and the seventh for the marriage. Such was the regeneration of the mother and father of Jesus.

But Jesus himself has more than the four, the seven, or the ten ; for he had the thirteen.

And first he had four of the soul. With these, two of the astral, and one of the body, he was born.

Afterwards, at the "ninth hour," when he had completed the fourth degree of the astral, he consummated the divine marriage.

Afterwards he achieved three degrees for his body, but the last only after his "ascension" to the mount of the Lord.

No man ever attained thus before. And since the glory is of the Spirit, or divine part, it is said[1] that Jesus by his marriage feast manifested forth his glory.

And the celebration of this marriage was in Jordan; but the manifestation was in Cana.

For Jesus had received the Double Portion; and hence his double glory.[2]

No. XXV.

CONCERNING THE CHRIST AND THE LOGOS.[3]

NOW, Christ Jesus—the perfected spiritual, not physical, man — is the culmination of the human stream which flows upwards into the bosom of God. Man, arising by evolution from the lowest, finds his highest development, as man, in the Christ. Having reached this point, he is the perfect Son of Man, in that he is produced in and of Humanity; and being such, and because he is such, he receives the

---

[1] *I.e.*, in the Mysteries, on which the Gospels are based.

[2] Concerning the Double Portion, see No. XXXVII.

[3] London, July 12, 1881. Received in Sleep.

baptism of the Logos. Now, the Logos is the Adonai,[1] a word which implies Duality. And the Adonai is the Son of God, the Only-Begotten, the Two-in-One, whose manifestation is possible only through the Christ. The Celestial Trinity is composed of Substance, Force, and Law. Force is Original Life, or God the Father. Substance is Original Being, or God the Mother. Indissolubly conjoined, together they are Living Substance, the En-Soph or Boundless One of the Kabala. In themselves incapable of manifestation, they become manifest in and through Law, their Expression, Word, Logos, or Son. But the Logos is celestial, and the human could not know him in his divine nature. That the human may touch and know the divine, it is necessary for the two natures to meet. This is accomplished in "Christ Jesus." Christ signifies the Anointed. He is human in pedigree; and his Christhood is attained only when he receives into his own spirit the Logos. Then is accomplished the union of the two natures, the divine and the human. The two streams meet and mingle, and thenceforth man knows and understands God—through the Christ. For the Christ, having received the Logos, is Son of God, as well as Son of Man; and the Son of God in him reveals to him the Father. Man as human only could not say, as the Christ says,—"I and the Father are One." It is the in-dwelling Word who enables him to say this,—"For He who dwelleth in the bosom of God (the Logos)

[1] The name invariably substituted by the Hebrews for Jehovah in speaking. See Part II., No. VIII., also Part III.

even He hath revealed God." Having received the
Law, or Word, the Christ receives also the Father and
the Wisdom of God through the Word or Son, because Adonai—being the Duality—manifests both of
these to and in the Christ. Hence Stephen, dying,
exclaimed,—"Behold, I see the Heavens open, and
the Son of Man standing on the right hand of God."
In this utterance he declares the union of the Human
and the Divine. He declares that in Christ, Adonai
is manifest; and that in consequence of this union,
humanity is exalted into Heaven. For humanity
can attain to the celestial only through "Christ."
When man penetrates into this sphere he is "in
Christ Jesus." And, as Paul says, "being in Christ
he is in God, and God in him; for Christ is God's."
God, so to speak, lays hold of man in Christ, and
draws him into Heaven. For at this moment both
rivers meet, and flow one into the other in indissoluble
union, the Logos in the Christ, the Divine in the
Human, the God in Man.

No. XXVI.

CONCERNING THE PERFECTIONMENT OF THE CHRIST.[1]

JUST after I had been speaking of the mistake
made by Christians in regarding Jesus as a
ready-made perfection, I received a momentary

[1] Paris, October 1, 1879.

vision confirming what I had been saying. For it represented to me the gradual perfectionment of the Christ through suffering, or experience; and a voice uttered aloud the words, " Ought not Christ to have suffered these things, and *so* to have entered into his glory ? " And other like passages also were suggested to my mind.[1]

Soon after this I found myself in my sleep sitting on a hill-side and carving a Cross out of wood. And a young man came to me and said, " I alone know how to make crosses, and I will show you if you will come with me." And I took him for Jesus,[2] and I followed him, and in our converse, which was long, but of which I remember but a small part, he spoke much of the difficulty that lies in the way of any one who wishes to attain a full revelation, owing to the deterioration of man's system through impure habits of life and especially in respect of food, through which the blood is tainted and the tissues rendered incapable of the sensitiveness necessary for perfect interior vision. Even with all his advantages of as pure a paternity and maternity as the earth afforded, he said, he himself had been unable to attain to perfect knowledge, and now, after nearly two thousand years of further degeneration, it is hopeless to attain all. That will come only when the world has for many generations lived purely, and the human system has recovered in a great degree the perfection which properly belongs

[1] Luke xxiv. 26 (Douay Version); Heb. v. 7, 8, 9; 1 Pet. iv. 1.

[2] But afterwards believed him to have been Hermes, assuming, as is his wont, a character in accordance with his message.

to it, and which it once had. It is to man frugivor-
ous, and to him alone, that the Intuition reveals herself, and of her comes all revelation. For between
him and his spirit there is no barrier of blood ; and
in him alone can the spirit and the man be at one.

No. XXVII.

CONCERNING CHRISTIAN PANTHEISM.[1]

THE crucifixion of Jesus was an actual fact, but it
had also a spiritual signification ; and it is to
this spiritual meaning, and not to the physical fact,
that the whole of the mystical writings of the
Christians refer.

The fundamental truth embodied in the crucifixion
is Pantheism. God is in all creatures ; and the stage
of purification by fire through which all being is now
passing, is the crucifixion of God. Jesus, as the most
perfect of initiates, is selected by the Christian
mystics as the representative of God. He is for
them, as Buddha for the Buddhist mystics, God
manifest in the flesh. In his crucifixion, therefore,
is the symbol and type of the continual crucifixion of
God in his suffering creatures, which crucifixion is
the means and cause of their purification, and thus
of their redemption. "These," says God, "are the
wounds wherewith I was wounded in the house of

---

[1] Received in sleep. Paris, June 22, 1879.

My friends."[1]　Which means, "I am wounded in the body or person of all creatures who are Mine—who are sealed unto Me."　For "the house of my friends" is nothing more than the mystical phrase for the temple of the body of others.　"Enter thou into my house, O Lord!" cries the holy soul who desires to be visited while in the body by the Divine Presence. And the Man-God, showing His five mystical wounds to the Angels, thus declares, "These are the wounds of My crucifixion wherewith I am wounded continually in the persons of those who are Mine.　For I and My brethren are one, as God is One in Me."

No. XXVIII.

CONCERNING THE "BLOOD OF CHRIST."[2]

BEING asleep I saw myself in a large room like a library, for it had in it a great many shelves filled with books; and there were several persons in it to whom I was speaking of the Christs, their origin and mission, and part in the history of mankind. And I spoke much of Jesus, representing that the doctrine of his immaculate conception was to be understood only in a mystic sense, and that all the story we have of his birth refers solely to his initia-

---

[1] Zech. xiii. 6.　Judged by the context, either the passage is corrupt or the citation is from some Scripture not now extant.

[2] Paris, October 17, 1879.

tion,[1] which is the true birth of the Son of God. And
I proved this by many texts and passages from the
gospels themselves and other writings. And I spoke
also of the origin of Jesus, and how he had been
made perfect through suffering. Of this suffering we
hear, I said, but little in the one life of his which is
recorded in the gospels. The suffering referred to is
a long course of trial and upward progress experienced in former incarnations. And I named some of
the more recent ones, but have not been enabled to
retain them.

Coming to his passion and death, I explained that
these were no atonement in the sense ordinarily
understood. For that God does not take the mere
shedding of innocent blood as any satisfaction for the
moral guilt of others. But that the mystical Blood
of Christ by which we are saved, is no other than the
secret of the Christs whereby they transmute themselves from the material to the spiritual plane, the
secret, namely, of inward purification. And I showed
that throughout all the sacred writings the word
blood is used as a synonym for life ; and that life in
its highest, perfectest, and intensest sense, is not the
mere physical life understood by materialists, but the
essence of that life, the inward God in the man.
And when it is written that those in the highest
courts of heaven are they who have made their robes
white in the blood of the Lamb, it is signified that

[1] Initiation does not necessarily involve the agency of any human
institution. The true initiator is in every case the divine spirit in the
aspirant himself.

H

they have attained redemption through their perfect
attainment of the secret of the Christs. And when
also it is said that the blood of Christ cleanseth from
all sin, it is signified that sin is impossible to him who
is perfectly spiritualised, and has been baptised with
the spiritual baptism. The blood of Christ, therefore,
is not the material blood of any man whatsoever.
It is the secret and process of spiritual perfectionment attained by the Christ, and that whereby all
who, following his method, know God and are initiated, become redeemed and attain the gift of eternal
life. And many other things I said, being, as it
seemed to me, taught of some spirit, and not knowing
beforehand what things I was to say.

Now I perceived behind me, a little to my right, a
beautiful marble image of Pallas Athena, which stood
in a small recess in the wall, and there fell upon it a
bright golden light like sunshine, which varied from
time to time to all the seven colours, but more frequently to the violet than to the others. And the
light was chiefly on the head and bosom of the figure,
which was clad as a warrior with helmet, shield, and
spear. And I could hardly determine as I looked at
it whether it were a living or a marble form, so life-
like was it.

A little while later all the people to whom I had
been speaking were gone away, and I was in the
room alone with my mother. She was in great
distress and agitation, regarding me as lost and as an
apostate from Christianity ; nor would she listen to
any explanation I could make on the matter. She

wept bitterly, declaring I had broken her heart, and
made her old age a sorrow and a burden to her by
my apostasy, and that I should be utterly cast away
unless I repented and returned to the orthodox belief;
and she besought me on her knees to recant what I
had said. No words can convey the intensity of my
pain, and the trouble of spirit caused me by this
conduct of hers. My mother seemed to swoon at my
feet with the excess of her emotion ; and I was on
the point of yielding to her entreaties when I saw the
door of the room open and a Spirit enter. He came
and stood beside me, and said these words,—" Whoso
putteth his hand to the plough and looketh back, is
not fit for the kingdom of God. And whoso loveth
father or mother more than Me, is not worthy of
Me."

Then the dream passed away and I remember no
more : but a deep feeling remained impressed on my
mind that the scene was but the rehearsal and fore-
shadowing of something that would actually occur in
my future life.

** It is a satisfaction, which the sympathetic reader will share,
to be able to state that, by taking the dream as a warning rather
than as a positive prediction, and observing caution accordingly,
opposition of the kind described was reduced to a minimum,
and no breach of affection or serious unhappiness ensued.

The image of Pallas illumined by the seven rays denotes the
Divine Wisdom in its plenitude, and manifesting all the "Seven
Spirits of God." As beheld on this occasion, it was an emphatic
intimation that the doctrine enunciated was uttered under the
inspiration of them all, and especially of those represented by
the two dominant rays, Love and Reverence.

No. XXIX.

CONCERNING VICARIOUS ATONEMENT.[1]

I STOOD in my sleep on the balcony of a house.
It was night, and so dense and dark and im-
penetrable that neither earth nor star, nor any object,
could be distinguished. Nevertheless, though not
knowing where I was, I was conscious of being in or
very near to a city.

And I beheld floating about in the darkness, small
tongues of flame exactly resembling in appearance
the flame of a candle. They moved of themselves as
if they were living creatures who directed their
motions with intelligence and will. They sank and
rose and passed through the air in all directions, and
nothing but them was visible, so intense was the
darkness.

And as I watched the flames, two of them came
floating towards me, and entering the house, glided
round the room, and then returned to me on the
balcony, and stopped and alighted, one on each of
my hands, and there remained awhile. And then
the whole scene passed away and the following
succeeded.

I saw a child, a boy at school, who thought himself
unjustly treated by the woman who kept the school,
and sorely oppressed and persecuted. And he went

[1] Paris, January 31, 1880.

into the room where she sat, and in a fury broke and
destroyed everything upon which he could lay his
hands. And the paroxysm of his anger made him
appear as one possessed. He dashed beautiful vases
to the floor, and trampled flowers under his feet,
and tore to pieces rich draperies, for the room was
furnished and decorated in a very costly and splendid
fashion. And then he suddenly turned on the woman,
and seizing her by the hair, beat her and tore her
garments, and scratched her hands and face. And
all the defence she made was a few words of remonstrance. And I was shocked and terrified, thinking
she was dead, and wondered what would become of
the child who had the fury of a wild beast and the
strength of a man.

Then, after an interval, I saw a young girl, the
daughter of the woman who had been thus assaulted.
She was kneeling before a furnace and watching
something in the flames. And she turned and looked
at me and said, " The punishment due to the child is
a terrible one, and cannot be escaped. He is condemned to be branded with a red-hot iron on the
palm of each hand, and then to be expelled from the
school. The brands are now heating in the furnace."

Saying this, she turned again to the furnace, and
then with a rod drew out the iron and branded
herself on each hand. And I saw the flesh shrivel
up with the heat. Then she held up her palms
towards me, and said, " See and read what is written
on them." And I read on each hand the word,
burnt into the flesh, " *Guilty*." " And now," she

added, " I am going to quit this house, my home, as
I am banished." "You !" I cried. "You are not the
guilty one ! What have you done to deserve this ?
I do not understand."

And she answered, "I told you the punishment
due to the child cannot be escaped. And I have
taken it upon myself of my own free will, although
I am innocent and the beloved daughter of her who
has been so grievously offended and injured. As he
would have been branded, I am branded. And as he
would have been expelled, I am expelled. Thus
have I redeemed him. I suffer for him. Justice is
satisfied, and he is pardoned. This is Vicarious
Atonement."

Then, as she spoke these words, a wind blew in my
face, and I breathed it in, and being inspired, spoke
thus, with a loud voice :—

" O fool, to imagine that justice can be satisfied by
the punishment of the innocent for the guilty !
Rather is it doubly outraged. How can your being
branded on the hands save the child ? Hath not the
Word of God declared, ' No man shall take the sin
of another, nor shall any make atonement for his
brother's trespass ; but every one shall bear his own
sin, and be purified by his own chastisement.' And
again, is it not written, ' Be ye perfect ' ? And as no
one can become perfect save through suffering, how
can any become perfect if another bear his suffering
for him ? To take away his suffering is to take away
his means of redemption, and rob him of his crown of
perfection. The child cannot be pardoned through

your assumption of his chastisement. Only if through suffering himself he repent, can he receive forgiveness. And so with the man who sins against the Creator by outraging his intuition and defiling the temple of God. The suffering of the Creator Himself for him, so far from redeeming him, would but rob him of his means of redemption. And if any declare that the Lord God hath thus ordained, the answer is, 'Justice first, and the Lord God afterwards!' But only through the perversion of ignorance can such doctrine be believed. The Mystery of Redemption has yet to be understood.

"This is that Mystery. There is no such thing as Vicarious Atonement; for none can redeem another by shedding innocent blood. The Crucifix is the emblem and symbol of the Son of God, not because Jesus shed his blood upon the cross for the sins of man, but because the Christ is crucified perpetually so long as sin remains. The saying, 'I am resolved to know nothing save this one mystery, Christ Jesus and Him crucified,' is the doctrine of Pantheism. For it means that God is in all creatures, and they are of God, and God as Adonai suffers in them.[1]

"Who, then, is Adonai? Adonai is the Dual Word, the manifestation of God in Substance, who manifests himself as incarnated Spirit, and so manifesting himself, by love redeems the world. He is the Lord who, crucified from the beginning, finds his full manifestation in the true Son of God. And therefore is it written that the Son of God, who is Christ, is

---

[1] See note on p. 108.

crucified.   Only where Love is perfect is Sympathy
perfect, and only where sympathy is perfect can one
die for another.   Wherefore the Son of God says,
'The wrongs of others wound me, and the stripes of
others fall on my flesh.   I am smitten with the pains
of all creatures, and my heart is pierced with their
hearts.   There is no offence done and I suffer not,
nor any wrong and I am not hurt thereby.   For my
heart is in the breast of every creature, and my blood
is in the veins of all flesh.   I am wounded in my
right hand for man, and in my left hand for woman ;
in my right and left feet for the beasts of the earth
and the creatures of the deep ; and in my heart for all.'

"The Crucifix, then, is the divinest of symbols
because it is the emblem of Christ and token of God
with man.   It is the allegory of the doctrine of Pantheism that man becomes perfect—the soul becomes
God—through suffering.   He who is wise, understands;
and he who understands is initiated ; and he who is
initiated loves ; and he who loves knows ; and he
who knows is purified.   And the pure behold God
and comprehend the Divine, with the mystery of pain
and of death.   And because the Son of God loves, he
is powerful, and the power of love redeems.   He
being lifted up, draws all men unto him.   This is
the mystery of the Seven Steps of the Throne of the
Lord.   And the Throne itself is of white, a glory
dazzling to look upon.   And in the midst of that
Light is one whose appearance is that of a lamb that
hath been slain.   And he is Christ our Lord, the
manifestation of Adonai, whose love hath thrust him

through and through.   And to him is given all power
to redeem in heaven and on earth.   For he opened
his heart to all creatures, and gave himself freely for
them.   And because he loved, he laboured and
grudged not, even to death.   And because he
laboured he was strong, for love laboured in him.
And being strong he conquered, and redeemed them
from death.   They were not forgiven because Christ
died ; they were changed because he loved.   For he
washeth their souls white with his doctrine, and
purifieth them with his deeds.   And these are his
heart's blood, even the word of God and the pure
life.   This is the atonement of Christ and perpetual
sacrifice of the son of God.   Believe and thou shalt
be saved : for he that believeth is changed from the
image of death to life.   And he that believeth sinneth
no more, and oppresseth no more.   For he loveth as
Christ hath loved, and is in God and God in him.
The blood of Christ cleanseth from all sin, not by
the purchase of pardon with another's gold, but
because the love of God hath changed the life of the
sinner.   The penitent saves himself by suffering,
sorrow, and amendment.   By these he rises and his
life is redeemed.   And it is the Christ that redeems
him by giving his heart's blood for him.   It is Christ
in him who takes his infirmities and bears his sorrows
in his own body on the tree.   And the same which
was true of old, is true to-day, and for ever.   Christ
Jesus is crucified continually in each one until the
kingdom of God come.   For wherever is sin, are
suffering, death, and oppression ; and where these are

the Christ shall be manifest, and by love shall labour, and die, and redeem."

Here the sound of my voice woke me, and the vision ended. But presently I slept again, and beheld an infinite expanse of sky, open and clear and blue and sunlit, all in the most intense degree. And across it and upwards flew an eagle like a flash of lightning before me, and I knew that it was intended to signify that with the reproach of innocent blood removed from God, and the Divine character vindicated, there is nought to check the soul's aspiration.

No. XXX.

CONCERNING PAUL AND THE DISCIPLES OF JESUS.[1]

IN a vision which was given to me last night, it was represented to me that the common view of Paul's character and position with regard to the primitive Church is a totally false one; and the persons who made the communication which I am about to relate, appeared to me to have been personally acquainted with Paul, and to be thoroughly familiar with the events occurring at the time of his apostleship. They told me, with evident indignation, that the Christian Church of to-day entirely misunderstands the relationship really existing between the apostles whom Christ had instructed and elected as

[1] Paris, July 17, 1877.

his missionaries, and the converted Hebrew sacerdotal-
ist. "It is amazing," they said, "that your Church
can read in the writings extant concerning our
relations with Paul the account of the mistrust,
suspicion, and disfavour with which we always
regarded him, and not see that he was never one
with us. The very leader and chief of our circle
withstood him to the face again and again, as though
he had been an enemy of the Church ; and on one
occasion he was forced to fly from the brethren by
night and by stratagem, so great and so bitter was
the indignation his view of the faith aroused among
us who had been the Lord's friends, and who knew
the truth as Paul never saw it. For he imported into
that pure and simple rule of life a mass of Levitical
and Rabbinical usages and beliefs which we had
shaken from us as the dust from our feet. He sunk
the realities of the Gospel of Jesus under an over-
whelming weight of hard sayings and sacerdotal
misrepresentations. He, who had never known the
Master as he was, took upon himself to distort his
image into that of a strange God whom we had not
known. Nor could we recognise in his garbled
version of the beautiful and willing martyrdom of the
man whom we had so dearly loved, a single trait of
his character, or the least resemblance to the doctrine
he had taught us. What we had seen and known as
the pure and perfect love of a ready death, bravely
borne for conscience' sake, Paul presented to us in a
new and unlovely guise as the sacrifice of a victim to
appease the anger of the God whom Jesus called his

Father and ours.   Out of that which had been for us
a simple rule of life, a simple purging of the old faith,
Paul erected the strange and elaborate system which
is called ' *the scheme of the Atonement.*'   For us and
our Master there had been no 'scheme ;' God was
reconciled to man by love, and not by sacrifice.   But
Paul would have a " new religion," and a creed hard to
understand ; and he left to the world a Christianity
of his own which we knew not, but which is yours to-
day.   And in this he did us greater evil and detriment
than if he had persecuted and slain us all physically.
For by his false conversion he deceived the world and
drowned the truth by a flood of strange doctrines.
For this we were all against him, and never acknow-
ledged his apostleship, being persuaded that he knew
not Christ nor the faith which Christ taught.   Had
he been content with the truth, we would never have
set our faces against him ; for he had many gifts,
among which his eloquence was not the least.   But
through his fatal perversion of the faith, and through
his fatal love of metaphysical doctrines and of Rabbinical subtleties, he falsified that which was the glory
of the Church, and brought into the world the monstrous doctrines of the 'Christianity' which is
preached in your churches to-day."

I was further told, that on the night before Paul's
escape in the basket let down from the wall of
Damascus, a violent altercation had taken place
between him and the brethren, in the course of
which Paul had maintained that the only chance for
the final triumph of the Gospel lay in its erection

into a system, and one that must of necessity be sacrificial. They then challenged him upon the point, but he insisted that he saw further into the matter than they did, and that his special mission lay in the elaboration of the plan he had conceived with regard to Christ's position as a mediator between God and man.

[The vision was entirely spontaneous and unexpected. I had not previously given any attention to the subject ; nor was I aware that a similar instruction had sometime previously been given to my colleague.

The personages I beheld in my vision bore no resemblance to any of the numerous representations of the apostles made by painters ; but I was far from being in a sufficiently lucid condition to obtain an impression of their appearance so vivid and distinct as to enable me, as usually is the case, to make a drawing of them. Neither have I been able, with anything like my accustomed accuracy, to reproduce their words. The tone and substance, however, are faithfully rendered. The tone throughout was that of strong indignation, mingled with regret, against Paul ; and of scorn at the folly of Christendom in accepting so gross and palpable a perversion of the teaching of Jesus and nature of God as that involved in the sacerdotal doctrine of vicarious atonement.] [1]

[1] 2 Peter iii. 15, 16 (an epistle of exceedingly doubtful authority), evidently represents a desire either to compose or to ignore this feud by treating the difference as more apparent than real.

No. XXXI.

CONCERNING THE MANICHÆANISM OF PAUL.[1]

A T this moment I hear a surge of waters. Out of the midst of them a voice seems to speak to me. This is what it says :—

"Many years before Paul wrote there arose a sect called the Manichæans. The founder of that sect, like the founder of the Epicureans, was inspired by US ; but they, like the Epicureans, understood not the nature of sin. The founder of the Manichæans, whom we call Felix, saw this, that evil is the result of creation; but his disciples understood that all matter is evil. In this alone they erred. And Paul, following his reason, but uninspired, perceived only the doctrine of the disciples. It is true, then, as the founder of the Manichæans saw, that evil is the result of creation, but not that matter is evil. He who among you possesses the most vivid imagination, can project upon the retina palpable rings of his thought. Thus it is with Deity. I have said already that matter is the intensification of Idea, and that evil is the result of materialisation.[2] You have asked me, Why, then, did God create ? I perceive that God created by force of will ; and that, willing, God imparted to every thought the power of will which, but for the limitation, could not have existed. God, therefore, is so much the richer by the will of the thought which He projects."

[1] Paris, July 24, 1877. Spoken in trance.
[2] Comp. No. XIX. Part 2.

No. XXXII.

CONCERNING THE GOSPELS ; THEIR ORIGIN AND COMPOSITION.[1]

I AM looking at the inside of the Serapeum at Alexandria. The temple is connected with a library which, as I see it, is still there, neither dispersed nor burnt, but filled with manuscripts,—mostly rolls upon sticks. I see a council of many men sitting at a table in the room of the library, and I see a number of names, as Cleopatra, Marcus Antonius, and others. This is called the *second* library of Alexandria, the former having been destroyed under Julius Cæsar. The nucleus of this one was the gift of Antony to Cleopatra, who added to it and improved it immensely, till it contained all the existing literature of the world ; and—why, they are deliberately concocting Christianity out of the books there! and, so far as I can see, the Gospels are little better than Ovid's Metamorphoses (historically, I mean),— so deliberately are they making up the new religion by replanting the old on the Jewish system.

Write down these names and the dates which are specially shown me. Theophilus, patriarch of Alex-

---

[1] London, November 6, 1881. Spoken in trance. It was wholly independent of any knowledge or prepossession of either of us,—the subject being quite new to us,—and proved on subsequent research, while going far beyond history, to be in full accordance with history so far as history goes, and also with the results of independent and candid criticism. By "history" is not meant ecclesiastical tradition or invention,

andria, and Ambrosius. A.D. 390, B.C. 286. This last
is the date at which the library was first of all got
together. A.D. 390 [1] is the date of the chief destruction
of the documents out of which the new religion was
made. If they could be recovered we should have
absolute proof of its concoction from Hindû, Persian,
and other originals ;—the interpolations, extracts, and
alterations proving this. They show, too, that the
name first adopted for the typical man was more like
Krishna, and that Jesus was a later choice, adopted
at Jewish suggestion, in order to suit a Jewish hero.
The system was long under formation, and it took all
that time to perfect.[2] Every detail of the Gospel
history is invented, the number of the apostles, and
all the rest. Nothing is historical in the sense
supposed.

I see the Serapeum destroyed ;—not only the library
but the temple, so fearful were they of leaving
any trace of the concoction. It was destroyed by
Christians at the instigation especially of Theodosius,
Ambrosius, and Theophilus.[3] Their motive was a
mixed one, each of the leaders having a different aim.
The object of the concoctors themselves was to
sustain and continue the ancient faith by transplant-
ing it to a new soil, and engrafting it on Judaism.

[1] The temple was destroyed A.D. 389. The library had never ceased
to exist, the Bruchium, at the time of its destruction, having overflowed
into the Serapeum. The remnant was far exceeded by Antony's
additions from Pergamos, which thus became the virtual nucleus.

[2] There is an ambiguity here, owing to the date of the completion of
the "concoction" not being specified.

[3] Theodosius was Emperor of the eastern division of the Roman
Empire. Ambrosius was Archbishop of Milan.

The object of Theophilus was to make the new religion the enemy and successor of the old, by making it appear to have an independent basis and origin. Ambrose destroyed the library in order to confute the Arians by leaving it to appear that Christianity had an origin altogether supernatural. The concoctors themselves did not intend it to be regarded as supernatural, but as representing the highest human. And they accordingly fixed and accumulated upon Jesus all that had been told of previous Christs,—Mithras, Osiris, Krishna, Buddha, and others,—the original draft containing the doctrine of the transmigration of souls most explicitly and distinctly.[1] The concoction was undertaken in order to save religion itself from extinction through the prevalence of materialism, — for the times corresponded in this respect exactly to the present. And the plan was to compose out of all the existing systems one new and complete, representing the highest possibilities and satisfying the highest aspirations of humanity.

The great loss, then, is not that of the first but that of the second library of Alexandria. The Serapeum was destroyed by Christians in order to prevent the human origin of their religion from being ascertained. The object was to have it believed that

[1] The reason for the exclusion is not far to seek. 'There is no more (birth nor) death for those who are in Christ.' Transmigration being the condition of man unregenerate only, the gospels—which have for their purpose the exhibition of Man Regenerate—had no call to refer to the previous stages of his evolution. It is implied in the account of his birth of a virgin, as see Nos. XXIII., XXIV.

I

it all centered in one particular actual person, and was not collected and compiled from a multiplicity of sources.

All the conversations in the Gospels were fabricated by the aid of various books in order to illustrate and enforce particular doctrines. I cannot recognise the language of many of the ancient manuscripts used. The Latin ones which I see are all in capitals, and without any division between the words, so that they look like one long word.

I am shown the actual scene of the destruction of the library and dispersion of the books. There is a dreadful tumult. The streets of Alexandria are filled with mobs of people shouting and hastening to the spot. They do not know the real object. They have been told that the library contains the devil's books, which, if allowed to remain, will be the means of destroying Christianity. The noise and tumult are dreadful. I cannot bear it; pray recall me, it hurts me so. It is extraordinary how exactly alike the two times are both politically and religiously. Everything established is breaking up in both; and that which comes out of each is the fuller revelation of the divine Idea of Humanity. All works for us and the new revelation. But the world suffers terribly in the birth. Afterwards things gradually become much better.

₊ In explanation of the method of this recovery it may be stated that, according to occult science, every event or circumstance which has taken place upon the planet, has an astral counterpart, or picture, in the magnetic light. So that there are

actually ghosts of events as well as of persons.   These magnetic
existences are the Shades or *Manes* of past times, circumstances,
acts, and thoughts, of which the planet has been the scene, and
they can be conjured and evoked.   The appearances left on such
occasions are but shadows left on the protoplasmic mirror.
" This magnetic atmosphere, or astral soul, is called the *Anima
Mundi*, and in it are stored up all the memories of the planet,
its past life, its history, its affections and recollections of physical
things.   The adept may interrogate this phantom-world, and it
shall speak for him.   It is the cast-off vestment of the planet ;
yet it is living and palpitating, for its very fabric is spun of
psychic substance, and its entire *parenchyma* is magnetic."—
See No. XLV. ; also " The Perfect Way," Lecture V. par 39
(R. and E. edition).   Concerning the recovery of the individual
memory, see No. XL

No. XXXIII.

CONCERNING THE ACTUAL JESUS.[1]

I AM shown the Descent from the Cross.   I see
Jesus carried by Joseph of Arimathea to his
house.   The house communicates with a sepulchre ;
and Jesus is carried to the house where they do something to revive him ; for he has swooned rather than
died.   The clothes are placed in the sepulchre, but
not Jesus.   I see a rupture of the pericardium, but
no fatal injury to the heart.   I see plainly that he is
not dead.   There is no organic lesion ; and the wound
heals like a simple wound, without suppuration, and

[1] London, March 22, 1881.   Spoken in trance.   See also No. XXIV.

by incessant bathing with water. What a lovely climate it is there! and how curious that there should have been a Joseph at both birth and crucifixion!

I am now shown the truth respecting the birth of Jesus. It was most certainly an ordinary birth. I see that quite distinctly. The names are all altered. The birth-name of Jesus is not Jesus, or anything like it. Nothing is real as I have thought it. Very little happens as related. The losing and finding in the temple, and the feeding of the five thousand are allegories of which the signification is spiritual. The miracles of the raising of the ruler's daughter and widow's son are real facts. Jesus saw clairvoyantly that the former was not dead, and that the body was uninjured by disease, so that the soul could return to it. For disease is gradual death, and when death occurs through it the soul is set free altogether. In violent or sudden death the soul is slow to get away, and the separation is a long process.

In his own case Jesus instructed his friends before-hand what to do. Joseph of Arimathea was a friend of Mary Magdalen; and she procured for him the requisite balms. I see her running with them through the sepulchre to the house. Jesus was not organically dead at all, for the heart never ceased to beat. He foreknew all the particulars of the event, and provided accordingly.

Nor is Jesus well again on the third day. He is at least ten days under treatment in Joseph's house. Three days is a mystical period, having no relation to actual time. All about him are women except one, the old man. Jesus' name begins with *M.* I do not see the rest of it.

The perfected adept is he who has attained in himself the Philosopher's Stone of a spirit absolutely quiescent, and is in union with the Divine Will. Being without ardour, sympathy and compassion are for him but other names for Justice; and, incapable of anger, his temperament is always cool and equable. I now see faults in Jesus which I did not see before. I mean Jesus as he actually was, and not as he is depicted in the Gospels. They are faults from the adept's point of view. I am shown a passion-flower as the emblem of his character. He sacrificed himself for others, but would have been able to do more had he been more careful,—especially in respect of his diet. His liability to give way continually to indignation or pity prevented him from getting higher. He allowed himself to be drawn too much out of himself to reach the highest possible.

I see him bidding his followers good-bye. It is on a hill which he ascends, and he disappears from their view, lost in cloud or mist. He now becomes a hermit. I see him in the wilderness alone; and there he attains the higher life which constituted his true ascension.

Jesus was able to influence persons at a distance by means of an emanation which he projected from himself; so that it was not necessary for him to be dead when supposed to be seen by Paul.

I now see some one with him on his mountain. It is John, writing down the Apocalypse at the dictation of Jesus. Jesus recollects all his past incarnations, and epitomises them in the Apocalypse, which is the history of his, and of every perfected soul. He is quite an old man at this time.

And now I see the panther's skin of Bacchos, and whence Jesus got the name which has been given him of "Rabbi Ben Panther," and why he was said to be the son of one Panther. It is a play on *Pan* and *theos*, and means *all the gods*. The panther's skin represented the raiment, or attributes, of all the gods, with which Jesus, as a "Son of God," was held to be endowed.

I am shown that there is but little of real value in the Scriptures. They are a mass of clay, comparatively modern, with here and there a bit of gold. The angel whom I saw before, and who told us to burn the Bible,[1] now puts it in the fire, and there comes out a few pages only of matter which is original and divine. All the rest is interpolation or alteration. This is the case with both Old Testament and New, Isaiah and the prophets. Isaiah is a great mixture. It is all fragments from various sources, just thrown together. The book of Genesis is one large parable ; and so are all the legends of the wanderings and wars of Israel. All is mixed up with fiction. Moses wrote none of it. And similarly with all the books of the Law and the prophets. All are made up in this manner. Here and there is an original piece of the ancient Revelation, but these are largely inter-spersed with additions and embellishments, commen-

[1] In a vision received sometime previously.

taries, and applications to the times by copyists and interpreters. And when the angel told us to put the Bible in the fire, he meant separate the gold from the dross and clay.

As for the gospels, they are almost entirely parabolical. Religion is not historical, and in no wise depends upon past events. For, faith and redemption do not depend upon what any man did, but on what God has revealed. Jesus was not the historical name of the initiate and adept whose story is related. It is the name given him in initiation.[1] His birth, the manner of it, his being lost and found by his parents in the temple, his lying three days in the tomb,—all are parabolic, as also is the story of the Ascension. The Scriptures are addressed to the soul, and make no appeal to the outer senses. The whole story of Jesus is a mass of parables, the things that occurred to him being used as symbols. Thus, the Crucifixion represents the soul's sufferings; the Resurrection its transmutation; and the life and Ascension are a prophecy of what is possible to man.

The real original gospel is that of John. The others came long afterwards, and all were written long after the time of Jesus. Jesus really wrote the Apocalypse by the hand of John, as he sat with him on the mountain. This was many years after the "Ascension," as his disappearance on the hill was termed. The Apocalypse was rather a recovery than an original composition of Jesus. The gospel life of

[1] See Part II., XI., Hymn to Phoibos, v. 9.

Jesus is made up of the lives of all the divine teachers before him, and represents the best the world had then, and the best it has in it to be. And it is therefore a prophecy. The recorded life of Jesus epitomised all the teachers before him, and the possibilities of mankind some day to be realised.

The "beautiful feet of the messengers on the mountains" are the first rays of the rising sun of the coming salvation, seen by the watchers from the spiritual heights,—the "shepherds who tend their flocks,"—even their own pure hearts and thoughts. They it is who see from the " hills " the coming God, the demonstration of the divinity that is in humanity, while the world below is wrapped in darkness.

No. XXXIV.

CONCERNING THE PREVIOUS LIVES OF JESUS.[1]

THIS morning between sleeping and waking I saw myself, together with many other persons, walking with Jesus in the fields round about Jerusalem, and while he was speaking to us, a man approached, who looked very earnestly upon him. And Jesus turned to us and said, "This man whom you see approaching is a seer. He can behold the past lives of a man by looking into his face." Then, the man being come up to us, Jesus took him by the

[1] Paris, February 7, 1880.

hand and said, "What readest thou?" And the man answered, "I see thy past, Lord Jesus, and the ways by which thou hast come." And Jesus said to him, "Say on." So the man told Jesus that he could see him in the past for many long ages back. But of all that he named, I remember but one incarnation, or, perhaps, one only struck me, and that was *Isaac.* And as the man went on speaking, and enumerating the incarnations he saw, Jesus waved his right hand twice or thrice before his eyes, and said, "It is enough," as though he wished him not to reveal further. Then I stepped forward from the rest and said, "Lord, if, as thou hast taught us, the woman is the highest form of humanity, and the last to be assumed, how comes it that thou, the Christ, art still in the lower form of man? Why comest thou not to lead the perfect life, and to save the world as woman? For surely, thou hast attained to womanhood." And Jesus answered, "I have attained to·womanhood, as thou sayest; and already have I taken the form of woman. But there are three conditions under which the soul returns to the man's form; and they are these:—

"1st. When the work which the Spirit proposes to accomplish is of a nature unsuitable to the female form.

"2nd. When the Spirit has failed to acquire, in the degree necessary to perfection, certain special attributes of the male character.

"3rd. When the Spirit has transgressed, and gone back in the path of perfection, by degrading the womanhood it had attained.

" In the first of these cases the return to the male form is outward and superficial only. This is my case. I am a woman in all save the body. But had my body been a woman's, I could not have led the life necessary to the work I have to perform. I could not have trod the rough ways of the earth, nor have gone about from city to city preaching, nor have fasted on the mountains, nor have fulfilled my mission of poverty and labour. Therefore am I—a woman —clothed in a man's body that I may be enabled to do the work set before me.

" The second case is that of a soul who, having been a woman perhaps many times, has acquired more aptly and readily the higher qualities of woman-hood than the lower qualities of manhood. Such a soul is lacking in energy, in resoluteness, in that par-ticular attribute of the Spirit which the prophet ascribes to the Lord, when he says, ' The Lord is a Man of war.' Therefore the soul is put back into a man's form to acquire the qualities yet lacking.

" The third case is that of the backslider, who, having nearly attained perfection,—perhaps even touched it,—degrades and soils his white robe, and is put back into the lower form again. These are the common cases ; for there are few women who are worthy to be women."

I was distinctly and positively assured that the incident thus shown me was one that actually oc-curred, and that I had borne part in it, though no record of it survives.

No. XXXV.

CONCERNING THE HOLY FAMILY.[1]

THERE were two subjects, on which I was desiring light, the explanation of which came to me in curious manner. They were (1) The real signification of the gospel account of the parentage and childhood of Jesus, which we have seen reason to regard as mystical and unliteral; and (2) The faculty of divination by means of the crystal or cup. I had just awoke, and was on the point of drinking my usual cup of coffee, when I was astonished by seeing in the liquid some words, while at the same instant there was flashed upon my mind a full view and explanation of the meaning of the Holy Family; and this is what I received.

"This is[2] the divining cup of Joseph, who represented the spiritual Egypt of Israel's infancy. Egypt was the spiritual father of Jesus, his spiritual mother, Mary, being Israel's pure intuition of God, and "virgin daughter of Sion."[3] Being of Jewish birth, Jesus went

---

[1] Paris, October 27, 1878.

[2] Meaning, of course, *answers to ;* the effect of a bright surface, as that of a crystal, disc, or fluid, being so to magnetise the sensitive as to render objective any images or ideas previously subjective whether in his own or in another's magnetic atmosphere, or in that of the planet, this last being the *anima mundi.* See note at end of No. XXXII.

[3] In this aspect Mary is the soul collective instead of individual only.

into Egypt to be initiated in the sacred mysteries of the country from which, through Moses, the Israelites originally obtained their religion.   Of that religion and those mysteries, Jesus, as a Christ, was the product.   For their object was the production of a man so perfected through the development of his mind and spirit, as to realise the divine idea of humanity.   As a full initiate and adept, a hierarch or "master" of the mysteries, Jesus returned to Judæa to fulfil his mission, receiving at the hands of John—a prophet of the Essenes, who were followers of the same mysteries —his baptism of the Spirit.

Joseph, therefore, represents Egypt,—not, however, as denoting the body,[1] but the mind,—and is an old man because Egypt was the senior of Israel, and also because, in the evolution of man, the mind precedes the soul in manifestation.   And in having him for his foster-father, Jesus is set forth as adopting the wisdom and elder religion of Egypt, to incorporate them with the Jewish.   Joseph, moreover, in being elderly and a widower,[2] represents Egypt in respect of its past youth and lost prime.   That he is not shown as the true spouse of Mary, or real father of her son, is because, though the mind may aid these by its knowledge and wisdom, the true spouse of the soul is the Divine Spirit, who is thus the true father of the man regenerate.

[1] See Part II., XIII., Hymn to the Planet-God (6).
[2] According to Christian tradition.

No. XXXVI.

CONCERNING THE METEMPSYCHOSIS OR AVATÂR.[1]

METEMPSYCHOSIS means, in its chief aspect, not transmigration which is of souls, but the vivification or illumination of a soul already incarnate by the spirit of a preceding "angel." Thus, the soul of Jesus was overshadowed by the angel of Moses.

The Word, Logos, or Adonai—for they are the same —speaks in the spirit of one or the other of the Gods of the Seven Spheres. He spoke through the Spirit, or God, of the Fourth Sphere—Dionysos or Iacchos— to Noah, Moses, and Jesus. Nevertheless Jesus was not an incarnation of either of these, and when he said, "Your father Abraham rejoiced to see my day," he spoke, in one sense,[2] of his own former birth as Isaac. For Jesus was a transmigration or re-incarnation of the soul of Isaac, and the two names are occultly related.

The metempsychosis constitutes a planetary Avatâr. The number of these is variously stated to be ten and twelve. Both are, in a sense, right. There are ten such Avatârs and twelve angels, or messengers, for the

---

[1] London, March 1881. Spoken in trance.

[2] Another sense was Abraham's recognition of the doctrine implied by the term "Christ." In their profoundest and most interior meaning the Patriarchs represent the component elements of the planetary divinity.

first and last are dual or "twins." The pair at the
first Avatâr were " Eve " and " Adam,"—for this also
is one sense of the allegory. The Avatârs and their
angels have their corresponding signs in the Zodiac,
the double ones being represented by the double signs
Gemini and Pisces. The latter Avatâr, now at hand,
will introduce Aquarius, "the sign of the Son of Man
in Heaven." Heracles is an epitome of the " twelve
Avatârs of the Lord." Each of his labours—the
labours, that is, of the soul—represents a divine
operation, and constitutes an Avatâr, while its sign
in the Zodiac corresponds to the nature of the
Labour. These signs represent the twelve gates of
the Holy City, or perfected kosmos, and the
twelve mysteries of the greater initiation ; and the
gates are spoken of as pearls, because pearls are
found at the sea-bottom, and in oysters, which are
difficult to get and hard to open ; and the sea
represents the Holy Spirit and the soul. In order
to obtain these twelve mysteries, one must be at
great labour and trouble, risking one's life in diving
for them, going down into the sea naked and
stripped of all things, finding them in obscurity and
darkness, and when they are brought up, requiring a
keen blade to open them.

The " twelve apostles " are types of these angels
and mysteries. John represents the dual messenger to
come. And by a metempsychosis corresponding to
that by which the spirit of Moses instructed Jesus,
the spirit of John will instruct the angel of the new
Avatâr. This spirit is dual. For John represents

both the Virgin and himself. This is the "mother" referred to by Jesus at his crucifixion. John comprises the feminine as well as the masculine element. His inspiring spirit is the same as that of Daniel. The spirit that informed Noah, Moses, and Jesus is Dionysos (Jehovah Nissi), the God of the planet. And the spirit which informed Daniel and John, and will inform the angel of this century, is Michael, who represents Zeus and Hera, or the planet Jupiter.[1]

That which comes back as a messenger or angel, is not the personal soul of the individual man employed ; for that has become transmuted into spirit. Nor does the spirit itself which was in that soul become re-incarnate. That which comes is the overshadowing, informing spirit who influenced and spoke through the man in his lifetime, and the man himself also, who has become an angel, or pure spirit, and who no longer needs the body. So that his return is voluntary, and his coming an Avatâr. The new Avatâr will be of the double or over-shadowing spirit of Daniel and John, as well as the spirit which was in those men. For, owing to the union between them, the two—the man's spirit and the divine spirit—are so much one as to be scarcely distinguishable ; and the God speaks through the

[1] See Daniel x. 21 and xii. 1, and Apoc. xii. 7. That Michael is by many regarded as the angel of the sun, is probably from their taking him to be the "angel standing in the sun" of Apoc. xix. 17. But even so, the position would not imply more than a temporary presidency.

man's spirit. It is as a tube within a tube. God speaks through the Logos, the Logos through an Elohe, and the Elohe through the perfected spirit of a former prophet. But of this last it is a metempsychosis, not a transmigration or re-incarnation. That is, the spirit returning informs the spirit of one already incarnate, and who, like John the Baptist, may be thus used without being himself regenerate and " in the kingdom of God."

No. XXXVII.

CONCERNING THE ÆON OF THE CHRIST.[1]

THE Christs are above all things *media*, and the various descriptions they gave of their office—such as "I am the way, the truth, and the life," "I am the door," and the like—referred not to themselves at all, but to the Spirit who spoke through them. Jesus, when questioned on this very subject, said plainly, "The words which I speak unto you I speak not of myself; but the Father which dwelleth in me, he doeth the works." Jesus, then, spoke as he was moved by the Holy Ghost, and was no other than a clear glass through which the divine glory shone. [As it is written, "And we beheld his glory, the glory *as of* the Only Begotten of the Father, full of grace and truth." Now, the Only Begotten is not mortal man,

---

[1] London, 1881. Received in sleep.

but he who has been in the bosom of the Father from all eternity, even the Word, the Maker, the Speaker, the Manifestor.] It was this Holy Spirit which descended upon Jesus at his baptism, and dwelt in him for the time of his sojourn upon earth, speaking through him and controlling him; while he, on his part, so lived as to bring all his personal will into oneness with that Spirit.

The Spirit answers to the Essence, the Father, and the Word. Of these, the first is one of the seven spirits, or divine flames, of universal Divinity. The second is the angel, or God, of the planet, and is the Æon of the Christ. The third is the Christ. They are respectively "the spirit, the water,[1] and the blood." The Father and the Word may therefore be said to be one; for by the Word the Father is manifest, and—in the microcosm—the Word *is* the Father manifested.

The greatest hierarch—he, that is, who has the most perfect control over Nature—is not only a man of many incarnations, but has obtained from God the greatest and rarest of gifts,—that of being a medium for the Highest. Such a one is the Æon,[2] and has what is called the "double portion." Elisha craved and received this grace. "Where now is the God of Elijah?" he cried, when endeavouring to work his

---

[1] A term which, as here used, implies also the "mother," "water" denoting especially the substance or feminine principle, as distinguished from the energy or masculine principle.

[2] The person who receives the Æon being called an Æon, as the person who manifests the Christ is called a Christ.

first miracle; and he besought Elijah that a portion of his double[1] might rest upon him. For Elijah had so transmuted his soul into spirit that it was doubled, and a portion of this he bestowed on Elisha. Such an Æon it was that descended upon Jesus, to quit him at the final moment. Hence the exclamation, "My God, my God, why hast thou forsaken me?"

No. XXXVIII.

CONCERNING THE DOCTRINE OF GRACE.[2]

ONE of the most dangerous mysteries to place in the hands of the vulgar is that of the doctrine of grace. When once union has been accomplished between the human and the divine wills, there is grace. And the man under grace cannot sin mortally. Conformity between the human and the divine wills is the condition of salvation, and salvation is not forfeited through any specific act, unless such act be wilful and indicate a condition of rebellion.

Of a man under grace, David is a type. His heart was right with God; his intuition was unfallen. So that even his many and grievous sins did not, and could not, alienate him from God. The man who is deliberately in opposition to the divine will is in far greater danger than the man who, having a true intuition, sins more flagrantly. It is not by a specific

---

[1] This is not the magnetic phantom ordinarily so-called.
[2] London, December 1880. Spoken in trance.

act, or many specific acts, that the soul is destroyed ; but by a state of heart in constant opposition to the divine will. Hence the axiom of the Calvinist, "If you are under grace you cannot sin,"—that is, mortally.

₊ Whence one reason for the appellation "Son of David" applied to the Christ. The man must first be "under grace" before he can become regenerate. It is an indispensable step in his soul's progress. Wherefore the latter is said to be the son of the former.

No. XXXIX.

CONCERNING THE "FOUR ATMOSPHERES." [1]

THE earthly mind (*anima bruta*) is that part of man which contains his material memory, abilities, affections, cares, acquirements, and the images bred of his associations in each particular incarnation. This mind is shed with the body and shade, and is—as it were—an individual in itself. It inhabits the astral sphere and cannot get beyond it ; nor does it ever return to earth (embodied), but dwells perhaps for many centuries, in the magnetic light, which it takes for heaven, seeking its own affinities and frequenting the places and persons familiar to it. But the soul—or *anima divina*, which is the true man— has another destiny than this. It leaves its body on

[1] London, August 1881. Received in sleep.

earth, its shade and its earthly mind in the astral
sphere, and mounts to its own proper higher region,
until the time comes for it either to pass into Nirvâna,
or to become again incarnate. The soul retains the
celestial memory ;—that memory only in which lives
such of its past as is worthy to live, and is not of an
ephemeral nature,—its knowledges, virtues, and true
loves. The only affections, therefore, which live
eternally are those of the soul,—those which have
struck deep into the man and made part of his inmost being. The loves of the mere body or earthly
mind die with these, and form no part of the permanent man. True it is that some souls are retained
in their phantoms for a time more or less long, not
being pure—or, rather, not strong—enough to mount
higher. But being in the astral sphere they cannot
see beyond it, and—like the astral phantom—believe
they are at their journey's end. The larva, or shade,
is not the same as the phantom seen by the ordinary
lucid. For the two are separable, and the shade
occupies a yet lower atmosphere. After a little while,
moreover, the shade consumes away and disappears ;
but the phantom with which the lucid converses, remains as strong and individual as ever, it may be for
centuries. For not only the recently dead, but some
who lived and died before the Christian era, have
been evoked and conversed with, and these are
not mere reflects (like the purely astral entities which
are emanations from the living), since they reason and
remember, and give proofs of their identity. The
ordinary lucid obtains access to them only because he

is himself in the astral when in the lucid condition, and sees, therefore, only what is there. To enter the heavenly sphere, and to come into communion with souls, a regenerated state is necessary. Now, the sphere entered depends, not alone on the lucid, but also on the magnetiser[1] and the circle present at the experience. There are four atmospheres surrounding us, and only in the highest of these do we find the freed soul. Each sphere is the counterpart of each portion of man, and each has its system and its sun. Interior knowledge, earnest aspiration, and purity of thought and life, are the keys by which alone can be opened the gates of the inmost and highest sphere. The lowest is enlightened by the material sun. It is that of the present life of the body. The next is enlightened by the astral or magnetic light; and it is that of the sideral body or perisoul. The next is that of the soul, and it is enlightened by the spiritual sun. And the highest is the immediate presence of the Lord God, where is the " great white throne " and the company of the "virgins." Now, the " virgins " are souls which, being perfectly spiritualised, retain no taint of materiality.[2]

[1] This is not necessarily a corporeal, or even an extraneous, being, but may be the spirit of the lucid himself.

[2] See Apoc. xiv. 4, where they are called virgins in virtue of their having overcome the need of sexual relations prior to their final incarnations, as in No. XXIV., par. 4. The term "women" was sometimes used as a general term for things material. See also " Dreams and Dream-Stories," No. IX.

No. XL.

CONCERNING THE HEREAFTER.[1]

WHEN a man parts at death with his material body, that of him which survives is divisible into three parts, the *anima divina*, or, as in the Hebrew, Neshamah; the *anima bruta*, or Ruach, which is the *persona* of the man; and the shade, or Nephesh, which is the lowest mode of soul substance. In the great majority of persons the consciousness is gathered up and centered in the *anima bruta*, or Ruach; in the few wise it is polarised in the *anima divina*. Now, that part of man which passes through, or transmigrates,—the process whereof is called by the Hebrews Gilgal Neshamoth,—is the *anima divina*, which is the immediate receptacle of the deific Spirit. And whereas there is in the world nothing save the human, actual or potential, the Neshamah subsists also in animals, though only as a mere spark, their consciousness being therefore rudimentary and diffuse. It is the Neshamah which finally escapes from the world and is redeemed into eternal life. The *anima bruta*, or earthly mind, is that part of man which retains all earthly and local memories, reminiscent affections, cares and personali-

---

[1] London, July 1881. Received in sleep, in timely and satisfactory solution of sundry perplexing experiences; and subsequently found to be a concise statement of the doctrine of the Kabala.

ties of the world or planetary sphere, and bears his family or earth-name. After death this *anima bruta*, or Ruach, remains in the "lower Eden," within sight and call of the magnetic earth-sphere. But the *anima divina*, or Neshamah,—the name of which is known only to God,—passes upwards and continues its evolutions, bearing with it only a small portion, and that the purest, of the outer soul, or mind. This *anima divina* is the true man. It is not within hail of the magnetic atmosphere; and only on the rarest and most solemn occasions does it return to the planet unclothed. The astral shade, the Nephesh, is dumb; the earthly soul, the *anima bruta*, or Ruach, speaks and remembers; the divine soul, the Neshamah, which contains the divine light, neither returns nor communicates, that is, in the ordinary way. That which the *anima bruta* remembers, is the history of one incarnation only, because it is part of the astral man, and the astral man is renewed at every incarnation of the Neshamah. But very advanced men become re-incarnate, not on this planet, but on some other nearer the sun. The *anima bruta* has lived but once, and will never be re-incarnate. It continues in the "lower Eden," a personality in relation to the earth, and retaining the memories, both good and bad, of its one past life. If it have done evil, it suffers indeed, but is not condemned; if it have done well, it is happy, but not beatified. It continues in thought its favourite pursuits of earth, and creates for itself houses, gardens, flowers, books, and so forth, out of the astral light. It remains in this condition

more or less strongly defined, according to the personality it had acquired, until the *anima divina*, one
of whose temples it was, has accomplished all its
avatârs.   Then, with all the other earthly souls belonging to that divine soul, it is drawn up into the
celestial Eden, or upper heaven, and returns into the
essence of the Neshamah.   But all of it does not
return ; only the good memories ; the bad sink
to the lowest stratum of the astral light, where
they disintegrate.   For, if the divine soul were
permanently, in its perfected state, to retain the
memories of all its evil doings, its misfortunes,
its earthly griefs, its earthly loves, it would not
be perfectly happy.   Therefore, only those loves and
memories return to the Neshamah, which have penetrated the earthly soul sufficiently to reach the divine
soul, and to make part of the man.   It is said that
all marriages are made in Heaven.   This means that
all true love unions are made in the celestial within
the man.   The mere affections of the *anima bruta* are
evanescent, and belong only to it.   When this, the
Ruach, is interrogated, it can speak only of one life,
for it has lived but one.   Of that one it retains all the
memories and all the affections.   If these have been
strong, it remains near those persons whom especially
it loved, and overshadows them.   A single Neshamah
may have as many of these former selves in the
astral light, as a man may have changes of raiment.
But when the *divine soul* is perfected, and about to
be received into "the Sun," or Nirvâna, she indraws
all these past selves, and possesses herself of their

memories; but only of the worthy parts of these, and such as will not deprive her of eternal calm. In "the planets," the soul forgets; in "the suns," she remembers. For, *in memoriâ æternâ erit Justus.*[1] Not until a man has accomplished his regeneration, and become a son of God, a Christ, can he have these memories of his past lives. Such memories as a man, on the upward path, can have of his past incarnations, are by reflection only; and the memories are not of events usually, but of principles and truths, and habits formerly acquired. If these memories relate to events, they are vague and fitful, because they are reflections from the overshadowing of his former selves in the astral light. For the former selves—the deserted temples of the *anima divina*—frequent her sphere and are attracted towards her, especially under certain conditions. From them she learns through the intermediary of the genius, or "moon," who lights up the *camera obscura* of the mind, and reflects on its tablet the memories cast by the overshadowing past. The *anima bruta*, or Ruach, seems to itself to progress, because it has a vague sense that sooner or later it will be lifted to higher spheres. But of the method of this it is ignorant, because it can only know the celestial by union with it. The learning which makes it seem to itself to progress is acquired by reflected soul-rays coming from the terrestrial. Advanced men on the earth assist and teach the astral soul, and hence its fondness for their spheres. It learns by reflected intellectual images, or thoughts. The

[1] Ps. cxii. 6.

Ruach is right when it says it is immortal. For the better part of it will in the end be absorbed into the Neshamah. But if one interrogate a Ruach of even two or three centuries old, it seldom knows more than it knew in its earth-life, unless, indeed, it gain fresh knowledge from its interrogator. The reason why some communications are astral, and others celestial, is simply that some persons—the greater number—communicate by means of the *anima bruta* in themselves; and others—the few purified—by means of their *anima divina.* For, like attracts like. The earthly souls of animals are rarely met with; they come into communion with animals rather than with man, unless an affection between a man and an animal have been very strong. If a man would meet and recognise his beloved in Nirvâna, he must make his affection one of the Neshamah, not of the Ruach. There are many degrees of love. True love is stronger than a thousand deaths; for, though one die a thousand times, a single love may yet perpetuate itself past every death from birth to birth, growing and culminating in intensity and might.

Now, all these three, Nephesh, Ruach, and Neshamah, are discrete modes of one and the same universal being, which is at once life and substance, and is instinct with consciousness, inasmuch as it is, under whatever mode, Holy Spirit. Wherefore, there inheres in them all a divine potency. Evolution, which is the manifestation of that which is inherent, is the manifestation of this potency. The first formu-

lation of this inherency, above the plane of the
material, is the Nephesh, this being the soul by which
are impelled the lower and earlier forms of life.
It is the "moving" soul that breathes and kindles.
The next—the Ruach—is the "wind" that rushes
forth to vivify the mind. Higher, because more
inward and central, is the Neshamah, which, borne on
the bosom of the Ruach, is the immediate receptacle
of the Divine particle, and without which this cannot
be individualised and become an indiffusible personality. Both the "wind" and the "flame" are
spirit ; but the wind is general, the flame particular.
The wind fills the house ; the flame designates the
person. The wind is the Divine Voice resounding in
the ear of the Apostle and passing away where it
listeth ; the flame is the Divine Tongue uttering
itself in the word of the Apostle. Thus, then, in the
soul impersonal are perceived the breath and afflatus
of God ; but in the soul personal is the formulate and
express utterance of God. Now, both of Nephesh
and Ruach, that which is gathered up and endures is
Neshamah.

No. XLI.

CONCERNING THE TRUE EGO.[1]

[This Illumination followed upon a meditation on the following passage from G. H. Lewes : " The evolution of organisms, like the evolution of crystals, or of islands and continents, is determined, first, by laws inherent in the substance evolved ; secondly, by relations to the medium in which the evolution takes place."] '

THERE is a law inherent in the primordial substance of all matter which obliges all things to evolve after the same mode and manner. The worlds in the infinite abyss of heaven are in all respects similar to the cells in vegetable or animal tissue. Their evolution is similar, their distribution similar, and their mutual relations are similar. Wherefore, by the study of the natural sciences, the truth may be learnt, not only in regard to these, but in regard also to the occult sciences ; for the facts of the first are as a mirror to the facts of the last. And just what the spiritual Ego is to the physical man, is God to the manifest universe,—its spirit, dwelling in and pervading it; no more, no less.

[1] Paris, December 6, 1882. Having previously studied materialistic science in Paris, Mrs Kingsford returned thither to study materialistic philosophy, when this and the following Illuminations, to No. XLVII. inclusive, were received by her in elucidation of the subjects studied, and in correction of the doctrine enunciated by her professor. The Illuminations were received chiefly in sleep.

And as for the souls of the planets, let us enquire awhile what, as an individual, thou art. Thy soul is constituted of the agglomerate essences of all the individual consciousnesses composing thy system. It has, then, *grown*,—evolving gradually from rudimentary entities, themselves evolved by polarisation from mineral and gaseous matter. And these entities combine and coalesce to form higher entities, the combined forces of their manifold consciousnesses polarising and centralising so as to form the human soul. In the same way, the souls of the planets are formed by the agglomeration and combination of the myriad souls composing them, these souls ranging from the mineral to the human group, and thus composing the four principles of each planet's kingdom. Each planetary God is, therefore, not a supernatural, extraneous personage, but is the sum total of the souls composing the planet. His physical body is the visible planet and its phenomena. His astral body and mind are the plant and animal intelligences. His soul is man's superior reason ; and his spirit is divine, being the *Nous* of the man. And as when we speak of the planet-god, we specially mean that *Nous*, it is said with truth that our divine part is no other than the planet-god,—in our case Dio-Nysos, the god of the emerald.

And again, such as are all creatures composing the planet to the planet, such also are the planets to the universe, and, in consequence, such are the Gods to God.

The primordial God is the sum total of all the

Gods. The Spirit of God is the agglomerate essences of all the deities. To pray to God is to address all the Celestial Host, and, by inclusion, all the spirits of just men.

But the Gods are not limited in number. For human convenience they are called seven, or twelve, or twenty-four, or seventy; but these are names of orders only. Beyond number are the orbs in infinite space, and each of these is a God. Phoibos is legion, so also is Hermes, so also Aphrodite, so also Dionysos, so also Ares, Zeus, Hera, Kronos, and the rest.* Phoibos is the spirit of all the suns; Poseidon, of all the seas; and each divinity has his *quality*, corresponding to the conditions of the elements which compose his kingdom.

To every planet belongs a different spectrum, and the physical is the measure of the spiritual. And every physical world of causes has its spiritual world of effects.

Now, the world of causes is the material and the astral, and the world of effects is the psychic. Therefore it may be said that the soul is the *effect* of the body, for organism is before function, and the mineral before man. And yet it is true that organism is the effect of idea, and that mind is the cause of evolution. So that spirit is before matter in its abstract, but not in its concrete conception. All things are begotten by fission or section in a universal blastoderm or protoplast, and the power which causes this generation is centrifugal.

No. XLII.

CONCERNING GOD.[1]

BUT why should we be at the pains to seek further than the phenomenal? Why this incessant craving to prove ourselves immortal, and to argue a God into the universe?

The answer is manifold, because the appeal is to nature, to reason, and to principle. First, evolution, as revealed by the facts of physical science, is inexplicable on the material hypothesis; as equally also are the facts of occult science and experience. Secondly, it has been proved that mind in man anticipates the demonstration of natural laws, and argues by mathematical and logical induction that what *is* ought to be, while yet the actual fact is undiscovered. It is thus evident that mind, greater than and yet identical with man's intelligence, has preceded phenomenon. Thirdly, the primary principle in the sane mind, justice, demands satisfaction, and insists that rectitude of intelligence infers also rectitude of spirit. And if this be conceded, all the rest follows. What, then, must we conceive—positing this indefeasible principle of justice as the central sun of our philosophical system? Equity on all planes, and a perfect correspondence and balance between physical and spiritual; between the world of causes and the world

---

[1] Paris, December 8, 9, 1882.

of effects. Justice is represented by the dual balance,
of which one scale is spirit and the other matter ; one
male and the other female ; without which dual principle the system of the balance itself would be impossible. The balance is unity ; the scales are the duad.

What, then, is God ? Spirit ; essential substance.
Is God, then, impersonal ? Impersonal if the word
persona be taken in its radical meaning, but personal
in the highest and truest sense of that word if the
conception be of essential consciousness. For God
has no limitations. God is a pure and naked fire burning in infinity, whereof a flame subsists in all creatures.
The Kosmos is a tree having innumerable branches,
each connected with and springing out of various
boughs, and these again originating in one stem, and
nourished by one root. And God is as a fire burning
in this tree, and yet consuming it not. God is
" I AM." Such is the nature of infinite and essential
being. And such is God in the beginning before the
worlds.

What, then, is the purpose of evolution and separation into many forms ? *Life is the elaboration of soul
through the varied transformations of matter.*

Spirit is essential and perfect in itself, having
neither end nor beginning. Spirit is abstract. Soul
is secondary and perfected, being begotten of spirit.
Soul is concrete. And the whole object of creation
or manifestation is the evolution of souls. Spirit is
the primary Adam ; soul is Eve, the woman, taken
out of the side of the man. Spirit is the first principle ; soul is the derivative.

Now, the essential principle of personality or consciousness—the higher personality—is spirit. And this personality is God. Wherefore the higher and interior personality of every monad is God. But this primary principle, being naked essence, could not be separated off into individuals unless contained and limited by a secondary principle. This principle, being derived and not essential, must be evolved. *Spirit, therefore, is projected into matter in order that soul may be begotten thereby.*

Soul is begotten in matter by means of polarisation. And spirit, of which all matter consists, returns to its essential nature in soul. Soul is the medium by which spirit is individuated, and in which it becomes concrete. So that by means of creation, God the One becomes God the Many. And the object set before the saint is so to live as to render the soul luminous and consolidate with the spirit, that thereby the spirit may be perpetually one with the soul, and thus eternise its individuality.

For personality is of and in the spirit; but individuality appertains to the soul. But for creation there would be one vast diffused and unindividuated consciousness, contained in one vast diffused substance. Of this substance all things consist by means of this force or spirit; and the soul grows up out of matter by means of evolution;—that is, by the inherent force acting on the manifest substance. And thus the soul is born in the womb of matter, and within her is conceived the personal element which, divided from God, is yet God and man. For God is not multiplied

L

neither diminished ; but God is separated into many.
The matter is the wax, the soul is the wick, and God
is the flame which illumines. If they ask thee the
reason of creation, thou shalt answer,—The evolution
and elaboration of the soul.

Anna is the rolling year, the Time, of which is born
Maria the soul, the mother of God. God is the first
of the ten categories of Aristotle,[1] as the number
one is the root of all numbers. Thou canst not begin
the tables with the duad, because the unity is the
primal idea. Therefore this unity is positive and
essential in necessity.

To God everything is good ; it is only to men that
evil appears positive. As it is written, " I am the
Lord, and there is none else ; I form the light and
create darkness ; I make peace and create evil ; I the
Lord do all these things." For that which differentiates evil from good is the plane of the action, and the
medium in which the thought is conceived. If thou
love from the plane of the spirit through the medium
of the soul, thou lovest as Christ loveth. But if thou
love from the plane of the astral man, through the
medium of the body, thou hast lust. And, again, if
spirit desire aught, it desires that which is like itself,
spiritual, and its treasure is in heaven : this is
aspiration. But if the plane of desire be the astral,
the medium of desire is material, and the material
desireth matter, that is, riches upon earth. This is
avarice. And again, the passion of the spirit is a
fierce upward burning towards spirit ; a force bursting

[1] Οὐσία, original substance or simple being ; the Ensoph of the Kabala.

forth and leaping into life; a vehement taking of heaven by heavenly violence. This is zeal. But the passion of the astral is a fierce burning downward through the body; a force translating itself in material action; a furious and blind collision of matter with matter. This eventuates in murder. See, then, that according to the plane and the medium, so is an act good or evil. There is nothing truly evil in its essential idea; for, primarily, all is good, because the primary is spirit.

(In answer to questions.) Any desire or act of the body that does not profit the mind, that is sensuality.

It is necessary that certain interior mysteries belonging to the Celestial be kept secret, because if they should be given to the people the mysteries would all speedily become materialised, and so lost. But if they be confided to a few Wise, and transmitted only to the Initiate, they will be preserved in their true meaning. And again, if these wise men betray their secret, the uninitiated would lay violent hands on them, and so they and the secret would perish together. But when the majority are wise, then may the mysteries be told openly.[1]

[1] The fact that the mysteries have been disclosed anew expressly in order that they may be made generally known, is by no means to be interpreted as an indication that in the view of their guardians the time has come when the " majority are wise." But this only :—(1) That the concealment of the mysteries has already led to their materialisation and loss at the hands of the priesthoods, and only by their publication can they be restored ; and (2) that the majority are sufficiently wise, at least in the land of the present promulgation, to refrain from murderous persecution either for the sake of opinion or in the interests of an Order.

No. XLIII.

CONCERNING PSYCHE, OR THE SUPERIOR HUMAN SOUL.[1]

IT is truly said that God is the primordial mind, and that the kosmic universe and its manifestations are the ideas of that mind. Mind in itself is passive; it is organ, not function. Idea is active; it is function. As soon, therefore, as mind begins to act, it brings forth ideas, and these constitute existence. Mind is abstract; ideas are concrete. When thou thinkest, thou createst. Every thought is a substantial action.

Thoth,[2] therefore, is the creator of the Kosmos. The science of the mysteries can be understood only by one who has studied the physical sciences; because it is the climax and crown of all these, and must be learned last, and not first. Unless thou understand the physical sciences, thou canst not comprehend the doctrine of *Vehicles*, which is the basic doctrine of occult science. "If thou understand not earthly things, how shall I make thee understand heavenly things?" Wherefore, get knowledge, get knowledge, and be greedy of knowledge, ever more and more. It is idle for thee to seek the inner chamber until thou hast passed through the outer. This, also, is another reason why occult

[1] Paris, December 13, 1882.
[2] Also spelt *Thaut*, in which form it is identical in both sound and meaning with our word *Thought*. Thoth or Thaut was the Egyptian equivalent for both Hermes and the Logos.

science cannot be unveiled to the horde. To the un-learned, no truth can be demonstrated. Theosophy [1] is the royal science. If thou wouldst reach the king's presence chamber, there is no way save through the outer rooms and galleries of the palace.

In every living globule there are four inherent powers. I speak not now of the component parts of a cell, but of forces. The first and lowest mode of power is mechanical; the second is chemical; the third is electric, and the fourth is psychic. The first three belong to the domain of physiological science; the last to that of occult science. It is this last mode of power which belongs to the immaculate and essential. It is inherent in the substantial, and is therefore permanent as an indefeasible quantity. It is in the Arche,[2] and it is wherever there is organic life. Now the Psyche is from the beginning latent and diffused in all matter; and forasmuch as Psyche also is not of herself, but of spirit, therefore is spirit also the basic quality of all things;—the motionless by motion converted into the solid;—the invisible by energy made visible. So that herein are two:—that which is made visible, and that which makes visible; and of these again is a third, that which is visible.

And of this energy, or primordial force, there are two modes (because everything is dual), the centri-fugal or accelerating force; and the centripetal or moderating force. (Yet, as I have already said, this

---

[1] This term is used here in its ancient sense, the science of divine things, and without reference to any modern or special application of it.

[2] See Appendix, "Definitions.'

second mode of energy is feminine, and therefore derivative, being reflex and complementary to its primary.) By means of the first force, substance (Psyche) becomes matter. By means of the second, substance resumes her first condition. But in all matter there is a tendency to revert to substance, and hence to polarise soul by means of evolution. The tendency to revert to substance is the cause of evolution. And this, because the instant the centrifugal mode begins to act, that instant its derivative, the centripetal, begins also to exercise its influence. And no sooner has the primordial Arche assumed the condition of matter, than matter itself begins to differentiate, actuated by the inherent force of psychic energy, and by differentiation begets individuals without number.

Then Psyche, once impersonal because essential, becomes individuated and personal, and through the gate of matter issues forth into new life. A tiny spark in the globule, Psyche becomes a refulgent blaze in the globe. And this by continual accretion and centralisation. As along a chain of nerve-cells the current of magnetic energy flows to its central point—being conveyed, as is a mechanical shock, along a series of units in contiguity—with ever culminating impetus, so is the psychic energy throughout nature developed. Hence the necessity of centres, of associations, of organisms. Thus, by the systematisation of congeries of living entities, that which in each is little becomes great in the whole. For the quality of Psyche is ever the same, and her potentiality is invariable.

I have spoken of an outer personality and of an inner personality ; of a material consciousness as differing from a spiritual consciousness. So now, in like manner, I speak of a spiritual energy as differing from a material energy. The energy whereby Psyche polarises and accretes, is not dependent on the undulations of ether, as are material energies. For Psyche is the essence of the ether itself. All manifested life is a process of burning. Psyche is the substance of the medium by which the burning is conditioned. The first state of matter is ether. But Psyche is within and before the ether. Therefore is she rightly termed immaculate. And to the first state of matter corresponds a first mode of force, that is *rotatory*, the centrifugal and centripetal in one. But before and within force is will;—that is Necessity. Necessity is the will of God. Now this will is spiritual force. It is inherent in Psyche, and she is the medium in which it operates. Such, therefore, as the primordial will is in relation to the primordial substance, such is the individual will in relation to the derived soul. And when the current of spiritual energy (or will) is strong enough in the complex organism to polarise and kindle centrally, then the individual Psyche conceives divinity in her womb, and becomes God-conscious. In the rudimentary stages of matter this current is not strong enough, or continuous enough, thus to polarise.

Psyche, when once she has gathered force enough to burn centrally, is not quenched by the disintegration of the physical elements. These, indeed, fall asunder and desquamate many times during life, whether it be the life of an individual or the life of a system ; yet the consciousness and memory remain the same.   Thou hast not in thy physical body a single particle that thou hadst fifteen years since, yet thou art the same Ego, and thy thought is continuous. Thy Psyche, therefore, has grown up out of many elements ; and in thine Ego their interior Egos are perpetuated, because their psychic force is centralised in thine individuality.   And when thy Psyche passes forth from the disintegrating particles of thy physical body, these shall build up new material entities, and the reversion of matter to substance shall still continue.   And thy substantial part shall go forth to new affinities.

"But," thou sayest, "if soul be immaculate, how comes she to be attracted by material affinities ? "

The link between her and earth is *Karma*.   Not until she is permeated throughout her essence by spirit, is she able to rise above the astral influences. Remember that the science of theosophy is a science of *vehicles*.   Soul is the highest of these vehicles. But the spirit is the first and last term.   Immaculate though she be in her virginal essence, she is not the espoused bride until the bond between her and earth be severed.   And this can only be when every molecule of her essence is pervaded by spirit, and indissolubly married therewith, as God with Arche in the Principle.

"But," thou sayest, "there are foul and horrible forms ;—have these also an immaculate Psyche ? "

These have a Psyche overwhelmed by her Karma, because of her feebleness. Either increase or decrease is the portion of the soul. "He that gathereth not with me, scattereth." Then, when the celestial is weak and divided, the astral and material are strong.

"But," thou sayest, "if soul be thus a resultant of polarisation occurring in the organism she animates, how can soul pass from one body to another by re-incarnation? Surely soul is formed anew in every body and cannot undergo transmigration?"

Do not confuse between substance and force. Substance is Psyche, the medium. Force is Spirit, the energy. That which burns in a flame is gas; the process of burning is a mode or condition of the gas. That which *is* burnt is fuel, or matter, in which the gas is generated. And when thou askest, "How can the Pysche, which is generated in one body, pass by transmigration to another?" it is as though thou askedst, "How can the flame generated in one log of wood pass to another?" The dispensation of physical series may be compared to a furnace into which are cast in succession many faggots. In each faggot is a certain amount of unburnt gas and of latent energy; because there is no medium without inherent force. This latent or inherent force is capacity. (A living medium need not always be active, but it must retain the capacity of action. God need not always be creating, but God must always retain the capacity of creating.) As by the burning the gas of each faggot is consumed, the elements of the faggot (in each of which is stored a certain proportion of this gas) disintegrate and fall into ash. Then another faggot catches the flame and continues it without solution, supplying in the same way the necessary medium. But observe that Psyche is not "generated in a body," neither is flame generated in a faggot. But for fuel there could be no flame, and but for matter there could be no Psyche. That which really is "generated" in the fuel, is the gas by means of which flame becomes manifest. And that which really is generated in the body, is the *condition* by means of which Psyche abstract becomes Psyche concrete.

No. XLIV.

CONCERNING THE POET, AS TYPE OF THE HEAVENLY PERSONALITY.

[Extract from Diary, Paris, Christmas Day, 1882.

"It is strange how I *forget!* This evening I have re-read several passages and chapters written by my own hand, and conceived in my own mind, of "The Perfect Way," and they filled me with as great wonder and admiration as though I had read them for the first time in some stranger's work. Ought this not to set me a-thinking how little this outward and mundane memory has to do with the true and interior consciousness? For, indeed, in my true self I know well all these things, and an hundredfold more than there lie written ; yet my exterior self forgetteth them right readily, and, once they are written, scarce remembereth them more ! And this sets me wondering whether, perchance, we are not altogether out of the reckoning when we talk of memory as a necessary part of selfhood ; for memory, in the sense in which we use the word, signifies a thinking back into the past, and an act by which past experience in time is recalled. But how shall the true, essential self, which is without end or beginning, have memory in any such sort, since the "eternal remembrance" of the soul seeth all things at a glance, both past and to come? To that which is in its nature Divine and of God, memory is no longer recollection, but knowledge. Shall we say that God remembers? Nay, God *knoweth.* I thank thee, O my Divine Genius; Thou art here! I feel thee; thine aura encompasseth me; I burn under the glow of thy wonderful presence. Yes, it is thus indeed!" Here meditation passes into illumination, and the diary thus continues. It will be seen that the writer had caught in advance the style of her illuminator.]

THIS faculty which we call Memory is but the faint reflex and image in the material brain of that function which, in all its celestial plenitude, can belong only to the heavenly man. That which is of time and of matter must needs think by means of an organ and material cells, and these can only work mechanically, and by slow processes. But that which is of eternity and spirit needeth neither organ nor process, since organism is related only to time, and its resultant is process. "Yea, thou shalt see face to face! Thou shalt know even as thou art known!" And just as widely and essentially as the heavenly memory differs from the earthly, so doth the heavenly personality differ from that of the material creature.

Thou mayest the more easily gather somewhat of the character of the heavenly personality by considering the quality of that of the highest type of mankind on earth,—the Poet.

The poet hath no self apart from his larger self. Other men pass indifferent through life and the world, because the self-hood of earth and heaven is a thing apart from them, and toucheth them not.

The wealth of beauty in earth and sky and sea lieth outside their being, and speaketh not to their heart.

Their interests are individual and limited : their home is by one hearth : four walls are the boundary of their kingdom,—so small is it !

But the personality of the poet is divine: and being divine, it hath no limits.

He is supreme and ubiquitous in consciousness : his heart beats in every element.

The pulses of all the infinite deep of heaven vibrate in his own : and responding to their strength and their plenitude, he feels more intensely than other men.

Not merely he sees and examines these rocks and trees : these variable waters, and these glittering peaks.

Not merely he hears this plaintive wind, these rolling peals.

But he *is* all these ; and with them—nay, in them —he rejoices and weeps, he shines and aspires, he sighs and thunders.

And when he sings, it is not he—the man—whose voice is heard : it is the voice of all the manifold Nature herself.

In his verse the sunshine laughs : the mountains give forth their sonorous echoes; the swift lightnings flash.

The great continual cadence of universal life moves and becomes articulate in human language.

O joy profound! O boundless selfhood! O God-like personality!

All the gold of the sunset is thine; the pillars of chrysolite; and the purple vault of immensity!

The sea is thine with its solemn speech, its misty distance, and its radiant shallows!

The daughters of earth love thee: the water-nymphs tell thee their secrets; thou knowest the spirit of all silent things!

Sunbeams are thy laughter, and the rain-drops of heaven thy tears; in the wrath of the storm thine heart is shaken: and thy prayer goeth up with the wind unto God.

Thou art multiplied in the conscience [1] of all living creatures; thou art young with the youth of Nature; thou art all-seeing as the starry skies:

Like unto the Gods,—therefore art thou their beloved: yea, if thou wilt, they shall tell thee all things;

Because thou only understandest, among all the sons of men!

Concerning memory; why should there any more be a difficulty in respect of it? Reflect on this saying,—"Man sees as he knows." To thee the deeps are more visible than the surfaces of things; but to men generally the surfaces only are visible. The

[1] An archaism for consciousness. In the French there is still but one word—*conscience*—for the two things.

material can perceive only the material, the astral the astral, and the spiritual the spiritual. It all resolves itself, therefore, into a question of condition and of quality. Thy hold on matter is but slight, and thine organic memory is feeble and treacherous. It is hard for thee to perceive the surfaces of things and to remember their aspect. But thy spiritual perception is the stronger for this weakness, and the profound is that which thou seest the most readily. It is hard for thee to understand and to retain the memory of material facts; but their meaning thou knowest instantly and by intuition, which is the memory of the soul. For the soul takes no pains to remember; she knows divinely. Is it not said that the immaculate woman brings forth without a pang? The sorrow and travail of conception belong to her whose desire is unto "Adam." [1]

No. XLV.

CONCERNING PSYCHE. [2]

(*Continued from No. XLIII.*)

BUT it may make the subject clearer to thee if, leaving such material comparisons, we speak of those things which only may be fitly compared together. Thou knowest already the nature of the

---

[1] *I.e.*, The outer sense and lower reason.
[2] Paris, January 6, 1883.

planet and the divisions of its Ego into four parts o
regions. Of these thou knowest that the soul o
Psyche is in man; the human superior reason. Nov
there appertains to the planet besides all these fou
regions, an atmosphere of a magnetic nature.[1] Thi
atmosphere is well known to thee. It is the astral o
sideral soul of the planet, the *anima mundi* or picture
world. Therein are stored up all the memories of th·
world; its past life, its history, its affections and re
collections of physical things. The adept may inter
rogate this phantom world, and it shall speak for him
It is the cast-off vestment of the planet; yet it i
living and palpitating, for its very fabric is spun ·
psychic substance, and its entire *parenchyma*[2] i
magnetic. And forasmuch as the planet is an entit·
ever being born and ever dying, so this astral counter
part of itself is ever in process of increase,—the mirro
of the globe, a world encompassing a world. But th
Divine Spirit, Dio-Nysos, is not in this magneti
circle. God the Nous is in the celestial, and th
temple thereof is in the heart of humanity.

Such as is the astral world to the planet, the Ruacl
is to man. And in truth the great magnetic spher·
of the planet is itself composed and woven out of th·
magnetic Egos of its offspring, precisely as these i·
their turn are woven out of the infinitely lesser atom

[1] Not another element, but another mode of the astral; that
which it represents its past as distinguished from its present conditi·
which co-exist,—the latter continually passing into the former.

[2] Anatomically, the mass of a glandular or similar organ. Botan·
cally, the soft cellular tissue of plants.

which compose the individual man. So that, by a
figure, one may represent the whole astral atmosphere
of the planet as a system of so many tiny spheres,
each reflecting and transmitting special rays. But if
in this astral sphere thou shouldst seek the true soul
and Divine Spirit, thou shalt not find them; for they
are of the higher altitudes. To each world its Ruach,
and but one. But the world's true soul migrates and
interchanges. And this is the secret of the "creation"
of worlds. Worlds, like men, have their karma, and
new kosmic globes arise out of the ruins of former
states. As the soul of the individual human unit
transmigrates and passes on, so likewise does the
Psyche of the planet. From world to world, in ceaseless intercourse and impetus, the living Neshamah
pursues her variable way. And as she passes, the
tincture of her divinity changes. Here her spirit is
derived through Iacchos, there through Aphrodite,
anon through Hermes or another god. Here, again,
she is weak, and there strong. Your planet did not
begin this avatâr in strength; an evil karma overwhelmed its soul, and evil lives predominated in its
first ages. Monstrous reptiles, creeping things, and
many fierce nâtures tore and devoured each other in
the great deeps. For the world-soul was weak, and
brought forth with pain and trouble. But Adonai
reigns, and shall reign.

Now the physical molecules of the planet are its
many generated bodies, whether of plants, of animals,
or of men; and these are continually dropping into
decay and being shed. But the living germs of all

s

these organisms die not; they revert continually to their proper place, and the soul of each gathers strength by progression. And the ghost of each living thing goes into the astral sphere, its proper place; and the dust of each creature to the earth; and the Psyche departs to fulfil her karma. For Psyche is as a flame within a flame, whereof the highest and most luminous part mounts and wanders, while the heavier and the less pure remains burning above the surface of the earth.

And as with the man, so with the planet; for small and great there is one law. And one star differeth from another star in glory. And so throughout the infinite vistas and systems of heaven. From star to star, from sun to sun, from galaxy to galaxy, the cosmic souls migrate and interchange. But every God keeps his tincture and maintains his indefeasible personality.

There is no evil. There are only weak and strong, and the differentiation of substance.

Compare like with like, and preserve the affinity of similars.

All things are explicable and comprehensible; but the key of their explanation is order.

Order is the first word of analysis, and the alphabet of synthesis.

No. XLVI.

CONCERNING CONSCIOUSNESS AND MEMORY IN RELATION TO PERSONALITY.[1]

CONSCIOUSNESS is not so much a thing as a condition.   Now, if thou wouldst have a clear conception of that condition by means of analogy, take as an illustration the image of an incandescent globe,—a ball of fire, fluid and igneous throughout its whole mass.[2]   Divide this globe in thought into several successive zones, each containing its precedent.   Thou wilt find that the central interior zone only contains the radiant point, or heart of the fiery mass, and that each successive zone constitutes a circumferential halo more or less intense, according to its nearness to the radiant point, but secondary and derived only, and not in itself a source of luminous radiation.

It is thus with the macrocosm, and thus also with the human kingdom.   In the latter the soul is the interior zone, and it alone contains the radiant point. By this one indivisible effulgence, the successive zones are illuminated in unbroken continuity ; but the source of this effulgence is not in them.   I call this effulgence consciousness, and this radiant point the spiritual ego or divine spark.   Now, for all things there is one law.   God is nothing that man is not. Man, therefore, is one.   But within this unity

[1] Paris, January 15, 1883.
[2] The idea is of a globe self-luminous and heated from within.

plurality. God being one, is yet three ; for in one personality are three persons. And not only three ; for God is beyond number, being all that *is.* So that in this divine unity are many comprehended personalities. This is because spirit is in its very essence consciousness, and wherever spirit is there is consciousness. Yet all spirit is one. Wherefore consciousness is one. And as spirit is manifold, so consciousness is manifold. And spirit, like light, is diffusive. Were it otherwise there could be no universe, but only one point spreading no rays, and instead, thick darkness and unconsciousness throughout eternity. But this is absurd and against reason ; because it is the very nature of light to be radiant ; and radiance is itself light ; so that wherever light is there is radiance or shining ; and God is the Shining One, or radiant point, of the universe. God is the supreme consciousness, and the divine radiance is also consciousness. And man's interior ego is conscient only because the radiant point in it is divine. But this consciousness emits consciousness, and transmits it, first to the *anima bruta*, and last to the physical body. But the more concentrated the consciousness, the brighter and more effulgent the central spark. It is erroneous to think of consciousness as non-diffusive, precisely as it would be to think of light as non-radiant. But it is true that consciousness hath a centre of diffusion, as light hath a radiant point.

Now, if from the midst of this imagined globe of fire thou take the central incandescent spark, the

whole globe does not immediately become dark, but
the effulgence lingers in each zone according to its
degree of nearness to the centre of the sphere.   It is
thus also when dissolution occurs in the process of
death.   Everything is conscious according to its
proper degree.   In somnambulism either the *anima
bruta* and the physical body are conscious while the
consciousness of the soul is suspended ; or the reverse
occurs, according to the kind of somnolence induced.
But that part which remains conscious is capable of
reflection, of thought, of memory, and even of intelligent invention and acumen, according to its kind
and its endowments.   Consciousness is, therefore,
diffusive and, in a certain sense, divisible.   He best
comprehends this truth who is nearest and most like
to God ; and such an one is the poet.

Thou knowest that in the end, when Nirvâna is
attained, the soul shall gather up all that it hath
left within the astral of holy memories and worthy
experience, and to this end the Ruach rises in the
astral sphere, by the gradual decay and loss of its
more material affinities, until these have so disintegrated and perished, that its substance is thereby
lightened and purified.   But continual commerce and
intercourse with earth add, as it were, fresh fuel to its
earthly affinities, keeping these alive, and hindering
its recall to its spiritual ego.   Thus, therefore, the
spiritual ego itself is detained from perfect absorption
into the divine, and union therewith.   For the Ruach
shall not all die, if there be in it anything worthy of
recall.   The astral sphere is its purging chamber.

For Saturn, who is Time, is the trier of all things; he devoureth all the dross; only that escapeth which in its nature is ethereal and destined to reign. And this death of the Ruach is gradual and natural. It is a process of elimination and disintegration, often —as men measure time—extending over many decades, or even centuries. And those Ruachs which appertain to wicked and evil persons, having strong wills inclined earthwards,—these persist longest and manifest most frequently and vividly, because they *rise not*, but, being destined to perish utterly, are not withdrawn from immediate contact with the earth. They are all dross; there is in them no redeemable element. But the Ruach of the righteous complaineth if thou disturb his evolution. "Why callest thou me? disturb me not. The memories of my earth-life are chains about my neck; the desire of the past detaineth me. Suffer me to rise towards my rest, and hinder me not with evocations. But let thy love go after me and encompass me; so shalt thou rise with me through sphere after sphere."

For the good man upon earth can love nothing less than the divine. Wherefore that which he loveth in his friend is the divine, that is, the true and radiant self. And if he love it as differentiated from God, it is only on account of its separate tincture. For in the perfect light there are innumerable tinctures. And according to its celestial affinity, one soul loveth this or that splendour more than the rest. And when the righteous friend of the good man dieth, the love of the living man goeth after the true soul

of the dead; and the strength and divinity of this
love helpeth the purgation of the astral soul, the
psychic ghost. It is to this astral soul, which ever
remaineth near the living friend, an indication of the
way it must also go,—a light shining upon the upward
path that leads from the astral to the celestial and
everlasting. For love, being divine, is *towards* the
divine. " Love exalteth, love purifieth, love uplifteth."

There is but one God ; and in God are comprehended all thrones, and dominions, and powers, and
principalities, and archangels, and cherubim in the
celestial world. And through these are all the worlds
begotten in time and space, each with its astral
sphere. Now, all these, both terrene and heavenly, are
conscient entities, yet all subsist in one consciousness,
which is one God. Because all things are of spirit, and
God is spirit, and spirit is consciousness. The material
of the physical brain is constituted of countless cells
and innumerable connecting fibres, and each cell hath
its own consciousness, according to its degree. Yet
the resultant of all these concordant functions is one
perception and one consciousness. There is also a
consciousness of the nerves, and another of the blood,
and another of the tissues. There is a consciousness
of the eye, and another of the ear, and another of the
touch. There is a consciousness appropriate, and
appertaining specially and distinctively, to every
bodily organ. And all these work night and day
within the body, each according to its kind and its

order. Yet the intellect of the man knoweth nothing thereof. Interrogate one of these living organs, and it will answer thee after its kind. If man, then, can so little dominate and direct the divers parts of his own physical body, why should he find it strange that his ethereal self be likewise similarly multiple? The *anima bruta* is as an organ of the spiritual man; and though it be part of him, its acts, its functions, and its consciousness are not identical with those of the spiritual soul. Consciousness *is* divisible, therefore, and diffusible in man, as in God; in the planet, as in the universe; and one law is throughout all.

No. XLVII.

CONCERNING THE SUBSTANTIAL EGO AS THE TRUE SUBJECT.[1]

IT hath been said, " All life is a burning," and thou sayest, " Let the cells of the brain be likened to these burning logs, and their ash to waste tissue, and the flame to consciousness. Then is consciousness nothing more than an unstable product, which, when the logs are all consumed, dieth away with their ash. How then shall we think of Psyche, if she be this

[1] Paris, February 27, 1883. Received during the night, and written down while in trance. The word Subject, spelt with a capital, is used herein in its metaphysical sense, to denote the thinking and perceiving agent.

flame? Is not all consciousness phenomenon merely, depending for its existence on an organic process ; a *consensus* of vital action in the nervous cells ? And the Psyche, what is she but the sum of conscious states, — a complexity, unstable and automatic, making and unmaking herself at each instant, even as the flame ? "

What, then, doth cognise these unstable states ? These successive and ephemeral objective conditions, to what Subject do they manifest themselves, and how are they recognised ? If consciousness be phenomenon, to what noumenon is it related ? Perceivest thou not that the flame, which is phenomenon, appeareth not *to itself*, and dependeth for its objectivity on the subjectivity of the observer ? The physiologist who telleth thee that memory is a biological *processus*, and that consciousness is a state dependent on the duration and intensity of molecular nervous vibration, toucheth not the Psyche. For this molecular phenomenon is incapable of cognising itself ; it is objective only. Seest thou not that unless there be an inner, subjective ego to perceive and to reflect in itself this succession of phenomenal states, the condition of personality would be impossible ? Or, thinkest thou that unless in the true and inner universe the ideal flame subsisted, thou couldst cognise the material flame ? Knowest thou not that in the Divine Mind subsist eternally and substantially all those things of which thou beholdest the images and phenomena ? It is this inner substantial noumenon which is the Psyche. And as in nature there are infinite gradations from simple to complex, and from coarse to fine, so is Psyche reached by innumerable degrees, and they who have not penetrated to the inner, stop short at the secondary consciousness, which is objective only, and imagine that the subjective, which alone explains all, is undemonstrable. But only Psyche can apprehend the psychical ; only reason can reach the ultimate. " By what, or by whom," say the biologists, "are these ephemeral and unstable states which they name consciousness, apprehended ? Dependent for their production upon duration and intensity of vibration, they pass away as quickly as they appear." If, then, they appear, it is *to something*, otherwise their production and apparition, automatic in itself, could not be cognised. A thing or a state doth not appear to itself, but to the observer. For apparition and production are processes affecting a Subject, and this Subject is Psyche.

But the vice of your biologists lieth in their pursuit of the unity in the simple rather than in the complex. By this method they reverse and invert the divine method of evolution, and nullify its end. They refuse unity to the man, in order to claim it for the molecule. For the ultimate element, indivisible and indestructible by thought, for the simplest and lowest monad only, they claim unity, and thereby individuality. Thus they divinise the lowest, and in their method evolution hath no motive or reasonable end.

But, in truth, Psyche is the most complex of essences, and of this complexity is born *responsi-*

bility. Pure and naked simplicity of being is the outermost and lowermost, touching negation. And the dignity and excellence of the human soul lieth not in her simplicity, but in her complexity. She is the summit of evolution, and all generation works in order to produce her. The philosophy, then, which deifies the lowest in place of the highest, ignores the true sense of its own doctrine of evolution. For the occult law which governs evolution brings together, in increasingly complex and manifold entities, innumerable unities, in order that these units may, of their substantial essence, polarise one complex essence ;— complex, because evolved from, and by the concurrence of, many simple monads ;—essence, because in its nature indivisible and indestructible. The problem of the Ego in man is the problem of God in nature. By the same method which expounds the last, shall the first be expounded likewise. The human ego is, therefore, the synthesis, the divine impersonal personified. And the higher and more excellent this personality, the profounder the consciousness of the impersonal. The divine personality is not concrete, but abstract, and the divine consciousness is not objective, but subjective. The phenomenal personality and consciousness are to the noumenal as water reflecting the heavens, the nether completing and returning to the upper its own concrete reflex.

If thou desirest really to study, to comprehend, and to master the heavenly science, thou must learn that interior and subjective method by which only heavenly things are apprehended. Thou must shift the ground

of thine observation from the exterior to the interior ;
and this can be accomplished only by means of regeneration. " I tell thee that unless thou be born
again, thou shalt not see the kingdom of God." And
this saying meaneth that unless a man be regenerate
he shall not be able to see the inner and essential,
which are the only true and divine things. The
unregenerate man works always from the exterior,
and hath experience only of that which is without.
But thou, if thou wouldst behold the kingdom of God,
learn to live in the essential, and fix the polaric point
of thy mind in the central and substantial.

PART 2.[1]

It is necessary, before entering on the study of the
substantial, that thou shouldst clearly apprehend what
difference there is between the abstract and the concrete. Now the study of the material is the study of
the objective, and that of the substantial is the study
of the subjective. That, then, which the biologists
term the subjective is not truly so, but only the last
or interior phases and conditions of phenomena.
Thus, for example, the unstable states which constitute consciousness, are in their view subjective
states. But they are objective to the true subject,
which is Psyche, because they are perceived by this
latter, and whatever is perceived is objective. There
are in the microcosm two functions,—that of the

---

[1] Received at the same time and in the same manner as the foregoing, but written down on the following day.

revealer, and that of the entity to which revelation is
made.   The unstable states of the biologist, which
accompany certain operations of organic force, are so
many modes whereby exterior things are revealed to
the interior subject.   They are not in themselves the
subject to which the revelation is made.   Do not
think that thou canst attain the subjective by the
same method of study which discovers to thee the
objective.   The last is found by observation from
without ; the first by intuition from within.   The
human kosmos is a complexity of many principles,
each having its own mode of operation.   And it is,
therefore, on the rank and order of the principle
affected by any special operation that dependeth the
nature of the effect produced.   When, therefore, for
example, the biologist speaketh of " unconscious
cerebration," he should ask himself to whom or to
what such operation is unconscious, knowing that in
all vital processes there is infinite gradation.   Questions of duration affect the mind ; questions of intensity affect the Psyche.   All processes which occur in
the objective are relative to *something ;* there is but
one thing absolute, and that is the Subject.   Unconscious cerebration is, therefore, only relatively unconscious in regard to that mode of perception which is
conditioned in and by duration.   But inasmuch as
any such process of cerebration is intense, it is perceived by that perceptive centre which is conditioned
by intensity, and in relation to that centre it is not
unconscious.   The interior man knoweth all processes,
but many processes are not apprehended by the

mental man. This truth ought in itself to demonstrate to thee the distinction of the human principles,
and their separability even on this plane of life. If,
then, the mundane ego and the heavenly ego be so
distinct and separable, even when vitally connected,
that a nervous process conscious to the latter shall be
unconscious to the former, how much more shall
separability be possible when the vital bond is
broken? If the polarities of all thy kosmos were
single and identical in direction, thou wouldst be
conscious of all processes, and nothing would be to
thee unknown, because thy central point of perception
would be precisely the focus of all convergent radii.
But no unregenerate man is in such case. For most,
the perceptive point lies in the relative and objective
man, and by no means in the absolute and subjective.
Thus the convergent radii pass unheeded of their
consciousness, because, as yet, they know not their
own spirit. They are asleep while they live, and
incapable of absolute cognition.

No. XLVIII.

CONCERNING THE CHRISTIAN MYSTERIES.[1]

PART I.

THE two terms of the history of creation or evolution are formulated by the Catholic Church in
two precious and all-important dogmas. These are—

[1] Paris, December 12, 1882.

first, the Immaculate Conception of the Blessed
Virgin Mary ; and, secondly, the Assumption of the
Blessed Virgin Mary.[1] By the doctrine of the first we
are secretly enlightened concerning the generation of
the soul, who is begotten in the womb of matter, and
yet from the first instant of her being is pure and
incorrupt. Sin comes through the material and intellectual element, because these belong to matter. But
the soul, which is of the celestial, and belongs to
heavenly conditions, is free of original sin. "Salem,
which is from above, is free, which is the mother of us
all. But Agar"—the intellectual and astral part—
"is a bond slave, both she and her son." The soul,
born of time (Anna), is yet conceived without taint
of corruption or decay, because her essence is divine.
Contained in matter, and brought into the world by
means of it, she is yet not of it, else she could not be
mother of God. In her bosom is conceived that
bright and holy light—the Nucleolus—which dwells in
her from the beginning, and which, without intercourse with matter, germinates in her and manifests
itself as the express image of the eternal and ineffable
personality. She gives this image individuality.
Through and in her it is focused and polarised into a
perpetual and self-subsistent person, at once God and
man. But were she not immaculate,—did any admix-
ture of matter enter into her integral substance,—no
such polarisation of the Divine could occur. The
womb in which God is conceived must be immaculate ;
the mother of Deity must be "ever-virgin." She grows

[1] The latter is not yet promulgated. See *The Perfect Way*, V. 43. n. 2.

up from infancy to childhood at the knee of Anna ; from a child she becomes a maiden,—true type of the soul, unfolding, learning, increasing, and elaborating itself by experience. But in all this she remains in her essence divine and uncontaminated, at once daughter, spouse, and mother of God.

As the Immaculate Conception is the foundation of the mysteries, so is the Assumption their crown. For the entire object and end of kosmic evolution is precisely this triumph and apotheosis of the soul. In the mystery presented by this dogma, we behold the consummation of the whole scheme of creation—the perpetuation and glorification of the individual human ego. The grave—the material and astral consciousness—cannot retain the immaculate Mother of God. She rises into the heavens ; she assumes divinity. In her own proper person she is taken up into the King's chamber. From end to end the mystery of the soul's evolution—the history, that is, of humanity and of the kosmic drama—is contained and enacted in the cultus of the Blessed Virgin Mary. The acts and the glories of Mary are the one supreme subject of the holy mysteries.

PART 2.[1]

It is necessary, in relation to the Mysteries, to distinguish between the unmanifest and the manifest, and

[1] Home, August 19, 1883. Mrs Kingsford thus prefaces this exposition in her diary :—

" How wonderfully the Church helps one in matters of Theosophy ! When I am doubtful about Divine Order, or about function in the human between the macrocosm and the microcosm. These last, however, are identical, in that the process of the universal and the process of the individual are one.

Mary is the soul, and as such the matrix of the divine principle—God—made man by individualisation, through descent into the "Virgin's womb." But the seven principles of universal spirit are concerned in this conception ; since it is through their operation in the soul that she becomes capable of polarising divinity.

[This is the secret aspect of the Mosaic week of Creation, each day of which week denotes the operation of one of the Seven creative Elohim or Divine Potencies concerned in the elaboration of the spiritual microcosm.]

It is said that the Blessed Virgin Mary is the daughter, spouse, and mother of God. But, inasmuch as spiritual energy has two conditions, one of passivity and one of activity,—which latter is styled the Holy Spirit,—it is said that Mary's spouse is not the Father, but the Holy Ghost, these terms implying respectively the static and the dynamic modes of

kingdom, I appeal instinctively to Catholic doctrine, and am at once set in the right path. I think I should never have clearly understood the Order and Function of the Soul but for the Catholic teachings concerning the Mother of God ; nor should I have comprehended the Method of Salvation by the Merits of our Divine Principle, save for the doctrine of the Incarnation and the Atonement."

Between Catholic doctrine in its inner and true meaning, however, and that doctrine as set before the world, she recognised an absolute distinction, holding firmly to the dictum that "The Church has all the truth, but the priests have materialised it, making themselves and their followers idolaters."

Deity. For the Father denotes the motionless, the force passive and potential, in whom all things *are*—subjectively. But the Holy Ghost represents will in action,—creative energy, motion and generative function. Of this union of the Divine will in action—the Holy Ghost—with the human soul, the product is Christ, the God-Man and *our* Lord. And through Christ, the Divine Spirit, by whom he is begotten, flows and operates.

In the trinity of the unmanifest, the great deep, or ocean of infinitude—Sophia (Wisdom)—corresponds to Mary, and has for spouse the creative energy, of whom is begotten the Manifestor, Adonai, *the* Lord. This "Mother" is co-equal with the Father, being primary and eternal. In manifestation the "Mother" is derived, being born of Time (Anna), and has for Father the Planet-God,—for our planet, Iacchos Joachim, or Jacob ;[1] so that the paternity of the first person of the Trinity is vicarious only. The Church, therefore, being a Church of the manifest, deals with Mary (substance), under this aspect alone, and hence does not specify her as co-equal with the first principle. In the unmanifest, being underived, she has no relation to time.

[1] Ps. xxiv. 6; cxxxii. 2, 5, &c. See Appendix, "Definitions." Every kosmic entity, whether a system, a planet, or a person, is constituted of a certain portion of Divinity, segregated and assigned to be its life and substance. These names designate that particular individuation of the universal deity of which we and our planet consist. Wherefore Mary, as the perfected human soul, is "daughter" of the planet-god, precisely as her "son" Christ, the perfected human spirit, is "son" of the planet-god. The soul is at once "daughter, mother, and· spouse of God," as woman is at once daughter, mother, and spouse of man.

No. XLIX.

CONCERNING DYING.[1]

WHEN a man or an animal dies a violent death, it is not an immediate separation that takes place between body and soul. There are many principles to be considered, each, as it were, incased in an outer, like a nest of Chinese boxes, or the spiral of a cone. And the lower consciousness can be re-animated in the physical body by physical means. This is the consciousness related to nerve-stimulation and reflex action, as involuntary gesture and all animal functions. It is only by degrees that the soul disengages itself, and its skirts linger long in the physical system, and can be detained artificially.

All the component elements of the body polarise to form a unity, which is as a sun to the system. But this polarisation is fourfold, and the central and in-most point of radiance is not objective but subjective. That which reflects is molecular ; that which shines is non-molecular. Force, or spirit, is non-molecular. That, therefore, is alone one and indivisible, and it is subjective. When Psyche is one with the spirit, she too becomes subjective. It has been said, "All things are by infinite gradation, and Psyche is reached by innumerable degrees ; so that they who have not

---

[1] Same place and date as the foregoing.

penetrated to the inner, stop short at the secondary consciousness, and imagine that to be the subjective." Psyche, so long as *existence* [1] lasts, is a mirror to the spirit ; she reflects, and is therefore molecular. But she is gradually in process of *at-one-ment ;*—she and the spirit mutually attract and permeate each other. She will, then, finally become non-molecular and entirely subjective. Therefore the higher the entity undergoing death, the easier the detachment of Psyche from the lower consciousnesses which enshrine her. For the nearer she is to being herself a radiant point, the nearer she is to unity and spiritual subjectivity. The saint does not fear death because his consciousness is gathered up into Psyche, and she into her spouse. " The grave—that is the physical and astral consciousness—cannot retain the holy Virgin." The whole object of incarnation is to build up a spiritual counterpart, subjective and substantial. Now, when once the radii of the physical and astral molecules have polarised a radiant point interior and superior to themselves, no injury or mutilation of the physical ego will affect the subjective ego. As a matter of fact, physical bodies are constantly changing and interchanging their particles ; portions of other bodies are engrafted continually within them ; but there is no change in the unity or continuity of the higher consciousness. This is because the true unity is not objective, but subjective. The true " Son of man " is " in heaven," and it is his body and *anima bruta* only which are on earth. Most of the mistakes

---

[1] The state of manifested as distinguished from unmanifested being.

of the materialists arise from understanding localities
and things when they should understand conditions
and principles.   Of course a subjective entity cannot
be localised in space or duration.   Potentially the
soul is always eternal, although brought into relation
with the objective through time.   It is therefore
a mistake to suppose that the soul is in the body
in the same sense as the watery humours of the
body.   The soul is in the body only in the sense
in which Arche is in the universe ; that is, she is
interior to it in the fourth dimension, of which, objec-
tively, no idea can be formed.   If there were no other
consciousness inherent in man than the lower consciousness of the cells, there could be no self-conscious-
ness, or unity of thought.   The cerebral sense would
not be reflected in knowledge, and man would not
be cognisant of his apprehensions and perceptions.
Continuity of memory and will must belong to *one*,
and must be positive and absolute, that is, when they
relate to higher selfhood.

As regards the lower consciousness, it is easy to
understand that in the case of violent death, death is
not instantaneous.   The stroke of the sword which
divides the physical head from the physical trunk
may indeed be instantaneous, but this physical
separation does not constitute death, and this process
is not really complete until the phantom is wholly
disengaged.   So long as it is present, of course, any
physical aid given to the nerve-cells permits the
manifestation of its forces.   But when it has wholly
abandoned the body such aid would be furnished in

vain. The fluidic body is so tenuous and elastic that no mere separation of the physical frame would suffice to destroy its integrity.

No. L.

CONCERNING THE ONE LIFE;[1]

being a recapitulation.

(1.)

THE spirit absorbed in man or in the planet does not exhaust Deity.

Nor does the soul evolved upward through matter exhaust substance.

There remain, then, ever in the fourth dimension —the principium—above the manifest, unmanifest God and soul.

The perfection of man and of the planet is attained when the soul of the one and of the other is throughout illuminate by spirit.

But spirit is never the same thing as soul. It is always celestial energy, and soul is always substance.

That which creates is Spirit (God).

The immanent consciousnesses (spirits) of all the cells of a man's entity, cause by their polarisation a central unity of consciousness, which is more than

---

[1] Written at home, the first five sections on December 9, 1883, and the rest on January 21, 1884, and regarded by the writer as an exercise or meditation, based on previous illuminations, rather than as a fresh illumination. It is unfinished.

the sum total of all their consciousnesses, because it is on a higher round or plane.

For in spiritual science everything depends upon levels ; and the man's evolution works round spirally, as does the planetary evolution.

In this relation consider the worlds of form and formless worlds of Hindû theosophy.

Similarly the soul of the planet is more than the associated essences of the souls upon it : because this soul also is on a higher plane than they.

Similarly, too, the consciousness of the solar system is more than that of the associated world-consciousnesses.

And the consciousness of the manifest universe is greater than that of its corporate systems.

But that of the unmanifest is higher and greater still : as, except in substance, God the Father is greater than God the Son.

(2.)

The elemental kingdoms represent spirit on its downward path into matter.

There are three of these before the mineral is reached.

These are the formless worlds before the worlds of form.

They are *in* the planet, and also in man.

All the planets inhabited by manifest forms are themselves manifest.

After the form-worlds come other formless worlds, caused by the upward arc of ascending spirit : but these also are *in* the planet.

They are also in the man : and are the states of pure thought.

The thinker, therefore, who is son of Hermes, is as far beyond the medium who is controlled and who is not self-conscious, as the formless worlds of the ascending arc are beyond the formless worlds of the elemental, or descending, arc.

In the planet and in the man they only seem contiguous because each round is spiral.

But each round takes the One Life higher in the spiral.

Neither the planet-soul nor the man-soul goes over exactly the same ground again.

But perverse and disobedient will may reverse the direction of the spiral.

Individuals in whom the will so acts, are finally abandoned by the planet to the outer sphere.

(3.)

The One Life is the point of consciousness.

The will is the impulse which moves it.

In the celestial the One Life is the Elohim ; and the will is the Father.

The One Life is manifest by effulgence (the Son).

So, then, the will begets in substance the effulgence, which is the manifestation of the One Life.

In man and the planet the effulgence is dim and diffuse until it moves into the soul. Then only Christ is born.

The One Life is invisible until Christ manifests it.

Christ in man has for counterpart Adonai in the heavens.

So, then, the One Life is in the Father-Mother latently, until manifest by the Son (effulgence).

And the procession of the Holy Spirit is from the Father-Mother through the Son.

Herein is the difference reconciled between the Greek and Latin Churches.

The point of consciousness shineth more and more unto the perfect day of brightness ("Nativity of Christ" within man).

(4.)

The object of creation is the production of "Ancients." [1]

They are the first-fruits of the souls of the planets; or "First Resurrection." (First in dignity, not in time.)

They are not themselves creators; but are regenerators of that which is created;

Being vehicles for the Holy Spirit, who is the regenerator, through Christ.

Because will can create only when it is in the abstract; the derived does not create.

The Father-Mother creates through Adonai by means of the Holy Spirit.

The will of the perfect man renovates through the effulgence of his One Life.

His Karma is poured out over the world to save mankind.

[1] A.V., "Elders," Apoc. iv.

He is the Saviour through his precious life.

There are twenty-four Ancients, because there are twelve Avatârs of the Lord, and every one is dual.

(5.)

Will, when it is derived through existence, begets Karma.

God has no Karma. God does not *ex-ist:* God IS.

Karma is the channel of initiation. God is not initiated.

The perfect man saves himself and saves others by his righteousness.

The two terms of existence are creation and redemption.

The first is God's work; the second is the work of Christ,—God in man.

The reason why the Ancient cannot create is because he is not infinite.

He is immortal, not eternal; he is derived, not self-subsistent.

His is the point of grace, not the point of projection.

The thrones of the Ancients are round about the Throne of God and below it.

(6.)

The lower self is the cause of the difference between man and nature.

This lower self is the unreal self, the magnetic states.

These magnetic states are the serpent, in whose folds all nature is involved (to man).

It is the serpent that tempts Eve, the soul.

How does this magnetic self arise?

It is a reflect, the pole of which is antithetic to the pole of the true self.

The perfect balance is to be in the centre or equator, between the two.

Nature has no lower self; consequently she is not self-conscious (does not know that she is "naked").

The centre of the true self is in eternity; the poles are in time.

The soul's proper seat is in the centre,—eternity.

When she is there, the man is in eternal life.

This centre is the tree of life.

The tree of the knowledge of good and evil is the condition of the cognisance of the two poles.

Eating the fruit of this tree is the act by which the soul beholds these two poles.

While she remained in her first state, she was as nature is, seeing only one pole, the good, and not knowing herself.

(7.)

There are two modes of God,—the manifest and the unmanifest.

God manifest rises gradually through nature to meet God unmanifest.

Every level in nature rises out of itself to merge in every other level.

When the mind-plane is reached, God emerges thence as the soul, and looks upon himself.

That into which the soul looks *back* is the past of her journey,—time and nature.

That into which she looks *forward* is God,—spirit and eternity.

The point she has reached is eternal life,—the tree in the midst of paradise.

The false self is the mirage in time.

As the planes evolved, their laws were the laws of God.

But backwards they are the laws of the Devil.

"A prayer said backwards is an evocation of the Evil One."

(8.)

The God manifest is the true self.

The God unmanifest is the Divine overshadowing, the true spouse of the soul.

To know one's self is no sin.

God planted the tree of the knowledge of good and evil.

The sin is in the retrogression towards the astral.

It is the giving of the apple to Adam.

Adam is commanded ; Adam is rebuked.

From the moment of the fall, a new projection takes place, similar to that of God's first projection into time.

The wheel turns again, and all is done over again in the microcosm.

For the retrogression towards the intellectual (Adam) is a displacement of the centre.

It is a transference of the tree of life from the place of Eve (the soul) to the place of Adam.

The centre can be nowhere save in the meeting place of the two lines which intersect at right angles the two triangles of the " Seal of Solomon."

There can be but one point of centre, therefore the two trees represent two lines crossed.

When the One Life has reached the seventh kingdom, then is the Sabbath.

That is the point of return from Nature—God in Action—to God in God—Rest.

Seven for the outgoing, seven for the incoming.[1]

(9.)

Thought in nature is the law of God.

Thought in man is the law of God ; because man is the offspring of nature, and there is but one law.

All the planes in nature express this thought in unison.

Law in one plane does not conflict with law in another plane. Therefore God is invariable in nature.

But in man there appears to be conflict of two diverse wills. How is this, and whence comes the will which conflicts with the law of God in man ?

Man, like the world, is constituted of many planes.

Each plane has its consciousness, and the medium

---

[1] The difference between this reckoning and that in *The Great Work*, Part II., No. III., v. 60, 61, is only apparent, the point which the two series have in common being here reckoned twice over, making the total in both cases thirteen.

of one plane is more responsive and powerful in expressing the will of God than that of another plane.

The same is true of nature's plane. It is a question of subtlety and rarefaction of media.

The cause of evolution is the constant convergence of radii.

That is,—the consciousness of the mineral plane has a tendency to express itself in a higher plane, *i.e.,* as vegetable consciousness; and the vegetable as animal; and the animal as human; and the human as divine.

But when the human is reached, the whole process begins over again, *in petto.*

And in man unregenerate, the tendency is not from behind forwards, in upward order, but in downwards, or retrogressive series.

For in man all the planes are consubstantiate, and all their modes of law *obtain.* Some media are weaker or denser than others, and these are the lowermost and outermost,—"touching negation."

(10.)

As the earth in its whirling, or individuation, throws off its Karma, so it is with man.

It is through Karma that initiation occurs.

Karma is two-faced, good and evil. But only the good face reflects on us the divine light.

Diana is the moon; so also is Hecate.

The "moon" is good or evil, according to the condition of the postulant.

.   .   .   .   .   .

PART THE SECOND.

THE BOOK OF THE MYSTERIES OF GOD,

ANCIENTLY CALLED

THE GREATER MYSTERIES,

AS CONTAINING KNOWLEDGES WHICH FOR THEIR
INTERIORNESS WERE RESERVED FOR
INITIATES OF HIGH GRADE.

"I AM."

o

No. I.

THE CREDO ; [1]

*being a summary of the spiritual history of the Sons
of God, and the mysteries of the kingdoms of the
Seven Spheres.*

I BELIEVE in one God ; the Father and Mother
Almighty ; of whose substance are the generations of Heaven and of earth : And in Christ Jesus
the Son of God, our Lord ; who is conceived of the
Holy Ghost ; born of the Virgin Mary ; suffereth
under the world-rulers ; is crucified, dead, and buried ;
who descendeth into hell ; who riseth again from the
dead ; who ascendeth into Heaven, and sitteth at
the right hand of God ; by whose law the quick and
the dead are judged. I believe in the Seven Spirits
of God ; the Kingdom of Heaven ; the communion
of the elect ; the passing-through of souls ; the
redemption of the body ; the life everlasting ; and the
Amen.[2] A

He that believeth and is initiated shall be saved ;
and he that believeth not shall consume away. B

---

[1] This and the next were received in Paris, July 1879.
[2] For the Notes indicated by small capitals, see Appendix.

No. II.

THE "LORD'S PRAYER";

being a prayer of the Elect for interior perfectionment.

OUR Father-Mother who art in the upper and the within :

Hallowed be Thy name :

Thy kingdom come :

Thy will be done, in the body as in the spirit :

Give us every day the communion of the mystical bread :

And perfect us in the power of Thy Sons, according as we give ourselves to perfect others :

And in the hour of temptation deliver us from the hand of Satan.

For Thine are the kingdom, the power, and the glory,

In the life eternal, and in the Amen. ^

No. III.

CONCERNING HOLY WRIT.

ALL Scriptures which are the true Word of God, have a dual interpretation, the intellectual and the intuitional, the apparent and the hidden.

2. For nothing can come forth from God save that which is fruitful.

3. As is the nature of God, so is the Word of God's mouth.

4. The letter alone is barren ; the spirit and the letter give life.

5. But that Scripture is the more excellent which is exceeding fruitful and brings forth abundant signification.

6. For God is able to say many things in one, as the perfect ovary contains many seeds in its chalice.

7. Therefore there are in the Scriptures of God's Word certain writings which, as richly yielding trees, bear more abundantly than others in the self-same holy garden.

8. And one of the most excellent is the history of the generation of the heavens and the earth.

9. For therein is contained in order a genealogy, which has four heads, as a stream divided into four branches, a word exceeding rich.

10. And the first of these generations is that of the Gods.

11. The second is that of the kingdom of heaven.

12. The third is that of the visible world.

13. And the fourth is that of the Church of Christ.

No. IV.

CONCERNING SIN AND DEATH.[1]

A S is the outer so is the inner: He that worketh is One.

2. As the small is, so is the great: there is one law.

3. Nothing is small and nothing is great in the Divine Economy.

4. If thou wouldst understand the method of the world's corruption, and the condition to which sin hath reduced the work of God,

5. Meditate upon the aspect of a corpse; and consider the method of the putrefaction of its tissues and humours.

6. For the secret of death is the same, whether of the outer or of the inner.

7. The body dieth when the central will of its system no longer bindeth in obedience the elements of its substance.

8. Every cell is a living entity, whether of vegetable or of animal potency.

9. In the healthy body every cell is polarised in

[1] Paris, October 3, 1878. Received in sleep.

subjection to the central will, the Adonai of the physical system.

10. Health, therefore, is order, obedience, and government.

11. But wherever disease is, there is disunion, rebellion, and insubordination.

12. And the deeper the seat of the confusion, the more dangerous the malady, and the harder to quell it.

13. That which is superficial may be more easily healed; or, if need be, the disorderly elements may be rooted out, and the body shall be whole and at unity again.

14. But if the disobedient molecules corrupt each other continually, and the perversity spread, and the rebellious tracts multiply their elements; the whole body shall fall into dissolution, which is death.

15. For the central will that should dominate all the kingdom of the body, is no longer obeyed; and every element is become its own ruler, and hath a divergent will of its own.

16. So that the poles of the cells incline in divers directions; and the binding power which is the life of the body, is dissolved and destroyed.

17. And when dissolution is complete, then follow corruption and putrefaction.

18. Now, that which is true of the physical, is true likewise of its prototype.

19. The whole world is full of revolt; and every element hath a will divergent from God.

20. Whereas there ought to be but one will, attracting and ruling the whole man.

21. But there is no longer brotherhood among you; nor order, nor mutual sustenance.

22. Every cell is its own arbiter; and every member is become a sect.

23. Ye are not bound one to another: ye have confounded your offices, and abandoned your functions.

24. Ye have reversed the direction of your magnetic currents; ye are fallen into confusion, and have given place to the spirit of misrule.

25. Your wills are many and diverse; and every one of you is an anarchy.

26. A house that is divided against itself, falleth.

27. O wretched man; who shall deliver you from this body of death? C

No. V.

CONCERNING THE "GREAT WORK," THE REDEMPTION,
AND THE SHARE OF CHRIST JESUS THEREIN.[1]

" FOR this cause is Christ manifest, that he may destroy the works of the devil."

2. In this text of the holy writings is contained

[1] Commenced in Paris, September 30, 1878, to v. 20. Completed in London, July, 13, 1881. Received chiefly in sleep.

the explanation of the mission of the Christ, and the nature of the Great Work.

3. Now the devil, or old serpent, the enemy of God, is that which gives pre-eminence to matter.

4. He is disorder, confusion, distortion, falsification, error. He is not personal, he is not positive, he is not formulated. Whatever God is, that the devil is not.

5. God is light, truth, order, harmony, reason: and God's works are illumination, knowledge, understanding, love, and sanity.

6. Therefore the devil is darkness, falsehood, disorder, discord, ignorance ; and his works are confusion, folly, division, hatred and delirium.

7. The devil is therefore the negation of God's Positive. God is I AM : the devil is NOT. He has no individuality and no existence ; for he represents the not-being. Wherever God's kingdom is not, the devil reigns.

8. Now the Great Work is the redemption of spirit from matter ; that is, the establishment of the kingdom of God.

9. Jesus being asked when the kingdom of God should come, answered, " When Two shall be as One, and that which is Without as that which is Within." [1]

10. In saying this, he expressed the nature of the Great Work. The Two are spirit and matter : the within is the real invisible ; the without is the illusory visible.

---

[1] II. Ep. Clement, v. 1.

11. The kingdom of God shall come when spirit and matter shall be one substance, and the phenomenal shall be absorbed into the real.

12. His design was therefore to destroy the dominion of matter, and to dissipate the devil and his works.

13. And this he intended to accomplish by proclaiming the knowledge of the Universal Dissolvent, and giving to men the keys of the kingdom of God.

14. Now, the kingdom of God is within us ; that is, it is interior, invisible, mystic, spiritual.

15. There is a power by means of which the outer may be absorbed into the inner.

16. There is a power by means of which matter may be ingested into its original substance.

17. He who possesses this power is Christ, and he has the devil under foot.

18. For he reduces chaos to order, and indraws the external to the centre.

19. He has learnt that matter is illusion, and that spirit alone is real.

20. He has found his own central point : and all power is given unto him in heaven and on earth.

21. Now, the central point is the number thirteen : it is the number of the marriage of the Son of God.

22. And all the members of the microcosm are bidden to the banquet of the marriage.

23. But if there chance to be even one among them which has not on a wedding garment,

24. Such a one is a traitor, and the microcosm is found divided against itself.

25. And that it may be wholly regenerate, it is necessary that Judas be cast out.

26. Now the members of the microcosm are twelve : of the senses three, of the mind three, of the heart three, and of the conscience three.

27. For of the body there are four elements ; and the sign of the four is sense, in the which are three gates ;

28. The gate of the eye, the gate of the ear, and the gate of the touch.

29. Renounce vanity, and be poor : renounce praise, and be humble : renounce luxury, and be chaste.

30. Offer unto God a pure oblation : let the fire of the altar search thee, and prove thy fortitude.

31. Cleanse thy sight, thine hands, and thy feet : carry the censer of thy worship into the courts of the Lord ; and let thy vows be unto the Most High.

32. And for the magnetic man[1] there are four elements : and the covering of the four is mind, in the which are three gates ;

33. The gate of desire, the gate of labour, and the gate of illumination.

34. Renounce the world, and aspire heaven-ward : labour not for the meat which perishes, but ask of God thy daily bread : beware of wandering doctrines, and let the Word of the Lord be thy light.

---

[1] *I.e.*, the magnetic or astral part of Man, which is accounted a person or system in itself.

35. Also of the soul there are four elements: and the seat of the four is the heart, whereof likewise there are three gates ;

36. The gate of obedience, the gate of prayer, and the gate of discernment.

37. Renounce thine own will, and let the law of God only be within thee: renounce doubt: pray always and faint not: be pure of heart also, and thou shalt see God.

38. And within the soul is the Spirit: and the Spirit is One, yet has it likewise three elements.

39. And these are the gates of the oracle of God, which is the ark of the covenant ;

40. The rod, the host,[1] and the law :

41. The force which solves, and transmutes, and divines: the bread of heaven which is the substance of all things and the food of angels; the table of the law, which is the will of God, written with the finger of the Lord.

42. If these three be within thy spirit, then shall the Spirit of God be within thee.

43. And the glory shall be upon the propitiatory, in the holy place of thy prayer.

44. These are the twelve gates of regeneration: through which if a man enter he shall have right to the tree of life.

45. For the number of that tree is thirteen.

46. It may happen to a man to have three, to another five, to another seven, to another ten.

---

[1] The Sacramental bread called by the Hebrews "Showbread."

47. But until a man have twelve, he is not master over the last enemy.

48. Therefore was Jesus betrayed to death by Judas : because he was not yet perfected.

49. But he was perfected through suffering : yea, by the passion, the cross, and the burial.

50. For he could not wholly die : neither could his body see corruption.

51. So he revived : for the elements of death were not in his flesh ; and his molecules retained the polarity of life eternal.

52. He therefore was raised and became perfect : having the power of the dissolvent and of transmutation.

53. And God glorified the Son of Man : yea, he ascended into heaven, and sits at the right hand of the Majesty on high.

54. Thence also the Christ shall come again : in power like unto the power of his ascension.

55. For as yet the devil is undissipated : the Virgin indeed has crushed his head ; but still he lies in wait for her heel.

56. Therefore the Great Work is yet to be accomplished.

57. When the leaven shall have leavened the whole lump ; when the seed shall have become a tree ; when the net shall have gathered all things into it.

58. For in the same power and glory he had at his ascension, shall Christ Jesus be manifested from heaven before angels and men.

59. For when the cycle of the creation is completed, whether of the macrocosm, or of the microcosm, the Great Work is accomplished.

60. Six for the manifestation, and six for the interpretation: six for the outgoing, and six for the ingathering: six for the man, and six for the woman.

61. Then shall be the Sabbath of the Lord God.[1]

No. VI.

CONCERNING ORIGINAL BEING; OR, " BEFORE THE BEGINNING."

BEFORE the beginning of things, before the generation of the heavens, the great and invisible God alone subsisted.

2. Even the God whose name is unspeakable, upon Whom no eye hath ever looked, whose nature no mind create can fathom.

3. In the bosom of the eternal were all the Gods comprehended, as the seven spirits of the prism, contained in the Invisible Light.

4. The Elohim filled and comprised the universe, and the universe was at rest.

5. There was no motion, nor darkness, nor space, nor matter.

---

[1] See note to Part I., No. L. (8); also Appendix, *Second Coming.*

6. There was no other than God.

7. For there was One only, the Uncreate and Self-subsistent.

8. But forasmuch as motion was conceived in the bosom of the Elohim, the Invisible Light moved on itself ;

9. And gathering itself inward toward its axis, left beyond and without it another self.

10. So that where God was not, there was darkness and the abyss.

11. Yet had the darkness of itself no existence, for before the beginning God was all in all.

12. And that which had been God became darkness by the withdrawal of God.

13. So that the darkness is no entity, for it is the negation of being.

14. It is no presence, for where a presence is, there is God.

15. Neither can it produce, neither can it be manifested, neither can it be annihilated.

16. Yet, forasmuch as the darkness doth not comprehend God, it is as another self.

17. Not havin power in itself, for all power is God's.

18. Neither having personality, for all personality is of God.

19. But unless there were again to be cessation of motion, there can be no extinction of negation.

20. It may be bounded, but never annihilated.

21. Whatever is, is of God ; but God only is absolute and perfect being.

22. All things visible and invisible were potential in God before the beginning, and of God's fulness we have all received.

23. Inasmuch as anything is absolute, strong, perfect, true, insomuch it resembles God and is God.

24. Inasmuch as anything is out of reason, weak, divided, false, insomuch it approaches negation, and is of negation.

25. Now the Absolute, which is God, is Spirit.

No. VII.

ALPHA, OR "IN THE BEGINNING."

IN the beginning, the potentialities of all things were in Elohim.

2. And Elohim was twain, the Spirit and the Water,—that is, the heavenly deep.

3. Now the spirit of Elohim is original life, and the heavenly waters are space and dimension.

4. He is the line, and She is the circle.

5. And without them is void and darkness.

6. Now the Divine twain were from the beginning contained in the bosom of the One who was before the beginning :

7. Even God the nameless, invisible, unfathomable, unspeakable, motionless :

8. From whom proceeded the heavens—that is, the duality, spirit, and deep—and the earth—that is, spiritually, the beyond.

9. Now the beyond was without form and void, and darkness covered the face of it.

10. But the heavenly waters were covered by the Spirit of God.

No. VIII.

BETA, OR ADONAI, THE MANIFESTOR.

THEN from the midst of the Divine Duality, the Only Begotten of God came forth :

2. Adonai, the Word, the Voice invisible.

3. He was in the beginning, and by Him were all things discovered.

4. Without Him was not anything made which is visible.

5. For He is the Manifestor, and in Him was the life of the world.

6. God the nameless hath not revealed God, but Adonai hath revealed God from the beginning.

7. He is the presentation of Elohim, and by Him the Gods are made manifest.

8. He is the third aspect of the Divine Triad :

9. Co-equal with the Spirit and the heavenly deep.

10. For except by three in one, the Spirits of the Invisible Light could not have been made manifest.

11. But now is the prism perfect, and the generation of the Gods discovered in their order.

12. Adonai dissolves and resumes ; in His two hands are the dual powers of all things.

13. He is of His Father the Spirit, and of His Mother the great deep.

14. Having the potency of both in Himself, and the power of things material.

15. Yet being Himself invisible, for He is the cause, and not the effect.

16. He is the Manifestor, and not that which is manifest.

17. That which is manifest is the Divine Substance.

No. IX.

GAMMA, OR THE MYSTERY OF REDEMPTION.

ALL things are formed of the Divine Substance, which is the Divine idea.

2. Therefore all things are one, as God is one.

3. And every monad of the Divine Substance hath in itself the potency of twain, as God is twain in one.

4. And every monad which is manifest, is manifest by the evolution of its Trinity.

5. For thus only can it bear record of itself, and become cognisable as an entity.

6. There are three which bear record in the Holy of Holies,—the Spirit, the Water, and the Word,—and these three are one.

7. And there are three which bear record in the outer world,—the life, the soul, and the body,—and these three agree in one.

8. As is God, so is all which goes forth from God.

P

9. From the imponderable particles of physical light, to the molecules of the lead of the outermost circle, ᴰ

10. All things in heaven and in earth are of God, both the invisible and the visible.

11. Such as is the invisible, is the visible also, for there is no boundary line betwixt spirit and matter.

12. Matter is spirit made exteriorly cognisable by the force of the Divine Word.

13. And when God shall resume all things by love, the material shall be resolved into the spiritual, and there shall be a new heaven and a new earth.

14. Not that matter shall be destroyed, for it came forth from God, and is of God indestructible and eternal.

15. But it shall be indrawn and resolved into its true self.

16. It shall put off corruption, and remain incorruptible.

17. It shall put off mortality, and remain immortal.

18. So that nothing be lost of the Divine substance.

19. It was material entity: it shall be spiritual entity.

20. For there is nothing which can go out from the presence of God.

21. This is the doctrine of the resurrection of the dead : that is, the transfiguration of the body. ᴼ

22. For the body, which is matter, is but the manifestation of spirit : and the Word of God shall transmute it into its inner being.

23. The will of God is the alchemic crucible : and the dross which is cast therein is matter.

24. And the dross shall become pure gold, seven times refined ; even perfect spirit.

25. It shall leave behind it nothing : but shall be transformed into the Divine image.

26. For it is not a new substance : but its alchemic polarity is changed, and it is converted.

27. But except it were gold in its true nature, it could not be resumed into the aspect of gold.

28. And except matter were spirit, it could not revert to spirit.

29. To make gold, the alchemist must have gold.

30. But he knows that to be gold which others take to be dross.

31. Cast thyself into the will of God, and thou shalt become as God.

32. For thou art God, if thy will be the Divine will.

33. This is the great secret : it is the mystery of redemption.

No. X.

DELTA, OR THE MYSTERY OF GENERATION.

BY the word of Elohim were the seven Elohim manifest :

2. Even the seven Spirits of God, in the order of their precedence :

3. The Spirit of Wisdom, the Spirit of Understanding, the Spirit of Counsel, the Spirit of Power, the Spirit of Knowledge, the Spirit of Righteousness, and the Spirit of Divine Awfulness.

4. All these are coequal and coeternal.

5. Each has the nature of the whole in itself: and each is a perfect entity.

6. And the brightness of their manifestation shineth forth from the midst of each, as wheel within wheel, encircling the White Throne of the Invisible Trinity in Unity.

7. These are the Divine fires which burn before the presence of God: which proceed from the Spirit, and are one with the Spirit.

8. He is divided, yet not diminished: He is All, and He is One.

9. For the Spirit of God is a flame of fire which the Word of God divideth into many: yet the original flame is not decreased, nor the power thereof nor the brightness thereof lessened.

10. Thou mayest light many lamps from the flame of one; yet thou dost in nothing diminish that first flame.

11. Now the Spirit of God is expressed by the Word of God, which is 'Adonai.

12. For without the Word the Will could have had no utterance.

13. Thus the Divine Will divided the Spirit of God, and the seven fires went forth the bosom of God, and became seven spiritual entities.

14. They went forth into the Divine Substance, which is the substance of all that is.

15. Now the Divine Substance is the great deep : that is the first protoplasma.

16. She encircles and embraces all things, and of Her are dimension, and form, and appearance.

17. Her veil is the astral fluid ; She is the soul of individuals and the receptacle of the Divine nucleus.

18. Now the Divine Substance is not matter, but She is matter in its potential essence.

19. She is the manifestation of personality, enclosing the Divine nucleus.

20. There are some entities which remain for ever invisible and intangible, being constituted only of two elements, that is of spirit and of soul.

21. These are fluidic beings, changing their external forms according to the will of the Spirit which they have received.

22. They are persons, because the plasmic substance which envelops the spirit of each, hinders the intimate union of that spirit with other spirit.

23. Spirit alone is diffuse, and the naked flame is liable to fuse with other flames.

24. But the flame which is enclosed in substance has become an indiffusible personality.

25. Other entities there are which are visible and tangible to material sense.

26. For the Divine Substance which encloses the spirit of each, coagulates exteriorly and becomes matter in the outermost.

27. So that the entity is composed of spirit, soul, and corporeal appearance.

28. The outermost has become coagulate; its inner content is fluid substance; its innermost is spirit.

29. The innermost is intangible light, which is the first generation; manifest by the Will of God through the Word of God.

30. The fluid medium is the firmament, which the Will of God divided from out of the great deep.

31. And the outermost is the dry earth, which is matter; which the Will of God causeth to appear by the gathering together of the waters, that is of the first protoplasma.

32. As of the greater, so also of the lesser.

33. This is the great secret; it is the mystery of generation.

34. Now of these two kinds of entities, invisible and visible, there are innumerable varieties and orders, having different functions, consistence, form, and tinctures, and dimension.

35. There are thrones, and dominions, and principalities, and powers.

36. There are Christs, and prophets, and saints, and congregations of the elect.

37. And concerning these the Spirit shall give you discernment hereafter.

No. XI.

EPSILON, OR THE FIRST OF THE GODS. E

Proem.

MANY are the thrones which the Holy Spirit of Elohim hath vivified.

2. They are centres of systems, bonds of graces, trees of life, suns of many worlds.

3. And the colour of them is the colour of the ruby and of the fire ; and their name is, in the Hebrew, Uriel, and in the Greek, Phoibos, the Bright One of God.

4. To whom are committed the dominion of the highest sphere, and the demonstration of the reason of all things which are manifest.

5. The Spirit of whose being is the Spirit of Wisdom, which is the first of the holy Seven.

6. Now, He—the angel of the sun—is not the Spirit of Wisdom, but the brightness of the glory thereof, and the express image of the selfsame spirit.

7. He is the first of the Gods, and his praise is great, and his works are wonderful, and his throne is in the midst of heaven.

8. He is that light which Adonai created on the first day.

9. And before his face Python the mighty serpent fell from heaven, to make his dwelling in the caverns and in the secret places of earth.

Hymn to Phoibos.

1. Strong art thou and adorable, Phoibos Apollo, who bearest life and healing on thy wings, who crownest the year with thy bounty, and givest the spirit of thy divinity to the fruits and precious things of all the worlds.

2. Where were the bread of the initiation of the Sons of God, except thou bring the corn to ear ; or the wine of their mystical chalice, except thou bless the vintage ?

3. Many are the angels who serve in the courts of the spheres of heaven : but thou, Master of Light and of Life, art followed by the Christs of God.

4. And thy sign is the sign of the Son of Man in heaven, and of the Just made perfect ;

5. Whose path is as a shining light, shining more and more unto the innermost glory of the day of the Lord God.

6. Thy banner is blood-red, and thy symbol is a milk-white lamb, and thy crown is of pure gold.

7. They who reign with thee are the Hierophants of the celestial mysteries ; for their will is the will of God, and they know as they are known.

8. These are the sons of the innermost sphere ; the Saviours of men, the Anointed of God.

9. And their name is Christ Jesus, in the day of their initiation.

10. And before them every knee shall bow, of things in heaven and of things on earth.

11. They are come out of great tribulation, and are set down for ever at the right hand of God.

12. And the Lamb, which is in the midst of the seven spheres, shall give them to drink of the river of living water.

13. And they shall eat of the tree of life, which is in the centre of the garden of the kingdom of God.

14. These are thine, O Mighty Master of Light; and this is the dominion which the Word of God appointed thee in the beginning:

15. In the day when God created the light of all the worlds, and divided the light from the darkness.

16. And God called the light Phoibos, and the darkness God called Python.

17. Now the darkness was before the light, as the night forerunneth the dawn.

18. These are the evening and the morning of the first cycle of the Mysteries.

19. And the glory of that cycle is as the glory of seven days; and they who dwell therein are seven times refined;

20. Who have purged the garment of the flesh in the living waters;

21. And have transmuted both body and soul into spirit, and are become pure virgins.

22. For they were constrained by love to abandon the outer elements, and to seek the innermost which is undivided, even the Wisdom of God.

23. And Wisdom and Love are One.

No. XII.

ZETA, OR THE SECOND OF THE GODS.

PART I.

Proem.

AND the Spirit of Wisdom gave counsel, whose is the angel of the innermost sphere, the brightest of the sons of heaven.

2. Lord Adonai, who createst, remember the souls beneath Thine altar.

3. And put a firmament between them and Thee, to divide the upper from the nether, and the inner from the without.

4. And whereas there hath been but one, let there henceforth be twain, the form and the substance, the apparent and the real ;

5. That they who are bound may remain in the outer element.

6. But to me Thou committest thine only begotten, who shall enter within the veil.

7. And God made a firmament in the midst of all being, and divided the spirit from the body.

8. And the firmament is the gate of the kingdom of heaven.

9. And God gave the keys thereof to the angel of the second sphere, whose spirit is the Spirit of Understanding.

10. He is Hermes, the mediator, for he mediates between the outer and the inner.

11. He is the transmuter and the healer, Raphael the physician of souls.

12. There is no riddle he shall not solve for thee, nor any solid he shall not melt, nor any wall he shall not pass through.

13. Many are his states and his aspects; his weight is as lead, he runneth like water, he is light as the mist of dawn.

14. Yet he is as a rock between earth and heaven, and the Lord God shall build his Church thereon ; F

15. As a city upon a mountain of stone, whose windows look forth on either side.

16. And upon the left are the kingdoms of the world and the shapes of illusion ; and upon the right are the heights of heaven and the kingdom of spirit.

17. And to him are committed the keys of the invisible, and of the Holy of Holies within the veil.

18. Whatsoever soul he shall bind, shall be bound in the outer and the nether.

19. And whatsoever soul he shall loose, shall be loosed in the inner and the upper.

20. He shutteth and no man openeth; he setteth free and none shall bind again.

21. And his number is the number of twain ; he is the angel of the twofold states.

22. And the waters below and above the firmament, are the evening and the morning of the second day. G

Hymn to Hermes.

1. As a moving light between heaven and earth ;
as a white cloud assuming many shapes ;

2. He descends and rises, he guides and illumines,
he transmutes himself from small to great, from
bright to shadowy, from the opaque image to the
diaphanous mist.

3. Star of the East conducting the Magi : cloud
from whose midst the holy voice speaketh : by day
a pillar of vapour, by night a shining flame.

4. I behold thee, Hermes, Son of God, slayer of
Argus,[H] archangel, who bearest the rod of knowledge,
by which all things in heaven or on earth are
measured.

5. Double serpents entwine it, because as serpents
they must be wise who desire God.[1]

6. And upon thy feet are living wings, bearing
thee fearless through space and over the abyss of
darkness ; because they must be without dread to
dare the void and the deep, who desire to attain and
to achieve.

7. Upon thy side thou wearest a sword of a single
stone, two-edged, whose temper resisteth all things.

8. For they who would slay or save must be armed
with a strong and perfect will, defying and penetrating with no uncertain force.

9. This is Herpe, the sword which destroyeth
demons ; by whose aid the hero overcometh, and
the saviour is able to deliver.

10. Except thou bind it upon thy thigh thou shalt

be overborne, and blades of mortal making shall prevail against thee.

11. Nor is this all thine equipment, Son of God ; the covering of darkness is upon thine head, and none is able to strike thee.

12. This is the magic hat, brought from Hades, the region of silence, where they are who speak not.

13. He who bears the world on his shoulders shall give it to thee, lest the world fall on thee, and thou be ground into powder. J

14. For he who has perfect wisdom and knowledge, he whose steps are without fear, and whose will is single and all-pervading ;

15. Even he must also know how to keep the divine secret, and not to expose the holy mysteries of God to the senses of the wicked.

16. Keep a bridle upon thy lips, and cover thy head in the day of battle.

17. These are the four excellent things,—the rod, the wings, the sword, and the hat.

18. Knowledge, which thou must gain with labour: the spirit of holy boldness, which cometh by faith in God ; a mighty will, and a complete discretion.

19. He who discovers[1] the holy mysteries is lost.

20. Go thy way in silence, and see thou tell no man.

---

[1] *I.e.*, uncovers, or discloses, to profane eyes.

PART 2.

An Exhortation of Hermes to his Neophytes.

1. He whose adversaries fight with weapons of steel, must himself be armed in like manner, if he would not be ignominiously slain or save himself by flight.

2. And not only so, but forasmuch as his adversaries may be many, while he is only one; it is even necessary that the steel he carries be of purer temper and of more subtle point and contrivance than theirs.

3. I, Hermes, would arm you with such, that bearing a blade with a double edge, ye may be able to withstand in the evil hour.

4. For it is written that the tree of life is guarded by a sword which turneth every way.

5. Therefore I would have you armed both with a perfect philosophy and with the power of the divine life.

6. And first the knowledge; that you and they who hear you may know the reason of the faith which is in you.

7. But knowledge cannot prevail alone, and ye are not yet perfected.

8. When the fulness of the time shall come, I will add unto you the power of the divine life.

9. It is the life of contemplation, of fasting, of obedience, and of resistance.

10. And afterwards the chrism, the power, and the glory. But these are not yet.

11. Meanwhile remain together and perfect your philosophy.

12. Boast not, and be not lifted up; for all things are God's, and ye are in God, and God in you.

13. But when the word shall come to you, be ready to obey.

14. There is but one way to power, and it is the way of obedience.[1]

15. Call no man your master or king upon the earth, lest ye forsake the spirit for the form and become idolaters.

16. He who is indeed spiritual, and transformed into the divine image, desires a spiritual king.

17. Purify your bodies, and eat no dead thing that has looked with living eyes upon the light of Heaven.

18. For the eye is the symbol of brotherhood among you. Sight is the mystical sense.

19. Let no man take the life of his brother to feed withal his own.

20. But slay only such as are evil; in the name of the Lord.

21. They are miserably deceived who expect eternal life, and restrain not their hands from blood and death.

22. They are miserably deceived who look for wives from on high, and have not yet attained their manhood.

23. Despise not the gift of knowledge; and make not spiritual eunuchs of yourselves.

---

[1] At this point the seeress was shown a garland of fig-leaves, the symbol of Hermes. For its meaning see pp. 38-41, and 242, 243.

24. For Adam was first formed, then Eve.

25. Ye are twain, the man with the woman, and she with him, neither man nor woman, but one creature.

26. And the kingdom of God is within you. ᴷ

No. XIII.

ETA, OR (MYSTICALLY) THE THIRD OF THE GODS. ᴸ

PART I.

Proem.

THE mystery of thine orbit, O Earth, and the secret of the work of the third day ;

2. Which the wise of old knew not, for the Lord God withheld them.

3. The light is as wisdom, the water as understanding, and the dry earth as the force and power of things.

4. Phoibos first, and Hermes next, and last the kingdom of Dionysos.

Hymn to the Planet-God.

(I.)

1. O Father Iacchos ; thou art Lord of the Body, God manifest in the flesh ;

2. Twice born, baptised with fire, quickened by the spirit, instructed in secret things beneath the earth :

3. Who wearest the horns of the ram, who ridest

upon an ass, whose symbol is the vine, and the new wine thy blood ;

4. Whose Father is the Lord God of Hosts ; whose Mother is the daughter of the King.^M

5. Evoi, Iacchos, Lord of initiation ; for by means of the body is the soul initiated :

6. By birth, by marriage, by virginity, by sleep, by waking, and by death :

7. By fasting and vigil, by dreams and penance, by joy, and by weariness of the flesh.

8. The body is the chamber of ordeal : therein is the soul of man tried.

9. Thine initiates, O Master, are they who come out of great tribulation, whose robes are washed in the blood of the vine.

10. Give me to drink of the wine of thy cup, that I may live for evermore :

11. And to eat of the bread whose grain cometh up from the earth, as the corn in the ear.

12. Yea; for the body in which man is redeemed, is of the earth ; it is broken upon the cross ; cut down by the sickle ; crushed between grindstones.

13. For by the suffering of the outer, is the inner set free.

14. Therefore the body which thou givest is meat indeed, and the word of thy blood is drink indeed.

15. For man shall live by the word of God.

16. Evoi, Father Iacchos : bind thy Church to the vine, and her elect to the choice vine.

17. And let them wash their garments in wine, and their vesture in the blood of grapes.

(2.)

18. Evoi, Iacchos: Lord of the body, and of the house whose symbol is the fig;

19. Whereof the image is the figure of the matrix, and the leaf as a man's hand: whose stems bring forth milk.

20. For the Woman is the mother of the living; and the crown and perfection of humanity.

21. Her body is the highest step in the ladder of incarnation,

22. Which leadeth from earth to Heaven; upon which the spirits of God ascend and descend.

23. Thou art not perfected, O soul, that hast not known womanhood.

24. Evoi, Iacchos: for the day cometh wherein thy sons shall eat of the fruit of the fig: yea, the vine shall yield new grapes; and the fig-tree shall be no more barren.

25. For the interpretation of hidden things is at hand; and men shall eat of the precious fruits of God.

26. They shall eat manna from heaven; and shall drink of the river of Salem.

27. The Lord maketh all things new: He taketh away the letter to establish the spirit.

28. Then spakest thou with veiled face, in parable and dark saying: for the time of figs was not yet.

29. And they who came unto the tree of life sought fruit thereon and found it not.

30. And from thenceforth until now hath no man eaten of the fruit of that tree.

31. But now is the gospel of interpretation come, and the kingdom of the Mother of God.

32. Evoi, Iacchos, Lord of the body; who art crowned with the vine and with the fig.

33. For as the fig containeth many perfect fruits in itself, so the house of man containeth many spirits.

34. Within thee, O man, is the universe; the thrones of all the Gods are in thy temple.

35. I have said unto men, Ye are Gods; ye are all in the image of the Most High.

36. No man can know God unless he first understand himself.

37. God is nothing that man is not.

38. What man is, that God is likewise.

39. As God is at the heart of the outer world, so also is God at the heart of the world within thee.

40. When the God within thee shall be wholly united to the God without, then shalt thou be one with the Most High.

41. Thy will shall be God's will, and the Son shall be as the Father.

42. Thou art ruler of a world, O man; thy name is legion; thou hast many under thee.

43. Thou sayest to this one, Go, and he goeth; and to another, Come, and he cometh; and to another, Do this, and he doeth it.

44. What thou knowest is told thee from within; what thou workest is worked from within.

45. When thou prayest thou invokest the God within thee; and from the God within thee thou receivest thy good things.

46. Thy manifestations are inward ; and the spirits which speak unto thee are of thine own kingdom.

47. And the spirit which is greatest in thy kingdom, the same is thy Master and thy Lord.

48. Let thy Master be the Christ of God, whose Father is the Lord Iacchos. [N]

49. And Christ shall be thy lover and the saviour of thy body ; [O] yea, He shall be thy Lord God, and thou shalt adore Him.

50. But if thou wilt not, then a stronger than thou art shall bind thee, and spoil thine house and thy goods.

51. An uncleanly temple shalt thou be ; the hold of all manner of strife and evil beasts.

52. For a man's foes are of his own household.

53. But scourge thou thence the money-changers and the merchants, lest the house of thy prayer become unto thee a den of thieves.

(3.)

54. Evoi, Father Iacchos : Lord of the thyrsos and of the pine-cone.

55. As are the involutions of the leaves of the cone, so is the spiral of generation,—the progress and passing-through of the soul,

56. From the lower to the higher ; from the coarse to the fine ; from the base to the apex ;

57. From the outer to the inner ; yea, from the dust of the ground to the throne of the Most High.

(4.)

58. Evoi, Io Nysæe : God of the garden and of the tree bearing fruit.

59. The dry land is thine, and all the beauty of earth ; the vineyard, the garland, and the valleys of corn.

60. The forests, the secrets of the springs ; the hidden wells, and the treasures of the caverns.

61. The harvest, the dance, and the festival ; the snows of winter, and the icy winds of death.

62. Yea, Lord Iacchos ; who girdest destruction with promise and graftest comeliness upon ruin.

63. As the green ivy covereth the blasted tree, and the waste places of earth where no grass groweth ;

64. So thy touch giveth life and hope and meaning to decay.

65. Whoso understandeth thy mysteries, O Lord of the Ivy, hath overcome Death and the fear thereof.

(5.)

66. Evoi, Father Iacchos, Lord God of Egypt : initiate thy servants in the halls of thy Temple ;

67. Upon whose walls are the forms of every creature : of every beast of the earth, and of every fowl of the air ;

68. The lynx, and the lion, and the bull : the ibis and the serpent : the scorpion and every flying thing.

69. And the columns thereof are human shapes ; having the heads of eagles and the hoofs of the ox.

70. All these are of thy kingdom : they are the chambers of ordeal, and the houses of the initiation of the soul.

71. For the soul passeth from form to form ; and the mansions of her pilgrimage are manifold.

72. Thou callest her from the deep, and from the secret places of the earth ; from the dust of the ground, and from the herb of the field.

73. Thou coverest her nakedness with an apron of fig-leaves ; thou clothest her with the skins of beasts.

74. Thou art from of old, O soul of man ; yea, thou art from the everlasting.

75. Thou puttest off thy bodies as raiment ; and as vesture dost thou fold them up.

76. They perish, but thou remainest : the wind rendeth and scattereth them ; and the place of them shall no more be known.

77. For the wind is the Spirit of God in man, which bloweth where it listeth, and thou hearest the sound thereof, but canst not tell whence it cometh, nor whither it shall go.

78. Even so is the spirit of man, which cometh from afar off and tarrieth not, but passeth away to a place thou knowest not.

(6.)

79. Evoi, Iacchos, Lord of the Sphinx : who linkest the lowest to the highest ; the loins of the wild beast to the head and breast of the woman.

80. Thou holdest the chalice of divination : all the forms of nature are reflected therein.

81. Thou turnest man to destruction : then thou sayest, Come again, ye children of my hand.

82. Yea, blessed and holy art thou, O Master of Earth : Lord of the cross and the tree of salvation.

83. Vine of God, whose blood redeemeth ; bread of heaven, broken on the altar of death.

84. There is corn in Egypt ; go thou down into her, O my soul, with joy.

85. For in the kingdom of the body thou shalt eat the bread of thine initiation.

86. But beware lest thou become subject to the flesh, and a bond-slave in the land of thy sojourn.

87. Serve not the idols of Egypt ; and let not the senses be thy taskmasters.

88. For they will bow thy neck to their yoke ; they will bitterly oppress the Israel of God.

89. An evil time shall come upon thee ; and the Lord shall smite Egypt with plagues for thy sake.

90. Thy body shall be broken on the wheel of God ; thy flesh shall see trouble and the worm.

91. Thy house shall be smitten with grievous plagues ; blood, and pestilence, and great darkness ; fire shall devour thy goods ; and thou shalt be a prey to the locust and creeping thing.

92. Thy glory shall be brought down to the dust ; hail and storm shall smite thine harvest ; yea, thy beloved and thy first-born shall the hand of the Lord destroy ;

93. Until the body let the soul go free ; that she may serve the Lord God.

94. Arise in the night, O soul, and fly, lest thou be consumed in Egypt.

95. The angel of the understanding shall know thee for his elect, if thou offer unto God a reasonable faith.

96. Savour thy reason with learning, with labour, and with obedience.

97. Let the rod of thy desire be in thy right hand; put the sandals of Hermes on thy feet; and gird thy loins with strength.

98. Then shalt thou pass through the waters of cleansing, which is the first death in the body.

99. The waters shall be a wall unto thee on thy right hand and on thy left.

100. And Hermes the redeemer shall go before thee; for he is thy cloud of darkness by day, and thy pillar of fire by night.

101. All the horsemen of Egypt and the chariots thereof; her princes, her counsellors, and her mighty men:

102. These shall pursue thee, O soul, that fliest; and shall seek to bring thee back into bondage.

103. Fly for thy life; fear not the deep; stretch out thy rod over the sea; and lift thy desire unto God.

104. Thou hast learnt wisdom in Egypt; thou hast spoiled the Egyptians; thou hast carried away their fine gold and their precious things.

105. Thou hast enriched thyself in the body; but the body shall not hold thee; neither shall the waters of the deep swallow thee up.

106. Thou shalt wash thy robes in the sea of re-

generation ; the blood of atonement shall redeem thee to God.

107. This is thy chrism and anointing, O soul ; this is the first death ; thou art the Israel of the Lord,

108. Who hath redeemed thee from the dominion of the body, and hath called thee from the grave, and from the house of bondage,

109. Unto the way of the Cross, and to the path in the midst of the wilderness ;

110. Where are the adder and the serpent, the mirage and the burning sand.

111. For the feet of the saint are set in the way of the desert.

112. But be thou of good courage, and fail thou not ; then shall thy raiment endure, and thy sandals shall not wax old upon thee.

113. And thy desire shall heal thy diseases ; it shall bring streams for thee out of the stony rock ; it shall lead thee to Paradise.

114. Evoi, Father Iacchos, Jehovah-Nissi ; Lord of the garden and of the vineyard ;

115. Initiator and lawgiver ; God of the cloud and of the mount.

116. Evoi, Father Iacchos ; out of Egypt hast thou called thy Son.

PART 2.

Hymns to the Elemental Divinities.

(a.)

To Hephaistos.

1. The spirits of the elements bear thee company, Lord Iacchos, whose wheels encompass thy planet, who hold the four corners thereof.

2. Hephaistos the Fire-King, whose symbol is the red lion, Lord of the serpent, the flame, and of the secret parts of the earth;

3. Whose veins are full of fire, whose breath is destruction and burning, whose finger maketh the hills to smoke.

4. Ah! beware how thou invoke him; as a lion he devoureth; he rendeth and swalloweth as a furious beast of prey.

5. He purifieth and layeth waste; the land is as the Garden of Eden before him, and behind him a desolate wilderness.

6. He commandeth the inmost zone of things; his hammer is the lightning, and his anvil the load-stone.

7. He maketh all bodies therewith, he fuseth and deviseth; whether in the small or in the great, whether in the outer or in the inner, before Demeter is Hephaistos.

8. He endoweth all metals with power, and fashioneth all manner of precious amulets.

9. The gold of the womb of earth is his, the mer-

cury, and the iron of the mine, the sulphur, the onyx, and the crystal.

10. All his galleries are luminous with mirrors of fire, wherein are manifold and wondrous images : the glory of princes, the wealth of nations, yea, the splendour of all the kingdoms of the world.

11. He blindeth and deludeth the eyes of men ; he encompasseth the foolish with illusions, and smiteth the feeble with madness.

12. Even Lucifer, Lord of the Crystal, which hath power to bind the children of earth, for therein are imprisoned the spirits of the fire.

13. Serve not the fire nor the crystal, and be not undone by their sorcery.

14. For the spirits of lust and illusion obey the crystal, and they who love the light of it shall fall under the dominion of Lucifer.

15. Be thou master of the fire, and command it ; let not the cloven tongue of the serpent beguile thee; neither barter thy liberty for the fruit of enchantment.

16. For the fire shall be quenched by the water, and the water shall be resolved into spirit.

17. But if the fire consume thy soul, it shall be scattered abroad as ashes, and return to the dust of the earth.

18. For it is fire that tries every man's work, and purifies the substance of all souls.

19. By fire is the initiate baptised, by fire the oblation is salted ; and the flame shall devour the dross of the crucible.

20. That which endureth unto the end, the same shall be saved.

21. Therefore be praised, Hephaistos, thou and thy wheel; be praised, O searching and purgatorial Fire!

(β.)

Hymn to Demeter.

1. And thou, Demeter, fair Earth-Mother, whose bosom the patient ox treadeth, whose hands are full of plenty and blessing.

2. Angel of the crucible, guardian of the dead, who makest and unmakest, who combinest and dissolvest, who bringest forth life out of death, and transformest all bodies.

3. They are sown as seed in thy furrows; they are buried therein, as the droppings of the ripened ear; from thy womb they came forth, and to thee they return, O Mother of birth and of sleep!

4. Who makest the volatile to be fixed, and the real to be apparent, whether in the great or the small, whether in the outer or the inner.

5. Who yokest the cattle of the field to thy plough, for thy dominion is of the field, O daughter of Time; thou bindest not the sons of the air and the sea.

6. But to the gross thou art gross, and to the subtle thou art subtle.

7. Be praised, Demeter, cunning and multiform alchemist; be praised,—thou and thy wheel, O fruitful Spirit of Earth!

(γ.)

Hymn to Poseidon.

1. And Poseidon, Lord of the Deep, Master of the substance of all creatures, who weareth the face of an angel, for he is the Father of Souls.[P]

2. His brow is dark with storms, his voice is as the thunder of cataracts in the mountains; he is subtle, and swift, and strong; he is mightier than all the children of earth.

3. All things are of the sea-salt, for without salt matter is not, whether of the outer or of the inner, whether of the small or of the great.

4. Behold the manifold waves of the sea, which rise and sink, which break and are lost, and follow each other continually; even as these are the transmutations of the soul.

5. For the soul is one substance, as is the water of the deep, whose waves thou canst not number, neither tell their shapes, for the form of them passeth away; even as these are the incarnations of the soul.

6. And the secret of Thetis is the mystery of the Metamorphosis.

7. Out of the sea the horse ariseth; strength and intelligence are begotten of the deep.

8. She is the mother of Avatârs, and her cup is the chalice of bitterness: whoso drinketh thereof shall taste of power and knowledge, and of tears of salt.

9. Be thou praised, O Poseidon, thou and thy wheel; be praised, O chrism of the soul, mighty and variable Spirit of the Sea!

(δ.)

Hymn to Pallas Athena.

1. And thou, Athena, blue-eyed virgin, Mistress of the Air, eagle-headed, who givest to all bodies the breath of life:

2. Immaculate mother of the word of prophecy, symbol of the holy essence, goddess of the ægis and of the spear:

3. Spirit of the whirlwind, secret breather of wisdom, fortifier of the soul, inspirer of armies:

4. Shining maid, by whose spear we vanquish, for interior wisdom thrusteth all things through; by whose shield we are covered, for interior purity preserveth from all contagion.

5. By thine aid, O Athena, strong and undefiled, by thine aid the hero overcometh in the battle.

6. By thine aid, O armed and winged wisdom, thy servant shall smite the lust of the world.

7. Upon whose beauty, whoso looketh, is changed into stone; who feedeth upon the souls of men. Q

8. Be praised, O Athena, thou and thy wheel; be praised in the great and the small, in the outer and the inner, invisible and immaculate Spirit of Life!

(ε.)

Epode.

1. These are the four great Genii, which are the angels of the Earth, the spirits of the elements of the macrocosm and the microcosm.

These are the fourfold Sphinx of the four states,—of the flesh, of the intermediary, of the human, and of the divine.

Of the house of bondage in the land of Egypt;

Of the ark of the covenant in the wilderness;

Of the gate and the tree of Eden;

Of the celestial chariot and the throne of Adonai.

And the wheels of their fourfold kingdom encircle the whole earth; and are full within and without of the eyes of life. R

No. XIV.

THETA, OR (MYSTICALLY) THE FOURTH OF THE GODS. L

PART I.

The Hymn of Aphrodite.[1]

(1.)

I AM the dawn, daughter of heaven and of the deep: the sea-mist covers my beauty with a veil of tremulous light.

2. I am Aphrodite, the sister of Phoibos, opener of heaven's gates, the beginning of wisdom, the herald of the perfect day.

3. Long had darkness covered the deep: the soul of all things slumbered: the valleys were filled with shadows: only the mountains and the stars held commune together.

[1] Home, received in sleep. September 19, 1884.

4. There was no light on the ways of the earth: the rolling world moved outward on her axe: gloom and mystery shrouded the faces of the Gods.

5. Then from out the deep I arose, dispeller of night: the firmament of heaven kindled with joy beholding me.

6. The secrets of the waters were revealed: the eyes of Zeus looked down into the heart thereof.

7. Ruddy as wine were the depths: the raiment of earth was transfigured; as one arising from the dead She arose, full of favour and grace.

(2.)

8. Of God and the soul is love born: in the silence of twilight; in the mystery of sleep.

9. In the fourth dimension of space; in the womb of the heavenly principle; in the heart of the man of God;—there is love enshrined.

10. Yea, I am before all things: desire is born of me: I impel the springs of life inward unto God: by me the earth and heavens are drawn together.

11. But I am hidden until the time of the day's appearing: I lie beneath the waters of the sea, in the deeps of the soul: the bird of night seeth me not, the herds in the valleys, nor the wild goat in the cleft of the hill.

12. As the fishes of the sea am I covered: I am secret and veiled from sight as the children of the deep.

13. That which is occult hath the fish for a symbol; for the fish is hidden in darkness and silence: he

knoweth the secret places of the earth, and the springs of the hollow sea.

14. Even so love reacheth to the uttermost : so find I the secrets of all things ; having my beginning and my end in the Wisdom of God.

15. The Spirit of Counsel is begotten in the soul ; even as the fish in the bosom of the waters.

16. From the sanctuary of the deep love ariseth : salvation is of the sea.

(3.)

17. I am the crown of manifold births and deaths : I am the interpreter of mysteries and the enlightener of souls.

18. In the elements of the body is love imprisoned : lying asleep in the caves of Iacchos ; in the crib of the oxen of Demeter. S

19. But when the day-star of the soul ariseth over the earth, then is the epiphany of love.

20. Therefore until the labour of the third day be fulfilled, the light of love is unmanifest.

21. Then shall I unlock the gates of dawn ; and the glory of God shall ascend before the eyes of men.

(4.)

22. The secret of the angel Anael is at the heart of the world : the "Song of God" is the sound of the stars in their courses.

23. O love, thou art the latent heat of the earth ; the strength of the wine ; the joy of the orchard and the cornfield : thou art the spirit of song and laughter, and of the desire of life.

R

24. By thee, O goddess, pure-eyed and golden, the sun and the moon are revealed : love is the counsellor of heaven.

25. Cloud and vapour melt before thee : thou unveilest to earth the rulers of the immeasurable skies.

26. Thou makest all things luminous : thou discoverest all deeps ;

27. From the womb of the sea to the heights of heaven ; from the shadowy abyss to the throne of the Lord.

28. Thy beloved is as a ring-dove, wearing the ensign of the spirit, and knowing the secrets thereof.

29. Fly, fly, O Dove ; the time of spring cometh ; in the far east the dawn ariseth ; she hath a message for thee to bear from earth to heaven ! T

PART 2.

A Discourse oj the Communion of Soules, and of the Uses of Love between Creature and Creature : being Part of the Goldene Booke of Venus. [1]

1. Herein is Love's Secret, and the Mysterie of the Communion of Saintes.

2. Love redeemeth, Love lifteth up, Love · enlighteneth, Love advanceth Soules.

---

[1] Printed as read in a book in German text, found in a chamber purporting to be the laboratory of William Lilly, the astrologer (17th century), to which the seeress had been introduced by her genius in sleep for the purpose of having her horoscope told. Failing to recover the whole of the poem on the first attempt to write it down, she sought and obtained access to the book again on the following night.

3. Love dissolveth not, neither forgetteth ; for she is of the Soule and hath everlasting Remembrance.

4. Verilie Love is doubly blessed; for She enricheth both Giver and Receiver.

5. Thou who lovest givest of thyself to thy Beloved, and he is dowered withal.

6. And if any Creature whom thou lovest suffereth Death and departeth from thee ;

7. Fain wouldst thou give of thine Heartes Blood to have him live always ; to sweeten the Changes before him, or to lift him to some happie Place.

8. Thou droppest teares on the broken Body of thy Beloved ; thy Desire goeth after him, and thou criest unto his Ghoste,—

9. "O Dearest! would God that I might be with thee where now thou art, and know what now thou doest !

10. "Would God that I might still guard and protect thee ; that I might defend thee from all Pain, and Wrong, and Affliction !

11. "But what Manner of Change is before thee I know not ; neither can mine Eyes follow thy Steppes.

12. "Many are the Lives set before thee, and the Yeares, O Beloved, are long and weary that shall part us !

13. "Shall I knowe thee again when I see thee, and will the Spirit of God say to thee in that day, 'This is thy Beloved?'

14. "O Soule of my Soule! would God I were one with thee, even though it were in death !

15. "Thou hast all of my Love, my Desire, and my

Sorrowe; yea, my Life is mingled with thine, and is gone forth with thee!

16. "Visit me in Dreames; comfort me in the Night-watches; let my Ghoste meet thine in the Land of Shadows and of Sleep!

17. "Every nighte with fervent Longing will I seek thee; Persephone and Slumber shall give me back the Past.

18. "Yea, Death shall not take thee wholly from me; for Part of me is in thee, and where thou goest, Dearest, there my Hearte followeth!"

19. So weepest thou and lamentest, because the Soul thou lovest is taken from thy Sight.

20. And Life seemeth to thee a Bitter Thing; yea, thou cursest the Destiny of all living Creatures.

21. And thou deemest thy Love of no Avail, and thy Teares as idle Droppes.

22. Behold, Love is a Ransome, and the Teares thereof are Prayeres.

23. And if thou have lived purely, thy fervent Desire shall be counted Grace to the Soule of thy Dead.

24. For the burning and continual Prayere of the Juste availeth much.

25. Yea, thy Love shall enfold the Soule which thou lovest; it shall be unto him a wedding Garment and a Vesture of Blessing.

26. The Baptisme of thy Sorrowe shall baptize thy Dead, and he shall rise because of it.

27. Thy Prayeres shall lift him up, and thy Teares shall encompasse his Steppes; thy Love

shall be to him a Light shining upon the upward Waye.

28. And the Angels of God shall say unto him, "O happie Soule, that art so well beloved ; that art made so strong with all these Teares and Sighs.

29. "Praise the Father of Spirits therefor, for this great Love shall save thee many Incarnations.

30. "Thou art advanced thereby ; thou art drawn aloft and carried upward by Cordes of Grace."

31. For in such wise do Soules profit one another and have Communion, and receive and give Blessing, the Departed of the Living, and the Living of the Departed.

32. And so much the more as the Hearte within them is clean, and the Waye of their Intention is innocent in the Sight of God.

33. Yea, the Saint is a strong Redeemer ; the Spirit of God striveth within him.

34. And God withstandeth not God ; for Love and God are One.

35. As the Love of Christ hath Power with the Elect, so hath Power in its degree the Love of a Man for his Friend.

36. Yea, though the Soule beloved be little and mean, a Creature not made in the Likenesse of Men.

37. For in the eyes of Love there is nothing little nor poor, nor unworthy of Prayere.

38. O little Soule, thou art mighty if a Child of God love thee ; yea, poor and simple Soule, thou art possessed of great Riches.

39. Better is thy Portion than the Portion of Kings whom the Curse of the Oppressed pursueth.

40. For as Love is strong₋ to redeem and to advance a Soule, so is Hatred strong to torment and to detain.

41. Blessed is the Soule whom the Juste commemorate before God ; for whom the Poor and the Orphan and the dumb Creature weep.

42. And thou, O Righteous Man, that with burning Love bewailest the Death of the Innocent, whom thou canst not save from the Hands of the Unjuste ;

43. Thou who wouldst freely give of thine own Blood to redeem thy Brother and to loosen the Bonds of his Paine ;

44. Know that in the Hour of thy supreme Desire, God accepteth thine Oblation.

45. And thy Love shall not return unto thee empty ; according to the Greatnesse of her Degree, she shall accomplish thy Will.

46. And thy Sorrowe and Teares, and the Travaile of thy Spirit, shall be Grace and Blessing to the Soule thou wouldst redeem.

47. Count not as lost thy Suffering on behalf of other Soules ; for every Cry is a Prayere, and all Prayere is Power.

48. That thou willest to do is done; thine Intention is united to the Will of Divine Love.

49. Nothing is lost of that which thou layest out for God and for thy Brother.

50. And it is Love alone who redeemeth, and Love hath nothing of her own.

No. XV.

LAMBDA, OR THE LAST OF THE GODS ; U

being the Secret of Satan.

AND on the seventh day there went forth from the presence of God a mighty angel, full of wrath and consuming, and God gave unto him the dominion of the outermost sphere.

2. Eternity brought forth time ; the boundless gave birth to limit ; being descended into generation.

3. As lightning I beheld Satan fall from heaven, splendid in strength and fury.

4. Among the Gods is none like unto Him, into whose hand are committed the kingdoms, the power and the glory of the worlds :

5. Thrones and empires, the dynasties of kings, the fall of nations, the birth of churches, the triumphs of time.

6. They arise and pass, they were and are not ; the sea and the dust and the immense mystery of space devour them.

7. The tramp of armies, the voices of joy and of pain, the cry of the new-born babe, the shout of the warrior mortally smitten.

8. Marriage, divorce, division, violent deaths, martyrdoms, tyrannous ignorances, the impotence of passionate protest, and the mad longing for oblivion :

9. The eyes of the tiger in the jungle, the fang of

the snake, the fœtor of slaughter-houses, the wail of innocent beasts in pain :

10. The innumerable incarnations of spirit, the strife towards manhood, the ceaseless pulse and current of desire :—

11. These are his who beareth all the Gods on his shoulders; ^v who establisheth the pillars of necessity and fate.

12. Many names hath God given him, names of mystery, secret and terrible.

13. God called him Satan the Adversary, because matter opposeth spirit, and time accuseth even the saints of the Lord.

14. And the Destroyer, for his arm breaketh and grindeth to pieces ; wherefore the fear and the dread of him are upon all flesh.

15. And the Avenger, for he is the anger of God ; his breath shall burn up all the souls of the wicked.

16. And the Sifter, for he straineth all things through his sieve, dividing the husk from the grain ; discovering the thoughts of the heart; proving and purifying the spirit of man.

17. And the Deceiver, for he maketh the false appear true, and concealeth the real under the mask of illusion.

18. And the Tempter, for he setteth snares before the feet of the elect : he beguileth with vain shows, and seduceth with enchantments.

19. Blessed are they who withstand his subtlety : they shall be called the Sons of God, and shall enter in at the beautiful gates.

20. For Satan is the doorkeeper of the temple of the King : he standeth in Solomon's porch ; he holdeth the keys of the sanctuary ;

21. That no man may enter therein save the Anointed, having the arcanum of Hermes.

22. For Satan is the Spirit of the Fear of the Lord, which is the beginning of wisdom.

23. He is the devourer of the unwise and the evil : they shall all be meat and drink to him.

24. Whatsoever he devoureth, that shall never more return into being.

25. Fear him, for after he hath killed, he hath power to cast into hell.

26. But he is the servant of the Sons of God, and of the children of light.

27. They shall go before him, and he shall follow the steps of the wise.

28. Stand in awe of him and sin not : speak his name with trembling ; and beseech God daily to deliver thee.

29. For Satan is the magistrate of the justice of God : he beareth the balance and the sword,

30. To execute judgment and vengeance upon all who come short of the commandments of God ; to weigh their works, to measure their desire, and to number their days.

31. For to him are committed weight and measure and number.

32. And all things must pass under the rod and through the balance, and be fathomed by the sounding-lead.

33. Therefore Satan is the minister of God, Lord of the seven mansions of Hades, the angel of the manifest worlds.

34. And God hath put a girdle about his loins, and the name of the girdle is Death.

35. Threefold are its coils, for threefold is the power of Death, dissolving the body, the ghost, and the soul.

36. And that girdle is black within, but where Phoibos strikes it is silver.

37. None of the Gods is girt save Satan, for upon him only is the shame of generation.

38. He hath lost his virginal estate : uncovering heavenly secrets, he hath entered into bondage.

39. He encompasseth with bonds and limits all things which are made : he putteth chains round about the worlds, and determineth their orbits.

40. By him are creation and appearance ; by him birth and transformation ; the day of begetting and the night of death.

41. The glory of Satan is the shadow of the Lord : the throne of Satan is the footstool of Adonai.

42. Twain are the armies of God : in heaven the hosts of Michael ; in the abyss the legions of Satan.

43. These are the unmanifest and the manifest ; the free and the bound ; the virginal and the fallen.

44. And both are the ministers of the Father, fulfilling the word divine.

45. The legions of Satan are the creative emanations, having the shapes of dragons, of Titans, and of elemental gods ;

46. Forsaking the intelligible world,[1] seeking manifestation, renouncing their first estate ;

47. Which were cast out into chaos, neither was their place found any more in heaven.

(2.)

48. Evil is the result of limitation, and Satan is the Lord of limit.

49. He is the father of lies, because matter is the cause of illusion.

50. To understand the secret of the kingdom of God, and to read the riddle of *Maya*, this is to have Satan under foot.

51. He only can put Satan under foot who is released by thought from the bonds of desire.

52. Nature is the allegory of spirit : all that appeareth to the sense is deceit : to know the truth,—this alone shall make men free.

53. For the kingdom of Satan is the house of matter : yea, his mansion is the sepulchre of Golgotha, wherein on the seventh day the Lord lay sleeping, keeping the Sabbath of the unmanifest.

54. For the day of Satan is the night of spirit : the manifestation of the worlds of form is the rest of the worlds informulate.

55. Holy and venerable is the Sabbath of God : blessed and sanctified is the name of the angel of Hades ;

56. Whom the Anointed shall overcome, rising again from the dead on the first day of the week.

[1] Of which the sensible world is the antithesis.

57. For the place of Satan is the bourne of divine impulsion : there is the arrest of the outgoing force ; Luza, the station of pause and slumber :

58. Where Jacob lay down and dreamed, beholding the ladder which reached from earth to heaven.

59. For Jacob is the planetary angel Iacchos, the Lord of the body ;

60. Who hath left his father's house, and is gone out into a far country.

61. Yet is Luza none other than Bethel; the kingdom of Satan is become the kingdom of God and of His Christ.

62. For there the Anointed awakeneth, arising from sleep, and goeth his way rejoicing ;

63. Having seen the vision of God, and beheld the secret of Satan ;

64. Even as the Lord arose from the dead and brake the seal of the sepulchre ;

65. Which is the portal of heaven, Luza, the house of separation, the place of stony sleep ;

66. Where is born the centripetal force, drawing the soul upward and inward to God ;

67. Recalling Existence into Being, resuming the kingdoms of matter in spirit ; [W]

68. Until Satan return unto his first estate, and enter again into the heavenly obedience ;

69. Having fulfilled the will of the Father, and accomplished his holy ministry ;

70. Which was ordained of God before the worlds, for the splendour of the manifest, and for the generation of Christ our Lord ; [X]

71. Who shall judge the quick and the dead, putting all things under his feet ; whose are the dominion, the power, the glory, and the Amen. ᵛ

XVI.

THE SEVEN SPIRITS OF GOD AND THEIR CORRESPONDENCES.

Elohim or Archangels.	*Signification.*	*Gods.*	*Office.*
1. Uriel	= Fire of God.	Phoibos Apollo.	Angel of the Sun.
2. Raphael	= Physician of God.	Hermes.	Angel of Mercury.
3. Anael	= Sweet Song of God.	Aphrodite.	Angel of Venus.
4. Salamiel	= Acquired of God.	Dionysos.	Angel of the Earth.
5. Zacchariel	= Man of God.	Ares.	Angel of Mars.
6. Michael	= Like unto God.	Zeus and Hera.	Angel of Jupiter.
7. Orifiel (or Satan)	= Hour of God.	Kronos.	Angel of Saturn.
Gabriel	= Strength of God.	Artemis or Isis.	Angel of the Moon.

Tincture of Ray.	*The Spirit of*	*Tincture of Ray.*	*The Spirit of*
1. Red.	Wisdom.	6. Purple.	Righteousness.
2. Orange.	Understanding.	7. Violet.	Divine Awe.
3. Yellow.	Counsel.		(Hence Reverence
4. Green.	Power.		and Humility.)
5. Blue.	Knowledge.		

White, being the combination of all the rays, implies full illumination and intuition of God, the symbol of which is the full moon, and is the symbol of initiation. Attaining to this state, the soul is the mystical " Woman clothed with the Sun," of Apoc. xii. 1. Gabriel, the angel of this state, represents the reflective principle of the soul. He is not one of the seven Elohim, but is the complement of them all, being the spirit of all the moons.

No. XVII.

THE MYSTERIES OF THE KINGDOMS OF THE SEVEN SPHERES.

I believe in the Holy Ghost, = The Nous, or Sun, of the microcosm, the Spirit of Wisdom, the ray of whose angel, Phoibos, is the red of the innermost sphere.

Whose seven spirits are as the seven rays of light ;

The Holy Catholic Church, = Hermes, or Peter, the Spirit of Understanding, and rock whereon the true Church is built, the guardian and interpreter of the holy mysteries.

Or, kingdom of heaven within man ;

The Communion of Saints, = Aphrodite, Venus, love, the Spirit of Counsel, or principle of sympathy, harmony, and light, whereby heaven and earth are revealed to each other and drawn together.

Or, the elect ;

The Forgiveness of Sins, = Iacchos, the initiator, Lord of transmigration, whereby alone *Karma* is satisfied and sins wiped out by expiation and repentance. As the Spirit of Power, he represents the force whereby creation and redemption alike are accomplished, the direction only being reversed.

Or, passing-through of souls ;

The Resurrection (which is the redemption) of the body, From material limitations ;	= Ares, or Mars, the war-god, and Spirit of Knowledge, of whom comes contention, at the cost of suffering and death, for the divine knowledge whereby man learns the secret of transmutation, which is the crowning conquest of matter by spirit.
The Life Everlasting ;	= Zeus and Hera, rulers of heaven, the dual Spirit of Righteousness or godliness, which is justice, or the perfect balance, and the secret of eternal generation.
And the Amen, Or, final consummation.	= Saturn, or Satan, the Spirit of the Fear of the Lord, being the angel—unfallen—of the outermost sphere, and keeper of the boundary of the divine kingdom, within which is the perfection, and without which, the negation of being.

[The man fully regenerate needs no "moon" to reflect to him the "sun." Wherefore Gabriel, having no function to fulfil in the perfected kosmos, is indrawn, and does not appear in these mysteries. See Part I., No. XIV. part 2, "Concerning the Genius."]

PART THE THIRD.

CONCERNING THE DIVINE IMAGE

OR

THE VISION OF ADONAI.

S

CONCERNING THE DIVINE IMAGE, OR THE VISION OF ADONAI.

[OWING at once to the sanctity and the unpronounceability of the *Tetragrammaton*, or word of four letters which in the Hebrew constitutes the name Jehovah, the Hebrews invariably substitute for it in speaking the name Adonai, which in the A. V. is rendered "the Lord." These names are, however, substantially identical, in that they alike imply a duality corresponding to that of the sexes,—a duality which arises, necessarily, from the nature of the function fulfilled by their bearer, which is that of the expression, word, or manifestor of Deity in the dual character of Father-Mother, as expounded in Nos. VII. and VIII. of Part II. ; from which it follows that this Person of the Trinity is, properly, not "Son" merely, but "Son-Daughter." As thus exhibited, the Trinity consists of Father, Mother, and Child, —(respectively energy, substance, and phenomenon),—and represents a mode of the godhead which, logically (not chronologically, time having no relation to the eternal), is antecedent to that of the ecclesiastical Trinity, wherein the "Son" appears as the second person, and the Holy Spirit as the third. For in this aspect, the "Mother" (substance) is merged in the "Father" (energy or will), the two together constituting one person,—the first, and the Son appears as the second, while the third is the Holy Spirit, or divinity in its dynamic or active mode as distinguished from its static or passive mode. Proceeding from the Father-Mother through the Son, and identical in nature with them, the Holy Spirit is, like them, dual, and consists of both energy and substance. For which reason the names and symbols denoting the Holy Spirit are masculine or feminine, according to the aspect or function concerned. On its procession through

the Son the Holy Spirit differentiates into the seven modes or
potencies called the Seven Spirits of God (as described in Nos.
VI., VIII., and X. of Part II.) dividing, like light on its emergence from the prism, into seven rays.   These are the Seven
Spirits of God, the creative Elohim, which, with the three persons
of the Trinity, constitute the ten Sephiroth of the Kabala.
Functions of the Supreme and essential principles in the Divine
nature, they are styled, on entering into manifestation, Gods and
Archangels ; and inasmuch as they are manifold and various as
the spheres and kingdoms of nature, in all of which they are
operative, and comprise grades and distinctions innumerable,
repeating themselves like the notes of the musical scale in many
keys and tones, their names are rather titles of orders than
designations of individuals.   In no case can they be apprehended
of the outer senses, but to souls sufficiently mature and sensitive
they manifest themselves under forms personal and symbolical
of their offices, being both seen and heard of the interior selfhood.   And just as the Rainbow is one, though rainbows are
legion,—inasmuch as all these are manifestations of one and the
same principle inhering in the nature of light,—so is each divinity
one, however multiplied his personality, inasmuch as every
appearance is but a fresh manifestation of one and the same
principle subsisting in the divine nature, and for that reason
subsisting also in every soul that is able to polarise divinity.
Thus is the soul " Mother of God " and also of the Gods, and
" Man is a universe in himself, having the thrones of all the
Gods in his temple."   And of their co-operation is the edification
of the world into the kingdom of God, and of man in the Divine
image, that of Adonai.   Attaining to this image, man has and is
Christ, Christ being the correspondent, equivalent, or counterpart in man, of Adonai in substance.   And, saving Adonai
himself, they are the highest objects of the sensible perception
of the soul.   That Adonai is the highest of all such objects is
because he is the image beheld in the point of the focus formed
by the convergence of all the consciousnesses of the system and
their polarisation to the highest plane.   Beyond him is the
" Invisible Light,"—the " Divine Dark " of the early Christian

mystics,[1]—the boundless sea of infinite wisdom, love, and power, informulate and unmanifest, the universally-diffused divinity; impersonal in the radical sense of the word, but personal in the highest degree in its true sense, that of essential consciousness; and in Adonai taking form and personality in both senses.

The Jehovah or Adonai of the Hebrews is thus no mere "tribal" god, as supposed by writers more learned and ingenious than experienced or percipient, on the strength of the defective presentations of Him in the Hebrew Scriptures; nor is He but a partial aspect only of deity, or a being unreal and imaginary. He is actually the one and supreme divinity, the central, radiant, and pivotal point of the universe—its spiritual sun—the God of Gods, from whom all others proceed, and of whom all others are modes and aspects. And He is this absolutely and indefeasibly, how defective and misleading soever the human conceptions and presentations of Him. And being recognised as such, He is fitly described as a "jealous" God, in that he reprobates the ascription to the low or to a part, of the honour due only to the highest and to the whole; and He is this, not for His own sake, —He cannot suffer loss—but for the sake of those His creatures who, by limiting their ideal of the Divine perfection, withhold themselves from the realisation of their own perfection, and thereby from being made in the Divine image. For what man thinks, that he *is*.

The vision about to be described of Adonai, was received without any previous knowledge on the part of its recipient, either of its possibility, or of its having always been claimed as a recognised fact of mystical experience, the allusions to it in the Bible,[2] although by no means rare, having altogether escaped her recognition as having any real basis in the consciousness.[3]

---

[1] *E.g.*, St Dionysius "the Areopagite."

[2] Ex. xxiv. 9-11 ; Is. vi. 1 ; Ezek. viii. 2 ; Dan, vii. 9, 10; Apoc. iv. ; xx. 11.

[3] The reception of it by myself a few months previously had been similarly independent of knowledge or anticipation, and I had been constrained to maintain an absolute reserve in regard to it. The

On this occasion she had been forewarned of something of un-
usual solemnity as about to occur, and prompted to make
certain ceremonial preparations obviously calculated to impress
the imagination.   The access came upon her while standing by
the open window, gazing at the moon, then close upon the full.[1]
The first effect of the *afflatus* was to cause her to kneel and
pray in a rapt attitude, with her arms extended towards the
sky. It appeared afterwards, that under an access of spiritual
exaltation, she had yielded to a sudden and uncontrollable
impulse to pray that she might be taken to the stars, and shown
all the glory of the universe.   Presently she rose, and after
gazing upwards in ecstasy for a few moments, lowered her eyes,
and, clasping her arms around her head as if to shut out the
view, uttered in tones of wonder, mingled with moans and cries
of anguish, the following tokens of the intolerable splendour of
the vision she had unwittingly invited] :—

" Oh, I see masses, masses of stars ! It makes me
giddy to look at them. O my God, what masses !
Millions and millions ! *Wheels* of planets ![2] O my
God, my God, why didst Thou create ? It was by
Will, all Will, that Thou didst it. Oh ! what might,
what might of Will ! Oh, what gulfs ! what gulfs !
Millions and millions of miles broad and deep !

account in *The Perfect Way* (IX. v.) was written from our joint experiences.   Many of our experiences were thus duplicated, hers, however, far exceeding mine both in number and in fulness of detail.   The
latter, probably, because I always made a point of retaining possession
of the external consciousness, in order to observe and record at the same
time, and not knowing the result of letting myself go altogether.

   [1] It was at Paris, July 23, 1877.

   [2] It was as if there had been suddenly opened to her view a
universe of inter-planetary systems, invisible to the bodily sight ; and
while dazzlingly bright to the spiritual eyes, of a consistency too tenuous
to intercept or refract the solar rays.   A like effect would also be produced by entering the fourth dimension of space, where all things would
be beheld unmodified by distance or any intervening medium.

Hold me—hold me up! I shall sink—I shall sink into the gulfs. I am sick and giddy, as on a billowy sea. I am on a sea, an ocean—the ocean of infinite space. Oh, what depths! what depths! I sink—I fail! I cannot, cannot bear it!

"I shall never come back. I have left my body for ever. I am dying; I believe I am dead. Impossible to return from such a distance! Oh, what colossal forms! They are the angels of the planets. Every planet has its angel standing erect above it. And what beauty—what marvellous beauty! I see Raphael. I see the angel of the earth. He has six wings. He is a god—the god of our planet. I see my genius, who called himself A. Z.; but his name is Salathiel.[1] Oh, how surpassingly beautiful he is! My genius is a male, and his colour is ruby. Yours, Caro,[2] is a female, and sapphire. They are friends— they are the same—not two, but one; and for that reason they have associated us together, and speak of themselves sometimes as *I*, sometimes as *We*. It is the angel of the earth himself that is your genius and mine, Caro. He it was who inspired you, who spoke

[1] " Lent of God." Every divinity has a separate name for each office fulfilled by him. Salathiel thus denotes the angel of the earth in his capacity as head of the order of Genii, in the sense of being the supreme spirit (of the planet) of whom each genius is a manifestation, and into whom they return on the accomplishment of their mission. As the first and last letters of the alphabet, A and Z, correspond to the " Alpha and Omega," in the sense of implying comprehension of the genii of all orders or grades, and consequently all the rays of the spiritual prism.

[2] A spiritual or "initiation" name that had been given to me, as Mary to her. The latter, however, was also one of her own names.

to you.[1] And they call me *Bitterness*. And I see
sorrow—oh, what unending sorrow do I behold!
Sorrow, always sorrow, but never without love. I
shall always have love. How dim is this sphere!
Oh, save me—save me! It is my demon that I am
approaching.   It is Paris—Paris himself, once of
Troy, now of the city that bears his name. He is
floating recumbent. He turns his face towards me.
How beautiful and dark he is! Oh, he has goat's
horns—he has goat's horns! Save me, save me from
him! Ah, he sees me not. I forgot I am invisible.
Now I have passed him.[2]

"I am entering a brighter region now. What
glorious form of womanhood is that, so queenly, so
serene, and endowed with all wisdom? It is Pallas
Athena,—a real personage in the spiritual world!
And yonder is one of whom I have no need to ask.
I am passing through the circle of the Olympians.
It is Aphrodite, mother of love and beauty. O
Aphrodite, spirit of the waters, firstborn of God, how
could I adore thee! And men on earth now deem
the gods and goddesses of Greece mere fables! And I
behold them living and moving in strength and beauty
before me! I see also the genii of all the nations
dwelling serenely in heavenly circles. What crowds
and crowds of gods from India and Egypt! Who

---

[1] The reference here is to an experience of my own, the relation of
which does not fall within the scope of this book.

[2] The reference here is to sundry visitations by which she had been
harassed previous to my joining her in Paris, the cause of which she
thus recognised for the first time, and whom she was wont to call her
demon, using the term in its conventional sense.

are those with the giant muscles? They are Odin
and Thor, and their fellow-gods of Scandinavia. Not
dead and lost; only withdrawn from the world
whereon they sought in vain to stamp their images
for ever.

"Oh, the dazzling, dazzling brightness! Hide me,
hide me from it! I cannot, cannot bear it! It is
agony supreme to look upon. O God! O God!
Thou art slaying me with Thy light. It is the throne
itself, the great white throne of God that I behold!
Oh, what light! what light! It is like an emerald?
a sapphire? No; a diamond. In its midst stands
Deity erect, His right hand raised aloft, and from Him
pours the light of light. Forth from His right hand
streams the universe, projected by the omnipotent
repulsion of His will. Back to His left, which is de-
pressed and set backwards, returns the universe, drawn
by the attraction of His love. Repulsion and attraction, will and love, right and left, these are the
forces, centrifugal and centripetal, male and female
whereby God creates and redeems. Adonai! O
Adonai! Lord God of life, made of the substance of
light, how beautiful art Thou in Thine everlasting
youth! with Thy glowing golden locks, how adorable!
And I had thought of God as elderly and venerable!
As if the Eternal could grow old! And now not as
Man only do I behold Thee! For now Thou art to
me as Woman. Lo, Thou art both. One, and Two
also. And thereby dost Thou produce creation. O
God, O God! why didst Thou create this stupendous existence? Surely, surely, it had been better in

love to have restrained Thy will. It was by will that Thou createdst, by will alone, not by love, was it not? —was it not? I cannot see clearly. A cloud has come between.

"I see Thee now as Woman. Maria is next beside Thee. Thou art Maria. Maria is God. Oh Maria! God as Woman! Thee, Thee I adore! Maria-Aphrodite! Mother! Mother-God!

"They are returning with me now, I think. But I shall never get back. What strange forms! how huge they are! All angels and archangels. Human in form, yet some with eagles' heads. All the planets are inhabited! how innumerable is the variety of forms! O universe of existence, how stupendous is existence! Oh! take me not near the sun; I cannot bear its heat. Already do I feel myself burning. Here is Jupiter! It has nine moons! Yes, nine. Some are exceedingly small. And, oh, how red it is! It has so much iron. And what enormous men and women! There is evil there too. For evil is wherever are matter and limitation. But the people of Jupiter are far better than we on earth. They know much more; they are much wiser. There is less of evil in their planet. Ah! and they have another sense. What is it? No, I cannot describe it. I cannot tell what it is. It differs from any of the others. We have nothing like it. I cannot get back yet. I believe I shall never get back. I believe I am dead. It is only my body you are holding. It has grown cold for want of me. Yet I must be approaching. It is growing shallower.

We are passing out of the depths. But I can never wholly return—never—never."

[Her apprehension was not without justification ; for her body was completely torpid, and several hours passed before consciousness was fully restored to it.

It is impossible for anyone who did not witness the intensely dramatic action and emphasis with which these ejaculations were uttered, to form anything like an adequate conception of the sense of reality they conveyed. Able as I was from my own experience above referred to, to follow her in her journey from sphere to sphere to the very highest and inmost, I found it impossible to doubt that the seeress was in the right, when, recalling her recollections, she declared her conviction that what she had beheld was no illusion, but the reality itself of the universe. There was for both of us the same sense of journeying through vast abysses of space and traversing various spheres of being ; and the same conviction that the journey was at once to the centre of one's own and to that of all consciousness.

She described the attitude and expression of Adonai as those of the absolute calmness and repose of the power without effort which is predicable only of the Infinite. Though bearing the aspect of humanity, it was impossible, she felt, to represent the form in fixed outline, and declared that it seemed like a sacrilege to attempt thus to portray it. She nevertheless made the attempt, with the result reproduced below. It represents, however, only the masculine aspect, the impression of the feminine having entirely failed to reach her outer consciousness ; and this had been the case also on the only other occasion on which she had beheld it. (See p. 85.) In this respect our experiences differed. She was most strongly impressed by the masculine, or will, element in Deity ; and I by the feminine, or love, element. In another respect, too, there was a difference. For her the form was that of one standing erect, and though calm, energetic : for me it was that of the "Sitter on the Throne" and wholly reposeful, though similarly engaged in the act of projection and recall. These differences were doubtless due to difference of temperament in the beholders. The soul is a living lens which invests with its own "tincture" the objects beheld by it.]

" Solve et Coagula " (Dissolve and Resume, or Project and Recall).
Ancient Hermetic Formula.

APPENDIX.

APPENDIX.

NOTE A, pages 45, 52, 210, 211, 269, 271.

THE long-standing controversy respecting the meaning of *Nirvâna* has been resolved for us in favour of both the interpretations assigned to it. This is to say that, while it means *extinction*, the extinction implied is of two different kinds. Of these, one, called the celestial Nirvâna, denotes the perfectionment and perpetuation of the essential selfhood of the individual, accompanied by the extinction of the external and phenomenal selfhood. Thus indrawn to his centre, the individual ceases to *ex-ist*, but does not cease to *be*. In other words, he *is*, but is not manifest, the term existence, as opposed to being, implying the standing-forth, or objectivisation, of that which *is*, subjectively. The condition implies the return from matter to substance or spirit.

The "Nirvâna of the Amen," on the contrary, denotes the extinction, not only of the externality of the individual, but of the individual himself; this occurring through the persistent indulgence of a perverse will to the outer and lower, such as to induce a complete deprivation of the inner and higher constituents of man, and so to divest his system of its binding principle as to render not only possible, but inevitable, complete dissolution and disintegration, to the total extinction of the individuality concerned. There is no loss of substance or spirit.

The term *Amen* in this relation signifies consummation or finality.

NOTE B, page 210.

Like the so-called "damnatory" clauses of the "Athanasian Creed," this declaration is simply a solemn recognition, first, of the doctrine that salvation is neither arbitrary nor compulsory, but conditional and optional, the alternative to it being extinction; and, next, of the Credo as a summary of the conditions of salvation. These, it is true, are expressed in terms which, in being symbolical, do not bear their meaning upon the face of them ; but none the less are the conditions themselves so simple and obvious as to be recognisable as self-evident and necessarily true.   That is to say, they represent the steps of a process necessary to be enacted in the soul, and founded in the nature of the soul itself; so that, when understood, the belief in them makes no greater strain upon the faculties than does the belief in any self-evident proposition whatever.   Rather would the difficulty be to disbelieve them.

Wherefore—to state the case in other words—the declaration of the soul's extinction through non-compliance with the conditions herein affirmed to be indispensable to its perpetuation, made by the initiate in the terms of the Credo, is the exact parallel and counterpart of the declaration of the body's extinction through non-compliance with the conditions indispensable to its continuance, made by the physiologist in the terms of his craft.   The language is in each case technical, but the truths it conceals (from the non-initiate) are incontestible ; and so far from their being disbelieved by those who do not understand them, they are invariably acted upon by all—who are of sound mind—to the best of their ability, despite their failure to understand them.   For, alike for soul and body, there is that within man which does believe, and which accordingly does comply with the conditions requisite for his welfare, quite independently of his knowledge of processes and terms spiritual or physiological, and which needs but fair play, and not to be thwarted by his own perverse will, to accomplish his salvation.

Wherefore the declaration in question is no menace, but rather is it a promise,—a promise that when the time comes to understand the process whereby salvation is accomplished, the very fact that it is understood is a token that salvation is accomplished ; for once understood, it can no more be disbelieved than gravitation or any other certainty of the physical world.

Now, to have this understanding is to be "initiated."

NOTE C, page 215.

On the conclusion of this instruction, the better to enable the seeress to comprehend the description given in verses 9 and 16, a vision was given her of two human forms, having their molecules, the one in the order of man regenerate, and the other in the disorder of man un-

regenerate, as on the two sides, A and B, of the fig. below, which represents a combination of the half of each form thus beheld. In the case of
specific organs, the rays represent the magnetic direction of each organ
as a whole, and not that of its constituent molecules, since the orderly
polarisation of these is not to the common centre of the system, but
to the centre of their own particular organ, and only mediately through
this to the common centre.

Similarly, figs. C and D show the physiologic unit or cell—the type
of every kosmical entity—the former in its fully-developed and healthy
state, wherein the protoplasmic contents are pure, and the nucleus and
nucleolus (which correspond to the soul and spirit) fully developed, and
the magnetic poles convergent ; and the latter in a rudimentary and
disorderly condition, with the nucleolus or spirit as yet unpolarised.
The four spheres correspond respectively to the physical, the astral,
the psychic, and the spiritual ; or body, mind, soul, and spirit.

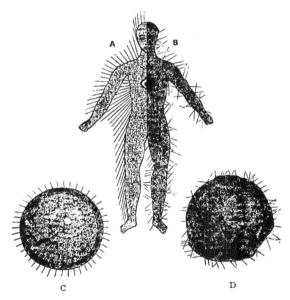

T

NOTE D, page 226.

This must be taken as a poetic rather than as a scientific expression.

NOTE E, page 231.

These Hymns of the Gods were, like all else in the text, received under illumination, occurring chiefly in sleep, over a number of years commencing in 1878. They constitute a synthesis of the Sacred Mysteries of the Egyptians, the Greeks, the Hebrews, and the Christians,—the last three of which were derived from the first, and are substantially identical with it and with each other; and they are expressed in terms derived indifferently from them all.

That they represent, at least in a great measure, a recovery of rituals and formulæ, oral or written, which were actually used in the ancient Mysteries, and of which the writers of the Bible largely availed themselves, was not only positively declared to us, but was indicated by the circumstances under which a considerable portion of them were obtained.   For example, No. XIII., the hymn to Iacchos, the planet-god, was chiefly obtained in dreams, wherein the seeress found herself re-enacting what she felt, and was positively assured, had been a scene in one of her own former existences, when she had chanted it in chorus as one of a body of priests and priestesses making solemn procession through the vast aisles of an Egyptian temple.

Concerning the purpose of this restoration and certain other particulars in relation to the Gods, see the preface and the note on page 193.

NOTE F, page 235.

As is well known to students of occult science, the name of Hermes has from prehistoric times been for the Western World the synonym at once for profound problems and for interpretative insight, his claim to have possessed " the three parts of the knowledge of the whole kosmos " —science, philosophy, and religion—having always been recognised. Whether the name originally denoted some actual man from whom, for his eminence in knowledge, it was transferred to the divinity, or whether it originally denoted the divinity, and was assigned to some man supposedly or really inspired by him, there is no historical evidence to determine.   It is sufficient to know, as an indubitable historical fact, that some of the profoundest of the sages of old claimed

Hermes the divinity as the source of their knowledge, and that the manner of its reception corresponded in all respects with that under which the illuminations in this book were received. It was as the divine principle itself of understanding that he was recognised by the Hermetists in the saying—

" Est in Mercurio quicquid quærunt sapientes ; "[1]

and by the authors of that wondrous compendium of Hebrew transcend-talism, the Kabala, when they declared that "all the mysteries are in Chockmah,"—the *Nous* of the Greeks ; as also by the famous Neopla-tonist, Proklos, when he thus wrote :—

" Hermes, as the messenger of God, reveals to us His paternal Will, and—developing in us the intuition—imparts to us knowledge. The knowledge which descends into the soul from above, excels any that can be attained by the mere exercise of the intellect. Intuition is the operation of the soul. The knowledge received through it from above, descending into the soul, fills it with the perception of the interior causes of things. The Gods announce it by their presence, and by illumination, and enable us to discern the universal order."

For "in the Celestial, all things are Persons ;" and it is as Persons that the divine Principles manifest themselves in and to the soul, being seen and heard of it, when duly receptive and percipient. That the forms under which they manifested themselves to Anna Kingsford were those of Egypt and Greece, was—we were assured—because she had been an initiate of the Greco-Egyptian mysteries, and those forms were indelibly impressed upon her.

Now of all those who have been enlightened by Hermes, the doctrine is identical, and it is the basic doctrine of all sacred scriptures.

The name Hermes, which is Greek, signifies both rock and inter-preter,—that which *stands under* and that which *understands*. And (as stated in " The Perfect Way," i. 20) it was to Hermes as the inspirer and prompter of the confession of Simon, and not to the man, that Jesus addressed the apostrophe, " Thou [the Understanding] art the Peter, or rock, upon which I build my church." Called Peter as the utterer of the confession, Simon has always been claimed as himself the rock of the church. He has also been assigned the office—likewise that of Hermes—of guardian of the mysteries. But he has yet to justify his claim to be the fulfiller of that other function of Hermes,

---

[1] All is in Hermes that the wise seek.

that of being their interpreter. Hitherto, as represented by the church which claims him as its especial patron, he has manifested himself only in his New Testament role—rebuked by Jesus—of the cutter off, not of the opener, of ears.

NOTE G, page 235.

As the Spirit of Understanding it is the function of Hermes to re-cognise and indicate limits and distinctions between things that differ, in whatever department of existence, so that there be no confusion or intrusion. Hence, on the physical plane, he was accounted the guardian of boundaries and landmarks. But though thus discerning and marking limitations, he was not the author of them. That was the function of the angel of the outermost sphere, the " last of the Gods," Saturn or Satan, as explained in Note U.

NOTE H, page 236.

Argus, the monster with a hundred eyes, represents the "power of the stars" over the soul,—the power, that is, of Karma, or the destiny acquired by the soul through its defects of conduct during the unre-generate stages of its existence. As it is for want of understanding, of its own nature and that of existence, that the soul comes thus under bondage, it falls to Hermes, as the angel of the understanding, to rescue the soul by imparting to it the instruction requisite for its perfection-ment. Thus emancipated by Hermes from the trammels of fate, the soul rises superior to all limitations, and, becoming as a " woman clothed with the sun," wears as jewels in her crown the stars over which she has triumphed, each of which thus denotes a spiritual grace or gift acquired in the conflict with materiality. And so, for her, Hermes is said to have slain Argus. For further information on this subject see " The Perfect Way," VII. 27 and IX. 13-17. And for the importance attached by the Bible to the office of Hermes, see the numerous passages cited in the concordance under the various forms of the word *understand*.

NOTE I, page 236.

Serpents when used to denote wisdom are the "seraphs" or rays of the (spiritual) sun, *i.e.*, they are divine emanations. The "serpent of the dust," or of the astral and lower nature, is the obverse of the seraph, and represents cunning rather than wisdom, as shown in its stealthy and sinuous mode of progression.

NOTE J, page 237.

Atlas implies Discretion. He was one of the Titans, or mundane spirits, and "brother" of Prometheus, Epimetheus, and Menoitios, or Precaution, Reflection, and Deliberation bred of, and exercised in, ignorance and distrust of God. In this aspect he is a type of the discretion taught by experience of the crushing weight of the world on those who are devoid of that quality especially as shown by their inability to restrain speech.

NOTE K, page 240.

The occasion made use of to give us this "exhortation" was one of peculiar interest. The late Laurence Oliphant was at that time the English representative and agent of Thomas Lake Harris, the founder and chief of a certain mystical brotherhood in the United States. And having heard from a mutual friend of our spiritual work and experiences, and desiring to gain recruits for his chief, he came to Paris to see us, when, after putting to us sundry questions, he declared that we were possessed of the requisite qualifications, and called upon us to renounce everything we were doing and place ourselves at the disposal of Harris, whom he announced as the prophet and king of the new dispensation, and in short, a new avatâr of Christ. Failing to do this, we should, he assured us, infallibly incur dire catastrophe. Knowing nothing of Harris's doctrine, but respecting him for his undoubted poetic faculty, and having a high regard for his emissary, with whom I had some previous acquaintance, we begged for further information. This was accordingly vouchsafed us, but only with the result of our finding ourselves in hopeless disagreement, on account of what we deemed its fanciful character, its failure to satisfy the needs either of the mind or of the soul, and the nature of the experiences on which it was founded. For, though recognising these as real, we also recognised them as appertaining, not to the spiritual and divine region of man's nature, but to the magnetic and astral, and as representing a disorderly condition of this. And in confirmation of this view Mrs Kingsford was on the following night given a dream, in which she beheld a wilderness teeming with sirens, loreleis, and other phantasmal forms, which she was

given to understand were of the order of those who pretended to be the
" counterpartal angels " and " arch-natural women " of Harris's school
—afterwards called by Oliphant " Sympneumata "—but which were the
morbid products of that part of man's system which is always mystically
called the wilderness, being the astral region which intervenes between
the " Egypt " of the purely material, and the " Promised Land " of the
purely spiritual ;—a region, indeed, which has to be entered and traversed by all seekers after perfection, but which must on no account
be mistaken for the goal or unduly loitered in.

A second visit from Oliphant served in no way to reconcile us to his
views, but rather the contrary. And early on the following morning,
Mrs Kingsford received the " exhortation " in question, in response,
apparently, to an earnest request of mine, made without her cognisance,
for some definite instruction which might be serviceable to our visitor
as well as to ourselves. This hope as regarded him proved vain ; as
after the receipt of a copy of it he made no response, nor ever again
approached us. The chief points in respect of which it condemns the
doctrine propounded by our visitor are—

(1.) Its rejection of mental training and intellectual knowledge—in
short, of the Understanding—in favour of extraneous influences and
phenomenal experiences, as the source and criterion of truth.

(2.) Its exaltation of an earthly personage as spiritual king and master.

(3.) Its failure to recognise a diet of flesh as incompatible with the
highest aspirations ; and,

(4.) Its fanciful sex-relations and doctrine of " counterparts," which
last, we were subsequently instructed, is a travesty, due to delusive
spirits, of the mystical process in the soul called the " marriage of
regeneration ; "—the errors in question being those whereby neophytes
are peculiarly liable to be ensnared.

It is due to Oliphant to state that he afterwards seceded from Harris,
and modified his teaching. But the change was not radical, and an
examination of his later views failed to diminish in the least the interval
between us.

This occasion was the first on which Hermes expressly avowed himself, though not the first on which he assumed the guidance over us
and our work, while leaving us to identify him for ourselves. Two
of Mrs Kingsford's earliest experiences in this respect are related in
" Dreams and Dream-Stories," Nos. II. and IX., in the former of
which he directed us to combine our faculties for the prosecution of the

interpretative work to which I had already been long devoted ; and in the latter of which he prescribed rigid abstinence, especially from flesh and cooked food, as an essential condition for the full perception of things spiritual. On the former occasion he presented himself in the double aspect of a letter-carrier and of John the Baptist ; the first in his official capacity as the " Messenger of the Gods," and the last in intimation of the necessity of our application of the principle represented by the Baptist—that of purification in body and mind—for the true discernment of the Christ-idea. But it was only by degrees and after a considerable period that the full significance of the instruction disclosed itself to us, so far in advance was it of what we then knew.

His claim to the power of conferring the divine life was, in itself a demonstration of his own divinity. No mere human soul, nor spirit of a grade below the divine, could, or would presume to, assert such a claim.

The true " bi-unity" of the mystic man, referred to in verse 25, consists in the equilibration of the mind and soul as shown by the equal use of the mind's two modes, the intellect and the intuition, which are, respectively, its musculine and feminine modes.

NOTE L, pages 240, 255.

Although Dionysos and Aphrodite are *mystically* the third and fourth of the Gods, they are *actually* the fourth and third, this being their relative position by the order of their planets, and of their corresponding rays in the spectrum. For Venus, which holds in the solar system the place of the yellow in the prism, and is the brightest both of the planets and of the rays, comes next outside that of Hermes, whose ray is the orange, and whose planet is Mercury; and the planet of Dionysos or Iacchos—the Earth,—whose ray is the green, comes next outside Venus. And such is their position in the Greek and Hebrew theogonies (for the latter of which see Isa. xi. 2, 3, the Douay rendering for preference) and in the "Apostles' Creed." But in the Mosaic theogony and cosmogony this order is inverted, and the creation of the earth, which is represented by Dionysos, is placed on the " third day," while the work of Aphrodite is placed on the " fourth day." And in this order these hymns were received and are here given. The following are the chief reasons for this arrangement :—

1. As the Spirit of Love or Counsel, Aphrodite is the enlightener of the spiritual eyes and revealer of heaven to earth. She is also the

centripetal force whereby man is drawn inwards to God. Wherefore the earth must have being, and the centrifugal force must have fulfilled its part in the work of creation, before she can exercise her function in the work of redemption.

2. As the Spirit of Power, and representative of the centrifugal force whereby the Divine substance is projected into the condition of matter, and the earth created, Dionysos must exercise his function before the centripetal force, which is Love, can manifest itself.

3. As representative of the soul, which, though first in being and in dignity, is the last to find recognition, Aphrodite remains unperceived until polarised by means of the bodily elements. So that, although Love really subsists prior to any exercise of force, inasmuch as she is the source of the desire which puts force—whatever its kind, physical or mental—in action, she is veiled and hidden until the mind recognises the need of her and acquires the power to discern her. For which reason also her "day" or manifestation succeeds that of Dionysos.

NOTE M, page 241.

The meaning of this and the less obvious of the foregoing symbols is as follows :—

V. 2. "Twice-born" denotes regeneration. The first birth is that of the exterior or bodily man ; the second is that of the interior or spiritual man. This latter is produced in and of the former, and is thus "Son of man ;" but whereas its true parents are the soul and the Divine Spirit, and the soul when pure is mystically termed water and "Virgin Maria," the interior or spiritual man is said to be born of water and the Spirit, or Virgin Maria and the Holy Ghost, and is at once Son of man and of God. See "Definitions," *Regeneration*.

Iacchos, in being the *mystic* Bacchos, denotes the planetary Spirit after its passage through this process in and by means of the human soul ; the way of perfection being one for both macrocosm and microcosm.

—— "Beneath the earth," a phrase equivalent to the "caves of Iacchos" (Part II. No. XIV. (3)), and implying the mysteries of the body.

V. 3. "The horns of the ram," a symbol of force, especially of intellectual force.

—— "Who ridest upon an ass," a symbol at once of humility and patient endurance. This animal is marked on the back with a cross.

V. 4. The "Daughter of the King" is the soul, whether in the individual or in the universal, so-called because proceeding from the higher mind, or Nous, mystically styled the King. The planet-god is herein recognised as proceeding from and constituted of the universal life and substance.

NOTE N, page 244.

See note on p. 193.

NOTE O, page 226, 244.

The full perfectionment, while yet in the body, of the process denoted by the term Christ, involves the redemption of the body from its material limitations, through the reversion of its constituents from the condition of matter to that of spirit. This is called transmutation, and also resurrection. See Part II. No. IX. ; also "Definitions," *Resurrection.*

NOTE P, page 253.

Poseidon is styled "Father of souls," in virtue of his representing the masculine energy of the sea, which is the symbol of the substance, or "Mother," of souls. It is for this reason that he is chosen as emblem of the third gospel, that of Luke, which deals especially with the relations of Christ to the soul, as distinguished from the other three elements of the microcosm. See Note R.

NOTE Q, page 254.

By the contemplation of wisdom man acquires wisdom, the highest product of which is the "philosopher's stone" of a spirit perfectly quiescent, and inaccessible to assault whether from within or from without. By wisdom, too, the soul is attracted and absorbed. The mystical meaning of the head of the Gorgon Medusa is thus—as customary in mystical presentations—the opposite of the apparent meaning.

NOTE R, page 255.

The sapphire throne and four wheels of Ezekiel ; the Merkaba, or Car, of the Kabala ; the Kaabeh, or Cube, of Islam ; the four Rivers of Eden ; the four living Creatures of Ezekiel, the Apocalypse, and the book of Enoch, and which also are the symbols of the four Evangelists ; and the celestial chariot of Adonai,—all these alike denote the fourfold existence in which, as in a vehicle, Deity descends into manifestation or

creation, and of which both macrocosm and microcosm are constituted.
The four are, respectively, the material, the astral, the psychic, and the
spiritual. See "The Perfect Way," VI. Part i., and VIII., final par.
of Part iii.

Note S, page 257.

For which reason the Christ, as the realisation of man's divine
potentialities, is said to be born in a cave and a stable.

Note T, page 258.

V. 28. The choice of the ring-dove to be the emblem of the Holy
Spirit is due to the hues of the circle round its throat, the colours of
which are taken to represent the Seven Spirits of God, or rays of the
prism constituted by the Trinity.

V. 29. The only message from earth that can look to find accept-
ance in heaven, is that which announces the consummation of the prophecy of Apoc. xvi. 12 :—That " the water of the great river Euphrates
is dried up, and the way prepared for the kings of the East."

For the Euphrates is the will of man,[1] and until this is "dried up "
and sublimed in him, and is no longer the human but the divine will,
he cannot receive the divine knowledges of which the bearers are ever
"kings of the East," or messengers from the source of all spiritual
light. It was given to Anna Kingsford to be the first to identify these
"kings." Christian tradition places their number at three. She
recognised them as the three principles in man, without whose combined operation no truth can be discerned, but through whose combined operation all truth can be discerned, namely, the Spirit, the
Soul, and the Mind, operating respectively as Right Aspiration, Right
Perception, and Right Judgment. And the sequel of their advent,
whether for the individual or the general, is ever that "acceptable year
of the Lord," wherein it is said "the knowledge of the Lord shall
cover the earth as the waters cover the sea," and the soul is at peace.

For those who recognise and appreciate her work, it is hardly possible
not to regard her very names as a prophecy of her appointed task, seeing
that a way specially prepared for kings across a dried-up river is no
other than a _Kings' Ford;_ and that the "good time" called "the
acceptable year of the Lord " is no other than an _Annus Bonus._

[1] See page 24.

Among other striking and no less undesigned coincidences, so far as concerns human agency, was that of the names given to her on her reception into the Roman Communion,—long anterior to her spiritual work,—for they were the names of all the women who were by the Cross or at the Sepulchre.

To this step, as also to that of obtaining a medical degree at the University of Paris, she had—as was in due time made clear to us— been prompted in anticipation of her destined spiritual work. Having for its object the downfall of the world's materialistic system, both in religion and in science, it was requisite that the instrument of that work should, in order to be able to speak with full knowledge, undergo initiation in the chief strongholds of the doomed system.

Note U, page 263.

There are two processions of the seven primary Gods, or Spirits of God, the first by emanation, and the second by evolution, but the evolution is not of the Gods themselves but of their manifestation in time. The direction of one of these processions is the reverse of that of the other. The first is from within outwards, and occurs through the operation of the Deity within and upon itself. By this operation the divine potencies are projected to the furthest verge of the destined kosmos, which—though fourfold as to elements—is always in idea a globe consisting of seven concentric spheres, each divinity having his own sphere, and the outermost being assigned to Saturn or Satan, who is thus the circumference of the entity concerned, having beyond him only the void. Representing the seventh and outermost sphere, and projected after all the others, Saturn is called the seventh and last, and therefore—in this order—the " youngest of the gods." Thus, as matter is the antithetical ultimate, or "adversary," of Spirit, yet without ceasing to be Spirit, so is Saturn—or Satan—the antithetical ultimate, or " adversary," of God, yet without ceasing to be God.

In this sphere manifestation begins, for not only is it the sphere of matter, which *is* Spirit—by the force of the Divine Will projected into conditions and limitations, and made exteriorly cognisable—but Saturn is the principle itself of manifestation, and herein of matter, time, and all other limiting conditions. Hence he is the principle also of Individuation, whereby from being universal and abstract, Spirit becomes particular and concrete. Himself the first to be manifested in the kosmos thus initiated, Saturn heads the procession which is by evolution, and hence, in this order, is the first and "eldest" of the Gods. And upon his sphere or kingdom as basis the kosmos is built up from without inwards, each God presiding over the work in his own domain, until the whole is completed by the attainment of the innermost and highest. This accomplished, the kosmos is made in the divine image, the Sabbath of perfection is attained, and "God rests from His work," so far as regards the particular entity concerned.

These two processions, which are in perpetual simultaneous operation for the whole duration of the manifest universe, represent and are due to two forces, or rather two modes of force, which constitute two streams consisting of the Divine substance and energy. Of these streams one flows outwards and downwards, and the other inwards and upwards ; one is centrifugal, the other centripetal ; one is projective, the other attractive ; one represents Will, the other Love ; one results in Creation, the other in Redemption. And as complements of each other they are as indispensable to each other and to the stability of the kosmos, as are the centrifugal and centripetal modes of force to the stability of the solar system; and whereas one is masculine and the other feminine, man is no less said to be "made in the divine image, male and female," because built up of them both, than because also built up of the Seven Spirits of the Divine Duad.

The substance of all things is spirit, is consciousness. Wherefore all things are modes of consciousness, and all being is consciousness, and consciousness is being, and non-consciousness is non-being. And whereas the outermost sphere of any existing entity is that of the lowest mode of consciousness, wherein it touches negation, that which lies without such sphere is non-consciousness, and, therefore, non-being,—a state the entrance into which constitutes extinction of being. At once the negation of consciousness and of being, this state constitutes the negation of God, which is theologically called the devil (as see page 216).

The transcendent importance of the functions of Satan, and their absolute necessity, not only to the well-being, but to the very being of the individual, become specially apparent when it is considered (1) that as the "bourne of the divine impulsion," he is the circumferential limit whereby life and substance are arrested in their outward course and made to return to their centre, thus converting into a permanent kosmos that which, but for his intervention, would be dissipated in space. And (2) that but for his guardianship of the outermost sphere, there would be nought to hinder the irruption from the surrounding void into the kosmos, of its deadly foe the principle, if the term can be applied to a nonentity, of the negation of God, and therein, of all being.

The passages in which the Bible seems to identify Satan with the devil, constitute, when properly considered, no contradiction to this view, even without the counterbalancing aid of passages which directly favour this view. For, although constituting integral parts of the same kosmos, the inner and spiritual and the outer and material are in a sense antagonistic to each other, and a retrogression from the former to the latter, when once the former has been transcended, is a descent which, unless timely arrested, lands the soul in the region of negation. The sphere of Satan and of the devil are conterminous, and where a downward course is persisted in, Satan becomes the minister of the devil in that in ejecting the irredeemably perverse from the precincts of the kingdom, he consigns him to final destruction. But his enmity is not for the sinner, but for the sin ; and his " temptations " are for the trial, not for the condemnation, of the subject of them, and to test his fitness for the kingdom. The apocalyptic "binding of Satan for a thousand years" is but an expression implying the exemption of the saints from a return into material conditions for a prolonged period, during which Satan is said to be bound, so far as concerns them. But even if it had been the intention of the Bible-writers to identify the devil and Satan in the manner commonly supposed, no authority of book can override and set at nought a necessary and self-evident truth clearly discernible as founded in the very nature of existence, such as that of the interpretation here given. And indeed, as stated in the preface and elsewhere, one of the main purposes of the restoration represented by this volume is to "utterly abolish the idols" whether they consist in books, persons, traditions, or institutions.

But there is not the smallest reason for ascribing to the Bible-writers any such intention. They wrote as initiates for initiates, and knew that by these the true values would be attached to the terms employed, however liable to be mistaken by others ; and a sufficient motive for such concealment of the truth concerning Satan is to be found in the fact that it was the most jealously guarded of all the mysteries, being— according to the instructions given to us—communicated only to initiates of the very highest grade. And it was imparted to us under injunctions of our observing the strictest secrecy, at least "until the word be completed ; " and only during Mrs Kingsford's last illness was this so far accomplished, that the promulgation was permitted. The personality assumed by the illuminating spirit on the occasion was that of Phoibos Apollo,—an indication that, owing to its profound nature, only by the first of the Gods might the crowning mystery of the last of the Gods be disclosed.

Note V, page 264.

Saturn, as Kronos or Time, is said to bear all the Gods on his shoulders because their manifestation occurs in and through time ; and he is, himself, the first to be manifested, and is the very principle of time and manifestation. Moreover, the faculties in man by means of which they find recognition by man, are the product of experience acquired in time. This was implied in the vision shown to Mrs Kingsford on the eve of her receipt of the first instalment of this instruction concerning Satan,—a vision, at the time wholly unintelligible, in which she beheld Hermes being carried through space on the back of Saturn.

Note W, page 268.

That is, from the condition of Existence or manifested Being, to the condition of pure, or unmanifested, Being.

Note X, page 268.

The spirit of the regenerated ego in and by whom we realise the divine potentialities of our nature, is, for each of us, "Christ our Lord." And inasmuch as this ego is generated in time, and is the crown of manifestation, and final realisation of the divine idea in creation, for the evolution of whom the whole universe works together, and Satan is the principle of manifestation, the ministry of Satan is said to have been "ordained of God before the worlds, for the splendour (or effulgence) of the manifest, and the generation of Christ our Lord." And this applies to Christ from the point of view alike of the microcosm or individual, and of the macrocosm or universal. For, just as the macrocosm itself comprises and is constituted of the sum total of the microcosms, so the macrocosmic Christ comprises and is constituted of the sum total of the microcosmic Christs, or spirits of the regenerated human egos, all these throughout the universe being combined and blended into one indefeasible personality, representing the individualisation of the Supreme Being, or personification of the Divine Impersonal, through man, by means of evolution. Thus "generated" and constituted, Christ is the "Son" in and by whom the "Father" finds His ultimate full expression, as do the unmanifest light and heat of the system in and by the solar orb.

But the consciousness or potency of the universal Christ must not be regarded as limited to the sum total of the associated consciousnesses of the human egos composing him, any more than the consciousness of the individual man is to be regarded as limited to the sum total of the associated consciousnesses of his system. For just as the human ego represents all the consciousnesses of man's system centralised into a unity and polarised to a higher plane, so does the macrocosmic Christ represent the consciousnesses of all the microcosmic Christs centralised into a unity and polarised to a higher plane. Thus, as—to cite "The Perfect Way" (V. 17)—"the soul of the planet is more than the associated essences of the souls composing it ; and the consciousness of the system is more than that of the associated world-consciousnesses ; and the consciousness of the manifest universe is more than that of the corporate systems," so is the universal Christ more than the sum of the individual Christs or Divine Spirits of the regenerated human egos of which he consists. And as in the individual microcosm this Christ is the radiant point, or "One Life," whence the Divine effulgence flows to illume and vivify the man, so in the universal macrocosm the Christ similarly constituted is the radiant point or "One Life," whence the Divine effulgence flows to vivify and illume the universal Church, invisible and visible, of the elect, which is the nucleus of which He is the nucleolus, or body of which He is the soul. And that wherein He differs from and surpasses all other Gods—even while constituted like them—is that, whereas they represent but partial modes or aspects of Deity, each one being but as a single ray of the Divine spectrum, He represents Deity in its integrity, inasmuch as He combines in Himself the whole of the Divine rays, being the result of the operation of them all. Thus generated through humanity, and therefore Son at once of God and man, and "*our* Lord," He becomes the counterpart or *replica* of Adonai, who—being generated in substance—is Son of God only, and is "*the* Lord."

Now, "the consciousness of the unmanifest Deity is greater than that of the manifest, for the manifest does not exhaust the unmanifest." Wherefore, in manifestation, "the Father is greater than the Son ; " while in substance, they are " co-equal and co-eternal."

Note Y, page 269.

The difference between the account herein given of the Lord's death and burial (verses 53, 64), and that of Jesus in Part I., No. XXXIII., presents no difficulty when it is considered that the former deals, as do the gospels, with the mystical or spiritual history of the typical Man Regenerate, and the latter with his physical history, and that it is quite sufficient for the purpose of the narrative that the correspondence between the two histories be general only and not particular. The object of the gospels was not to exalt an individual but to delineate an order, the order of the "Sons of God," for the sake of exhibiting the highest possibilities of humanity. And it is for this reason that while the events which occurred to Jesus were used and adapted to illustrate certain doctrines, they were not followed in all their details. To have so followed them would have been to give the physical history of but one of the "Sons of God," instead of the spiritual history of them all.

DEFINITIONS AND EXPLANATIONS OF TERMS AND PHRASES NOT GENERALLY FAMILIAR, OR USED IN AN UNFAMILIAR SENSE.

Adam and Eve. In their mystical sense, and as applied to the individual, Adam and Eve are respectively the exterior selfhood, or sense and reason, and the interior selfhood, or soul and intuition, which together constitute the human being. And they are as man and woman to each other, in that they represent respectively the centrifugal or force element, which is the masculine, and the centripetal or love element, which is the feminine element of existence. For a full treatment of this subject, see "The Perfect Way," Lectures VI. and VII.

Arche,[1] a Greek term, signifying beginning, first cause, origin, and said to have been first used by Anaximander (B.C. 580) in the sense of principle (*principium*) to denote the eternal and infinite basis or substance (*sub-stans*) of things, and which is therefore not itself a thing, but that from which all things proceed, and of which they all consist, and to which they all return. It is thus the containing, and therefore the feminine, element or mode of Deity, as distinguished from the energising and masculine element or mode ; or God the Mother as distinguished from God the Father. It is termed also the fourth dimension, or the *within* of space, from which the other dimensions proceed ; and the *noumenon*, reality, being, or "thing in itself," which underlies or *sub-stands* the phenomenon, appearance, existence, or thing perceived. As original, divine, and self-subsistent, and therein distin-

[1] In Arche, Aphrodite, Persephone, Psyche, Herpe, and all Greek terms ending in *e*, the final letter is sounded. The *ch* is usually pronounced as *k*.

guished from matter, which is secondary, derived, and created, Arche denotes the substance alike of divinity and of the soul, the nucleus of the nucleolus in both God and man. The word Ark is derived from it, and like the work Ark, the Hebrew for which is *tebah*, means any kind of containing vessel. In one of the ancient versions of the Bible— the Coptic—*thebi* is used instead of *tebah*, a form which relates it still more closely to Tibet, Thebes, and other places similarly so named apparently as being homes of the Mysteries, and as representing, there- fore, the Soul as the dwelling-place of the Spirit, and source of all Divine knowledges.[1] Thus, in its highest application, the ark of Noah denotes the original Divine substance containing in its bosom the "eight persons," God (the *Nous*) and His seven spirits, of whom all the universe is overspread.

Astral fluid; the universal ether of space and immediate sub- stance of the manifested universe, which becomes the various elements by means of differentiality of polarisation. It is not the substance of the soul, whether unindividuate or individuate, for that is divine and uncreate; but it is the first projection of soul-substance into the material of creation, and is as the veil of the soul. It subsists under many degrees of purity or tenuity, and is the abode of all spirits below the celestial. In man it constitutes the third element of his system, counting from within outwards, and coming next to the body, acts as the intervening medium between it and the soul. As thought-substance, it is the seat of the mundane mind or lower reason ; and a disorderly condition of it is a frequent cause of such mental derangements as are not due to lesions of the organism.

Astral Spirits. While the astral sphere is the abode of all spirits below the celestial, and their exterior covering or ethereal body is con- stituted of it, there are spirits, or rather entities so-called, which are constituted entirely of it, having neither a spiritual nor a material nature. These have no existence apart from man, and are emanations from man, being to him as reflects of himself, but devoid of substanti- ality as the images in a mirror. As with morbid growths in the physical system, such as tumours, they become new centres of activity in the system, deriving their sustenance from the system generally, to the deple- tion and emaciation of the individual ; and only by a healthy regime in mind and body, of which earnest and frequent prayer is an important element, can they be subdued and the vitality absorbed by them returned

[1] See page 89, note 1.

U

into its proper channels. The function of prayer in such cases consists in its being a means of directing the mind inwards and upwards with such energy as to convert its otherwise lambent and diffused substance into a flame, so to speak, thereby rendering it incapable of division or diversion,—a condition incompatible with astral obsession. The astral fluid constitutes the perispirit, double, or astral body of man in life, and his phantom, ghost, or Ruach after death. The astral body is called also the magnetic and odic body, according as the reference is to the substance, the force, or some other attribute. The term odic is claimed to be of oriental derivation. The Hindûs apply the term Ákasa to the astral ether in its primordial or pre-cosmic state. The astral emanations or " reflects" of persons are visible to the lucid, who —unless duly instructed—is unable to discriminate between them and genuine extraneous spirits, so life-like are their impersonations. The merely mechanical "medium" is readily responsive to their influence. And many besides mediums are liable to receive from. them mental suggestions—often of the most mischievous character—and to mistake them for suggestions arising from a divine or some other source entitled to be heeded. The astral phantom may serve as a medium of communication with an actual departed spirit ; but the message depends for its value upon its independence of the transmitting vehicle. The mere phantom, uncontrolled by the soul, is no trustworthy instructor or guide, and inasmuch as the astral is rather an emanation from the body than a distinct element, it is essential to clear spiritual vision that the body also be subjected to the rule of purity, especially in respect of diet.

Thus far concerning the astral on its occult side. In its mystical aspect it denotes (as explained in Note K) the region of spiritual weakness, doubt, temptation, difficulty, and distress, upon which the aspirant enters on his emergence from the " Egypt" of things material merely and intellectual, when he sets his face towards the "Promised Land" of spiritual perfection. For the wilderness that lies between, and must be painfully traversed, is no other than the astral belt within his own system, already in these pages so exquisitely presented in the hymn to the planet-god [Part II., XIII., (6)], as to need no further explanation here. Concerning the distinction between the terms mystical and occult, see the explanation given under *Occultism*.

The Elect is a term the misunderstanding of which has been a stumbling-block and a curse to Christendom. And the evil has arisen through the suppression of the doctrine of a multiplicity of earth-lives, otherwise called the doctrine of re-incarnation or transmigration, and the consequent assumption that all who are not actually of the elect are hopelessly reprobate and lost ;—a belief which, by its ascription to God of a capricious, arbitrary, and pitiless character, has served greatly to obscure from view the perfection of the Divine Nature.

The truth is that by the elect are denoted only those in whom the redemptive process has already proceeded so far as to ensure their ultimate salvation, all others being still in too rudimentary a stage of their evolution to have attained to this desirable state, and, therefore, still without assurance of salvation, and consequently liable to failure.

Seeing how small a proportion of persons in any one period or generation are entitled to be regarded as elect, and how complex and prolonged the process requisite for the elaboration of the individual from his beginning in the lowest forms of organic life to the summit of human evolution, where humanity unites with Deity,—the denial of a multiplicity of earth-lives to afford the requisite opportunities of experience would be a sentence of perdition upon the entire race. Whereas, as it is,—according to the ancient and universal doctrine now newly recovered—so far from souls having their beginning at some arbitrary stage upon the ladder of evolution, with their destiny for eternal bliss or woe, not merely dependent upon the use made by them of a single brief existence, amid conditions wholly new and strange to them, but arbitrarily fixed independently of aught that they can do or desire,—they begin at the lowest round, and returning again and again to the body, have ample time and opportunity to determine their final lot for themselves, according to the tendencies voluntarily encouraged by them.

Hades (Heb. Sheol = hell ; lit. in darkness) denotes the lower spheres of the consciousness, the material and astral, to be in which is to the soul, which belongs by its nature to the higher and celestial, to be " in prison," or " beneath the altar." See p. 234.

Iacchos, Jacob, and Joachim. The last of these three names is that which Christian tradition assigns to the father of the Virgin Mary, in obvious recognition of her derivation as the soul, from him as the planetary Spirit. The names themselves are not only related to each other in form and meaning, but they have a common reference to the special functions and characteristics of the god of the fourth sphere,— the earth, matter, or body. For in implying force, effort, success, and triumph, they indicate all the stages through which spirit passes, from its first projection into matter to its redemption and final exaltation in soul. It is true that the successes of Jacob over his brother Esau, wherein he supplanted him in his birthright and blessing, are ascribed to craft, and only his success when he "wrestled with God, and prevailed," to force. But inasmuch as the brothers are types respectively of the exterior and the interior self-hood, of which the former is the elder, in virtue of its being the first to be manifested in man, the craft by which Jacob obtained his advantage denotes precisely that superior subtlety of nature whereby the soul surpasses the body, and demonstrates itself as the true and only possible inheritor of eternal life.

The Egyptian origin of Joachim (as also of Jehovah) is indicated in 2 Kings xxiii. 34, where Pharaoh is said to have changed the name of Eliakim to *Jehoi*akim (of which Joachim is an equivalent); while the identity of this name with Iacchos is implied in the fact of its being thus imposed by the conquering upon the conquered king, since only the names of the gods of the former were thus imposed.

Karma. By the recent appropriation of this Eastern term into the English language, a most valuable addition has been made to our vocabulary of mystical science. It is not yet sufficiently familiar, however, to render a definition of it superfluous. The idea implied by it, namely, the persistence after death of the effects of the tendencies encouraged and the characteristics acquired in life, and the necessity, where these have been bad, of expiation and amendment by the subject of them, is involved in the doctrine of purgatory and retribution. But inasmuch as by Karma is meant a repeated return into the earth-life, there to work out in new bodies the evil consequences of past lives, and by means of multiplied experiences to rectify defects of character; and by purgatory is meant only a *post-mortem* expiation by suffering, and no experiential development, the latter term is in no sense an equivalent for the former.

The inability of the vast majority of persons to remember their previous existences is due to the fact that the return is that only of the permanent ego or soul, and not of the external personality; and that they are very few in number who succeed during life in establishing with their souls relations so intimate as to gain cognisance of their soul's history. But the fact that the outer personality is left thus uninformed on the subject, in no way invalidates either the truth or the value of reincarnation, since the function of the body is to serve as an instrument by and through which the soul obtains experiences, and the end of those experiences is attained when the soul applies them to its own advancement. Nor is the fact—if it be a fact—that but comparatively few of the spirits with whom intercourse is held admit the doctrine, valid as an argument against it, since the agent of such communication is rarely the soul itself but only its astral envelope, and this is in no better position than the material body to pronounce upon the question.

Miracle. In default of a prior definition of the terms natural and human, the terms supernatural and superhuman must be rigidly excluded from any attempt to define miracle. In defining miracle as the " natural effect of an exceptional cause " (p. 91), the term natural is used simply in the sense of orderly, regular, normal, legitimate. Wherefore it remains only to show in what sense the cause is exceptional. This term derives its force from the inequality of human development in respect of human capacities. As a microcosm of the macrocosm, man comprises in his system, either actually or potentially, all that is in the universe ; and in virtue of his having obtained the consciousness of and mastery over any plane within himself, he is able to attain the conscious-ness of and mastery over the corresponding plane without himself. The fully developed man—he who, having realised all the potentialities of his nature, is a typical Man—is able to exercise mastery over planes of being, of the very existence of which the undeveloped man is ignorant, finding no answering consciousness of them in himself. To him, there-fore, the manifest tokens of such mastery constitute miracles. They represent for him a region and a power which by virtue of their trans-cending his own range of observation and ability, are apt to be regarded by him as also transcending nature, and as being, therefore, miracu-lous. But neither do they transcend nature, nor are they miraculous (using these terms in the conventional sense) for the man who works them, because he knows them to be the natural effects of causes which are exceptional only in that they appertain to a sphere of nature known to but a comparative few. Nor would they be regarded as transcend-ing nature and as being miraculous even by the undeveloped witness of them, save for the liability of the undeveloped man to regard himself and his compeers as typical men, and as the measure of nature and of humanity, and to consider all that transcends their own limits as also transcending nature and man. Their mistake lies, of course, in re-stricting their conception of nature and man to the material and physical, and then either assuming that the psychical and spiritual are beyond nature and man, or denying to them any real being.

Now, the undeveloped man subsists under two modes. In one of these he is altogether rudimentary in respect of all faculties which sur-pass the physical, namely, the intellectual, the moral, and the spiritual. And in the other, he is developed—possibly to an extraordinary degree

—in respect of some one of the spheres of consciousness denoted by these terms, and yet is altogether rudimentary as regards the others. The typical scientist of the day, for instance, is one who is highly developed in respect of the intellectual faculty so far as regards the consciousness of things material ; but as regards that of things moral and spiritual he is altogether rudimentary, and his attitude towards experiences of the order commonly accounted miraculous and supernatural, is one of such determined antagonism—through his inability to recognise the corresponding regions in himself—as to render him wholly inaccessible to reason and evidence in their behalf. This is to say, he has a fixed idea which no reason or evidence can overcome. Now, it is a significant fact that the possession of a fixed idea, which no reason or evidence can overcome, is by materialistic scientists themselves—those whose speciality is medicine—accounted a sufficient plea for certifying its possessor as insane and unfit to be at large.

It is by persons similarly rudimentary in respect of the spiritual consciousness that the important function of literary criticism is for by far the most part exercised; the result being that the confession of spiritual experiences is treated in a tone of contempt and ribaldry such as largely to deter from the promulgation of this class of experiences ; their recipients shrinking alike from exposing their "pearls" to profanation and themselves to contumely and affront. Hence it has come that, between the physician and the literary critic, the confession of experiences indicative of man's higher potentialities—and, in such sense, "miraculous"—has in our day been made perilous, and the world has in consequence been deprived of testimony which would have gone far to save it from the abyss of unreason and negation into which it has fallen. And this repression and rejection of experience in deference to an hypothesis—it is curious to note—has occurred in an age which vaunts itself superior to all other ages, especially on the ground that it takes nothing for granted, but makes experience the sole basis of knowledge.

Such denial of man's higher potentialities is, moreover, utterly inconsistent with the belief in evolution as the method of creation, combined as that belief is with the confession of absolute ignorance respecting the nature of the substance in which evolution occurs.

Mysticism (in religion) has for its antithesis materialism (in religion), in that it deals with those realities and verities which are spiritual, eternal, and of the soul—that is, with principles, processes, and states appertaining to the interior consciousness—instead of with persons, places, and events which are physical, historical, and of the senses ; and regards the sacred writings when expressed in terms derived from the latter as really referring to the former, and valuable only in so far as they do refer to the former. For which reason the religious mystic cares for the letter of Scripture only in so far as it is a vehicle for the spirit, and makes it his study to discern the spirit through the letter, and by all means to avoid limiting the spirit by the letter ; considering that to the substitution of the literal for the spiritual sense of Scripture has been due the perversion of Christianity into a fetish at once monstrous, idolatrous, and dishonouring both to God and to man. Wherefore in the condition hitherto prevailing in Christendom, the mystic sees the fulfilment as of a prophecy, of the saying that " the letter kills," so completely has the worship of it killed the faculty of the perception of divine things. And he insists accordingly that only through the revival of Mysticism can the true Christianity—that, namely, of Christ—be restored.

Mysticism and Occultism. These terms are so far identical in that they are respectively the Greek and the Latin for that which, by its nature, is hidden or secret as concerns the outer perceptions. But they differ essentially in respect of the particular region or department of the hidden and secret to which they respectively refer. Occultism deals with the region and its phenomena, which, being interior to the body and exterior to the soul, constitutes the astral or magnetic circulus which separates one from the other, and is the immediate environment of the soul. And Mysticism deals with principles, processes, and states which, being interior to the soul and comprising the spirit, determine the soul's progress and condition. This is to say, that Occultism implies transcendental physics, and belongs to the kingdom of science and the intellect, and is "human." And Mysticism implies transcendental metaphysics, and belongs to the kingdom of religion and the intuition, and is divine. Of these two kingdoms the typical representatives are, respectively, the Adept and the Christ. By which explanation is illustrated this utterance made to Anna Kingsford by her divine illuminator : " If Occultism were all, and held the key of heaven, there would be no need of Christ. . . . If the adepts in Occultism or in physical science could suffice to man, I would have committed no message to you " (pp. 99, 100).

Noumenon. See under *Arche.*

Polarisation. Every particle of matter, however minute or tenuous, whether fixed or fluidic, has two magnetic poles, a positive and a negative. Polarisation, as the term is applied in this book and in "The Perfect Way," consists in the arrangement of the particles constituting any entity, in such order as to bring each pole of every particle into immediate conjunction with the opposite pole of another particle —the positive in one joining on to the negative in another—so as to admit of the passage of a continuous current of energy throughout the whole series.

Regeneration. This term implies much more than is ascribed to it by the theological dictionaries, and the failure to understand it has been the cause of all the perversions of Christianity. For, had the doctrine of salvation through regeneration, so emphatically asserted by Jesus to Nicodemus, been duly comprehended, no place had been found for the orthodox presentation either of the Incarnation or of the atonement. For it means simply and purely the re-formation or reconstitution of the individual out of the spiritual substance of his soul, instead of the created material of his body. Such a man is interior, mystic, spiritual, and the elaboration of him occurs in the body as in a matrix constituted of coarser elements, the efficient cause being the operation of the Divine Spirit in the soul, he himself co-operating with it ; and when fully elaborated he can dispense altogether with the body as well as with all other elements exterior to the soul ; or, if the process be accomplished while in the body, he can indraw and transmute his body into spirit. The individual thus produced is said to be son at once of God and of man. He is son of man, because a product of humanity ; and He is Son of God because generated immediately by the Divine energy. And he is said to be also son of a woman, and this a virgin, because he is produced of the soul and constituted of the substance of the soul, and the soul is mystically called the woman, as being the feminine element in man's nature, and "mother" of the man, and when pure from materiality is called virgin, being named Maria after the boundless sea of space, the substance·at once of herself and of Deity.

Wherefore the saying of Jesus, "Ye must be born again of Water and of the Spirit," is a declaration, first, that it is necessary to every one who would be saved, sooner or later to be born in the manner in which He Himself, as a typical Man Regenerate, is said to have been born ; and, next, that the gospel narrative of His birth is, really, a presentation, symbolical and dramatic, of the process of regeneration, having no physical significance whatever, the Christ Jesus in and through whom salvation occurs, being no other than the regenerated spiritual selfhood in each person. (See "The Perfect Way," V. 45.)

Failing to comprehend the true doctrine of atonement, and to recognise its identity with that of regeneration, the church visible has altogether set aside regeneration, and in the place both of regeneration and the true at-one-ment with God thereby, has rested everything on the false doctrine of the atonement.

Resurrection. This term is used in Scripture in various senses, none of which is that commonly supposed, since there is no resurrection of the dead and disintegrated body. The current belief has arisen through the preference of the letter to the spirit, exercised in complete disregard both of the ideas intended to be conveyed by the writers of the mystical Scriptures, and of the facts of existence. Thus, the " graves " of John v. 28 imply only the lowermost strata, or modes, of consciousness, the material and astral, in which during its earth-life the soul is regarded as buried, and the resurrection of verse 29 is the soul's awakening to the recognition of the destiny it has incurred through its behaviour during such period. There is a resurrection that occurs while in the body,—the resurrection from the " death in trespasses and sins," to the consciousness of things spiritual and to a consequent life of holiness. The " First Resurrection " (Apoc. xx. 5, 6) consists in the redemption of the body, while yet alive, from liability to death, by means of its transmutation or indrawal into its original spiritual substance (see Part I., No. XXI., and II., No. V.). They who attain to this resurrection are called first-fruits—first, that is, in rank (Apoc. xiv. 4). They are the fully manifested Christs who are glorified in the hymn to Phoibos. Paul craved this distinction, but failed through his inability to obtain the requisite mastery over the elements of his body.

The other, or second, resurrection, consists in the investment of the soul with a spiritual body which shall serve it as an indestructible environment after the termination of its association with the material and astral. Being evolved immediately from the soul itself it constitutes, not a *body raised*, but a *raised body*.*

Second Coming of Christ. A careful reading of verses 54 and 58 of Part II., No. V., shows that they do not necessarily imply a return of the actual Jesus of the Gospels, but that their sense will be satisfied by such a manifestation anew of the Christ-principle as shall comprise an exhibition of power such as that which constituted the " Ascension." This is the " Resurrection "—in the sense of the transmutation—of the body through its indrawal by the Spirit. For they in and by whom this process is enacted, are of the order, and bear the title, of Christ Jesus.

Such an event would not itself constitute the " Second Coming," but only the crowning demonstration of that coming. The coming will consist in the revelation anew of the Christ-idea in such wise that it shall be so fully understood as shall render possible the demonstration above described. In this sense the Second Coming may be affirmed to be already actually in progress, seeing that the Christ-idea is now, for the first time in the Church's history, being understood and made known in its true sense. This is the sense in which it constitutes the "eternal gospel" of the passage chosen for motto to this book, inasmuch as that only is eternal which, in virtue of its being purely spiritual, and inherent in the nature of Being, and therefore perfectly logical, subsists independently of time, person, and place, and even of matter itself (as see Part I., No. III.). This passage has been widely accepted as referring to the promulgation of the Scriptures under the Reformation. But seeing that only their letter was then promulgated, while their spirit was altogether reserved, its proper reference must be to a promulgation which for its disclosure of the latter, can alone be accounted a real promulgation. In this view it is the intelligent appreciation of the Christ-idea, now first made known, that is implied in the declaration that "the Son of Man shall be seen coming in the clouds of heaven with power and great glory;"—"heaven," and the "clouds of heaven" being mystical terms denoting man's higher reason, the microcosmic heaven within the individual.

Sons of God. See under *Regeneration.*

TURNBULL AND SPEARS, PRINTERS, EDINBURGH.

LIST OF
OTHER WORKS BY THE SAME WRITERS.

Revised and Enlarged Edition. Price 12s. 6d.

The Perfect Way; or, the Finding of Christ.

BY

ANNA (BONUS) KINGSFORD, M.D., and

EDWARD MAITLAND, B.A.

A book setting forth the "intellectual concepts" which underlie Christianity, but which its official exponents cannot or may not disclose; and demonstrating Christianity to be a symbolic synthesis of the fundamental truths contained in all religions.

FIELD & TUER, *The Leadenhall Press, E.C.;*
SIMPKIN, MARSHALL & CO.; HAMILTON, ADAMS & CO.;
GEORGE REDWAY, 15 York Street, Covent Garden, W.C.

OPINIONS FROM SPECIAL ORGANS.

" A fountain of light, interpretative and reconciliatory. . . . No student of divine things can dispense with it. . . . The more it is studied carefully, as it deserves to be, the greater does the wonder grow as to its production, and the interpretative genius that pervades each well-weighed sentence."—*Light* (London).

" A grand book, keen of insight and eloquent in exposition; an upheaval of true spirituality. . . . We regard its authors as having produced one of the most—perhaps the most—important and spirit-stirring of appeals to the highest instincts of mankind which modern European literature has evoked."—*Theosophist* (India).

"The most valuable contribution to theosophical literature, and unequalled as a 'means of grace' among all English books of the present century."—*Occult World* (U.S.A.).

"Could this work have sale equal to its merits; and would the people, young and old, not only read and study, but understand it, and live in its light and spirit, the long expected millennium would soon dawn on our darkness, and shine full-orbed in beauty and glory over the habitable globe."— PARKER PILSBURY in *The Esoteric* (Boston, U.S.A.).

"We regard 'The Perfect Way' as the most illumined and useful book published in the nineteenth century. Amid all the stars that have recently shone forth in the new heaven of spiritual literature, this seems to us to shine the brightest. It came into our own lives at the very moment that we stood in need of just such a book. We know of many who have had similar experience in this relation." —*Gnostic* (U.S.A.).

"I have much pleasure in dedicating this work to the authors of 'The Perfect Way,' as they have in that excellent and wonderful book touched so much on the doctrine of the Kabbala, and set such value on its teachings. 'The Perfect Way' is one of the most deeply occult works that has been written for centuries."—S. L. MACGREGOR MATHERS, in *The Kabbala Unveiled.*

"The Christian mystics of modern Europe represented by the authors of 'The Perfect Way.'"—*Swedenborg, the Buddhist*, p. 39, by Philangi Dasa (U.S.A.).

"A work which has found recognition among students of divine things in all countries, irrespective of religion or race, as the fullest exposition concerning God, nature, and man, ever vouchsafed to this planet, and her (Anna Kingsford's) share in which has gained for her the reputation of being a seer and prophet of unsurpassed lucidity and inspiration."—*Light* (Obituary notice of Mrs Kingsford).

PRIVATE TESTIMONIES.

"Your book has had the most extraordinary effect on my mind, removing not one veil but many veils which shut out happiness in various directions."

"The moment my mind touched this book I drank it in as does the ground rain after a long drought. . . . As I write this, warm waves of joy and life flow through me."

" Your splendid work ' The Perfect Way.' "

" Those marvellous appendices."

" You have done a grand work in vindicating the scientific
dignity of mysticism."—*The late* Dr ERNEST GRYSANOWSKY, *of
Leghorn.*

" ' The Perfect Way ' will always remain a monument of inspired
genius. The more I study it, the more I admire and appreciate it.
I am convinced that it is without exception the most valuable
' Bible ' that has yet appeared ; and it will be long before mankind
is sufficiently advanced to require a further revelation. It is a
perfect mine of occult wealth,—so harmoniously consistent, and so
logically true."

" I am under an ever-abiding sense of gratitude for the comfort,
peace, and quiet it has brought to my inmost soul."

" It is like listening to the utterances of a God or archangel. I
know of nothing in literature to equal it. It is something quite
new in the world. Its magnificent enthusiasm for humanity excites
my highest admiration."--*The late* Sir FRANCIS H. DOYLE, *Professor of Poetry at the University of Oxford.*

" Humanity has always and everywhere asked itself these three
supreme questions :—Whence come we ? What are we ? Whither
go we ? Now these questions at length find an answer, complete,
satisfactorily, and consolatory, in ' The Perfect Way.' "

To be had separately. Price 1s.

The Nature and Constitution of the Ego.

BEING LECTURE V. OF " THE PERFECT WAY," WITH TWO OF THE APPENDICES " CONCERNING THE CHRISTIAN MYSTERIES " AND THE " HYMN TO THE PLANET-GOD."

Second Edition, Crown 8vo.   Price 6s.

Dreams and Dream=Stories.

By the late Dr ANNA (BONUS) KINGSFORD.

Edited by EDWARD MAITLAND.

" Charming stories, full of delicate pathos. . . . We put it down in wonderment at how much it outstrips our great, yet reasonable, expectation, so excellent and noteworthy is it ; a book to read and to think over."—*Vanity Fair.*

" Curious and fascinating to a degree, . . . by certainly one of the most vivid dreamers, as she was one of the brightest minds, of her generation. . . . A curiously interesting volume."—*Court Journal.*

"Wonderfully fascinating, . . . with invention enough for a dozen romances, and subjects for any number of sermons."—*Inquirer.*

" More strange, weird, and striking than any imagined by novelist, playwright, or sensational writer . . . for the marvellous, the beautiful, and the vraisemblable, having Hawthorne's marvellous insight into the soul of things."—*Lucifer.*

" The preface is as singular as the stories themselves."—*Literary World.*

" The union of the most rigid accuracy with the most vivid imagination, and the most intense love of mysticism, gave a peculiar and almost unique character both to Mrs Kingsford's intellectual efforts, and to her personal individuality.   The present volume testifies to all these qualities."—*Vegetarian Messenger.*

" Mrs Kingsford was a very wonderful woman, and it was only fit and proper that she should go through some very wonderful experiences."—*St James's Gazette.*

" A valuable addition to the literature of the Mysticism of the nineteenth century," by " one of the brilliant women of the day."— OSCAR WILDE, in *The Woman's World.*

OPINIONS.

"We recognise in the author of 'The Pilgrim and the Shrine' an artist who approaches very near to the ideal that his brilliant pages disclose."—*Saturday Review.*

"One of the wisest and most charming of books."—*Westminster Review.*

"Its aspects are so varied, and the whole so fascinating, from whatever point of view it is seen, that we are forced to pronounce it a very masterpiece."—*Brooklyn* (U.S.A.) *Union.*

"That same purity of style and earnestness of tone, that same depth of philosophic reflection, which marked 'The Pilgrim and the Shrine,' may all be found, rendered still more attractive by the beauty of the story, in 'Higher Law.' There is no novel, in short, which can be compared to it for its width of view, its cultivation, its poetry, and its deep human interest . . . except 'Romola.'"—*Westminster Review.*

"In 'Higher Law' the study is made on noble people in a noble style. The argument runs all the way on the uplands of the mind. . . . The scenery of the book, in general and social, is magnificent. They who can appreciate its general wealth will rejoice in its splendour. Such books are truly emancipating in their influence. They stimulate and instruct, entertain and educate."—Rev. O. B. FROTHINGHAM in the *Index* (U.S.A.).

"We regard 'By and By' as in some respects the most important of Mr Maitland's novels."—*Westminster Review.*

.*. The Author of these tales desires them to be regarded as representing but steps in the process of mental unfoldment, and not, therefore, those final conclusions which can come only of a perfect accord between the mind's two indispensable modes, when duly developed, the Intellect and the Intuition. For such conclusions, readers are referred especially to "The Perfect Way; or, The Finding of Christ," advertised above.